Loving In The Offbeat

A Novel

PATRICIA HOPKINS

Loving In The Offbeat (The sequel to *Living In The Offbeat*)

Visit website at http://www.wanderlustbooksllc.com

Copyright © 2013 Patricia Hopkins

Published in the United States by Wanderlust Books
Cover art photo Shutterstock / holbox / 75417679

ISBN-10: 0985761385
ISBN-13: 978-0-9857613-8-7

for Zander…
one of God's most precious miracles

Also by Patricia Hopkins

~~~Novels~~~

Living In The Offbeat
More Than A Notion

~~~Short Stories Collection~~~

I Am The Shadowman (And Other Supernatural Tales)
Old Graciola Young (eBook)

A Life With Regrets

Regret living my life not fully living my life;
waiting for you to change when
I should have changed myself.
Gave up when I could have gotten up and
pulled away instead of pushing forward.
Regret the day I said good-bye instead of hold-up.

Regret the day you let me go because I let you go first.
Could have held on a little bit longer;
for one more day would have made a difference.
Did we put a period where we should have paused?
Ended us before we had a chance to begin?
Regret not letting you love me the best way you knew how.

Regret the day I shut down my heart, my mind, my soul
to the person who was my best friend.
Allowed life's misunderstandings ruin a good thing.
Sadly, the lost years can never be recovered;
And time marches on even though we did not.
What I most regret is...
Living a life filled with regrets.

~~~Patricia Hopkins

Chapter One

"*R*onnie, have you seen my car keys?" Luis darted from one room to the next of their spacious Mediterranean-style home.

"You left them on the table near the door, remember?" Ronnie replied calmly, chuckling at how often he misplaced his keys.

"Found them!" he shouted from the hallway.

"Knew you would!" She sang out from the kitchen. She spread cream cheese on a bagel and placed it on the table next to a cup filled with his favorite coffee.

"They were in my nephew's hand print," he said, referring to a dish given to him by his nephew a few years ago when they visited the Dominican Republic. *Another plant? I don't remember seeing that yesterday... I swear it feels like this woman is trying to turn this house into a jungle.*

"I'm not surprised. That's where you put them when you came home last night."

Luis returned to the kitchen. "What would I do without you?"

"You would probably be late every morning."

He picked up the cup and took a sip. "Ah, now *this* is a good cup of coffee. Strong and black." Taking a bite of the bagel, he said, "I see you've added another plant to the collection."

"Well, since we haven't made it back to the DR, those plants are probably the closest I'm going to get to being there." She glanced at him sideways. "What's wrong? Don't you like them?"

Luis replied nonchalantly, "There's plenty of plants in the backyard, but if turning this house into a greenhouse makes you happy, I'm all for it."

"When *are* we going back to the DR, anyway?"

"We'll go back someday. I promise."

"You say that every year, but somehow we never seem to get there. Whatever happened to those yearly reunions with your family? It's going on three years.... I hope you didn't stop going because of me."

"Nothing could be further from the truth. It's just that I have been busy with work and trying to keep my business going."

"I understand. And as the politicians like to remind us, this country is still in a recession..."

"Yeah... don't I know it. Business has dropped way off. I've lost so many clients."

"Things will pick up soon." *I hope.* Ronnie poured the remaining coffee in a travel mug and handed it to him.

He planted a kiss on her cheek. "I need to get going. I have an early appointment."

"Hey, remember we're having dinner with Kiara and her friend this evening. They should be here by seven. I haven't seen her in weeks, so I am really looking forward to this."

"I'll be back way before then. Who is this guy she's bringing, anyway? Must be serious if she's introducing him to us."

"I don't know how serious it is, but I believe she said she met him last year at the university. Don't know how long they've been dating, though."

"Well, I for one think it's good for her to have another man in her life. She's a grown woman, yet Travis hovers over her like she's still a little girl."

"Don't be so hard on Travis. Anyway, twenty-one ain't really grown, so in his eyes she *is* still a little girl. Now get out of here before you end up being late." She nudged him from the kitchen.

"All right, I'm going. I love you."

"I love you, too. Have a wonderful day, papi."

He hesitated at the door. "Speaking of Travis, you going to the office today?"

"Yeah, I'm feeling better so I told him I'd put in a few hours to finish up that report I started."

"Just make sure you don't overdo it and have a relapse."

"I'll be fine, now get out of here. It's almost eight."

He glanced at his watch. "You're right, I'd better get going. I'll give you a call later. Bye." She watched Luis back out from the driveway. *I am so lucky to have Luis in my life. Three years have passed and I still love him as much as the first day we met. What more do I need? I have a man who loves me, respects me, and is willing to go out of his way to please me. I know one thing... No matter what happens in this lifetime, I am never letting his ass go.*

Chapter Two

As soon as Luis made it to his office, he phoned Tomas to voice his concerns about his morning appointment.

Tomas picked up on the first ring. "Hello."

"Look man, I'm doing you a huge favor by interviewing this woman, so you'd better not be sending me another one of your so called "ladies". You remember how upset Ronnie was when she found out that woman you recommended was the first place runner up for Miss Rio de Janeiro. That girl was fine as hell, but she couldn't do secretarial work if her life depended on it."

Tomas responded to Luis' tirade with silence.

"We may be cousins and all, but the last thing I need is another distraction like that in my life."

Dripping with sarcasm, Tomas responded, "Good morning to you, too, *primo.*"

"Sorry man… I'm having one of those mornings. Now tell me again about this woman—Miss Sanchez."

"Carmen Sanchez has over ten years experience as an administrative assistant. Her husband is a good friend of mine from back home, so you needn't worry about her being one of my "ladies". He and I got to talking and he mentioned something about his wife needing a job, and I thought about you needing an assistant."

"Okay, her being married makes me feel a little better…" Luis said.

"I learned my lesson the last time I recommended one of my girls for your company. Trust me, man; I don't ever want to face the wrath of Veronica again. That woman has a temper when she gets fired up!" exclaimed Tomas.

"I thought Ronnie was going to explode when she walked into my office and saw that Brazilian beauty sitting behind the desk with her breasts almost popping out of her dress." Luis was now able to laugh at the memory, but vowed to never put himself in a situation like that again.

"Well, she may not have been much of a typist, but she sure could work the rest of that body. I could pound that ass all night long! Man, I remember this one time…"

Luis cut him off. "Anyway, like I said, I hope this woman is qualified to do the job and isn't just another 'ho you want to sleep with."

"You are not listening to me. I am not interested in her. Furthermore, I haven't even laid eyes on Carmen."

"Fine. What else do you know about her?"

"Carmen is in her early thirties and they have three kids. Her husband told me she has tons of ambition and needs to hook a decent job. She is even fluent in Spanish. And since you've let your language skills slip, you need someone who can communicate with the locals."

"Unfortunately, you're right. Lately, I am beginning to feel more Californian than Dominican."

"Don't tell me you're turning into a *coconut?*" Tomas joked. "I hope you realize that a man without a connection to his roots tends to lose his soul, as well."

Although Tomas' observation was right on, Luis chose to let it slide. "Anyway… So she is married with three kids? Bilingual? And she has experience? If she can pass the Ronnie test, she's hired!" Luis laughed.

"Hey man, just give her a chance. If you don't think she's going to work out, then don't hire her. At least I tried. What time is the interview?"

"Nine o'clock."

"I have a feeling that Carmen is going to be perfect for the position." Tomas wanted to make amends for his last screw up.

"Yeah, I've heard that before!" Luis laughed again. "I've got to go. I'll call you later."

"*Primo*, tell Veronica I said *hola.*"

"Sure thing."

"You know I'm going to take that beautiful lady from you if you don't make an honest woman out of her soon."

"Whatever man... Ronnie and I have an understanding. We don't need to be married to be happy, so don't sweat me."

"I'm just saying that no matter what a woman says about not wanting to be married, she is lying. No woman wants to be in a long-term relationship without having a ring involved. Either that or she's waiting for someone better to come along. You'd better take care of that situation before someone else does."

"Tell me, Mr. De La Cruz, why should I take advice from you— someone who has never been married?"

"Because I know women and the only reason I am not married is because I haven't found anyone I want to settle down with. Most of the women I meet are not *wifey* material. If you know what I mean."

"Unfortunately, I do…"

"You guys have been together for how many years?"

"We met over three years ago. Been together just as long."

"My point exactly. It looks like neither one of you is going anywhere, so why not make it official? She is not getting any younger, you know. And pretty soon she'll be going through "the change". You know how horrible women are when that happens. Bet you won't get any action then."

"Man, I don't get you. One minute you're flirting with Ronnie and the next you're dissing her. What is it with this *love-hate* thing?"

"There is no love-hate anything… But I'll bet she's the reason you quit hanging out with me."

"No, Tomas. That wasn't Ronnie's decision, it was mine. Your idea of a good time is hopping into bed with as many women as you can and I gave that up a long time ago."

"Okayyyy… Your loss. Anyway, after that last hen you married, I expected you to end up with a more traditional woman this time. Perhaps, a nice Spanish-speaking Catholic girl."

"Uh, okay…" Luis looked at the phone as if his cousin had lost his mind.

"Veronica is beautiful and intelligent; yet, she is much too headstrong for my tastes." Tomas was enjoying getting Luis riled up.

"What do you mean *for your tastes*? Look man, that's my woman you're talking about." Luis tolerated many things from his cousin, but disrespecting Ronnie wasn't one of them.

"All I'm saying is, personally, I could not tolerate my woman being so bossy, that's all." He laughed. "On the other hand, perhaps there's something to dating a strong woman. Letting her take control."

"Watch it cousin…"

"Getting back to the subject, you know how much your mother disapproves of you two living together. She is always telling your sister, 'he needs to get married to that woman or he will spend an eternity burning in hell.'"

"Is that right?" Luis had about all he could take.

"When are you going back home anyway? You have stayed away much too long…"

"I don't believe you put my mama into this conversation."

"All right, I can take a hint."

"¡*Adiós*, Tomas!"

"Just don't say I didn't warn you…"

"Don't worry, I won't. Later." Luis hung up the phone, hanging onto the threads of their conversation.

He leaned back in his ergonomically designed leather chair, listening to the background music, and allowed random thoughts to go through his mind. Years ago, he had upgraded the piped in music from hits of the 60's and 70's to a contemporary jazz station after complaints from the staff. It was meant to be white noise. However, lately he often found himself daydreaming when a familiar song played.

Strains of Daryl Hall's, *Eyes for You (Ain't No Doubt about It)* played on in the background. He got caught up in the words of the song and the beat of the music.

Memories of the first time he and Ronnie met rushed back. Luis recalled how lovely Ronnie looked sitting in the dining room of that resort in the DR—all alone, trying to convince everyone that she preferred it that way. Her quiet confidence attracted him towards her table. After their first conversation, he intentionally made a pest of himself by getting on every excursion she signed up for, just to get to know her better.

Another song droned on in the background, and he fondly recalled their cross country road trip from her mother's house in Oklahoma to California, desperately trying to make Kiara's graduation on time. *We used to be so spontaneous. Used to make plans about moving to the DR. Used to make time for one another. What happened to us? Lately it seems we don't have much fun at all. I can't even remember the last time we actually spent any quality time together.*

A year ago, he and Ronnie decided they didn't need to get married because their current living arrangement was working well for both of them. And, after living together, Ronnie seemed even more adamant than ever about not being married. In spite of their agreement, Luis loved Ronnie and only wanted to make her his wife. Unfortunately, no matter how often he brought up the subject, her response was always the same. *"Why should we get married? We're not trying to have babies and we're happy with each other. Why mess up a good thing by getting married?"* Even so, the veiled words of wisdom from his cousin reverberated in his head.

Missing his woman, he picked up the phone and dialed her cell. Just as he pressed the last button, a knock at the door caused him to pause, interrupting his phone call.

He stopped what he was doing and stared at the woman standing in his doorway. She was a knockout in every sense of the word. With skin the color of caramel and eyes as black as coal, she was positively gorgeous. Her voluptuous body was slamming every which way in a tightly fitting red dress and her pretty face was framed by shoulder length, curly black hair.

"Hi, can I help you?" Luis said to the woman, trying his best to maintain his composure.

"*Si señor* My name is Carmen Sanchez. *Señor* De La Cruz referred me for a position—I mean a job, with *Señor* Duarte. That couldn't be you now, could it?" she said in a sensual, sexy voice, licking her full lips.

"*You're* Mrs. Sanchez?"

She nodded.

"Oh… I am *Señor* Duarte…I mean Luis Duarte." His voice cracked with unexpected nervousness. He swallowed the hard lump stuck in his throat. Thankfully, the lump formed an obstacle to prevent him from making a complete fool of himself by responding inappropriately.

"Oh really? I wasn't expecting someone as handsome as you. May I come in?" She purred like a cat in heat.

"You are right on time. P-p-please have a s-s-seat." He absentmindedly replaced the phone on its receiver; not realizing Ronnie had already picked up.

"Hello? Luis? Are you there? Luis? What the hell? I know he didn't just hang up on me." Unbeknownst to Luis, Ronnie had overheard the exchange on the other end, noticing an unfamiliar tone to Luis' voice. And she had never heard him stutter before. She immediately tried calling him back, first on his work phone and then his cell. He answered neither.

Luis heard both phones ring, but had put all calls on hold, which is what he typically did during business meetings. In his current state of mind, he forgot all about the call to Ronnie and focused on his task at hand—interviewing the beautifully tantalizing Carmen Sanchez.

"Mrs. Sanchez, Tomas tells me you've recently moved to California."

"*Si*, that is correct," she replied using an unrecognizable Spanish accent. It wasn't Dominican, nor was it Puerto Rican. He couldn't put his finger on where she was from.

"Uh, tell me a little bit about yourself." Luis willed his professionalism to return and not allow himself to be distracted by the sex appeal oozing from the woman's every pore.

She leaned forward in her chair, tossed her hair back and seductively replied in a low voice, "*Senor* Duarte, I can do anything you need me to do. Just tell me what you want." She licked her juicy red lips again and smiled.

Carmen was playing an all too familiar role—pretending to be a reluctant seductress in order to land a job. She eyed Duarte and thought, *he's really good looking. I think I'll switch up and be the innocent, helpless woman this time. He seems to be the sort of man who tries to save women in order to help them. This is going to be so easy and so much fun!* Times like this, her husband looked the other way, ignoring the fact that his wife often sold her body for money. At first, it began purely out of necessity. Though lately, her conquests seemed to be more for her own pleasure than cash. And when the man was both handsome and successful as Luis Duarte was, seduction was all the more interesting.

As for Luis, he studied the woman and realized she was trying her best to seduce him. He noticed her hands nervously tugging at her dress and she chewed her bottom lip—an adorable nervous tic. In spite of her actions, she seemed slightly uncomfortable—almost vulnerable. He would have laughed if it wasn't so pathetic. And as tempted as he was to see how far Carmen would go, he decided to put her out of her misery.

"I am looking for an experienced administrative assistant. Tomas tells me you have experience in this position, which is the *only* reason he referred you to me and the *only* reason I would hire you. Please tell me about your previous jobs and any qualifications you possess that will convince me to hire you."

Carmen sat back in her chair. *So this is how he wants to play it? All right…he isn't like the others. Ai caramba! This man sure is fine! I wouldn't have minded much if he had agreed to let me seduce him, but I really do need this job so I guess I should behave myself.*

In one swift motion, she pulled her hair upwards into a ponytail, securing it with an elastic band she kept on her wrist. She retrieved her glasses from her purse, perched them on the tip of her nose; and magically produced a light sweater and shrugged into it. In the span of a few minutes, she transformed herself from a hoochie mama to a professional businesswoman.

"I apologize if I may have offended you, but I need this job so badly I am willing to do anything to get it," she explained in a soft-spoken voice. *Especially with a man as handsome as you.* "And please call me Carmen. Mrs. Sanchez is my mother-in-law's name."

Luis also softened his tone. "I understand, but you should never be willing to compromise your morals for a job. Please tell me about yourself."

Over the next hour, Carmen filled him in on her qualifications as an administrative assistant. She also told Luis all about her husband and children, beaming as she did. Explained how she, a native of Dallas, ended up marrying a man from the Dominican Republic and how they had lived on the island for the past ten years. Told him that she became fluent in Spanish while she was a teenager growing up amongst her Mexican-American friends. She said they relocated to California, because the children were getting older and they wanted them to have a quality education.

"Mrs. Sanchez, I mean...Carmen, I think you are perfect for this job. You possess all the right skills and have the experience that I am looking for in an administrative assistant. And the fact that you are fluent in Spanish is a huge bonus. So, I've made the decision to hire you. When can you start?" He extended his hand.

"I can begin as soon as you need me. Today? Tomorrow?" Carmen stood up and grasped his hands in gratitude.

"Next Monday will be fine. I'll give you a new employee packet that includes all the forms you need to complete. Just bring those in with you when you return."

"*Señor* Duarte, thank you so much! I promise I will not disappoint you. My husband will be so pleased. I will see you on Monday."

"You are very welcome." He walked her to the exit.

She dropped her head in shame before she spoke, "I am so sorry for how I behaved earlier. Tomas always brags to my husband about the many beautiful women he dates. He tells my husband about the good deals he has gotten based on the women he associates with. I thought doing business with you would be the same."

Luis was not surprised by his cousin's brazenness. In fact, he felt like laughing out loud, but he didn't because this wasn't the right time. He'd catch up with Tomas later. "You have no need to apologize. As far as I'm concerned, *that* never happened. I will see you Monday morning at eight o'clock."

"Thank you so much. You have no idea what this means for my family, because we never realized how expensive it is to live in California." She laughed after realizing she overlooked one of the most important aspects of the interview. "I forgot to ask, what does this job pay?"

"Do not worry about the pay. I make it a point to make certain my employees are well compensated. Better pay means fewer turnovers. We will discuss salary and benefits when you return."

"Thank you again, *senor*. I will see you next week. *¡Adiós!*"

Luis watched Carmen saunter across the street. He expected her to get into a car and drive off, but apparently she didn't own one because she headed to the bus stop. Part of him wanted to offer her a ride, but the more rational half stepped in before he could make a fool of himself. She gave a little wave. A little voice inside whispered, *be careful with this one.*

Julio, Luis' office manager, passed Carmen as she was leaving the main office. He stopped so abruptly he almost got whiplash from turning his head so fast. "Daaaamn!!! Boss, who is that?!"

Luis watched Carmen board the bus. He also watched the men who were watching Carmen. That is when the reality of the situation slapped him across his face. *Oh no! What have I gotten myself into? Just wait until Ronnie sees Carmen. She is going to lose her mind!*

Even when Carmen tried to look plain, her natural beauty made her stand out from any crowd. There was no way in hell he was going to convince Ronnie that Carmen was *only* an employee. "Uh, that's my new secretary Carmen Sanchez."

"Yeah right… Don't tell me she's another one of Tomas' women!" Julio laughed, thinking Luis was kidding around.

The strained expression on Luis' face told him all he needed to know.

"Boss? You didn't..." Julio shook his head in disappointment. There was nothing he hated more than drama at work. He got enough of that at home. Considering the last time his boss hired a woman recommended by his cousin and all the problems it caused, he thought for sure Luis would be smarter this time. Guess he was wrong…

Chapter Three

*R*onnie pulled up to the *J. Bradford Rehabilitative Center*. The tall Madrone trees formed a canopy over the parking lot only letting fragments of sunshine through. *This place is so peaceful.* She rolled down the windows and watched several species of birds flit from one tree to the other. *Birds have it so easy. Nothing to worry about except where their next meal is coming from and staying out of the rain.*

Still fuming from earlier, she tried to put the exchange between Luis and the woman aside. She recalled the last time Tomas tried to land a job for one of his sluts, including the backlash that followed. *There is no way Luis would let something like that happen again, would he?*

As she embraced every unimaginable situation, a purple butterfly landed on the hood of her car. It had been ages since she'd seen one. "Hello, little butterfly. Where did you come from?"

The butterfly distracted her only for a moment before the negative thoughts resurfaced. "That Tomas is nothing but trouble. Seems like he can't be happy for us. And intentionally or not, he seems to want to sabotage our relationship. The worst part is Luis doesn't realize how manipulative his cousin can be. That asshole even tried to hit on me a few times."

The last time this happened, Luis swore up and down he wasn't interested in that bitch Tomas sent over. He tried to convince me that 'ho was nothing more than his receptionist. I must have had stupid plastered across my forehead. If she was just his employee, why did he feel the need to keep her secret? Letting me find out only by showing up at his office felt like a slap in the face. After he got rid of that woman, who could barely type or speak a lick of English, Luis promised to never let his judgment slip like that again.

"Lord, my father always told me that You use butterflies to remind us how something ugly can become beautiful in time. And purple was my daddy's favorite color... So I'm going to try my best to give Luis the benefit of the doubt."

Unfortunately, after overhearing the conversation with him and his so called appointment, her every instinct told her differently. Although she wanted to trust Luis, she understood that some men were weak when it came to a very determined woman. She looked at the clock on the dashboard. She exhaled her frustration away because it was time to go inside.

Ronnie walked past the receptionist and sang out, "Good morning, Kaylee. How is that adorable baby of yours?"

"He started walking a few days ago. Now we've got to baby proof the apartment."

"Your baby is walking already? Where did the time go?"

"I don't know, but before I know it he'll be starting school... Oh, I almost forgot to tell you, Travis is running late this morning. He'll be in later."

"Okay, thanks. Well, I have a lot of work to catch up on. Please let me know when Travis gets in."

"Sure thing," Kaylee replied.

Ronnie made it to her office. She dropped her bags on the floor behind her desk before settling down. "Good morning, Trudy."

"Veronica?! Good morning, dearie. I didn't expect you back today. How are you feeling?" Trudy asked with motherly concern.

"I'm feeling much better. Still a little under the weather, but I'm able to keep light food down. Must have had a touch of the stomach flu. Or something."

"I am glad you're back. Travis has had me running all over the place looking for this file or that file... He has been a nervous wreck ever since he found out we're being audited."

"What do you mean we're being audited? Since when?"

"Let's see... You've been out for a week, so... Let me think, I believe it was... Oh dear, I forgot. Perhaps, it is on his calendar... I'll pull it up. Now what is the password? Oh, there it is... What was I looking for again?" She began pecking at the keyboard, stopped abruptly, and then went to a file cabinet and started flipping through files.

Trudy was in her early seventies and was slowly losing what remained of her memory. Lord only knows why Travis kept her on. Most days she couldn't remember what she did from one day to the next so Ronnie ran the office and assigned her the most simplest of tasks. But when her mind was fully engaged, she was one sharp cookie.

Ronnie watched her elderly coworker dart from one place to the next without rhyme or reason. A brunette wig styled in a fashionable short bob was perched crooked atop her head. Fine white hairs peeked from underneath. Despite her advanced years, she took extra care in her choice of clothing, sparing no expense.

"Don't worry about the audit, Trudy. I'll catch up with Travis when he gets in."

Ronnie checked a week's worth of emails, and then corrected several errors made by Trudy in the weekly status report. After her work was finished, she tried calling Luis several times, but couldn't get through. He simply would not, or chose not to, answer his phone.

The phone rang, shifting her focus back to work.

"Business admin office," she answered, wishing Travis would enter the 21st century and purchase phones that came with caller ID.

"Veronica, its Kaylee. Travis is in his office now." The old phone lines made Kaylee's voice sound like she was miles away instead of just a few offices down.

"Thanks, Kaylee," she replied, disappointed it wasn't Luis. "Trudy, I'll be right back. I'm going to see Travis."

"All right dearie, I'll be here when you get back." Trudy smiled, showing a mouthful of bright white dentures.

Ronnie poked her head around Travis' office door. When she didn't see him, she called out, "Travis, you in there?"

"Yes, I'll be right out. Come in and have a seat," he answered through the closed bathroom door.

Ronnie compulsively began straightening up his cluttered office. A vase of dead flowers sat in one corner with dried-up brown petals littering the space surrounding it. She emptied the flowers into the trash can and made a mental note to get the cleaning crew in there.

"Ronnie! Good to see you. How are you feeling?"

"Much better, thanks."

"Good, that's really good to hear. Well, everyone is happy you're back. Now I know who really runs this place and it's not me." He chuckled, good-naturedly.

"I'm glad to be back. I'm not used to being at home sick." She eyed Travis, noticing he also seemed tired. "Anyway, Trudy tells me the center is being audited. What's up?"

"I received the notice in the mail last week. The state of California audits nonprofit agencies every few years and unfortunately, it's our turn. I've asked Trudy to gather the necessary documentation, but she couldn't seem to locate what I needed. I've been a nervous wreck because I don't know where anything is."

"When is the audit?" asked Ronnie.

"In two weeks. We have an accounting firm lined up to review our records to make sure everything is in order prior to the audit. Can you pull the files I need by tomorrow?"

"Sure. Everything is stored on the hard drive. I'll download the files onto a thumb drive and send Kaylee out for the hard copy printouts. They can make the reports as fancy or as simple as you like."

"Is that all there is to it? Why doesn't Trudy know this? She's been searching for those files for the past few days."

"Actually, I *have* explained to Trudy where to locate the files *and* how to download them many times. She has access to everything that I do—just in case I'm out sick, like last week."

"I can't believe it was this simple…"

Ronnie cleared her throat before continuing, "Travis, about Trudy… She's not, um, very… To be perfectly honest, she's getting very forgetful. I think this job may be more than she can handle."

"I think you may be right. And thanks to this audit, I've seen how inefficient Trudy is. I'd hate to let her go because she's such a sweet lady."

"I'm not saying you should fire her, but maybe you should place her in a position with less responsibility. Your decision…" Ronnie raised her hands in surrender.

She was careful not to overstep her boundaries with Travis concerning his hiring decisions. Although their relationship was at one time personal, unless it now pertained to Kiara, it was strictly business.

Distracted by the thoughts running through her mind, she stared over his shoulder and out the window at a bougainvillea vine draped alongside a wrought iron fence. The dark pink color was so vibrant; it looked as if the plant wasn't real.

"I'll think about it. However, because you work with her more closely than anyone else, I will take your comments into serious consideration."

"The only reason I said anything is because I am concerned—for her health, as well as the centers'."

"I understand. Since you've been here, you've gotten everything so organized, the office practically runs itself. And about the report brochures, we usually use Luis' company for that. Kaylee has the secretary's number. She can run over there as soon as you get the files prepared."

The mention of Luis' name reminded her she needed to speak to him as soon as possible. "Consider it done. Oh, did I mention that Kiara is coming over for dinner tonight?"

"No, but that's great. She rarely takes time to do anything fun anymore. It's usually school and work."

"I know. I don't see her as often as I'd like to, so tonight will be extra special." Ronnie decided not to mention Kiara's friend, just in case Travis didn't know about him.

"Will you please ask that daughter of ours to call her old man? She used to call me all the time, now I'm lucky if I hear from her once a month. Even luckier if I get to see her…"

"She *is* growing up, Travis."

"Don't I know it?" His eyes momentarily glazed over. "Anyway, I'm glad you're back. I've got a teleconference this morning and need to review for it. See you later?" he asked.

"Sure. I'll start working on those files right away."

"Thanks." Travis looked like the weight of the world had been lifted from his shoulders.

He redirected his attention to his computer and Ronnie returned to her office. With thoughts of Luis and that woman's conversation still on her mind, the first thing she did was pick up the phone and call Luis.

Chapter Four

*L*uis' cell phone rang. He picked up when he saw it was Ronnie. "Hey sweetheart, how are you?"

"I'm good. I'm returning your call from this morning."

I started to call her this morning, but hung up before the call went through. Damn, did the call go through? "Oh, I see you've called several times. Sorry I wasn't able to get to the phone. I've been in meetings most of the morning."

"You've been in meetings? With whom?"

"Oh, nobody special. Had a meeting with a new client. Just the usual work stuff."

"So…you've been *working* all morning? It's almost lunchtime. Why didn't you call me back earlier?"

Luis knew when Ronnie's BS detector was up. She never tracked his whereabouts or his time. "Baby, what's wrong? What's with all the questions?"

Just at that moment, Kaylee entered the office talking a mile a minute about the files needed for the audit. "Veronica, is the flash drive with the financial files ready? What kind of report should I request? Are they supposed to be in black and white or color? Does he want charts…?"

Ronnie raised a finger to ask Kaylee to hold on. "Luis, we'll continue this conversation at home. I've got to get these files downloaded so Kaylee can run them over to your office for printing."

Luis breathed a sigh of relief. "Sure, we'll catch up later. Do I need to stop by the store to pick up anything for dinner?"

"Nope, I've got everything already taken care of. Just be sure you're home before seven."

"I will. I love you, baby."

"Yeah, I love you, too. Bye." Ronnie hung up the phone still pissed off. *Luis didn't sound like he was trying to hide anything. But I am not crazy. I heard how that woman spoke to him and she is definitely up to something, I just know it. A woman who is all about business does not speak that way during an interview.*

"Sorry, I didn't mean to interrupt your conversation," Kaylee apologized.

"Don't worry about it. What do you need?"

"Travis said you were getting the files ready. He told me you would tell me what I needed to have printed."

"Let's get Trudy over here so she'll know how to do this." Once again, Ronnie patiently showed Trudy the step-by-step process of how to locate and download the files while Kaylee waited.

"Oh dear, perhaps I should be taking notes... Kaylee, be a dear and hand me a pad and pencil. Now, what did you say I need to do, dearie?" She looked up at Ronnie with confused, rheumy eyes.

Trudy became so flustered trying to follow along that Ronnie finally gave up. "Never mind. I'll have Kaylee finish."

"If you're sure..." Trudy looked relieved.

Ronnie reassured her, "Don't worry. We'll take care of it."

Kaylee sighed loudly in frustration. "That's right, Trudy. We got it."

"Here you go, Kaylee. I printed out the instructions in a work order. Give this to the secretary. She'll know what to do. Thanks."

After the crisis of the audit was taken care of, Ronnie finished up several projects in the office and headed home to prepare dinner.

* * *

Luis reflected on how much he loved Ronnie. She was the only woman for him and he wanted to spend the rest of his life with her. For whatever reason—maybe it was listening to Carmen talk about her family, or possibly Tomas' words from this morning reverberating over and over again in his mind—he decided to do something about it once and for all.

Despite their earlier conversation, he needed to speak to his cousin. Tomas was the closest male friend he had and most of the time, being related was an added bonus. Without hesitation, he picked up the phone. "Hey Tomas, you got a minute?"

"Sure, *primo*. What's up? How'd the interview go? Wasn't Carmen as talented as I said she would be?"

"Yeah, yeah, she was great...."

"Did you hire her?"

"Yes, I did, but that's not why I'm calling."

"No, *que pasa*?"

"I've been thinking about what you said this morning... About me and Ronnie getting married."

"Is that right?"

"Yes. I'm going to get a ring and propose."

"Seriously? Man, I was just joking earlier. I wasn't serious."

"Maybe so, but it makes perfect sense for us to get married. We've been together awhile now and we belong together. I love that woman."

"Are you sure you want to give up your freedom to get hitched? You know how women change once they have a ring on their finger. Veronica may be cool now, but wait until she becomes your wife. Don't forget what happened the first time you got married. She turned out to be a first rate gold digging bitch."

"You must have forgotten that you introduced me to that bitch in the first place. Ronnie is different. I thought you would be happy for me—for us."

"I'm just saying that women change once they get married. I've seen it too many times. Why do you think I'm still single? There are too many fine women out here for me to get tied down to one."

"What do you know about marriage? *I* must be crazy for asking your opinion, anyway."

"*Primo*, with your credentials, you can have your pick of the litter. I'll bet Veronica would dump your ass in a hot minute if some rich guy came along. That's what woman do. They look for a man who can take care of them so they can lie around on their asses and get fat."

"Tomas, you sound like you're still in your twenties. When are you going to grow up?"

"If growing up means getting married, you can plan on me being a child forever."

"Whatever man. You and I may be related, but we are as different as night and day. I love Ronnie, she loves me, and I want to be with her. Period."

"If that's what you want… "

"I'll catch up with you later."

"Did you tell Veronica about Carmen?"

"Not yet."

"You'd better get her to say yes before you spring *that* news on her. Women don't like competition, especially when it's that close. Or that fine." He chuckled at the naivety of his cousin.

"*Adios* Tomas, I am not going to let you piss all over my parade." Luis hung up and tried to not let their conversation bother him. He asked his reflection in the window, "Why do I always let Tomas get to me?"

* * *

Ronnie pulled out virtually every dish in the kitchen cabinets searching for the paella pan. Paella was Kiara's favorite dish, therefore, that's what she was going to prepare. It wasn't often her daughter stopped by to visit, so when she did, Ronnie made it into an event.

As she set the heavy skillet on the stove, Ronnie's heart was weighed down with the circumstances and conversations of the morning. She needed to talk to someone. Setting the food aside, she picked up the phone and dialed.

"Hello?" Joie answered on the third ring.

"Hey, girlfriend? What's going on?"

"Ronnie? I haven't heard from you in months! How you doing?"

"I'm good. You know… Just living my life in the offbeat."

"How's the family?"

"Everyone's fine. I'm getting over a touch of the flu. Kiara is stopping by this evening for dinner. Luis is good—staying busy with work and all. I started my novel but haven't gotten very far. Been too busy with everything else."

"I understand about being busy because that's all I am. So you and Kiara have really bonded?"

"Yes, like we were never apart…."

"That's great." Joie knew her friend well enough to realize she would eventually get to the point of the phone call. Until then, she'd settle for small talk. "So what are you cooking for dinner?"

"Kiara loves paella and I'm baking my mother's famous 7up cake for dessert. In fact, I'll have to call her for the recipe after I hang up with you."

"Girl, I've been planning on visiting you since you moved out there. Hopefully, I'll make it before this summer is over."

"Joie, I'd love for you to come visit. Just let me know when." Ronnie sighed heavily. "Yeah, everybody's doing okay…"

"Uh oh, I know that sound. What's wrong?" asked Joie.

Ronnie started to laugh. Even after years of being apart, Joie still knew her very well.

"I'm fine, really. How are my Godchildren?"

"Girl, these kids are doing great. Still driving me crazy most of the time, but I wouldn't have it any other way." She laughed. "At the moment they're with Derek's parents. They spend a couple of weeks with them every summer, so right now I'm just enjoying the quiet."

"I am so happy that Derek's parents have finally connected with your children."

"Me too."

"Lord knows Maya and Trey have been through more than enough in the last few years. It's about time they can just be kids again."

"Cedric still stops by to get them. Not as often as he used to, but they still call him Daddy."

"Well, he is the only daddy they've ever known..."

"Ronnie, I miss him so much, but I guess after three years, it's gotta be time to move on."

"It's hard letting go of someone you once loved. But like you said, it is time to move on. Has he?"

"Who? Cedric? Yeah, he's messing around with some woman. I try my best to *not* keep track of what's going on in his life."

"I hear you, girl. After me and Derek got divorced, the last thing I wanted to hear about was how happy he was without me. There was many a night I wanted to do a drive by and throw a Molotov cocktail on their lawn." Ronnie chuckled. "On yours too, come to think of it."

"I know I probably deserved that and more, but I am so happy we are still friends. There aren't many women who would have been as forgiving as you."

"Trust me, Joie. It wasn't easy."

"Well, the only good thing that did come from my indiscretion was my kids." Joie paused, remembering the pain.

"I guess what they say about time healing all wounds is true. Having Luis in my life also helped me move on."

"It also doesn't hurt that Derek is no longer living. Don't want to speak ill of the deceased, but that man was something else..."

"That is true. But calling on the awesome power of forgiveness, does tend to take the edge off of hating someone." Ronnie recalled how many years it took her to forgive Derek. It was quite a few.

"Amen! And speaking of forgiveness, Maya and Trey picked up a few half brothers and sisters, a couple of new grandparents and a slew of aunts, uncles, and cousins in the process."

"Tell them Auntie Ronnie sends lots of hugs and kisses."

"I will." Joie paused and asked, "Now, girlfriend, tell me what's *really* up with you?"

"It's probably nothing, but you know how you can tell when your man is keeping something from you?"

"Something like what?"

"Well, like I said, it's probably nothing, but earlier today, I overheard a conversation between Luis and a woman. She was in his office and sounded like she knew him. But not really... Their conversation was similar to how you and Cedric used to role play."

"You had to mention me and Cedric's role playing, didn't you. I sure do miss those days".

"What got my attention was she was talking all sexy and he sounded nervous. He actually hung up on me."

"What do you mean he hung up on you? Why would he call you while he's role playing with some woman?"

"That's just it. It was like he dialed my number, but didn't know I was on the line. He must not have heard me pick up."

"Did you call him back and ask him about it?"

"Yeah, I tried calling a few times. When he finally did pick up, he said he had been in meetings all morning."

"Meetings my ass… Okay, I was willing to give the man the benefit of doubt until you said that. What the hell, Ronnie? I know this man ain't messing around on you."

"No, I don't think he is. We've been doing really well together. It's just that…"

Joie had enough experience with lying, cheating, no good men to smell one a mile away; and in this case, fifteen hundred miles away.

"Girlfriend, if I was you, I'd straight out ask his ass about who he had meetings with today. If he lies, then you know he's up to no good."

"You're right. That's the only way I'm going to find out what's going on. I'll have to ask him point-blank."

"I hope what's going on with Luis is nothing, but my cheat-on-a-bitch instincts tell me differently. I have had too many instances of dealing with d-o-g-s to last a lifetime. In fact, that's all I've run into lately. Can't find a good man to save my life. They're either married and steppin' out on wifey, on the down-low, or just a broke assed niggah with no dreams or goals. I'm tired of these good for nothin' brothas, so I've given up on 'em."

"Damn! You have really become cynical."

"That's what life has done to me, so I focus on taking care of my kids and every now and then pull out Mr. Johnson to scratch that itch. I ain't trippin' no more on finding Mr. Right when Mr. Johnson will do."

"Joie, you are truly crazy. Sounds to me like you just haven't found the right one. Don't get all bitter on men and become some crazy-assed man-hater."

"Oh, that ain't never gonna happen. Your girl loves men too much to go that route."

Ronnie felt her stomach lurch. "Girl, I've got to go. I think I'm going to be sick again. Ugh, I thought this stomach flu was over."

"Okay, you take care of yourself and call me anytime."

"Thanks Joie. Talk to you soon."

Ronnie ran to the bathroom and promptly threw up the remains of her lunch. Apparently, she overdid it by going to work, which resulted in a relapse of her illness. After she recovered, she returned to the kitchen and spent the next several hours preparing the paella. It was going on three and she still needed the recipe for the 7up cake. Time to call her mother.

"*You've reached the Pierce residence. We are unavailable to take your call…*" answered the male recording. Years ago, Dianna asked her neighbor, Mr. Smith, to setup her voicemail message so people wouldn't know she lived alone. It was his voice that greeted her on the answering machine.

"Mama, pick up. It's Veronica," Ronnie stated, knowing her mother screened all her calls to avoid telemarketers.

"Hi baby. I'm here," replied Dianna.

"Hey, Mama… How you doing?"

"I'm fine. What about you?"

"Pretty good, except I can't seem to shake this stomach flu. It's been a week and I'm still getting sick to my stomach. I called because I'm making Kiara dinner tonight and I need the recipe for your 7up cake."

"That flu ain't nothing to play around with. It's unusual to get it this time of year, ain't it?"

"Yeah, but I picked it up somewhere."

"You been to the doctor lately?"

"No, it's not that serious to go to the doctor. I've been taking it easy and watching what I eat. Hopefully, it will go away soon."

"Well, if it lasts any longer, you should see your doctor. Maybe you're pregnant," teased Dianna.

"Mama, don't even joke about something like that. You know I am too old to be even thinking about having babies." Ronnie counted backwards to her last period. They tended to be irregular and she couldn't remember her last one.

"I'm not joking. I have heard of forty-three year olds having babies. Never say never."

"Mama, please... I am not pregnant. I'm going through early menopause, if anything. I'll be fine in a few days."

"If you say so..."

"Now what about your recipe? I only have a couple of hours to get the cake made and in the oven."

"All right, all right... First make sure the eggs and butter are room temperature. Then you get yourself three cups of flour..." Dianna explained her recipe, step-by-step, and provided additional instructions on the importance of setting the oven temperature just so.

After Ronnie had copied down all the ingredients on her kitchen chalkboard, she said, "Thanks, Mama. I'll be sure to let Kiara know it's your recipe. She'll get a kick out of that."

"You're welcome. Give my best to Luis and Kiara. I'm going to try to get out there to visit later this year, so have my room ready."

"I will. Take care and I'll talk to you soon. Love you."

"I love you, too. And don't forget to make an appointment with your doctor," she added before hanging up.

Ronnie pulled out her calendar and started counting backwards. Luis' two Boxers padded into the kitchen searching for food. She stared down at the dogs and asked, "When *was* my last period? I can't remember. Doesn't matter. I'm not pregnant—can't be." She shook off the possibility. "Enough of that foolish talk. I've got to get this cake baked before everyone gets here."

Both boxers checked their dish, seeing there was no dog food in their bowls because it wasn't feeding time. The dogs stared at Ronnie and cocked their heads to the side as if they totally understood. They squeezed through the doggie door to get outside.

"Well, just to make sure it's nothing more than a virus, might as well see the old doc. It's time for my annual anyway." With that she picked up the phone and made an appointment.

Chapter Five

"*B*aby, I'm home!" Luis was greeted by the aroma of seafood paella and freshly baked cake wafting from the kitchen. He went straight to Ronnie standing by the stove, stepped behind her, and slid his arms around her waist.

"You sure are in a good mood this evening. Did you have a good day?" Ronnie turned the cake upside down on the cooling wire rack. The cake slid out from the Bundt pan without sticking.

"I had a wonderful day, but I missed you terribly." He kissed her neck up and down.

Succumbing to his kisses, Ronnie almost forgot she was still angry with Luis. She was about to question him about his mysterious conversation when the doorbell rang. She glanced at the clock. "They're early. Can you please get the door?"

Luis turned Ronnie around and kissed her passionately. "We'll finish this later," he said, obviously aroused.

What in the world has gotten into that man? He hasn't kissed me like that in a long, long time. I wonder if it's got anything to do with this morning. Has some other woman revved up his engine and now he's ready to finish with me?" She pushed the thoughts away and focused on finishing the meal.

"Hello mother dear," Kiara called out, coming into the kitchen. She gave Ronnie a great big hug before peeking into the pot. "Mmm, it smells delicious in here. You made paella? I love you, I love you, I love you!" She squealed, jumping up and down.

"You're always talking about how much you love it, so I made it especially for you."

"You baked a 7up cake, too?" Kiara pinched crumbs from the plate.

"Sure did. From your grandmother's special recipe."

"Are there strawberries to go with it?"

Ronnie nodded. "Freshly whipped cream, too."

"Awesome! You have no idea what I've been eating lately. *When* I have time to eat..."

"I can see you've lost a few pounds. You need to come by more often so I can feed you." She loved seeing her daughter so happy.

"Have you talked to Daddy lately?"

"Uh huh, I saw him today, as a matter of fact. He wants you to call him."

"I know I should call more often, but he's always so busy with work. He needs to let someone else take over for awhile so he can relax."

"Considering I'm the only one who knows what goes on in that office, I can understand his concern."

"What about his assistant? And there's always Trudy," said Kiara.

"His assistant spends most of his time on the road. And Trudy can sometimes be a bit, um…forgetful."

"I know what you mean. I used to, like get away with so much because Trudy didn't seem to remember most of the things I did while I was in the office."

Ronnie laughed at her mischievous daughter. She could only imagine how she was as a child. "Where's your friend?" Ronnie peered over Kiara's shoulder. "Who is he? Anyone special?"

"He's in the living room talking to Luis. His name is Gerald Quinn, but we all call him GQ. We've been seeing each other like off and on now for about a year."

"GQ, huh? Well, I can't wait to meet him. Does your father know you have a boyfriend?"

Kiara rolled her eyes. "Are you kidding? Daddy would like kill me if he knew I was dating—especially a man who goes by his initials. He's so conservative, you know."

"Conservative? Who? Travis?" Ronnie laughed out loud. "Child, your father is anything but conservative. You would be surprised by some of the things we used to do while we were dating. And I've gotten to know him all over again since I've been in California. Remember, you only know him from a daughter's perspective which is coming from a very protective place. That does not mean conservative. Not by a long shot. Give your father a chance, he may just surprise you."

"If you say so… I'll let you be the judge once you meet GQ, then you can tell me how you think Daddy will react."

"Well then, I guess I'd better go meet Mr. GQ." Ronnie untied her apron, turned the stove down to warm, and went to meet Kiara's date.

The two men sat across from one another sharing work stories over a couple of drinks. GQ was an attractive man with a head full of long dreads that hung down towards the middle of his back. Ronnie took notice that Luis seemed to have taken an immediate liking to GQ because he let him sit in his favorite chair.

"There he is. What do you think?" whispered Kiara.

Her "boyfriend" looked to be several years older than Kiara. No, not just several—more like fifteen. In fact, he appeared to be closer to her age than her daughter's.

Kiara went and stood next to him. "GQ, I want you to meet my mother, Miss Veronica Pierce."

"I'm pleased to meet you, Miss Pierce, but you can't be Kiara's mother. You look young enough to be her sister!" he exclaimed in genuine disbelief.

Kiara and Luis snickered because this wasn't the first time they had experienced that same reaction from others upon meeting Ronnie and her daughter.

"Well, I am her mother, but thank you for the compliment." She motioned towards a chair. "Please, sit down."

GQ took his seat in Luis' favorite chair and Kiara perched near him, on the chair's arm. Ronnie sat on the loveseat next to Luis.

"Sweetheart, Gerald was just telling me about his travels. He's been all over the world volunteering in poor countries—doing missionary work," said Luis.

"Is that right? Missionary work, huh?" Ronnie eyed the man up and down.

"Yes, ma'am, I've been to numerous countries. As a matter of fact, I spent several months last year in Port-au-Prince helping to rebuild the city. Their problems began a long time before that earthquake hit. And years later, there is still much that remains to be done." GQ sipped what was left of his drink and placed the empty glass on the coffee table.

"That's quite a lot of life experience. I assumed you two met in school." Ronnie furrowed her brow.

GQ glanced at Kiara. "School? Didn't Kiara tell you?" he asked, watching Kiara squirm.

"Tell me what?" Ronnie said.

"How we met," he answered.

"No, she didn't. So tell me daughter, how *do* you two know each other?"

"We did meet in school, Mom. GQ is an Assistant Professor of Cultural Anthropology at UC Santa Elena. I, like uh, took his class during freshman year. We've been dating on and off for the last year."

Ronnie and Luis exchanged a look that spoke volumes. Her maternal instincts kicked into high gear providing her with a suspicion that there was more to this story than Kiara had initially revealed. She'd get to the bottom of it later.

"Uh, Luis, please show Gerald where he can freshen up. Kiara can help me set the table. The food should be ready in about fifteen minutes."

GQ grabbed Kiara's hand and gave it a playful tug. She giggled shyly and pulled away to follow Ronnie to the kitchen.

"What do you think? Isn't GQ great?" Kiara gushed.

"Uh huh, he seems to be very nice. I had no idea he was so much older than you... How old is he anyway?"

Kiara paused before speaking. She took a huge breath and stated, "GQ is really cool. He's like super smart and is always trying to help those less fortunate. In fact, he wants me to go with him to Haiti when school is out."

Ronnie did a double-take. "What? He wants you to go to Haiti? Next month? Have you spoken to your father about this?" Ronnie studied the woman-child standing before her. In so many ways, Kiara reminded her of herself at that age.

"Um, not exactly. I was like hoping you could be there when I do. Daddy's like much more practical when you're around."

"I don't know, Kiara. You're still kind of young to be traveling to a foreign country with a man we know nothing about. What in the world could you do in Haiti that you can't do here?"

"Mom, I am not a child..." she protested. "As for what I'll do there, he says I can like help wherever I am needed."

"Umph! Really? You still haven't said how old he is." Ronnie removed a stack of plates from the cupboard.

Kiara hesitated again before answering, "GQ is thirty-five, but his age doesn't matter to me. Anyway, he says I'm mature beyond my age." She went behind Ronnie to massage her tense shoulders. "I'm just trying to spread my wings, that's all. Don't you want me to experience life and all it has to offer?"

"Oh, now I get it. You think you can butter me up and get me on your side. Well, young lady, I think your being involved with this man is a bad idea for so many different reasons. I am sure Gerald has good intentions and means well..." She exhaled loudly. "Kiara, I have to just say it; I think he is way too old for you."

"I thought you'd be the last person to hold his age against him. Mom, I want you to be okay with my decision—Daddy too. I'm twenty-one years old and I don't really need you guy's permission. But I would like your support. It's a good opportunity for me to get outside my little bubble and experience the real world."

"Look, we need to discuss this further. For now, let's just put this conversation on the backburner until we can talk to Travis. How 'bout we just enjoy dinner and I will take this opportunity to get to know Gerald better." Ronnie handed Kiara a stack of plates and silverware to set the table. She turned the paella into a serving dish and motioned for Kiara to follow her to the dining room.

"Yeah, okay. It's just that he's so great. All my girlfriends say how lucky I am to be dating him. He's smoking hot, right?"

"Yes, Kiara. He's hot," replied Ronnie, marveling at her daughter's youth and naivety. "You practicing safe sex?" she added without missing a beat.

Kiara blushed five shades of red, "Of course, we are. Dang, what do you think I am? Stupid?"

"Not stupid, sweetheart, just young," replied Ronnie.

* * *

"What do you think about this GQ character?" Ronnie asked Luis as she slathered lotion on her feet. Lately, it seemed as if every part of her body required extra moisture.

Luis propped the pillow behind his head, anticipating a long discussion. "He appears to be legitimate. Got a good head on his shoulders. He also seems to really care for Kiara."

"Luis, he's fifteen years older than she is. Don't you think he's too old for her?"

"Um, not really. My father was thirteen years older than my mother when they got married. Things worked out okay for them."

"That is not a good example. Your parents were from a different era *and* another country. Life was different back then."

"Let me ask you this; do you trust your daughter?"

"Yes, I trust Kiara. I trust her to do only what her sheltered life will tell her is okay. I *can* say that I do not trust her grown-ass boyfriend. He has to have an ulterior motive. What could a thirty-five year old man possibly see in a twenty-one year old besides the obvious?" It pained

Ronnie to speak of Kiara in that context, but the situation called for realism and she would not permit herself to think of it any other way.

"She is a very smart young lady, even if she did live a sheltered life. I've known her for several years and I think going to Haiti will do her a world of good. She has good instincts."

"You're right, but…"

"Look, if it'll make you feel any better, I have a few relatives in Port-au-Prince who can look out for her if she decides to go."

"Knowing that makes me feel a little better. But I still have reservations about any thirty-five year old man who calls himself 'GQ'". Ronnie slid underneath the covers and snuggled up against Luis.

"Darling, the man's name is Gerald Quinn. GQ just happens to be his initials. My advice is to trust your daughter. She comes from good stock on both sides." Luis snuggled close anticipating finishing what they started earlier.

Ronnie pushed up on her elbows and said, "Speaking of trust, what happened this morning at work?"

"Uh, what do you mean? Nothing happened at work today. What are you talking about?"

"Are you sure? Because you hung up on me after a woman came into your office. I heard you."

Luis' mind went into overdrive. With everything else that happened during the day, he had completely forgotten about hiring Carmen Sanchez. "Oh, I forgot to tell you that I hired a new administrative assistant today."

"Oh, really?"

Luis frowned trying to remember everything that happened earlier. "You say I hung up on you?"

"Yes, you hung up on me. I heard your entire conversation and the woman on the other end didn't sound like someone coming for an interview."

"My love, I do not know what you *think* you heard, but all I did today was interview a young lady who needed a job to help out her family."

"Luis, I overheard your conversation. That woman sounded like she was coming for more than a j-o-b. And you sounded like you wanted to do more than hire her." Ronnie scoffed.

Luis snickered nervously. "It's not what you think. Tomas recommended her because he works with her husband…"

"Did you say Tomas recommended her? Oh, hell naw! If your cousin knows her, then she must be a first rate 'ho," Ronnie declared. She felt any remaining self-control slowly slipping away. At this point, it was too late to care. Ronnie tossed the covers away and jumped from the bed.

He pushed himself up and sat up straight. "Ronnie calm down. You're getting yourself wound up. Let me explain…"

"Don't tell me to calm down!" She hissed.

"Fine, I won't tell you to calm down. Sit down and hear me out. Please…" He pleaded, not wanting the situation to escalate any further.

"Wait a minute… I know you didn't hire some bitch that Tomas recommended!" Ronnie saw Luis avert his gaze. "You hired her?! What the fuck, Luis?! Did you forget what happened the last time you hired one of Tomas' freaks? It damn near broke us up!"

"Of course, I didn't forget." *How could I?* "Please, just listen for a moment."

"I'm listening…" She folded her arms across her chest and twisted her mouth sideways.

"What you overheard this morning was a simple misunderstanding. Carmen Sanchez is an American—a sister. She knows how Tomas uses women to get to men, so she played the part. It took only a minute to straighten her out and let her know I was only interested in her secretarial skills and nothing else. After I let her know I wasn't about to play that game, she changed her tune. I am not about to let any woman come between us. Believe it or not, she was relieved to discover I wasn't anything like Tomas," Luis explained.

Ronnie studied closely Luis for any obvious signs of deception. When she didn't see any, she began to relax. Thankfully, he was a lousy liar and she could pick up on his lies a mile away.

Noticing her anger had subsided, he continued. "Her husband works with Tomas. They recently moved here from the DR with their three small children so the kids could attend an American school. She has over ten years of experience as an admin assistant and she's bilingual—fluent in Spanish. I wouldn't have hired her if she wasn't qualified."

"All right, well, I still want to meet her. And she better not be no big tittied skank like the last one." Anger blazed from her eyes.

"Okay, I have no problem with you meeting her because I love you and only you."

"You wouldn't let someone come between us, would you? Step out on me and have an affair?"

"Never." He shook his head.

"You promise?"

"I promise. Now come sit next to me. I want to give you something." Luis went to the closet. He retrieved something from the right pocket of his blazer. After returning to Ronnie's side, he knelt down on one knee.

Ronnie sat on the side of the bed. She watched Luis kneel before her in seemingly slow motion. He held a small red velvet box in his hand. All thoughts of this morning went out the window when she realized what was about to happen. She almost forgot how to breathe.

"Veronica Indigo Pierce, I love you and have loved you since the moment my eyes connected with yours on that beach in the Dominican Republic. You have made my life into what it is today and I want to spend all my remaining days loving you and making you happy. My day begins and ends with that beautiful smile on your face. No day is complete without having you near. I want you to be my wife, if you'll have me." Luis opened the box to reveal a two carat, round diamond solitaire ring set in an antique platinum setting.

Various thoughts raced through Ronnie's mind as she stared at the ring nestled in luxurious white satin. Memories from her first marriage threatened to overtake her happiness, but she pushed them away to focus on the man in front of her now. She loved Luis and knew in her heart he was the only man for her. Each and every day, he proved his love in so many ways. She planned to spend the rest of her life with him, loving only him, living in the offbeat of life together. Yes, he was the man for her and she knew it deep within the depths of her soul. "Baby, I love you so much." She took a deep breath, and with happy tears streaming down her face, she replied, "Yes Luis, I will marry you."

"You will?" Luis removed the ring from the box and placed it on her finger. "Darling, you have just made me the happiest man in the world."

"I know I always said I never wanted to get married again, but this time it feels so right." She kissed every inch of his face."I love you."

"I'm not going to ask what changed your mind; I'm just happy you did." He returned her kisses and slipped back beneath the covers.

Ronnie nestled her head against Luis' chest feeling the quiet beat of his heart. She played with the short, curly hairs, listening to the thump, thump, thump. In the offbeat, she felt at home with the man she loved unconditionally. The man who would make her his wife. The man who promised his love to her and her alone. Luis draped his arm across her back and enjoyed the simple wonderfulness of the moment.

"My ring is so beautiful. Look how it sparkles." She stretched out her arm and admired the light bouncing from the diamond. "Come here big boy and give the future Mrs. Veronica Duarte some of that good loving."

"I am more than happy to take care of that, Veronica Duarte."

Chapter Six

*R*onnie woke up before Luis. A wave of nausea suddenly overtook her, sending her running to the bathroom. When there was nothing left to throw up, she rinsed her mouth, brushed her teeth and checked her reflection in the mirror. Her mother's words bounced around her head. *Maybe you're pregnant...* She dismissed the thought as quickly as it came.

"Ronnie? You okay in there?" Luis called out when he heard retching noises coming from the bathroom. He peeked inside.

"Yeah, I probably overdid it last night. Shouldn't have had that extra helping of paella. I'm okay now." She kissed Luis and removed her nightgown. The rough edges of the ring's setting snagged on the satin fabric. The engagement ring felt unfamiliar on her finger, and yet she couldn't wait to get used to it. She turned on the shower waiting for the water to get hot.

"You've been feeling poorly for over a week now. Don't you think it's time to see your doctor?"

"Already made an appointment for this afternoon. I'm going after I get off work."

"That's a good idea. I can't have my future wife getting sick on me. I have a meeting down in San Diego, but I can cancel and go with you to the doctor instead."

"No, don't do that. I'll be okay."

"If you're sure..."

"I'll be fine." She hooked her finger inside his pajamas. "Making love was excellent last night. Let's do it again later, okay?"

"You don't have to ask me twice. How about I bring home a bottle of champagne to celebrate our engagement?"

"Yeah, champagne sounds great. And I'll order in some of that Thai food you like so much." She tested the water again and stepped in. "I'll be out in a few minutes." Ronnie belted out an off-key version of an unrecognizable upbeat tune.

Luis piddled around the bedroom waiting for Ronnie to finish, smiling at her funny song. "Leave the water running, I'm getting right in."

Five minutes later, she was finished. "Shower is all yours, papi."

After drying off, she selected her favorite pair of slacks and a light sweater. Oddly enough, when she tried to zip her pants, she discovered they were too tight. *I must have put on a few pounds since I wore these pants last. I really don't feel like wearing a dress today. Oh well, time for the ole' safety pin under the zipper trick,* she thought. She quickly fixed her pants and finished getting dressed.

Luis met Ronnie down in the kitchen. He grabbed her hand to admire his selection. "That ring really does look great on your finger."

"I know. It's gorgeous. I can't wait to show it off."

Luis began patting the outside pockets of his jacket. "Have you seen my car keys?"

She laughed. "They're where they always are. In the dish in the hallway."

"No, not those. Since I'm driving to San Diego, I'm going to take the Jeep."

"In that case, I think the spare set for the Jeep is in the kitchen junk drawer. Or I can give you my set."

"That's okay. Got 'em!" He remarked after opening and closing three different drawers. "I think I'll call my family on the way down and tell them the good news about our engagement."

"I'll call my mother first thing this morning, too. She'll be so happy for us. She always liked you from the start. And wait until I tell Kiara... I know she's going to be thrilled."

"What about Travis? How is he going to take the news?"

"What do you mean? Why should Travis be anything but happy for us?"

"Baby, in spite of what you think, Travis has never really gotten over you. I know he won't admit it, but I can tell by how he reacts when you're around. Whereas he is overprotective of Kiara, he seems to have the same protectiveness when it comes to you." Luis raised an eyebrow, pecked Ronnie on the cheek, and grabbed his briefcase.

"Well, I think you're wrong. Travis couldn't care less who I am with or that I'm marrying you." She tied a colorful scarf around her hair to keep her natural hair tamed.

"I hope you're right. I'm just concerned how he's going to handle his daughter dating an older man who wants to take her to Haiti and on top of it, finding out that you and I are getting married."

"Oh my God, Luis, you sound just like a woman! Travis has moved on from "us" years ago. I don't know where you get these ideas, but they're ludicrous."

"I hope you're right."

"You have nothing to worry about. Trust me."

"I've got to get going. Call me as soon as you leave the doctor." Luis grabbed a banana from the fruit bowl and headed out the door. "Love you, baby."

"I love you, too. See you this evening."

* * *

Ronnie's cell phone rang just as she was about to merge onto the freeway. Kiara's smiling face appeared on her screen.

"Good morning, my darling daughter. This sure is an early call."

"Good morning. It is kinda early, but I was thinking about our conversation at dinner. I need to tell Daddy about GQ and my trip to Haiti. A group of us are going from the school and today is the final deadline to sign up as a volunteer."

"Did you say a *group* is going?"

"Uh huh."

"Are they all students?"

"Yeah, didn't I like tell you that yesterday?"

"Nooooo, you said *Gerald* asked you to go to Haiti with *him*. Traveling with a group of students is a lot different than just you and he going."

"Oh, did I forget to mention that I'm going with a group? There's like eight of us volunteers and GQ is our sponsor. Why?"

Ronnie chuckled, imagining the expression on her daughter's face. "Kiara, that makes all the difference in the world. Knowing that you're going to be with other students will make your father much more likely to accept the news. Why didn't you tell me this yesterday?"

"I don't know. I guess I didn't think it like made a difference. Daddy is so protective of me that he doesn't want me too far from him. *Ever.*"

"I understand, but we need to talk to him this morning. When can you break away from class?"

"I don't have class until this afternoon. I can meet you at the center and we can talk to him this morning. Is that okay?"

"I think that will be all right. I'll check Travis' schedule and will let you know." Ronnie was just about to say good-bye when the sunlight hit her ring, turning the diamond into a hundred dazzling points of light. "Hey Kiara, I've got some good news to share."

"What's up?"

"Last night after you guys left, Luis asked me to marry him."

"For real? Congratulations… That's great… Luis… He's… uh…a great guy. When is the big day?" Kiara responded without any hint of real enthusiasm.

Ronnie picked up on Kiara's tone. "We haven't set a date yet, but I'll let you know. Of course, we want you to be involved in the wedding…"

"Awesome… I'd like that. Well, I've got to run. Let me know when it's a good time to stop by. I'll bring a couple of brochures with me so you guys can take a look at the charity's mission."

Ronnie was dismayed by the abrupt end to their conversation. "Okay, I'll send you a message when he's available. Love you."

"Thanks, Mom. Love you, too. Bye."

Now what was her cool reaction about? I thought Kiara would be happy for me. Maybe she's preoccupied about her trip. Yeah, that's all it is, she convinced herself.

Ronnie exited the freeway and pulled up to the center. She removed the engagement ring from her finger and safely tucked it away in the center console, thinking that Kiara's news would be enough of a surprise for Travis this morning. She noticed he seemed a bit off lately.

Once she got in her office, she logged in and checked Travis' schedule. His morning was completely free, so she blocked off an appointment from nine to ten o'clock for Kiara.

Chapter Seven

*L*uis stopped by his office to pick up samples of brochures to take with him to his meeting in San Diego. He was feeling on top of the world since Ronnie had agreed to marry him, never imaging she would actually say yes, because she had been adamant about not getting married for so long. In the end, it really didn't matter what changed her mind, he was just ecstatic that she did. Just as he was about to leave the office, Tomas knocked on his door.

"What's up, *primo?*" Tomas was grinning from ear to ear, as if he were laughing at his own private joke.

"Hey Tomas, I was just headed out the door. What are you doing here? Aren't you supposed to be at work?" Luis eyed his cousin up and down, noting his disheveled appearance.

"Naw, I called in sick. Had too much of Melinda last night. If you know what I mean."

"I can only imagine," replied Luis.

"She works in the gentleman's club over on Las Flores and man can she move her body. There should be a law against somebody that fine working as a stripper."

"So what brings you here so early?" Luis ignored Tomas' comments, not wanting to be dragged into his world so early in the morning. Most days he was amusing. Today he was not.

"I'm a little short this month on my rent. Can you spot me a grand?"

"A thousand dollars? Isn't that half your rent?"

"Yeah, I got behind paying some other bills because of an investment opportunity I'm looking into. I'm good for it. You know I always pay you back."

"Yes, you do. Okay, when do you need it?"

"Um, today if you have it." He looked away sheepishly.

"Now?" Luis checked the time and pulled out his checkbook. "This is the last time I'm going to do this, man. I am not your bank." He quickly wrote out a check and handed it to Tomas.

"*Gracias.* Check it out; I've got some deals in the works that should bring in a load of *dinero.* I'll get this back to you next week. Promise."

"Yeah, yeah, yeah… Get it to me when you can. I have a meeting in San Diego. I've got to go before I'm late."

"I won't hold you up. So what happened with Carmen? Is she going to work out?"

"Carmen? Yes, thanks for recommending her. And for the record, I would've hired her even if she hadn't come on to me. I don't operate my business that way."

"Oh that… I advised her to use her *assets* to get your attention."

"She tried, but I wasn't biting. After I convinced her I wasn't like you, the interview went well."

"I had no idea Carmen was so fine. I met her when I dropped her old man off after work. I'm telling you…if she wasn't married…watch out!"

Luis changed the subject, not wanting to encourage Tomas any further. "I hired her because she has the skills I'm looking for."

"*Chévere!* I think you made a good choice. Uh, you *have* told Veronica about hiring Carmen, right?"

"Yes, I did and she's fine with it. Oh yeah, speaking of Ronnie, I took your advice and asked her to marry me. She said yes."

"Luis, you old dog! Congratulations! Look, forget what I said yesterday about getting married. I'm just jealous, that's all."

"Thanks man. Well, I've got to go. We cool?" Luis turned and locked his office door. He walked Tomas to the exit.

"Yeah, we're cool. You and Veronica are getting married? I'll be damned!" He scratched his scruffy face.

Luis checked his watch again, "Hey man, I'll catch up with you later. Got to run."

"Thanks again for the loan." Tomas clutched the check in his hand and headed out the door.

Chapter Eight

Kiara arrived promptly at nine, dressed in her typical Bohemian fashion. A vibrant scarf encircled her head, leaving her hair springing forth like long-haired, fluffy seeds of a mature dandelion. Draped over her shoulder was a well-worn knapsack bursting at the seams with bits and pieces of her life. She bounded into Ronnie's office with a huge smile on her face.

"Good morning, sunshine," Trudy blurted out. "What brings you here so early?"

"Good morning, Miss Trudy. Hey Mom." Kiara plopped down in the chair near Ronnie's desk. "I came to talk to my pop," she explained to Trudy.

"Oh good! He's always saying he never sees you anymore."

"Hold on. I'll see if he's free." Ronnie dialed Luis on the intercom. "Travis, you got a few minutes?"

"Sure. C'mon down," he replied.

"I'm not alone. I'm bringing a special visitor with me," she hinted.

"A special visitor, huh?"

"Yep, that's right."

"I can hardly wait to see who it is."

"We're on our way." She quickly stood and as she did, another unexpected wave of nausea hit her, causing the room to spin.

"I'll see you when you get here." Travis' voice crackled over the intercom.

Kiara jumped to Ronnie's side and eased her to a chair. "Are you okay?"

"Yeah, thanks...I'm fine. I just can't seem to shake this flu." She held her hand to her forehead. "Guess I came back too soon."

"Maybe you should go back home and rest, dearie," added Trudy. "I can finish up here."

"Um, maybe you're right. I have a doctor's appointment this afternoon. I should be fine until then."

"Do you need me to drive you to the doctor? I can skip my classes the rest of the day. If you're getting dizzy, you shouldn't be driving."

"No, I'll be all right..."

"Does Luis know you're still under the weather?"

"No, I told him I was better. But, come to think of it... You're right about me not driving."

"We can talk to Daddy later. I should probably take you home."

"I'm fine. The lightheadedness comes and goes. Anyway, you have to meet with your group today, right?"

"Yeah, this afternoon is the deadline for final payment. I have the money; I'm just worried about Daddy's reaction."

"No time like the present. Let's go talk to Travis."

"Are you sure you're all right?" Kiara asked with concern.

"Yeah, I feel better, now. That's what's so crazy about this. It comes and goes with no consistency. C'mon, let's get this trip arranged so you can visit Haiti."

Unexpectedly, Trudy screeched out, "Haiti? Who's going to Haiti? Not our little Kiara, I hope!" She shook her head in disapproval. "Oh no dear, that will never do… There are too many diseases down there. Do they even have running water? What about indoor plumbing?" She wrinkled her nose in disgust. "I saw on the news that country is filled with nothing but filthy criminals. Don't hold your breath about Travis letting you go. I wouldn't let any child of mine go to such a horrible, horrible place." As she regarded Kiara and Veronica, she twisted and turned her head in quick short movements, resembling a bird pecking the ground in search of delicious earthworms. She redirected her attention to her computer screen.

Ronnie took a huge breath and replied with quiet restraint, "Trudy, we appreciate your concern, but this decision is between me, Travis and Kiara. Volunteering to assist those less fortunate is going to be a rewarding experience, and I am proud that my daughter wants to be part of something like this."

"I'm sorry dear… What did you say? What's this about volunteering?" she asked, already forgetting her part of the conversation.

"Kiara is going to Haiti to volunteer," Ronnie repeated.

"Oh my! That is such an awful place…" Trudy continued her previous rant.

Kiara smiled warmly at the old woman's forgetfulness. She threw her arms around Ronnie's shoulders. "I love you, Mom."

"I love you, too. C'mon, let's get this done."

"Tsk, tsk, tsk." Trudy once again voiced her displeasure with Kiara's decision, before reluctantly returning back to work.

Ronnie headed towards Travis' office with Kiara trailing closely behind. During the short walk down the hallway, Kiara seemed to revert back to her childhood shyness.

She knocked at his door. "Hey Travis, look who I brought with me," said Ronnie.

His face lit up when he noticed Kiara standing besides Ronnie. "Well, look at you! What a nice surprise! Come on over here and give your old man a hug."

"Hi Daddy." Kiara dutifully went to her father and showered him with love and affection.

"I was just about to put in a call to the nurse recruiting agency. My head RN just told me she's taking another position so I have to fill the spot quickly. Nurses with credentials like hers are hard to find. Anyway, so what brings you two here this morning? As happy as I am to see you, I suspect this isn't just a friendly visit. What's going on?"

Kiara didn't make any motion to speak so Ronnie began for her. "Well, Travis, Kiara stopped by for dinner last night, as I told you yesterday. When she was there, she brought up a trip she'd like to go on this summer." Ronnie turned to Kiara, "Go ahead, tell him about it."

Travis turned his full attention to Kiara. "I'm listening. Where's the trip? Paris, Rome, London… More importantly, how much is this going to cost me?" He laughed, pulling out his checkbook.

Kiara fidgeted in her seat. Beads of perspiration popped up on her forehead, trickling down her face. She opened her knapsack, pulled out a stack of colorful brochures, and plopped the stack down on Travis' desk.

"What's all this?" he asked.

Looking to Ronnie for support, she uttered, "Um, Daddy… Well, I've actually volunteered to go to Haiti. A group of students from my school are going for the summer to help out where we can. As far as how much it's going to cost, all I have to pay for is airfare. The mission charity takes care of the volunteer's room and board fees."

Travis glared coolly at Ronnie. "You're all right with this?" He picked up the brochures and flipped through the ones describing the agency, the mission, and what was expected of the volunteers.

Ronnie said, "I must admit, Kiara took me by surprise when she first told me."

"Volunteering in Haiti, huh? That's a long way from home, don't you think?"

"The more I thought about it, the more I think this will be good for Kiara. It'll give her an entirely new perspective on what's really important. And she won't be alone; the group will be chaperoned by one of the teachers."

Kiara shot Ronnie a questioning look. "Yeah, that's right... We'll be chaperoned by Professor Gerald Quinn. He was one of my teachers last year."

"I know Quinn. He and I crossed paths occasionally when I was teaching seminars at the university."

"*You* know Professor Quinn?" Kiara asked, warily.

"Not well, but I know who he is. So tell me, darling daughter, how do you intend to live without the luxuries you have grown accustomed to? If you go, you will be roughing it down there. Are you willing to give up daily bathing, clean clothes, fine dining? How about your manicures and hair appointments? How do you intend to live without those luxuries?"

Kiara exhaled her youthful annoyance. "Daddy, in case you've like forgotten, I've been living in a dorm with three other women. I gave up manicures, pedicures, and hair appointments a long time ago. I eat pizza or ramen noodles at least five times a week now. For the past couple of years, I've gotten used to living without the luxuries. I want to do this. More importantly, I need to do this..."

"It sounds like you've already made up your mind," he replied, drumming his fingers on his desk. "Okay, you're right. I think getting out of your sheltered world will do you good. I've got to admit that you're behaving more like your old Mom and Dad every day. This sounds like something we'd have done when we were your age. You remember, Ronnie?"

Ronnie smiled at the shared memories from her college days spent with Travis. She said, "Remember that time we all protested because they wouldn't let that band play on campus?"

"Oh yeah, I forgot all about that. What was the name of that band?" Travis reminisced.

"I don't remember, but I can't believe we were so fired up over something that ended up being so insignificant."

"Banning a group from playing on campus doesn't sound insignificant to me. Denying someone's freedom of speech should never be downplayed," interjected Kiara.

"Sweetie, you don't understand. They weren't banned because of their music; they were banned because at previous concerts they stripped down to nothing and played in the nude. Then they'd pull members from the audience to perform live sex on stage," explained Ronnie.

They allowed their laughter to subside upon noticing that Kiara hadn't joined in their little trip down memory lane. She gawked at her parents as if they were dinosaurs from the prehistoric age.

Travis cleared his throat and returned to the subject at hand. "Um, so when do you leave?"

"We leave after classes are over. Those pamphlets I put on your desk will explain just about everything there is to know."

"Got it. How much do you need?" He reached for his checkbook again.

"Nothing. I'm paying for this out of the money I saved from my job. The agency sets us up with room, board and meals. Plus, we're getting a huge discount on the flight, so it really doesn't cost much at all. Anyway, I feel it's time I started paying my own way."

"It looks like my little girl has grown up." Travis relished the enormity of the moment. Kiara had walked into his office a child, but was leaving as an adult.

"I am going to make both you guys so proud of me. Just wait and see." She grabbed her knapsack, kissed Ronnie and Travis on their cheeks and floated out of the office as happy as could be.

"She's something else, huh?" asked Travis.

"I gotta admit I was hesitant at first about agreeing to let her go, but Travis, this is going to be good for her. Lord knows, I'm not knocking your parenting skills, but Kiara needs a good dose of reality. She's been living in a bubble. There is an entirely different world outside of southern California that she should know about."

"No offense taken. I know I've kept her sheltered from the harsh realities of life. After everything she went through as a child, I didn't want to expose her to the ugly truths of the world."

"I understand. It can be brutal out there, but she's old enough— and smart enough to avoid trouble. The only way for her to learn about life is to live it."

"She's been through so much… I just want her to be happy. And safe."

"She'll be fine. You know the teacher. And she won't be on her own. There will be several other students traveling with her."

Travis still wasn't convinced.

"If it makes you feel any better, Luis has family in Port-au-Prince and he says he'll have someone watch over her."

Travis concluded, "I'm losing my daughter. When did she stop trusting me? She even came to you first to discuss this…"

Ronnie thought long and hard before responding. There wasn't a single cell in her body that wanted Travis to think he had been "replaced". All those years it had been just the two of them, going through life's trials and tribulations together. Alone and without her involvement. Ronnie understood her role was fairly recent.

"Kiara came to me first because she was concerned about your reaction. She knows how protective you are of her—and rightly so, but because of her strong feelings about doing this, she wanted my input. Wanted to know what I thought before approaching you. She loves and respects you so much, Travis. You're not losing her. She will always be your little girl. Just give her room to grow into the woman you and I know she can be."

Ronnie pretended not to notice the moisture that suddenly appeared in the corners of his glistening eyes. He casually wiped the tears away with the back of his hand.

"You're right… She'll be fine." He quickly changed the subject. "So, how are *you* feeling today?"

"Better. The dizziness comes and goes, as does the nausea. Since I felt sick again this morning, I'm going to see the doctor this afternoon."

"That's probably a good idea. By the way, how is Luis?"

"He's fine."

"Is he taking you to your appointment?"

She shook her head. "No, I'll be okay."

"Your being dizzy means you probably shouldn't drive yourself." He leafed through the pamphlets Kiara left on his desk.

Ronnie toyed with the idea of mentioning her recent engagement, but thought better of it considering Travis' current fragile state. "Travis, I'm all right. And actually, Luis is on his way to San Diego for an important meeting."

"Well, if you need a ride I can have my driver take you." He offered.

"Thanks for the offer, but I'm sure I'll be okay." *I think I'll let Kiara's offer to drive me to the doctor slide. That girl was so distracted when she left, that I'd be better off driving myself.* "Well, I've got to get back to it." She rose from her chair.

"Yeah, me too. I've got to get in touch with this agency and find another nurse ASAP. We'll talk soon." He hesitated then continued, "Thanks for being there for Kiara. It was good seeing how well you two have connected."

"No need to thank me. It was my pleasure. I have a lot of time to make up for, so whenever I get an opportunity, I'm going to be there for her. See you later."

Travis smiled and gave a brief wave before returning his attention to locating a qualified RN.

Chapter Nine

*T*he waiting room of the doctor's office was decorated in warm earth tones and contained comfortable, overstuffed chairs and loveseats. Several decorative flameless candles threw off an aromatic vanilla scent into the cozy space.

Ronnie observed the other people in the room. It was filled with women of various ages and the men who accompanied them. Many of the women were obviously pregnant, while others may have been there for annual checkups. There was no way to tell just by looking.

After updating various insurance forms, Ronnie plopped down in an empty chair next to a very pregnant woman who appeared to be close to her age. The woman rubbed her swollen belly and smiled unabashedly at Ronnie, as if she possessed some deep inner secret to all of life's mysteries. Ronnie smiled in return and picked up an old dog-eared magazine to avoid getting into some profound philosophical conversation with the woman about the meaning of life. She merely wanted to get in, see the doctor, and get out as quickly as possible—unscathed and with a clean bill of health.

Just as she was feigning interest in an article about canning homemade rhubarb jam, her phone vibrated with a text from Kiara. It read, *Mom, I am so sorry. I forgot all about taking you to the doctor. If you still need a ride, please give me a call. I just left the school after paying for my trip. Call me.*

She texted back, *I was feeling better so I drove myself. I'll call you later.* Ronnie smiled thinking about Kiara's youthful enthusiasm. She prayed it would be a very long time before she lost it.

"Miss Pierce? Miss Veronica Pierce?" called out the nursing assistant.

"Right here," answered Ronnie. She replaced the magazine on the end table, smiled at the older mother again, and then followed the assistant to the exam room.

After checking her blood pressure and taking other vital signs, the nursing assistant instructed, "Please strip down to your underwear and put this on." She handed Ronnie a paper gown. "The doctor will be with you shortly."

Ronnie undressed and sat on the edge of the exam table, swinging her feet, trying to ward off her nervousness. She twisted the engagement ring around and around her finger; occasionally outstretching her hand near the light to catch the radiance of the diamond. Her cell phone vibrated loudly. It was Luis.

"Hey..." she answered.

"Hello, my love. Are you at your appointment yet?"

"As a matter of fact, I am. I'm in the exam room waiting for the doctor. Where are you?"

"I'm close to downtown San Diego—almost there. But I'm having a bit of trouble locating the street."

"Well, it's a good thing you have GPS." A gentle knocking at the door drew her attention. "Hey baby, the doctor's here. I've got to go. Let me call you back."

"All right. Call me as soon as you find out what's going on. Love you."

"I love you more..." The doctor knocked again. "Come in," Ronnie called out.

In walked a petite, middle-aged, Chinese woman whom Ronnie didn't recognize. The woman's salt and pepper hair was fashioned in a Chin-Length Bob with bangs that skirted the top of her frameless glasses.

"Hello Miss Pierce, my name is Dr. Chung and I will be examining you today. Now what seems to be the problem?" asked the doctor as she washed her hands.

"Uh, hi... Pardon me doctor, but where is Dr. Foster?" Ronnie hated when her HMO switched doctors without notice. If she didn't absolutely need to be seen, she would have hopped down from the table, pulled her clothes on, and walked out the door. But she didn't because she needed to find the cause of her ailment. Adding emphasis to her need to stay, the medicinal smell from the antiseptic soap caused her stomach to lurch.

"Oh, didn't the nurse tell you? Dr. Foster retired a couple of months ago. She bought a vineyard up north and is spending her days making wine. Is there a problem?"

"No, I was just expecting to see Dr. Foster, that's all," Ronnie said, instead of expressing her true thoughts.

"I understand... So what brings you here today?" Dr. Chung sat down at the computer and pulled up Ronnie's health records.

Ronnie discussed all her symptoms with the doctor making certain she didn't leave anything out. Dr. Chung asked all the right questions and appeared to not only be knowledgeable and thorough, but also displayed an appropriate level of concern.

"I want to check you over. Make sure everything is hunky-dory. Okay?" She smiled a genuine warm smile.

"Sure."

After the physical exam was complete, Dr. Chung said, "Miss Pierce, there are no obvious signs of any illness or disease, but just to be on the safe side, I'd like to run a few more tests and get your blood tested. When was your last menstrual cycle?" she asked, entering instructions into the computer.

"Um, I really don't know. During my last appointment, Dr. Foster explained I would soon begin early menopause and my periods would become more and more infrequent. I think the last one was a couple of months ago. Why?"

Dr. Chung frowned and peered over her glasses. "You're only 43. No reason to believe you're going through perimenopause so soon. How old was your mother when she went through the change?"

Ronnie had to admit that question had never come up before. And Dianna was not one to offer up that information in polite conversation. "I'm not really sure. You don't think I'm going through menopause?"

The doctor appeared puzzled. "Let's check one more thing. Please lie back down."

Ronnie laid on her back as instructed. The doctor pressed on her stomach in several places and looked upwards as if the answers to her questions resided in the design of the ceiling tile. She said, "I want to do a pelvic exam, if that's okay with you."

"A pelvic exam? Why? I don't understand, Dr. Chung. What's wrong with me?"

* * *

Travis replaced the phone's receiver in frustration after hours of trying to locate an experienced rehabilitation nurse. Seemed like every agency he called had the same response. "I'm so sorry, Mr. Bradford, unfortunately there is a shortage of nurses all over the country—especially ones with the particular skills you're looking for. We will put you down on our list; if one becomes available, we'll be sure to call."

"Good thing I still have a month to find a replacement. I can always run an ad in the local paper," he sighed.

Time was going by much too quickly and Kiara had totally knocked his world off balance with her announcement about wanting to go to Haiti. *Before I know it, she'll be getting married, moving hundreds of miles away, and having children of her own. When that happens, I really will be all alone.*

Travis peered out the window at the waning daylight. He watched as the wife of one of his male patients lovingly helped him maintain his balance, while they strolled through the garden enjoying what remained of the pleasant afternoon. *I wonder what life would have been like had Ronnie and I gotten married. In so many ways, I still care for her—even still love her. Today we were parents making decisions for our daughter. That's the way it's supposed to be. The way it should've been all along. I wonder if it's too late.* He decided to call Kiara.

"Hi Daddy," she answered. She had just completed her last class and was headed to the parking lot.

"Did you get all the arrangements for your trip taken care of?" he asked, wanting to get the small talk out of the way.

"Yes, I did. It is like so exciting! I've got to get my shots and my passport should arrive any day now. Mr. Quinn had me expedite the processing due to our short time frame."

"I know you've got a handle on everything, but if you need help, you know where to find me." He took a deep breath and exhaled. "Kiara, can I ask you a question?"

"Sure Daddy, what is it?" She rolled down the windows and made herself comfortable, because whenever her father said, *"Can I ask you...?"* she knew a long conversation was about to occur.

Travis bounced ideas off his daughter all the time, so asking her opinion on important issues was normal. However, because of his ulterior motive, this particular question was anything but normal. "Um, how are you and Ronnie getting along?"

"We're doing fine. Couldn't be better... Why?"

"I was just wondering how it feels having her back in your life—as a mother? Is it everything you hoped it would be?" he asked, realizing he was now the one beating-around-the-bush.

"It's great. She's an awesome person and a super Mom. I'm thrilled to have her in my life."

"That's good to hear honey. Speaking of Ronnie, how are she and Luis doing? They getting along?"

Uh oh! I know where this is going, she thought. From the moment they all had reunited in that restaurant at the Santa Elena Pier three years ago, Kiara suspected her dad still had feelings for Ronnie. She admitted that at first she entertained those childhood wishes; hoping Ronnie and her father would get married and make them into a real family. It was the dream of most children when their parents split. However, after spending time with her mother, she quickly realized Ronnie was trying to make a life with Luis—not her dad. The old Veronica Pierce had moved on and the only relationship she wanted to pursue with the Bradfords was the one with her daughter.

On numerous occasions, Kiara had closely gauged her father's reactions when he was near Ronnie. And whether it was intentional or not, he seemed to patiently await the demise of Ronnie and Luis' relationship so he could possibly step in. Kiara understood that would never happen, especially since Ronnie told her that Luis had asked her to marry him. Unfortunately, maybe Travis did not. The time had come to set her father straight.

"Daddy, Ronnie and Luis are doing just fine," she told him. "They seem to be very happy and I am happy for them both." Kiara wondered if Ronnie told her Dad about her engagement to Luis. Or on a more personal note, about *her* relationship with GQ.

"That's great. Ronnie's happy. Good to know…" After hearing the tone of Kiara's response, Travis felt foolish asking his daughter whether she thought he had a chance with Ronnie. She didn't want him decades earlier, and couldn't possibly want him now, especially in his current physical condition. "So you had a good time at dinner last night? With the two of them?"

"Yes Daddy, it was fun." She broached the subject. "Um, did you and Ronnie get a chance to like discuss anything else this morning? I mean, besides my trip to Haiti?"

"She just mentioned she had a doctor's appointment. Why? Were we supposed to discuss something else this morning?"

"Uh, not really, she just seemed to have a lot on her mind. Why are you asking about Ronnie and Luis, anyway?"

Travis sighed wearily. He glanced at the photo of Kiara and Ronnie that he kept on his desk. Feeling he had nothing more to lose, he asked his daughter outright, "Do you think I will ever have a chance with Ronnie? Of us being together again? I mean… Does she ever talk to you about me?"

Kiara didn't respond right away—she couldn't. As much as she suspected that her father still cared for Ronnie, she *wasn't* expecting him to ask *her* such a direct question. *Why is he asking me this now? Does it have anything to do with my going to Haiti?* "Daddy, I'm not sure I understand. Why are you asking about getting back together with her now?"

"To tell you the truth, I suppose I never stopped loving Ronnie. Those years we spent together were magical and our relationship ended so abruptly. I thought I had gotten over her years ago, but now that I see her everyday… All those feelings of love have resurfaced and I just want to know if she ever thinks about me."

"Daddy, you do remember she *lives* with Luis? And they *are* involved in a very serious relationship." *Not to mention he asked her to marry him.*

He gave a brief nod. "Okay…?"

She continued, "I think you might be feeling sad because I'm like going away for the summer, but I'll be back. I know Ronnie cares for you, but more like a friend. She loves Luis and he loves her."

Travis tried to laugh it off. "You're right. I'm being a bit overly sentimental because you're growing up. Ronnie *is* happy with Luis and I'd be a fool to try to come between them. Forget I said anything. See, even your old man needs some good advice every now and then." Feeling deeply embarrassed, he wanted to quickly hang up the phone and put his mind on anything else.

"Are you sure you're okay? I can stop by later if you'd like to talk more."

"No, that won't be necessary. I just needed to get that off my chest. Like I said earlier, forget I said anything."

"Well… All right… If you're sure you're okay…"

He attempted to sound upbeat. "As a matter-of-fact, I'm on my way out the door as we speak. I think I'll stop by and see my brother and Lexi on the way home. I haven't spent much time with them lately, so this is as good a time as any. I'm also considering taking off for a couple of weeks. I could use a real vacation."

Though Kiara remained skeptical, she acquiesced. "A vacation sounds perfect. I think you should like seriously consider it." She watched as the parking lot slowly cleared of cars. Most of the classes were over for the day, so faculty and students were taking off to go do other things. "Okay, Daddy, I will talk to you later. Tell Auntie Lexi I said 'hi'. And if you need to talk…"

"I know… You're just a phone call away." He laughed. "You're starting to sound more like your old man every day."

She joined in his laughter, "I love you, Daddy."

"I love you, too. Talk to you later." He hung up the phone and rested his head on the cool desk. *She must think I'm a damn fool! After all these years, here I am talking about getting back together with her mother.*

Travis stared at the picture of Kiara and Ronnie embracing one another full of joy and laughter. *This was supposed to be a family portrait of the three of us. Wouldn't you know it! Just when I have Veronica Pierce back in my life, she's with someone else. How about that for irony?*

*   *   *

Ronnie reclined on the living room couch nervously awaiting Luis' return. Every five minutes or so, she peeked through the blinds waiting for his car to come up the driveway. Unable to sit still, she paced the floor, rechecking the clock every few minutes. Luis said he would be home by three and it was almost six. She tried calling him several times, but each call went straight to voicemail.

To quell her nerves, she put on one of her favorite CDs and tried to relax by getting lost in the offbeat of the music. Whereas listening to music usually worked to relieve her stress, today it didn't. Not even the mellow sounds of Chris Standring's sax could put her at ease. She was startled by the shrillness of the house phone ringing. Fully expecting to hear Luis' voice on the other end, she was surprised to hear Joie's.

"Hey lady," said Joie.

"What's up, Joie?" Ronnie asked, distracted by her personal issues.

"Girlfriend, after talkin' to you yesterday, I realize how much I miss you. So, I was wondering if I can come out there in a week or so—just for a few days to visit. The kids will be with their grandparents and I have a week's vacation due."

Half listening to Joie's chatter, Ronnie heard a car door slam. She ran to the window to see Luis removing a couple of boxes from the trunk. "Yeah, yeah, yeah… That sounds like a great idea," she replied absentmindedly.

"Okay, I'll make the flight arrangements and let you know when I'll be there. I've got to jump on these tickets now before the price goes up."

"Sure, that's cool. Hey look, I can't talk now. I'll give you a call tomorrow. Okay?"

Joie stared at the phone. "You did hear me say I wanna come out and visit?"

"Uh huh, I'll call you back tomorrow, Joie."

"Okay... Well, I'll go ahead and order my tickets then."

"Yeah, do that. Hey, I've got to go. We'll catch up later." Ronnie ended the call.

Joie hung up the phone and pulled up the website to order her tickets. From previous experience, she knew that trying to snag cheap airline tickets within a week of a flight was nearly impossible. The online special fare was going to expire at midnight and she had to act now or chance paying double.

Ronnie replaced the cordless phone in the base. She ran to the door, met Luis, and threw her arms around him. Happy to see him, relieved he was home safe.

Luis stepped inside and was met by Ronnie's embrace. He dropped his briefcase on the floor. After he accepted her hugs and kisses, he gingerly pushed her away before letting loose a rant about his day.

"I am so glad to be home. You wouldn't believe how awful the traffic was getting back here. There was an accident outside of Oxnard and traffic came to a complete standstill for over two hours. My cell phone totally died and I wasn't able to recharge it because I didn't have my car charger. But that wasn't even the worst part of my day. To top everything off, the company's representative, who I gave the presentation to, only spoke Spanish. Here I am in the middle of an opportunity of a lifetime and their rep didn't understand half of what I said."

She shrugged. "I thought you were fluent in Spanish."

He glared at her. "Do you know how rusty my Spanish is? And Dominican Spanish is way different from Mexican Spanish! *Coño!* What a fuckin' waste of a day! I need a fuckin' drink!" He pulled off his tie and tossed it on the couch. Afterwards, he let out a long string of expletives in Spanish as he searched the liquor cabinet.

Ronnie stood by patiently listening to Luis' uncharacteristic tirade, waiting for it to dissipate. Amused by his behavior, she knew once he started there was nothing she could do except listen, especially when he swore in Spanish. After a few minutes, he finally calmed down and perched on at the bar sipping on a snifter of cognac. She went behind him and gently kissed his scruffy cheek.

"Mmm, that feels nice. I missed you today… Sorry I wasn't able to call. I left my cell phone charger in the other car. Of all days to not have my phone fully charged."

"I missed you, too. I was so worried when I couldn't get through." She refilled his glass and joined him at the bar.

"You're not drinking with me? You okay? What did the doctor say?" He set his glass down and gave Ronnie his full attention.

"Well, first of all I am going to be fine. I'm not sick and my symptoms are perfectly normal." She smirked.

"What do you mean 'perfectly normal'? Perfectly normal for what?" he asked, evenly spacing his words.

She grinned and replied, "Perfectly normal for a 43 year old expectant mother."

Luis gasped loudly and nearly slipped off the barstool. Ronnie reached out and grabbed his arm to break the fall. After regaining his composure, Luis stood up and stared at Ronnie with a shocked expression on his face.

"Luis, I'm pregnant! We're going to have a baby!"

Chapter Ten

"**D**addy, I'm leaving for Haiti soon. When are you coming home?" asked Kiara. "I can't leave without saying good-bye."

"I'll be back before you leave. I promise."

"You've been in Arizona for over a week. I thought you'd be back by now. I miss you." She pouted, resorting to the guilt-inducing tactic that always worked in the past.

"I miss you, too. But I'm having a good time and this getaway is exactly what I needed."

"Good for you, Daddy."

"This resort is wonderful and I am really enjoying my vacation. Thanks for asking," he retorted sarcastically. "And I met a very nice couple who introduced me to their daughter. Believe it or not, she works here—at the spa."

"That's nice. So you met a woman… Is *she* why you're staying away for so long?"

Travis chuckled. "Don't tell me you're jealous. Anyway, *she* is a rehabilitation nurse on staff and is looking to relocate. She's seems to be very interested in our center, but that's not the reason I've been here so long. Do you realize I haven't had a real vacation in years?"

Kiara tried her best to empathize with her father's predicament. He had dedicated his life primarily to raising her, and secondly to running the *J. Bradford Rehabilitative Center*. She thought back over the years and realized that what he said was true. Any of his free time was spent with her. All of his vacations involved Kiara. The last time he had anything that resembled adult fun was on his honeymoon with Janelle. And even that was just for a weekend.

"You're right, I'm being selfish. Are you like having a good time?" she asked with genuine interest.

"Like I said, this getaway is exactly what I needed. Though, this started out purely for fun it ended up as a working vacation. I'm learning all types of various programs and techniques that can benefit our center."

"That's good. So when *are* you coming home?"

"My flight leaves late tomorrow afternoon. I'll call you when I get home. Okay?"

Kiara perked up. Despite how grown she wanted everyone to believe she was, she was still daddy's little girl. "Okay, I can't wait to see you. Have a safe flight back. I love you."

"I love you, too. I'll see you tomorrow."

Travis parked his wheelchair near the side of the swimming pool. He thoroughly enjoyed watching bikini clad women strut their half-naked tanned bodies past him in an endless parade of bronzed flesh. It didn't matter to him that the vast majority of those women got their firm bodies compliments of plastic surgery or with a little assistance from *Botox*. To him, all women were beautiful—something to be appreciated.

He watched a couple of blondes, dressed in skimpy bikinis that left nothing to the imagination, slather suntan oil on each other as he sipped on a refreshing concoction of healthy fruit juices. One of the women slipped her hand under the other's bikini top, allowing her fingers to linger on the woman's firm breast. Images of what they did in the privacy of their room threatened to send him to his for relief. Although his legs didn't work, the rest of his equipment worked just fine—even if it had been awhile since he had an opportunity to use it. He thought, *nice to know I am still a man, with or without the functionality of my legs I can still get an erection that would satisfy them both.*

The resort didn't serve alcoholic beverages and that was perfectly fine with him. Relaxation without intoxication was their motto. He raised his glass of fruit juice and toasted the ladies; thanking them for the opportunity to get a rise out of 'lil T. Without realizing their contribution to his good mood, they both smiled and returned the gesture.

Because Ronnie had taken several days off recuperating, Travis wasn't able to share his vacation plans before he left. Just as well... Seeing her may have caused him to change his mind or express aloud intimate thoughts that were better left unsaid. In any case, he hoped whatever illness she had had run its course.

He had to admit, time away from the center had done him a world of good. And by the end of the week, he was ready to return, refreshed and recharged. He took the vacation getaway as an opportunity to put his feelings for Ronnie into perspective. Despite how much he loved Ronnie then—and continued to love her still, he had to find a way to let go. A wise man once told him that the best way to get over loving someone was to find another person to love. And that's exactly what he intended to do.

Chapter Eleven

*E*ver since Luis discovered Ronnie was pregnant, he became super attentive; responding to her every whim. He even took off work to help around the house. Unfortunately, Ronnie was starting to feel as if she couldn't brush her teeth without giving Luis a play by play update. His attention was slowly suffocating her.

The morning Luis asked Ronnie about the regularity of her bowel movements was the day she decided enough was enough. It was time for Luis to go back to work. There was no way should could survive the next six months with him hovering over her.

Luis brought a tray of fresh fruit and croissants to the bedroom. He sat the tray on Ronnie's lap and opened the blinds to let the sunshine in.

Ronnie shielded her eyes from the sudden change in brightness. "Hey baby, when are you going back to work? I'm feeling much better now." She wanted to broach the subject of his returning to work tentatively—not wanting to hurt his feelings or appear to be ungrateful for his attention.

"Don't worry about me. I am going to be home with you as much as possible. I can start working part-time if I need to. You and the baby's health are what are most important. Julio can handle the backlog."

She cleared her throat and replied sweetly, "Um, sweetheart, don't take this the wrong way, but I'm not sick, I'm just pregnant. The doctor says that once the morning sickness passes, I'll be fine. Of course, she's going to watch me closely and run a few more tests because of my age, but for the most part she says I should have a healthy, normal pregnancy. So there's no need for me to quit work or for you to either."

Luis sat on the side of the bed, clasped his hands, and tapped his thumbs together. He seemed to be searching for the right words to say. "Ronnie, I do not want you to return to work."

She gaped at Luis as if he grown a third eye. "Uh, what do you mean *you don't want me to return to work?*"

He looked her squarely in the eyes and stated matter-of-factly in what Ronnie referred to as *Latino machismo*, "No pregnant wife of mine is going to work. You should be home taking care of yourself and preparing to bring our child into this world. You don't *need* to work, so why should you? Now that you are going to be my wife, the only place you will work is in our home."

"Really?" she asked, wide-eyed.

"My mother stayed home to raise us and so did her mother before her. In fact, Duarte women rarely work outside the home, and if they do, it was purely to keep from being bored. As far as I'm concerned, you should be no exception."

Observing his reaction, she half expected Luis to start pounding his chest like a gorilla. *Well, I ain't your wife yet!* "Excuse me, but I have worked all my life and am not about to let my pregnancy change that. As long as the doctor says I am healthy, then I intend to keep on working until I no longer can. Since when did you become so traditional anyway?"

"Why are you being so stubborn? I can afford to take care of all of us comfortably. What is the big deal, anyway? I know hundreds of women who would rather stay home than work. They would jump at this opportunity."

Ronnie almost brought up his gold-digging, high maintenance ex-wife, but changed her mind. There was no comparison between the two women. This they both knew. Although Ronnie hated when Luis behaved like a throwback to cavemen, at the same time, she loved how protective he was of her.

Luis patiently awaited her response.

"Baby, look, I know you can take care of me—of us. It's just that I love my job. I love working at the rehab center. It gives me a sense of fulfillment and purpose. To me, it isn't work."

He replied in a somewhat patronizing tone, "Darling, you do realize you are at higher risk for complications because of your age, right? You know that and I know that. Why take a chance if you don't need to?"

"I'm not doing anything at the center that prevents me from working."

"Working stresses you out and you definitely don't need to be feeling any sort of stress." He scooted behind her and began massaging her shoulders.

Ronnie toyed with the idea of staying home. It was tempting, but she knew she'd be bored silly after the first month. Anyway, back at her old job in Virginia, she knew women who worked up until the time of delivery. For them though, it was out of necessity, rather than choice.

"Just promise me you will think about it."

"Okay, how about if I cut my hours back to part-time. Or only work a few days a week. If it gets to be too much, then I'll quit."

"Or you can tell Travis that you're pregnant and won't be able to work at all. You could do that. When are you going to tell him anyway?"

"He's in Arizona on vacation. Kiara says he should be back any day now."

"Do not let too much time pass. I want to share our good news with the world. Have you told her yet?"

"No, I haven't told anyone. I wanted to get past the critical first trimester first. You know…" She relaxed into his massage, closing her eyes to get the full sensation.

"You like that, huh." Luis kissed her neck. "How much longer before we can make the official announcement? I'm dying to tell my family that I'm going to be a father." Luis moved the tray to the nightstand.

"My next appointment is in two weeks. If Dr. Chung says all is well, we can tell everyone then. Think you can keep a secret for another couple of weeks?" She purred, feeling her passion rise.

"Um…possibly." He ran his hand under Ronnie's silk top and lovingly cupped her breast.

She felt his erection stiffen against her back. "That feels nice. Why don't you come back to bed? Since you're taking all this time off, you may as well put yourself to good use."

Luis laughed out loud. "Good use, huh? I'll show you what I can put to good use." He pulled his t-shirt over his head and dropped his pajama pants. His erection stood at full attention. "You want me to put this to good use?"

"Oh yeah… Come here, papi," she purred.

* * *

The sound of the doorbell rudely interrupted their lovemaking. It rang once, twice more, and then continued as if the person pushing the button had lost their ever-loving mind. As Luis and Ronnie were in the throes of passion, they attempted to ignore it. Unfortunately, whoever was at the door was determined to get their attention. The ringing of the doorbell was interrupted by a continuous loud pounding on the door.

"*Coño*! Who in the hell is that banging on my door at this time of the morning?" Luis untangled his legs from Ronnie's and pulled a robe taut around his nakedness. Still half erect, he peeked out the bedroom window. A taxi cab was pulling way.

"What in the world?" she asked sitting up in bed. "Do you see anybody?"

"Ronnie, are we expecting company?"

"No, I don't think so. Who do you think it could be? Someone from work? Maybe Kiara?" She wiped the sweat from her brow and headed to the bathroom to freshen up. The pounding on the door continued.

"I don't know, but whoever it is better have a damn good reason for knocking on my door like that." Luis stormed off towards the living room.

Ronnie used the bathroom and shrugged into her bathrobe. She headed down the hallway to the living room to see who dared disturb their peace and more importantly their lovemaking. She stopped dead in her tracks when she heard the familiar voice of her old friend.

"You must be Luis." Joie cleared her throat and stifled a giggle. "Uh, do you have a gun underneath that robe or are you just happy to see me?"

"What the...?" asked Luis, confused as to who the loud, obnoxious woman standing at his front door was. He tightened the belt on his robe, but that action only emphasized his rapidly disappearing erection.

"Hi, I'm Joie, Ronnie's girlfriend. She said I could come out for a visit. I guess she forgot to tell you, huh?" Joie smirked. She looked past him into the house.

Oh shit! It's Joie! Damn, I forgot all about her saying she was coming out. Luis is going to kill me! "Joie, hey girl... What are you doing here?" Ronnie pushed past Luis.

"You said I could come out. Did you forget?" Joie asked, looking from Luis to Ronnie.

"I'm sorry Joie. I had so much going on that I guess I did forget. We last spoke—what was it? A couple of weeks ago?"

Joie replied indignantly, "No, it was just last week. Well, if I had known it was going to be a problem..."

"Girl, get in here! I'm just surprised, that's all." She reached for Luis' hand and said, "Baby, this is my best friend, Joie. Joie, this is Luis."

"Yeah, I figured as much. Nice to meet you, Luis. Finally." Joie looked him over from head to toe and nodded in approval.

Luis reached out and shook Joie's hand. "You too. I've heard so much about you, Joie. And any friend of Ronnie's is welcome in our home any time. I'll get your suitcase and Ronnie can show you your room later." He glanced sideways at Ronnie, picked up Joie's bags, and headed towards the guest house.

"You look good, Ronnie. Did you lose weight?"

"Yeah girl, I dropped a few pounds when I stopped eating all that fast food."

"Did I catch you at a bad time?" whispered Joie. She raised her brow and added, "Y'all both have that after sex glow going on."

Ronnie laughed. "Still the same old Joie. You always did have bad timing."

Joie joined in. "I'm sorry. I tried to call but kept getting your voicemail. I took the first flight out of Norfolk at 5 o'clock this morning. Girlfriend, I forgot all about the three hour time difference between the east and west coasts, that's why I'm here so early. Sorry…"

"Don't worry about it. We can always pick up where we finished later." Ronnie adjusted the belt around her robe and smiled happily.

"Well, well, well… Go on with your bad self! It appears that my girl is finally getting some on a regular basis. Now, that's what I'm talkin' about. Luis must be all right."

Ronnie stood grinning from ear to ear listening to Joie. Both recalled that it wasn't long ago when it seemed that Ronnie's life was spinning out of control, churning in a bottomless pit of unhappiness. Fortunately, all that was in the past. "Girl, come on in and let me show you around the house. How long are you staying?"

"That all depends on how long you can stand having me here." She chuckled. "But for real, my return flight is a week from today. Momma and Daddy got the kids and said they'd keep 'em for me until I got back. Gonna take 'em to summer camp and everything. So what *does* your schedule look like? Since you forgot I was coming out…"

"I'm only working part-time and thinking about cutting my hours even further. But since you're here for a week, this is as good a time as any to tell Travis I need to reevaluate my schedule." Ronnie gave the quick tour and ended up in the kitchen.

"Oh, so you got it like that? You can cut your hours down to nothing and still make a living? Luis must be doing all right if y'all ain't hurting for money. And by the looks of this house and this neighborhood, y'all must be doing all right." Joie surveyed the living room and hallways filled with original art.

"We do okay." Ronnie motioned to a stool. "Sit down and make yourself comfortable."

Joie sat at the breakfast bar.

"You want some coffee? I was just about to put on a pot for Luis." Ronnie took down a can of *Bustelo* from the top shelf, put in a filter, and scooped out enough for a full pot. She took down two cups and placed one in front of Joie.

"What? You're not having any?" Joie sat her purse down on the counter and peeked out the French doors into the garden. She saw Luis headed back in their direction. *Hmm, not bad. Ronnie's got herself a very nice looking brotha.*

"No, I've given it up. I'm only drinking tea, now."

"Are you okay? You used to be a Starbucks addict. And if my memory serves me right, you couldn't get your day started without a tall cup of dark roast with a shot of espresso." She noticed the engagement ring on Ronnie's finger.

Ronnie dropped her chin towards her chest, trying her best to hold back a mischievous grin.

Joie studied her friend closely. She watched her cross her arms protectively over her stomach. And just as Luis returned to the kitchen, she guessed Ronnie's secret. "You're pregnant!"

Luis stopped mid-step and stared incredulously. "You told her?"

"No, Luis, she didn't tell me. For your information, I know this woman like the back of my hand. Veronica Indigo Pierce is a workaholic and after she told me she was cutting back on her hours at work, I became suspicious. But when she said she gave up coffee, I knew there could only be one reason. She is pregnant! Am I right?"

Ronnie looked up at her friend and displayed the biggest shit-eating grin she could muster. She joined her friend by jumping up and down excitedly. "Yeah girl! We were going to wait to tell everyone until I was sure everything was going to be okay. But since you already guessed… Yes, we're going to have a baby!" she screamed in delight.

"Congratulations! That is awesome!" Joie hugged them both individually. "Why didn't you tell me you were engaged?"

"No reason. Got a lot going on and I've been so preoccupied with everything else, I guess I just forgot to call. Plus, it's only been a week since he asked." Ronnie raised her hand to allow the light to bounce off the brilliant crystal. "Isn't it gorgeous?"

Luis hung back and took in the sight of Ronnie and her friend enjoying each other's company. They both looked so happy. He didn't want to get in their way. "Baby, I think I'm going to head in to work and leave you two to visit, if that's okay with you."

Ronnie said a silent thank you. "Sure love, getting back to work will probably do us both some good. You know what they say about couples spending too much time together…"

"No. What do they say about couples spending too much time together?"

"Too much of a good thing can ruin a relationship. We need balance. That's all I'm saying," she replied, hoping she wasn't treading on thin ice.

"Is that right? So you think we've been spending too much time together?" he asked, looking slightly hurt.

Joie, realizing that they needed privacy, excused herself to the bathroom. She crept down the hall and opened all the doors until she found the right room.

Ronnie weighed her response carefully because that *was* exactly what she thought. Over the past week, practically every time she turned around, she had almost bumped into Luis. She couldn't even go to the restroom without him coming to look for her. "All I'm saying is that it's good for us to spend time apart so that when we get back together, we have something to look forward to."

"What are you saying?" Luis felt hurt in spite of himself.

"Sweetheart, I'm not saying this to hurt your feelings. I love you and I love having you near me. It's just that I do need some time alone. It will make the moment we see each other again all that much sweeter."

"Sorry, I didn't realize I was smothering you. I thought I was just being helpful, considering your condition. But if space is what you need, then I'll make sure you get it. I can find something to do at work and at the same time give you room to breathe."

"Don't be mad…"

Luis walked over to Ronnie and gave her a quick peck on her cheek. "I'm not angry. And I understand. I will give you space, especially since your friend Joie is here."

"Thanks. I love you."

"I love you, too." Luis passed Joie coming from the bathroom. She stopped him in the hallway.

"You've made her so happy. I can tell she really loves you."

"Thanks, Joie. That's good to know. Well, I've got to get dressed so I can get out of here. Ronnie can show you to the guest house where you'll be staying."

"Okay. Well, I'd better get back in there with the new expectant mother. I am so excited for you guys. Ronnie has always wanted to be a mommy and finally she's going to be able to experience it."

"You do realize she *does* have a daughter? Kiara's her name…"

"Yeah, I know about Kiara. But she didn't raise Kiara from a baby. She needs to experience holding that little precious baby in her arms and feeling the softness of its skin. Needs to know how it feels to get up in the middle of the night to soothe away the crying. Feel what it's like to kiss the hurt away. She never had the chance to go through that. Know what I mean?"

"I think so." He pondered her insightful words. "We're both excited and I cannot wait to be a father."

"I can feel in my heart that you guys are going to be great parents."

"Thanks, and for what it's worth, I'm glad you're here. We both are. I'll see you later."

Joie returned to the kitchen. Ronnie poured a cup of coffee for her and decaf tea for herself. She slid two croissants in the toaster oven to warm and plopped her butt down at the island counter. A smile of contentment was plastered across her face.

"You're really happy, aren't you?" asked Joie.

"Joie, you have no idea how happy I am."

"Girlfriend, I'm all ears…" Joie had never seen her friend in such a state of pure bliss. All the misery she had lived with in Virginia seemed to have been replaced with an undeniable spirit of peace. Living in the offbeat appeared to suit her best friend just fine. And for that, Joie was truly ecstatic.

Chapter Twelve

"*C*armen? Julio? Could you both please join me in my office?" Luis shouted through the open door.

"We'll be right there, boss," Julio answered for them both.

Over the past several days, Luis had been in very close contact with his prospective client in San Diego. After their last visit, which Luis thought ended in total disaster, the owner somehow changed his mind and agreed to sign on with *Duarte Graphics* if Luis would customize his company's brochures and pamphlets to his liking. Problem was, the owner only spoke Spanish and with Luis' language skills being as rusty as they were, important aspects were being lost in translation.

Carmen entered his office first. "*Senor* Duarte, Julio said you called for us..." It was only her second week on the job. The first week was spent with Julio because Luis had taken the time off to be with his woman.

"Please sit down," instructed Luis. He pointed to the two chairs positioned in front of his desk.

"What's up boss?" Julio walked in at Carmen's heels.

"Do you remember when I went down to San Diego a couple weeks ago to meet with the Hernandez group? They're that Mexican-owned company that is looking to expand into the United States and is looking for a graphics design company to complete their marketing portfolio. The president was impressed with our work..."

"That's great, Mr. Duarte," Carmen interrupted.

"Yeah, I remember the Hernandez account and how upset you were about it," Julio said. "What's up?"

"I told you how rusty my Spanish has become over the years..."

"Hey, I've offered to tutor you, but you were always so busy..." Julio teased.

"Is there anything I can do to help?" asked Carmen.

"Hold on one moment, Carmen. This is where you come in."

"Okay..." She patiently awaited Luis' explanation.

"Well, I have to head back to San Diego first thing tomorrow morning to meet with the owners. *And* we have another large order that goes out in a couple of days. I can't be in two places at once, so I want you to take over for me while I go to San Diego to seal this deal."

"Sure, boss. I'll do whatever you need me to do. What's the problem?" asked Julio, looking perplexed.

"I'm thinking about taking Carmen with me. She speaks Spanish fluently and according to you, she's caught on very quickly in the front office. Do you think she's ready to assist me on this deal?" Luis scrutinized Julio's reaction.

Carmen searched Luis' face to see if he were serious. Then she took one look at Julio. He didn't appear to be pleased at all with his bosses' request.

Julio knew exactly what Luis was asking and it had nothing to do with Carmen's administrative skills. His boss was asking how it would appear for him to take his secretary—his drop dead gorgeous secretary—to San Diego. Not only how it would look to his workers, but more importantly to Ronnie. Business trip or not, it wouldn't look good.

"Hey Carmen, can you please go pull the file for tomorrow's shipment? It's under *Inexpensive Gourmet Foods.*" Julio sent her away.

"Uh… Of course, I'll be right back." Fully aware of the reason behind Julio's request, Carmen left the two men alone to discuss her.

Julio closed the door. "Boss, you do remember how dealing with one of Tomas' women almost destroyed your relationship, right?"

"But this isn't like that." Luis defended his decision.

"You even slept in your office a few nights because you were so fucked up over Ronnie leaving you. And now you're considering taking *Carmen* to San Diego with you? Uh, have you looked at her lately?"

Luis interlaced his hands behind his head and leaned back in his chair. "Yes… Unfortunately, I have. That's why I'm talking to you now."

"Boss, I have a lot of respect for you and everyone knows how smart you are when it comes to business, but you don't know a damn thing about women." He chuckled and swiped his hand over his face.

Luis knew Julio was right, yet he felt the need to justify his position. "I know what you're saying, but this situation isn't like that. Carmen is an asset to this company and I need her language skills on this transaction. What I need to know is do you think Carmen's professional skills are polished enough to pull this off?"

"As far as your question… Yeah, I think Carmen's ready. She is a quick learner and seems to have a good head for business. Too bad she's so good looking."

Carmen returned to the office. The two men immediately stopped talking, allowing an awkward silence to settle in the room. Without being privy to the conversation, she knew what this situation was about because she had been here too many times. No matter how much she downplayed her appearance, men and women alike, seemed only to focus on her looks. Despite how she felt in the beginning, she enjoyed working for Luis' company and wanted to be sure her position was secure. She wondered if *Senor* Duarte would take her with him. Or would he buckle like previous bosses and not include her just because their wives or girlfriends felt threatened.

"Carmen, I have an opportunity for you," stated Luis. Whenever he looked at Carmen, he tried to think of her only as his employee and not a gorgeous woman. So far, it hadn't worked.

"*Si*, what is it *Senor* Duarte?" She gave Julio the file he sent her out for and took a seat.

"I have a major deal going down in San Diego. It's very important for the company and I need you to attend with me—because of your fluency in Spanish and your knowledge of my company. We'll only be gone for a couple of days, but I have to be down there tomorrow afternoon. Do you think you can make it?"

"Go to San Diego with you? Um, I don't know. I must check with my husband first…" She hesitated, unsure of where this was headed, or of the infinite opportunities the situation presented.

Luis offered an explanation. "Please… I don't want you to get the wrong idea… This trip is strictly for business and I will even throw in a nice bonus if we get the deal. Clear it with your husband if you need to. But we've got to leave first thing tomorrow morning."

"All right. I'll check with him and let you know," replied Carmen rushing from the room with a cell phone in her hand.

Julio leaned against the wall with his arms crossed, shaking his head. Luis shot him a warning look. He uncrossed his arms, threw his hands up in defeat, and uttered, "Hey, it's your funeral…"

Luis realized he was putting himself in a precarious position by including Carmen Sanchez in his plans to San Diego, but he didn't have much of a choice. The last time he visited the company, he missed out on half of what was said. He needed someone to help translate for him and the most obvious person was Carmen.

"Look, if I didn't need her, I wouldn't take her," he explained.

"You asked for my opinion. I think taking Sanchez with you is a mistake," Julio said.

He'd explain the situation to Ronnie later. After all, it was she who said they were spending too much time together. A little time apart would do them both good. And with Joie visiting, Ronnie probably wouldn't care if he were home or not. He quickly dismissed Julio's concerns and managed to convince himself that the trip would be good for everyone involved.

Carmen returned to the office to give Luis the news. "*Senor* Duarte, I spoke to my husband. He is okay with me going with you as an interpreter. I told him we would be back day after tomorrow. Is that right?"

"Yes, we will meet with Mr. Hernandez tomorrow afternoon and return the following day."

* * *

Joie was working on her second cup of coffee and picking at a freshly toasted bagel. "Girlfriend, what have you been up to besides getting all pretty out here in California? You let your hair grow out and your skin has such a healthy glow to it. What's your secret? It's gotta be more than just a regular dose of good dick."

Ronnie laughed realizing Joie hadn't changed a bit. "That's part of it—being in love. But seriously, I'm just happy. When I'm happy I eat healthier, exercise more, and take better care of myself."

Joie nodded. "Sounds like I could use some of what you got."

"I love having Kiara right up the road and Luis is perfect for me. I love my life!"

"I'm so happy for you. And what's up with the rock on your finger? I thought you swore off marriage forever."

"I did, but Luis asked me in a weak moment and I agreed. I'm not going anywhere and neither is he. The way I figure, we may as well make our relationship official. And now that I'm pregnant, it really feels like the right thing to do."

"Did he ask you before or after he found out you were pregnant?" asked Joie.

"Before. Why?"

"I'm just checking that's all. You wouldn't want to marry Luis just because he felt obligated after getting you knocked up."

"Please… It wasn't anything like that. In fact, we weren't even trying to have a baby. I thought I was going through the first stages of menopause. Talk about having a mid-life crisis… Instead of getting rid of my period, I'm going to have a mid-life baby."

"How are you really dealing with this?"

"To tell you the truth, I am scared." Ronnie placed the breakfast dishes into dishwasher.

"You don't have nothin' to be scared of. There are lots of women in their forties having babies. Medical technology has caught up to help make sure you have a healthy baby. I think you're going to make a terrific mommy."

"Thanks for saying that." She offered Joie more coffee. "I haven't told Kiara yet. We were going to wait a couple of weeks before saying anything to anybody."

"I understand and my lips are sealed." Joie made a zipping motion across her mouth. "So you and Kiara have gotten tight, huh? Doing mother-daughter stuff?"

"Yeah, we've really connected." She sipped her remaining tea and picked up the phone. "Speaking of Kiara, I want you guys to meet." Ronnie punched in the first five digits of her daughter's cell.

"Okay, I'm looking forward to it."

Ronnie explained, "She's leaving for Haiti next week for the summer and is getting ready to go, but I'm sure we can hook up for lunch while you're here."

"Sounds good. Before I forget, did you ever get that situation straightened out with Luis?"

"Hmmm? What situation?"

"You called and told me about Luis having had some woman come to his office. You asked what I thought you should do. Did you ever find out what that was about?"

"Oh that? Yeah, Luis was interviewing administrative assistants. It's cool." *I hope.*

"As long as you're cool with it, so am I." Joie's phone rang and she interrupted her conversation with Ronnie to take the call. "It's my mother. This'll only take a few minutes."

"Take your time; I'm going to jump in the shower after I get off the phone. I also need to stop by work for a few minutes to talk to Travis," she whispered, still holding the phone in her hand, waiting for Kiara to pick up.

Joie acknowledged her, all the while giving instructions about the twins to her mother. After she got off the phone, she found her way into the guest cottage where she also showered and changed. She met Ronnie back at the main house.

"Guuurl! That guest house is the bomb! And y'all don't have nobody living there?"

"No, Luis doesn't like the idea of strangers living so close. I lived in the apartment for a few months after I first moved here. Now it mostly sits empty except when we have out-of-town visitors."

"Forgive me for being nosey, but you know how I am. I have to check out my surroundings no matter where I go." Joie smacked her lips together.

"What are you talking about, Joie?"

"Okay, I admit I was snooping. It looked like there was an office set up in that purple room. Are you working on your book?"

Ronnie was embarrassed at how little she had accomplished. "Kind of. When Luis and I first met, I told him that I wanted to be a writer. He thought it was a cool idea so he set up a writer's studio in the guest house for me."

"That's great... So when *are* you going to start writing? It's only been three years." Joie sipped on the now cold cup of coffee. "What's holding you up?"

Ronnie shrugged. "I don't know. Time? Life? Or maybe I just don't have it in me to become a real writer. It takes much more focus and creativity than I ever imagined."

"Well, I think you should pursue it. Nothing ventured, nothing gained."

"Easier said than done." She countered with another cliché. "Are you ready to go? I'm supposed to be at work in a few minutes."

"I'm ready. Let's roll," replied Joie.

* * *

Fifteen minutes later, they pulled up to the gates of the center and Ronnie entered her special code into the keypad. The large metal gates parted as if they were welcoming them into a magical hidden kingdom.

Joie admired the beautifully landscaped grounds. "Is *this* where you work?"

"It's nice, huh? Travis started this all on his own," Ronnie replied with a sense of pride. "He oversaw every detail from selecting the building design to hiring the finest medical staff in their field."

Joie cooed, "Very nice. This place looks like one of those expensive spas."

Ronnie laughed at Joie's reaction to the center. It was refreshing to see the center through someone else's eyes for a change. It was exactly the reaction Travis hoped for when he approved the landscape design. He felt his patients would recuperate faster if they were in a beautiful, eye-pleasing, relaxed atmosphere. Thus far, it was working.

"So y'all still cool working together after all those years? Most importantly, is *Luis* cool with you working closely with your ex?"

Ronnie dismissed Joie's concerns with a wave of her hand. "We straightened all that mess out a long time ago. The good work Travis does here is bigger than any of our petty problems. Once we all realized that, the drama never happened."

"Good for all of you, then," Joie replied. "Go on in. I'll follow you."

"Oh, I forgot to tell you, Kiara is going to meet us later."

"Oh good! I can't wait to meet her," said Joie as she followed Ronnie through the entrance. "I'll bet you she's just like her mother."

"In some ways, yes. In other ways, absolutely not."

Joie surveyed the rehabilitative center, noting the soothing décor. It was the perfect combination of spa and health center.

"Hey Kaylee, is Travis here today?" Ronnie asked the receptionist.

"Yeah, he got back in this morning. Would you like for me to see if he's available?"

"Yes. Tell him I'll be in my office, please."

"Do you want me to wait here?" Joie asked referring to the admittance waiting room.

"If you don't mind. This shouldn't take too long. Help yourself to another cup of coffee and a scone. Kaylee brings them in fresh every morning."

"Ooh scones! Haven't we come up in the world?" Joie teased.

"Whatever…" Ronnie laughed. "I'll be right back."

* * *

A week had passed since Ronnie was in the office. Trudy had taken the day off, leaving the office neat and tidy in her absence. She took a seat behind her desk. She logged into the computer. After updating the calendar and reviewing some of Trudy's work, she felt confident about cutting back her hours.

She heard the whir of the wheelchair's motor. Travis appeared at her door looking tan and healthy. He seemed relaxed and content. Apparently, his vacation had worked.

His heart skipped a beat when he saw Ronnie sitting there. In that moment, he realized how much he had missed her. Seeing her smiling face somehow made his day that much brighter. "Well, hello stranger. You're looking much better." He grinned.

"Thanks, I am feeling much better. And you don't look bad yourself. How was your vacation?" Ronnie gazed down to her hands resting on the keyboard and suddenly felt self-conscious about wearing her engagement ring. She covered her ring with her free hand and leaned forward.

"It was wonderful. I finally took time to do only what I wanted to. I put the center into my assistant's hands and you know what? He did fine." He noticed her hands resting awkwardly on the desk. Something was different. He frowned. She was hiding something.

"Great! Looks like the time off did you a world of good."

"Yes, it did. Oh, I was just reviewing the results of the audit. So far, we've done really well. The state auditors reviewed our books and gave us a clean bill of health. Hiring that accounting firm was money well spent."

"That's great news, Travis. I don't know why you were worried anyway." She exhaled and decided to put her business out there because beating around the bush was getting her nowhere. "Travis, there's a couple of things I need to discuss with you."

"All right, I'm listening…"

Her stomach flip flopped with unanticipated nervousness. "Well, I've got some news I'd like to share,"

"I hope it's good news," he replied.

"I think it is." *Oh well. I might as well just spit it out…* "Luis and I are getting married." She stretched her hand forward showing off her ring.

Travis leaned back in his wheelchair stunned, momentarily unable to speak. For several seconds, he forgot how to breathe.

"Travis?" she asked with concern.

Upon realizing he was holding his breath; he forced the air out from his lungs, forced it in again, and then continued until breathing was once again a natural reflex. He swallowed hard and managed to say, "Congratulations. When is the big day?"

Ronnie never imagined telling Travis about her engagement would be so difficult. After all, she and Luis *had* been together for three years. Getting married should not have been a surprise to anyone, least of all, Travis.

"We haven't set a date yet." She noticed his blank stare. "Hey, are you okay?"

He responded in a tightly controlled voice. "Yes, I'm fine. Just surprised is all." He turned his chair away from her and towards the window.

Ronnie broke the silence. "Travis? Are you all right?"

"Yeah, yeah…I'm fine. Have you told Kiara yet?"

"She knows."

Still facing the window, he tried to find the words to offer an appropriate response. "T-T-That's really great news. I'm happy for you two…"

Ronnie wished there was a better way to break the news, but there wasn't. She pressed on. "I'm also going to need to cut my hours to part-time. I can do a lot of work at home." At this point, mentioning her pregnancy might have sent him over the edge.

"Sure, take all the time you need… Uh… I have an important meeting to prepare for." He turned his chair towards the door, still unable to face her. The initial happiness he felt had all but evaporated into a deep sadness. *Kiara warned me that Ronnie was very happy with her life. Who am I to stand in her way?*

"Travis, what is it?" she asked. Usually Travis took everything in stride and was always the voice of reason.

Ronnie rose from behind the desk to walk Travis out, but he put his hand up to stop her. It felt like there was no air in the room to breathe. Ronnie's news was so unexpected that it totally caught him off guard. She stood before him with happiness oozing from every pore. He realized that back then, even on their best days, making her this happy was something he could never do.

He imagined himself saying, *When you first came here to work, I put all those old feelings to rest. I convinced myself that what we had was in the past. Over and done with. But lately, especially with Kiara going off on her own, I started to fantasize about us being together. You and me. Thought about how it would have been to be a family—like we always spoke of. You were going to be my wife twenty something years ago, yet you ran away from me like a little girl. Now you tell me that you've given your heart to someone else... What am I supposed to do now? I still love you!*

Instead he merely uttered, "It's nothing Ronnie. I wish you and Luis all the best. We'll catch up later."

"Thanks... You sure you're okay?" she asked again, now feeling awful.

He gave a little wave as he made his way out the office without saying another word.

She listened to the whir of the motorized wheelchair until it was barely audible and he was no longer visible. In a whisper she declared, "Travis, although I have given my heart to Luis, there will always be a space left for you. You were my first love and the man I planned to marry. We have a child together who shall always bind us to the other. You rescued Kiara from a life of uncertainty and for that reason alone I will always love you. I pray you find a woman who loves you as deeply as you love her." She wiped away the lone brave tear that had the courage to travel down her cheek. The tear was shed for a life with a man that never was and never would be. Their time had come and gone. Hopefully, in time, Travis would also come to know this simple truth.

Ronnie locked up the office, took a few files with her to work on at home, and returned to the waiting room to find Joie. She found her friend in deep conversation with a young family whose oldest child, a girl of around eight years old, sat strapped motionless into a miniature wheelchair. They were all laughing as if they were in an amusement park instead of a rehabilitation center. And for just a moment, Joie had eased the family's burdens and left them all in stitches.

"Bye! Y'all take care of each other," Joie said to the family as she joined Ronnie at the entrance.

The young family called out in unison, "See ya later, Joie."

Joie noticed Ronnie was unusually quiet when they strolled outside. Despite the raw emotions she felt after meeting the family, she had the presence of mind to take notice of her friend's state. "You all right, girlfriend? Is everything okay with Travis?"

"Yeah, yeah, I'm okay. I just had to take care of a sensitive matter. Anyway, I see you've made yourself some new friends."

"Friends? No. Matter-of-fact, I didn't even catch their names." Once they were inside Ronnie's car, Joie's timid smile was quickly replaced with quiet tears that ran down her face as she looked towards the building.

"Joie, are *you* okay?" Ronnie asked tenderly.

"That little girl was about the same age as Maya. I don't know how that family is dealing with it. It's tragic, Ronnie. That baby hasn't even had an opportunity to live yet. She's going to be in that goddamn wheelchair for the rest of her life."

Ronnie attempted to console her friend. She totally understood Joie's angst because for the first year or so, she'd come home sobbing to Luis about the injustice of it all. Why some and not others? Spinal cord injuries were almost always a permanent state of disability. Very, very few patients ever recovered to their full capacity. Fortunately, over the years, she came to accept that part of her job. Nonetheless, the most difficult and heartbreaking cases usually involved children.

She explained to Joie, "That's why the center is here—to help families deal with the pain. We help patients adapt and live with their disabilities. We can't cure them. Not yet. But we do our best to make their lives as comfortable as possible. The center not only deals with their physical injuries, but the psychological ones as well."

"I don't get it. What made Travis interested in this particular area? Does he know someone who was injured?" She wiped her nose with her sleeve. Ronnie handed her a tissue from the glove compartment.

"Oh my goodness! You *haven't* met Travis. I would've introduced you to him today, but he had a full schedule."

On the way back to town, Ronnie relayed the story of Travis' injury and how he came to build the *J. Bradford Rehabilitative Center*. Joie's reaction indicated she was impressed and a bit in awe of how someone could take an idea and transform so many lives as a result of it.

"It sounds like Travis Bradford is an amazing man." Joie looked at Ronnie from the corner of her eye. "You sure he ain't the one you supposed to be with? I mean, you should hear the way you speak about him. You're practically gushing!"

"Shut up! I'm just telling you what he did. And *it is* impressive. I can't help it if I sound like I'm bragging on him. I am proud of him. So what?" Ronnie glanced over at Joie who seemed to see right through her. They both started giggling.

"Be careful is all I'm saying.... It is hard to be in love with two men at the same time and love either one the right way. Trust me, I know."

"Okay, I'll admit I still love Travis, but not the way you think. I love Travis for who he is—for everything he has accomplished. For being a man and raising our daughter in spite of all the obstacles placed in his path."

"I knew it!"

"But I am *in love* with Luis. There is a difference. That's why I'm marrying Luis and not Travis."

"I hear ya. Just let me share some advice my momma gave me. When you fall in love and decide to get married, always let the man love you just a little bit more than you love him."

"What the...? That doesn't make an ounce of sense, Joie."

"Yes, it does. Look at it this way; men need to wonder if they have you. Because if they are one hundred percent totally certain that they got you, most of 'em will stray the first chance they get. Momma said to keep 'em on the hunt in pursuit of your affection."

Ronnie snickered. "I'm not trying to be mean *or* disrespectful, but girlfriend; you are probably the last woman I'd take advice about men from. Your record with the opposite sex hasn't been exactly, ahem... How shall I say...admirable."

"You got me there. Nevertheless, I gave you the advice my mother gave me. I didn't say I followed it, but there ya go."

"I get what you're saying. Some men need that challenge of a woman they're not sure they can hold on to. I don't agree with it because to me it sounds like both of them have a problem with trust and commitment. Sounds like playing games to me."

"Anyway... What do you have planned for us today?" Joie asked, changing the subject to something a little less confrontational.

"I got in touch with Kiara. We're on our way to have brunch with her and her man. I can't wait for you to meet my daughter."

"Did you say 'her and her man'? She's hooked up with somebody already?"

"Yeah girl. His name is Gerald Quinn but he goes by 'GQ'. He used to be her professor."

"Whaaaat?! Her professor? Does her daddy know this?"

"Travis knows Quinn, but he doesn't know about Quinn and Kiara. And I didn't tell him."

"Keeping secrets from daddy, huh? He must be an older man if he used to be her professor. You okay with this?"

Ronnie made a right turn into the parking lot of a local restaurant that served breakfast all day. "No, I'm really not 'okay' with her dating him. He's got fifteen years on Kiara *and* he was her teacher last year. On the other hand, I've met Quinn—I mean GQ, and he seems cool. He is a very intelligent man, but I just can't get over the teacher-student thing."

Joie's cynical expression mirrored Ronnie's true feelings.

"Girlfriend, Kiara is so naïve when it comes to the ways of the real world. That's why I—we, agreed to let her go to Haiti with him. The trip will expose her to how other people live…"

"She's going with him to Haiti? I don't know if that's a good idea…"

"Actually, he's taking a group of students and unfortunately, we cannot stop Kiara from going. That child is like a dog with a bone when she sets her mind to something. I've just got to pray she has enough sense to keep her skirt down and panties up," replied Ronnie.

"Amen!" replied Joie, nodding in agreement. "From everything you've told me, she has a bright future ahead and babies are not in the equation at the moment."

Chapter Thirteen

*T*he family owned restaurant was fairly empty considering it was late morning. A waitress sporting a head full of red and blonde dreadlocks held back with a tie-dyed scarf, reacted as if they had interrupted her coffee break. She took several more sips from her large mug before acknowledging their presence.

With the aid of another waitress, the woman remembered she was not at home sitting at her kitchen table enjoying a morning cup of coffee. She warmly greeted the ladies, picked up a couple of menus, and showed them to their table.

Ronnie spotted Kiara and GQ sitting at a booth with their heads bent towards one another, lost in an intense kiss.

"Ahem!" Ronnie loudly cleared her throat to get their attention.

"Oh, I'm sorry. We didn't see you guys standing there." Kiara grinned, wiping the remnants of the kiss from the corners of her mouth.

"Miss Pierce, good to see you again," replied GQ, making room in the booth.

GQ was fashionably dressed in faded blue jeans, a long sleeved cotton shirt topped off by a funky vest, and comfortable loafers graced his sockless feet. He used a cloth napkin to discretely wipe away Kiara's ultra glistening pink lipstick. Kiara wore her usual Bohemian outfit, and this time her wild hair was left untamed and free. The handsome couple seemed to fit well together.

"Good to see you, too. Joie, this here is my daughter Kiara and her friend Gerald..."

"Mom, he goes by GQ, remember?" interjected Kiara.

"I'm sorry. Of course... Guys, this is my very good friend, Joie Parker. She just flew in this morning from Virginia and will be visiting me for the week."

"Nice to meet you, Miss Parker," they responded in unison and started to laugh as if they had a private joke going on.

Joie smirked. She glanced at Ronnie before responding, "Nice to meet you both. I've heard so much about you, Kiara."

Kiara smiled warmly at Joie. *I think this is the first time I've seen Mom with a girlfriend.*

"Have you two been here long?" said Ronnie. She perused the mostly empty restaurant, suspecting the crowd would swell in just a couple of hours.

"No. We've been here like about fifteen minutes. We were just going over some information about the trip."

"Kiara, I remember how excited your mom was when she first found out about you."

Ronnie kicked Joie's shin underneath the table and shot her a look that meant "keep your mouth shut". The twenty year separation was still a sensitive subject in spite of the leaps and bounds made in their mother-daughter relationship. And because the memories of her earlier years without a mother were still very painful for Kiara, Ronnie and she had silently agreed to refrain from that topic of conversation.

The unexpected pain shot up Joie's leg. "Oww!" Joie grabbed her shin and tried rubbing the pain away. She shot darts with her eyes at Ronnie that silently asked, "What the fuck did you kick me for?"

Kiara hesitated before responding. "Miss Parker, you have no idea how thrilled I am to have my mother back in my life. It's been like awesome over the last few years."

"I feel the same way... Kiara is all grown up now and concentrating on finishing college. We're all so proud of her," Ronnie furrowed her brow and pierced her lips at Joie.

"As well you should be." Joie ignored Ronnie's stare and refocused her attention across the table. "So, Gerald…"

"Please… Call me GQ." Almost immediately he could tell that Joie was the type of woman who could cut you every which way with words alone.

"All right, GQ it is. So…*GQ*, Ronnie tells me you're a professor and that you're taking a group of students with you to Haiti." She studied him intently as if she were trying to read his mind.

GQ rested his elbows on the table and interlaced his fingers. "That's right, Joie. Um, may I call you Joie?"

"Sure," she replied.

"I think you have a very beautiful name. Does *Joie* have a French pronunciation?" He attempted to win her over with charm, because it usually worked on most women.

Joie smirked, replying in a dismissive tone. "No, sweetheart. It's pronounced like *Joy*. I changed the spelling when I was in my twenties, because j-o-y sounded too plain. And I am anything but plain."

GQ was not impressed. *Would you look at this ghetto queen trying to be exotic?* "Pardon me for the faux pas, *Joie.*"

"Easy mistake to make…" She shrugged it off.

"As I was saying, we're leaving next week. Our group will join with others to help rebuild one of the schools the earthquake destroyed. Right now, the children are using a tent for a classroom and as you can probably imagine, it is very difficult to learn under those austere conditions."

"I think it's commendable what you're doing—helping those devastated by that awful earthquake." *I wonder what's in it for him,* Joie thought.

"The Haitian people can still use all the international help they can get," he replied. GQ imagined he was making inroads with Joie. He momentarily relaxed.

Joie wasn't buying his holier than thou attitude. Ronnie may have refused to see the snake sitting next to her daughter ready to strike at a moment's notice, but she knew better. She studied the menu for a minute, sucked her teeth, and then blurted out unapologetically, "GQ, let me ask you this… How in the hell did you get involved with Kiara? Ain't you kinda old to be with someone so young? Are you one of those men who only like 'em young and fresh? Or is it because you're intimidated by women your own age?" she asked, unfazed by the group's reaction to her questions.

Ronnie kicked Joie in the shin again and shot her another menacing look.

Joie winced in pain and whispered loudly, "Heifer, if you kick me one more time, I swear to God I'm gonna come straight across this table and whup that ass! So help me…"

"I'm sorry girlfriend, but damn…! Don't you have any tact? Guys, please excuse Joie. When she wants to know something, she just comes right on out and asks, no matter who she offends."

Kiara narrowed her eyes at Joie. She was at a total loss for words. Never in her life had she met anyone like the vulgar woman who sat before her. She didn't understand how her mother could ever call someone who acted so uncouth a friend. After only a few minutes in her presence, Kiara decided she didn't care much for her mother's long-time friend.

Kiara glanced over at GQ and sweetly said, "I'll answer that."

Ronnie touched her daughter's arm. "You don't have to explain anything to us. Neither does Gerald. I mean GQ." Secretly Ronnie was glad Joie had asked the questions that swirled around in her mind. *If I wasn't so afraid of offending her, I would have asked the same questions last night.*

The redheaded waitress with the serious coffee addiction interrupted the dramatic scene that was sure to follow. "Good morning folks. My name is Amber and I will be your waitress today." Standing with her tablet poised to take orders, she suspected she had approached the group at the worst possible moment. "Do you need a few more minutes? I can come back later."

Amber? Seriously? What an absurdly appropriate name for a redhead. Ronnie spoke for the group. "Yes, please give us a few more minutes. Thanks."

Kiara took back the floor. "As I was about to say before I was interrupted, GQ and I have been dating for like about a year. Yes, he was my teacher, but we weren't seeing each other then. As far as him being older, it doesn't bother either one of us, so why should it like bother you?"

"You certainly are your mother's child," Joie responded in pleasant surprise. "Not afraid to speak your mind. Girl, you are gonna go far in this world. I can see that now. If you like it, I love it."

Kiara blushed. She had surprised herself by sticking up for her relationship with GQ. And to show his approval, he raised his water glass in a toast to her.

The waitress watched the group from across the room, gauging when it was safe to return to take their orders. Once the group's uncomfortable silence was replaced with cheerful laughter, she bounced over to the table and turned on her tip-the-waitress-well charm.

* * *

"Be right back. I think I drank way too much coffee and juice." Joie tossed a couple of twenties on the table.

GQ picked up the money and handed it back to Joie. "I'll get this. My treat." GQ wasn't trying to befriend Joie anymore; he was merely being the gentlemen he prided himself as.

"Thank you, um… GQ," she responded and headed towards the sign pointing to the restroom.

"No problem," said GQ. Joie's sideways glance would have caused someone with less confidence to pause, but it didn't faze GQ at all. He was used to women like her. *That's* why he was with a woman like Kiara.

"Brunch was fun. And I guess she's not so bad after you get to know her, right?" Kiara watched Joie head towards the toilet. "I must admit my first impression was not that great." They trailed GQ to the cashier.

Ronnie replied, "Joie is kinda rough around the edges, but she has a good heart. We have been through some hard times, but in the end we're still friends."

GQ settled the bill and returned his attention to the women. "Miss Pierce, once again, it was such a pleasure visiting with you. I want to assure you that I am going to watch out for Kiara while we are in Haiti. She'll be in good hands, so no need for you or Travis to be overly concerned about your daughter's welfare."

"I can't promise you that we won't worry, but I certainly appreciate you keeping an eye on her."

Kiara rolled her eyes and remarked, "I'll be fine. It's not like I'm the first American woman to like volunteer in Haiti. Jeez!"

"Baby, don't get upset. Your mother is simply concerned about your welfare. I think it's endearing," GQ whispered into her ear and lovingly kissed her cheek.

Kiara snuggled closer to GQ and giggled.

Oh brother, thought Ronnie. *My child is in way over her head.* "Um, sweetie, when are you going to tell Travis that the two of you are dating? Don't you think he should know?" She posed the question to Kiara.

"I'll speak to Travis." GQ rubbed his chin nervously. "I'm sure he'll understand—once I explain."

"Don't be so sure of that," added Kiara. "Daddy can sometimes be very irrational when it like comes to me. So it would be better if I like told him first."

Joie rejoined the group. As she squirted a dollop of lotion on her hands from a tube she kept in her purse, she casually blurted out, "Okay, you lovebirds. Break it up. I've got to get the little mother here back home so she can take a nap. We can't let her get all tuckered out now—especially in her condition."

Kiara's eyes grew wide at the news. She looked directly to Ronnie and gasped, "Little mother? You're pregnant?"

Joie realized her mistake as quickly as the sound of her voice reached Kiara's ears. It was too late to take it back. She went to Ronnie and said, "Me and my big mouth. I'm so sorry…"

"Well?" asked Kiara wide-eyed.

There was no use in lying or sugar coating the news. *Best to be honest now that the secret was out.* "Yes, I am. About ten weeks. I was going to tell you after I had my next checkup."

"Wow!" Stunned by the news, she groped for a chair. GQ eased her into the nearest one. "Are you sure?"

Ronnie nodded. "The doctor confirmed it a couple of weeks ago." She nervously wrung her hands. This was not how she wanted to break the news to her daughter.

"You mean I'm going to have a little sister? Or maybe a brother? This is like frickin' awesome news!" She looked up with tears in her eyes.

"Does this mean you're happy?" asked Ronnie.

Kiara jumped up and wrapped her arms around her mother. "Of course, I'm happy! First I find out you're like getting married and now you're going to have a baby…"

"I didn't want you to find out this way. I'm an older mother so I wanted to make sure everything was fine before I told anyone." She cut her eyes at Joie.

"What do you mean? Is the baby going to be all right?" Kiara asked, alarmed.

"I'll know more after the first trimester is over. The doctor will probably want to run a few tests to make sure the baby is healthy, but I'm in good shape and I've been taking very good care of myself. I'm confident the baby will be fine. After all, The Lord wouldn't have allowed this to happen if it wasn't meant to be."

"I can't wait! I'm going to spoil it rotten." Kiara laughed.

"I'm sure you're going to be a wonderful big sister." Ronnie kissed her on her cheek. "C'mon, I'll walk you to your car. Joie, GQ, give us a moment, would ya?"

GQ and Joie trailed behind them. In spite of how they felt about one another, they discovered they had a mutual fascination with action hero lunchboxes after they spotted a collection in a storefront window.

"Are you sure you're all right?" asked Kiara. "Is something about the baby bothering you?"

"No, I'm fine. It's not me I wanted to talk to you about. It's Travis."

"What's wrong with Daddy?"

"Nothing. He's fine. It's just that when I told him about me and Luis getting married he didn't react the way I imagined he would. I thought he would be happy for us."

"What did he say?"

"Well, it wasn't *what* he said. It's *how* he reacted. Like he was shocked or hurt or that I had given him horrible news."

"Mom, you must know that Daddy still loves you. He never stopped loving you. He talks about you all the time. In fact, before he went on vacation, he asked if I thought there was a chance for you two to get back together."

"He did? What did you tell him?"

"I told you you and Luis are very happy together."

"Yeah, that is very true. We are happy." She held Kiara's hand. "Listen, I never meant to hurt Travis. He means the world to me. I never imagined he still had feelings for me. Not like that anyway. Especially after all these years."

"Daddy will be okay. He needs to move on and let you go. In fact, it would probably be a good idea if you stopped working at the center all together. As long as you're nearby, it's almost impossible for him to like move forward. And now that you're pregnant…"

"You're right. I was planning on quitting anyway."

Kiara sighed wearily, "I'll talk to Daddy. Don't worry, he'll be all right."

"I know, he will."

Joie and GQ caught up with them.

"We've got to head back to the university. I have a class in forty-five minutes and GQ has a lecture to give."

"You still have a few more days, right? If you need anything before you leave, give me a call, okay?" Ronnie stopped besides GQ's car. He opened the door to let Kiara get in.

"Okay Mom. See you later. And get some rest!" she shouted.

Once again, no thanks to Joie and her big mouth, disaster had been averted. Ronnie jabbed Joie in the arm and shook her head in disbelief.

"Damn it! I told you not to hit me no more."

"That's for opening your big mouth. And what if she wasn't okay with it? Then what?"

"Woman, you better be glad you're pregnant. Otherwise, I'd beat the shit out of you." Joie pretended to be upset.

"I wanted to break the news to her gently, not hit her over the head with it at a restaurant."

"Kiara is excited about being a big sister, so you have nothing to worry about."

"That's true. She did sound excited."

"Now, c'mon so I can get you home. I don't want to tucker you out—little mommy."

Chapter Fourteen

*L*uis called Ronnie with news about his upcoming trip to San Diego. "Baby, it will be a quick trip down there and back. I'd take you with me, but your friend is here visiting."

"Why are you going back to San Diego? I thought you said it was a waste of time meeting with the Hernandez group." Ronnie hated it when Luis left town.

"Last time it was, but this time I'm taking an interpreter with me—someone who speaks Spanish fluently and therefore will make the meeting more productive."

"Okay, fine. So what time are you getting home tonight?"

"It'll probably be late because we need to go over the presentation and make sure the documents are as close to perfect as possible."

"Yeah, I know what "late" means. It means I probably won't see you at all tonight. I wanted us to go out to dinner to celebrate Joie's first night here."

"I'm sorry, but this meeting in San Diego is very important. And remember it was you who wanted us to spend less time together."

"You know how I hate it when you use my words against me."

"I'll be home before you know it."

"All right, me and Joie will go to the Pier by ourselves."

"That's a good idea, love. You girls should go out and have fun. Every now and then think about me and poor old Julio working overtime to get this presentation together. I'll call you later."

"Okay, I love you."

"Love you too, baby."

* * *

The drive to the Santa Elena Pier took them past the busy boardwalk where dozens of people were still jogging and riding bicycles, despite the sun having already set. Tourists milled about, sampling the gorgeous scenery and filling their shopping bags with interesting, yet overpriced souvenirs.

"Ronnie, I love this restaurant. The décor is too funky for words and being on the water is fuckin' cool."

"This is my favorite seafood restaurant. The food is very good and most importantly, fairly inexpensive." Ronnie approached the hostess.

"I hear ya. Lately, price is the most important part of eating out, especially when I'm paying the bill," Joie joked.

"Since you're my guest, I'll pick up the tab."

"Thanks. I'll take care of you next time."

For the second time that day, a waitress showed the ladies to a table. She handed them menus and explained the dinner specials. "I'll be back in a minute to take your orders."

Joie surveyed the laidback crowd. She whispered softly, "I can see why you like living in Santa Elena. It's really nice out here, but where are the Black men? I've seen White, Asian, Mexican, Indian, Arab, and everything in between, but no Black men. What's up?"

"They're here. Not as plentiful as the east coast, but they are here. You just have to look a little harder."

Another waitress approached the table and placed two martinis before the women.

"I'm sorry, but we didn't order any drinks." Ronnie told the waitress.

"The gentleman seated over there…" The young woman pointed in the direction of the bar. She continued, "He asked me to bring these drinks over."

Joie glanced towards the bar and inhaled sharply. "Lawd have mercy! I spoke too soon!" She raised her glass at the fine brotha and mouthed, "Thanks, sugah."

"You have got to be kidding me!" Ronnie exclaimed at seeing who had sent over the cocktails.

"You know him? If you do, I'd advise you to invite him over. That is one fine specimen of a man." Joie laughed, licking her lips.

"Ugh! That's Tomas, Luis' cousin. I swear to goodness he gets on my last nerve. That man is nothing but trouble."

"Mmm, I think I might want to get myself into a "little trouble" while I'm here," Joie cooed.

"You do not want to get mixed up with Tomas. Trust me." Ronnie pushed the drink to the side.

"Shoot, I'm on vacation." Joie downed her martini and picked up Ronnie's. "Don't mind if I do… Waste not, want not."

Tomas strode over as if he owned the world. He looked Ronnie up and down and then fixated his gaze on Joie. "*Buenos tardes*, Veronica. *Come esta?* Mind if I join you?"

"Well, actually, we were just about to…"

Joie cut her off. "No, we don't mind at all. Please pull up a chair." She motioned for the waitress to bring an additional seat.

"*Hola*, my name is Tomas. I don't believe I've had the great pleasure to make your acquaintance, *senora*."

"Tomas, Joie. Joie, Tomas." Ronnie made the introductions, rolling her eyes.

"Nice to meet you," replied Joie. *Damn this man is finer than fine. And that accent of his is to die for. Lawd have mercy! A black man who speaks Spanish…*

"The pleasure is all mine," replied Tomas.

"What are you doing here? You waiting on somebody?" Ronnie asked sarcastically, looking behind him for the ever present lady friend. Tomas was the type of man who was never alone. There was always a model or two hanging off his arms wherever he went.

"No, I just stopped by to have a drink and a light dinner."

"Is that so?"

"Yes, that is so."

"Umph!" Ronnie replied. "I doubt that."

"Veronica, I hear congratulations are in order. Luis told me you finally accepted his proposal."

She softened her tone when she responded. "Yes, we are getting married."

He whistled as he checked out her ring. "I think that is wonderful. My cousin is a great guy, but he still doesn't deserve a woman as lovely as you."

"Thanks," Ronnie replied. She had become immune to Tomas' charm years ago when she realized he poured it over anything wearing a skirt.

"And where did you find this lovely woman?" he asked, refocusing on Joie.

Joie extended her right hand. "I'm here for the week visiting my best friend, Ronnie."

"Oh yeah? Where are you visiting from?"

Ronnie wanted to stop this before it went any further. "Look Tomas, Joie is here from Virginia for just a few days. She doesn't have time to get caught up in whatever it is you're offering." She waved her hand dismissively.

"I'm just trying to be friendly…"

"I don't mean to be rude, but Joie and I haven't seen each other in years and we just want to take this time to catch up."

Tomas pushed the chair back and rose from the table. "I'm sorry, Veronica. I did not intend to be rude. I just thought it would be nice to have dinner with two beautiful ladies." He sneered at Ronnie, even though he tried his best not to.

"It's okay," said Joie. "She's just going through some stuff."

Tomas was insulted by how Ronnie had spoken to him, especially in front of Joie. There was something about Joie that attracted him in ways other women hadn't. She intrigued him and he wanted to explore her further. To show his displeasure, he decided to give Veronica one last zinger before he left. He knew it was probably childish, but so what?

"Veronica, I think it's admirable how well you have accepted Carmen Sanchez as Luis' new assistant. It takes a very strong woman—a woman secure in her relationship, to allow a woman as striking as Carmen to work with her man."

Ronnie nearly choked on the breadstick she was nibbling on. "What are you talking about?"

"Carmen Sanchez, his assistant."

In the blink of an eye, she regained her composure and said, "Look, don't even try it. I *trust* my man." She refused to fall into his trap.

"Like I said, you must be a strong woman." He bent down to Joie and whispered in her ear. She giggled and took a card from his hand.

They both watched Tomas walk away. Joie with stars in her eyes and Ronnie with daggers in hers. "Ugh, I can't stand his ass. He is always trying to start some shit between me and Luis."

"Well, I think he's charming. And look, he gave me his card."

"Sorry to tell you this girlfriend, but he probably has the phone number of half the women in town."

Joie waved the card in front of Ronnie's face. "I didn't give him my number—he gave me his," she stated matter-of-factly. "So there!"

Ronnie tried to ignore Tomas' comment about Carmen. She knew he was just stirring the pot as he always did. Because she had yet to meet the woman, she had nothing to go on. Unfortunately, the harder she tried to ignore her feelings, the angrier she became. "Too bad I can't drink. That martini is exactly what I need right now to calm my nerves."

"I know you didn't let that remark about that woman get to you. He was just trying to push your buttons because you didn't want him to have dinner with us."

"You don't know Tomas. He was the one who sent that hoochie mama to Luis the first time. And he's always doing some underhanded shit to undermine us. I don't trust him."

"Do you trust Luis?" Joie sipped the remainder of Ronnie's martini.

Ronnie paused before answering. "Yes, of course I trust Luis, but if you had seen that last 'ho Tomas sent over there…"

"Well, how about we go over and meet with Miss Thang while Luis is out of town? That way *you* can check her out and make sure she knows to keep her skankish hands off your man."

"I'm so glad you're here, Joie. I missed you and your craziness."

"Ain't that what girlfriends are supposed to do? I got your back. Now let's eat; I'm starving."

* * *

The gentle noise from the shower woke Ronnie from a sound sleep. She checked the clock on the nightstand, seeing it was a little after midnight. The bathroom door was slightly ajar. She peeked in and saw Luis getting out of the shower.

"Baby, are you just getting in?" She yawned.

"Yeah, sorry. I didn't mean to wake you. After we finished up in the office, I helped Julio in the warehouse and ending up covered with dirt."

"Well, hurry up and come to bed. I'm exhausted and you have an early morning." Ronnie noticed his rumpled clothes on the floor. They didn't look dirty. She pushed the troubling thoughts aside and returned to bed.

* * *

Early the next morning, Luis was up bright and early going through his usual routine of running around like a madman. He had inadvertently overslept and was now trying his best to make up for lost time.

"Honey, can you please throw a couple of shirts and ties into my suitcase," he yelled from the bathroom.

"Which ones?"

"You choose. Also, please pack my dark grey slacks."

She carefully folded his clothes and tucked them into the carryon bag. Noticing he hadn't packed a change of underwear, she tossed in a couple pairs of briefs, an undershirt, and socks. He hurried from the bathroom with a bloodied piece of tissue stuck to his face.

"Luis, please slow down. Look at your face. You cut yourself shaving. You never do that."

He touched the cut. "I'll be all right."

"Are you sure you're okay?"

"Why didn't you wake me? Damn it... Now I'm going to be late!"

"Excuse me, but you didn't tell me what time you had to get up and the alarm clock still works last time I checked."

"It's already after nine and I was supposed to be at the office by now." He grabbed his suitcase from the bed and brushed past Ronnie.

"You're welcome!" she shouted.

Luis returned to the bedroom. "Baby, I'm sorry for yelling at you. I'll call you when I get on the road."

"It's okay..."

"Look, I've got to go. I'll see you in a couple of days."

"A couple of days? Aren't you coming back tomorrow?" she asked, trailing him down the hallway.

"Yes, that's what I meant, unless something else comes up with the presentation that requires addressing."

She walked him to the door. "Tell Julio I said 'hi'."

Luis appeared confused, yet responded, "Sure. I'll tell him when I see him." He kissed Ronnie and headed to the car.

"You're not taking the Jeep?" she yelled. But it was too late because he had already started backing out of the driveway. *That's strange; he always takes the Jeep when he goes out of town.*

Ronnie went to the kitchen, noticing Joie hunched over the counter sipping from a cup of coffee. "What?"

"Nothing. I am just being a fly on the wall..."

Ronnie turned and accidently stubbed her toe on the briefcase sitting near the sofa. "Aw shit! Luis was in such a hurry this morning, he left his briefcase. Maybe it's not too late for him to turn around to come get it." She picked up the house phone and called his cell. Within seconds, the phone on the counter began to vibrate.

Joie asked innocently, "So, whatcha gonna do now."

"Get dressed. I've got to get this to his office. He needs his briefcase and cell for this trip."

"Slow down woman. Take a look. I'm already dressed. You forget I'm still on east coast time. I've been up for hours."

"Oh, right... Give me a few minutes." Ronnie returned to the kitchen wearing a baggy pair of sweats and an old t-shirt. She didn't have time to fix her hair, so she tied it down with an old scarf.

One look at Ronnie and Joie erupted in laughter. "For his sake, I hope you at least brushed your teeth."

"Kiss my ass!" remarked Ronnie. "Just get in the car."

Ronnie fired up the Jeep and drove like a maniac to get to the office before Luis got on the road. "Anytime he gets rushed like this, he would forget his head if it weren't attached."

"Hold up, girlfriend. It ain't that serious. He's probably already realized he's left his phone." Joie double-checked to make certain her seatbelt was securely fastened.

Ronnie zipped through a red light and arrived at Luis' office in no time flat. She pulled up just in time to see him opening the passenger door for a very pretty woman. She parked the car askew in the entryway.

"What the fuck?! Who the hell is that, Joie?"

"You're asking *me*? I think you'd better ask your fiancée that question."

Ronnie stepped out from the Jeep and angrily approached the car. Luis visibly jumped when he saw Ronnie coming towards him.

"R-R-Ronnie? W-w-what are you d-d-doing here?" He looked first at Carmen, then to Julio who stood in the doorway taking it all in. He wanted Julio to come out to diffuse the situation, however, Julio didn't budge.

There's that fuckin' stutter again. "You left your briefcase and cell phone at home. I know you needed both for your trip so I damn near broke my neck trying to get them to you before you left," she explained in a cool, icy tone.

"Oh... Thanks. I didn't realize I had left either." He laughed nervously. Still distracted by the task at hand of driving to San Diego, getting into an argument with Ronnie was the last thing on his mind.

"Maybe if you weren't in such a fuckin' hurry to get here you would have noticed." Ronnie stared at Carmen.

"Thanks. Once again you saved my ass." He glanced at his watch.

"Excuse me, but don't you have something to tell me?" Ronnie stood with her hands on her hips and glared at the man who had only proposed just a few days ago.

"Um...yeah...I...I... We'll be back tomorrow. Hopefully early." He started walking towards the car and as an afterthought he added, "Oh, I almost forgot to tell you I love you."

Ronnie screamed, "Luis! Didn't you forget to introduce me to the woman sitting in *our* car?! Are you taking *her* to San Diego?!"

"Who? Her? Oh, that's Carmen Sanchez, my new administrative assistant."

"*Your what?*! Is that the skank you were talking to when you hung up on me the other day?"

"Ronnie calm down. You are blowing this way out of proportion. Just let me explain." Luis requested in a calm voice.

"Don't you dare tell me to calm down!" she screamed. "Why the fuck are you taking her to San Diego? I thought you said Julio was going with you."

Joie walked to Ronnie and stood by her side. She didn't say a word, just wanted her girl to know she was there for her.

"Ronnie, I never said anything about Julio going with me." He held his hands up in defeat and shouted, "Carmen could you join us, please?" Luis realized the only way to put an end to this was to introduce the two women. He had to explain who Carmen was and what her position at the company was.

Ronnie thought, *my hormones might be raging out of control and causing me to behave unpredictably, but I'll be damned if I let them make a fool out of me!*

Carmen reluctantly stepped from the car and approached the angry trio. *Here we go again... Me having to explain myself to some man's crazy heifer of a wife. I am so sick and tired of this mess. Look at her. Couldn't even take the time to comb her damn hair. I wouldn't blame Luis if he stepped out on that.*

Luis made the uncomfortable introductions. "Ronnie, this is Mrs. Carmen Sanchez. She is my new administrative assistant and will be accompanying me to San Diego to participate in a presentation to the Hernandez Group. Carmen has been working extensively with Julio to get up to speed on the company. She's done great work in a short amount of time. Since she is fluent in Spanish, she will assist me in the meeting."

Ronnie swiveled her neck and uttered, "Umph!"

"Carmen, this is my lovely fiancée, Veronica Pierce."

Carmen extended her hand to the crazy looking woman whose eyes burned holes through her. "Pleased to meet you, Miss Pierce. I've heard so much about you."

"I can't say the same about you." Ronnie did not return the handshake. Based on her intuition, she didn't trust Carmen no matter how many men touted her accomplishments. As a woman, she understood how easily manipulated some men could be by a pretty face and a hot body.

At that very moment, a black sports car pulled into the parking lot, sending a plume of dust into the air. It was Tomas. He put the car in park and got out to lend his flair for drama to the group.

"*Buenos dias,* everyone. What's going on?" he asked, seemingly oblivious to the situation at hand.

"Tomas, uh, we're in the middle of something. What do you need?" asked Luis.

"I'm just returning what I borrowed from you." He handed Luis a white envelope.

"Cool man. Thanks," he replied.

"What's going on here?" Tomas eyed the tense group. "Hey Carmen, how's the job going? I told your husband that you were fitting in very well."

"*Hola* Tomas, I was just meeting Miss Pierce. She seems to be as friendly as you told me she was." Carmen wanted to respond in a well-deserved sarcastic tone, but thought better of pouring fuel on the fire.

"*Que pasa,* Veronica. Joie." He addressed the ladies who weren't smiling.

Ronnie crossed her arms and sarcastically replied, "Hey Tomas. What a coincidence seeing you again. So soon…"

"Veronica, coincidence *is* all this is. I had no idea you and Joie would be here this morning." He noticed the briefcase sitting at Ronnie's feet. "*Primo,* what's going on?" he asked again.

"I was on my way to San Diego for a business trip. Carmen is going with me. I forgot my briefcase and my sweet and kind fiancée was thoughtful enough to bring it to me. We were just in the middle of introductions when you pulled up." He looked at his watch again.

"Oh, I see…" Tomas fell silent.

"Baby, I would love to continue this conversation, but I cannot afford to be late for this very important meeting."

Ronnie vacillated between the fight or flight response. Both emotions tugged at her heart, causing her to feel like she was being ripped apart.

"I promise you I will make up for this little misunderstanding, but for now I've got to go." Luis pleaded, once again noting the time.

All eyes were fixated on Ronnie; waiting for her response to see if she would blow up again. "Fine. We'll talk later and go over this *little misunderstanding* as you call it." She threw the cell phone at Luis, gave the evil eye to Carmen, and stomped off to the Jeep.

Luis picked up the briefcase and Carmen returned to the car. He hesitated momentarily before starting the engine and driving off. Feeling the need to say something more, he beeped the horn and yelled out the window, "Ronnie, *te quiero!*"

Yeah. Right. Whatever… Fuck you! Ronnie watched Luis drive off with Carmen, occupying the seat that was usually hers, headed to San Diego with her man. As Luis merged into traffic, Ronnie imagined she saw a smirk appear on Carmen's face. She blinked twice to clear her vision; to convince her mind that what she'd just seen didn't happen.

"Is she going to be all right?" Tomas asked Joie.

"I don't know. Considering what we just witnessed, she could to go off any minute. And my girl sure don't need to be under any stress right now, especially in her condition."

"What do you mean *her condition?*"

"Oh shit! Ronnie is going to fuckin' kill me!" Joie clamped her hands over her mouth to keep from saying anything more.

"She's pregnant?" Tomas' eyes nearly popped out of their sockets. "That's great news!"

"Me and my big mouth. Tomas please don't say anything to anybody. This was supposed to be a secret, but I keep opening up my big-ass mouth. She would kill me if she knew I accidently told you. Promise me you won't say a word. Let them be the ones to tell you. Promise?" Joie pleaded.

"I promise, but only if you promise to join me for dinner this evening." He smiled, showing his pearly whites.

"All right, I think I can swing it. What time?" Her heart softened at the sound of his voice.

"Pick you up at seven?"

"Okay. But for now, I've got to see about Ronnie."

"I understand." He started walking towards his car. "Hey Joie?"

"Hmm, what's up Tomas?"

"I'm not as bad as Veronica says I am."

"I know, Tomas. I know… I'll see you later."

Joie approached the driver's side. She peered through the window and insisted, "Hand over the keys. You are not driving me anywhere in your current state of mind."

Ronnie surrendered the keys to Joie and slid over to the passenger's seat. "Do you think he's telling the truth? Should I believe him?" she whispered, while nibbling on her fingernails.

"What do *you* think Ronnie? You know that man better than any of us."

"That's the problem, Joie. I don't know what to think. I really don't."

Chapter Fifteen

*T*ravis was visibly shaken after hearing Ronnie's news of her engagement. Despite what he told her, there was no scheduled meeting to prepare for; he just needed to get away from Ronnie and her overwhelming joy. In time, he might feel some sort of happiness for her and Luis' impending nuptials. Or maybe, he wouldn't.

Although Ronnie's news had sent him into a state of minor shock, there was still very important business to attend to. The center would soon be without its head nurse so he went about his business with rectifying the situation.

"Kaylee, would you please get Miss Moore on the phone?" He relayed the number on the card given to him by the couple he met at the resort in Sedona.

"Got it. Give me a few minutes and I'll buzz you right back," replied Kaylee.

Travis flipped the card over and over in his hand. Although Rachel Moore was a very attractive woman, at this particular point in time, he needed an experienced RN more than he needed a girlfriend. Rachel's parents had introduced Travis to their daughter, hoping for some kind of love connection. When that didn't happen, they seemed to be satisfied with the possibility of having their daughter work at a world renowned rehabilitation center, instead.

His intercom crackled with electricity. Kaylee said, "Travis, Miss Moore is on the line."

"Thanks, Kaylee." He pulled up his email. "Good morning Rachel, this is Travis Bradford from the *J. Bradford Rehabilitation Center* in Santa Elena, California. We met at the Sedona resort a week ago..."

"Hello Travis, how are you?"

"Fine thanks. The reason I'm calling is to see if you're still interested in coming to work at the center. I've reviewed the resume you sent and I have spoken with several of your references. It appears that you're really good at what you do."

"Thank you. And yes I am still interested in working there."

"Very good. Well, at this point I'd like for you to come to the center, meet the staff and a few of the patients. If you decide to work with us, I want you to be comfortable with your decision."

"Thanks, I appreciate that. I can be there next Friday. Does that work for you?"

"Friday morning will be fine. I look forward to seeing you."

"You too. Bye now."

Travis dialed Kiara's number. He hadn't seen nor spoken to his child since he returned from his trip. At first it seemed as if she couldn't wait for him to get back and now she wouldn't even answer her phone.

He left a message. "Kiara, it's your father. I made it home yesterday and will be in the office all day today. Call me when you get this message. I love you."

Travis noted the time. Thirty minutes had passed and he still hadn't heard from Kiara. He called and left another message, "Sweetheart, I know you're probably in class, but call me when you get a break. We need to catch up."

He called a few more times but eventually decided to give up. Knowing his daughter, she was still angry with him for taking a vacation. For leaving her behind, as she liked to say.

* * *

"Your mother is really cool. I'm surprised by how much I like her. And her friend Joie is off the chain." GQ lit up a joint, then blew the pungent smoke in Kiara's face.

"Yeah, she is. I just wish her and Daddy had gotten back together. Luis is cool and all, but Daddy waited around for Ronnie for years. It would have been great to be a real family again."

"You've got both parents in your life. A lot of kids these days don't, so just try to appreciate what you have." He untied a dread that held the rest secure, freeing them. The long locs cascaded to the middle of his back.

"You're right." She inhaled. "Babe, I have a question I've been like wanting to ask you."

"Ask away."

"Do you think our age difference is a big deal? I mean, Joie did seem bothered by it. That probably means my mother is also. I don't even want to think about what Daddy is going to say."

"It doesn't bother me if it doesn't bother you. Fifteen years isn't that much of a gap between a man and a woman. Anyway, we're both adults. Why do you ask?"

"I don't know. Some of my friends think it's like kind of gross for me to be with someone so old."

GQ laughed out loud. "*Old?* You think I'm old?" He took a long drag from the joint, squinting to avoid the sting of the smoke.

"No, I don't think you're *that* old. Just older than me." She took the joint from his hand and took a hit. "Never mind, it's not important."

"You still excited about our trip to Haiti? We're leaving in less than a week, you know."

"Yes, I am. And like you suggested, I've done some research on where we're going. Those poor people… I can't imagine having to live under those conditions for so many years."

"It is difficult, but the people are resilient. They have a history of overcoming hardship. Each time I go down there, I'm inspired by the Haitians—young and old."

Kiara felt the mellowing effects of the herb taking over. She moaned in contentment and turned over on her stomach. "I just hope that I can make a small difference while I am there."

GQ never tired of seeing Kiara's nude form, as she lay stretched out in his bed naked in all her exotic and erotic glory. Her youthful long, lean body somehow managed to be curvy and muscular at the same time. He couldn't seem to get enough of her. It was almost as if her youth, helped him to maintain his.

He marveled at her carefree attitude towards life, remembering how he was at that age. *When you're twenty-one years old, everything is a possibility and nothing seems out of reach. Most of the women my age are into their careers and looking to get married. Settle down, make babies and shit. Always nagging about this or that—tripping because I'm not ready to make a commitment. Not my beautiful Kiara. She is as free as a bird and has no intention of settling down anytime soon. And having sex with her is like discovering hidden treasures over and over again.* Sometimes they would skip classes just to spend the day in bed.

Kiara took another long drag of the joint and held the smoke in. She allowed the drug to work its way into her bloodstream, putting the worries of the world behind. "Daddy is going to like kill me when he finds out we're dating, GQ. Every boy I ever brought home, he found flaws with them. None were good enough. So imagine what he's going to think once he knows you're more than just my teacher."

"Sweet K, let me handle your father. Travis and I are professional colleagues and after I explain to him about us, I know he'll accept it.

Just you wait and see." He took another puff and passed it back to her.

"Okay, but even if he doesn't approve of me being with you, I'm not going to stop. I am like a grown woman. I'm not his little baby girl anymore."

"But you're *my* baby girl." GQ snuggled Kiara closer to his chest. Her skin was as soft as the fuzz of a ripe peach and she smelled like fresh air. All her pubic hair had been waxed away except for a narrow strip leading to her ecstasy. He had been the first and only man lucky enough to have enjoyed her body and that was just the way he liked it. "Umm, my luscious honey pot," he whispered, inhaling her musky fragrance.

Kiara noticed GQ's thick penis rise upwards standing at attention. The little blue pills he took earlier had kicked in and he was ready for action. She fingered the curly hairs on his chest, loving how they sprang to life when she pulled them straight. He wore earthy musky cologne that made her forget all about her father. She felt herself become aroused as well.

"That's right. Mmm, you sure do feel good, GQ." She climbed on top, straddling his chest and bent down to kiss him. "How about we do it one more time before I leave?" Her thick hair flopped over his face, tickling his moustache.

"Oh yeah, baby. One more time? Yeah, I'd love to. Just tell me how you want it."

"You make me feel so good that I want it however you can give it to me." Kiara purred and slipped him inside.

Kiara was a virgin when she met GQ. Before her first sexual encounter, she didn't understand what all the fuss was about. Now that she'd experienced GQ's magical golden penis, she couldn't get enough of it. She wanted him morning, noon, and night as her sexual needs were insatiable. They could go on for hours or as long as GQ could hold on to his erection. At first, he wasn't able to keep up with her, but the medication helped solve that problem.

Inside her purse, her cell phone vibrated several times with missed calls. Bzzz, bzzz, bzzz… It continued on and on. They both heard it ringing, but chose to ignore the phone as they were both close to orgasm. Soon the constant banging of the headboard against the wall had the neighbors on the other side screaming for them to finally put an end to their "fucking session". GQ and Kiara ignored anything that wasn't in that room with them—including the neighbors. And for several more hours, the couple continued exploring each other's bodies every which way possible.

GQ's light snoring awoke Kiara from her well-needed nap. The clock radio on the dresser indicated it was a little after four in the afternoon. After experiencing several hours of sex and smoking too many joints to remember, she was virtually starving. She pulled on one of GQ's t-shirts and padded into the kitchen. She peered into the refrigerator. It was empty except for spoiled milk, a couple of old Chinese food cartons, and a case of beer. She opened the cabinets and discovered they were just as bare.

"Dang, GQ, I can understand my not having food in my house. After all I'm like a starving student. You on the other hand are like an adult."

She stared at the dozens of take-out menus pasted to the refrigerator door with magnets. "I'm going to have to do something about this—go grocery shopping or something. Why don't you have any food in his place?" She wondered aloud.

"I don't keep food in my refrigerator because I eat out. Or I have it delivered," he responded, standing in the doorway—totally naked.

Kiara jumped. "Oh my! You startled me." She held her chest and looked closely at GQ. She didn't like the way he looked minus clothing. He had a little round beer belly, funny looking bird legs—that needed lotion badly, and a high round butt that was covered in hair bumps, reminding her of chicken skin.

However, the absolute worst part of GQ's body was his feet. They were crusted with layers upon layers of dry dead skin. His long yellowed toenails needed trimming, badly. She absolutely hated it when he accidently scraped his feet against her legs. And on occasion when he walked around without any clothes on, his flaccid penis flopped up and down like it had a mind of its own. Clothes on, he was sexy. Clothes off, he was gross. *Well, except when his dick is erect and inside me; making me call out his name.* She chuckled to herself.

He shut the refrigerator door. "Sorry baby, I didn't mean to frighten you. Hey, we can call in for delivery if you'd like. Pizza, Chinese, Mexican…"

"Um, I'm not feeling any of that…"

"We can stay in the apartment the rest of the day in bed." He grinned. "I don't mind skipping my last class."

"Um, no, that's all right, I've got a test to like study for tomorrow. I really do need to get back to my dorm. I'll pick up something along the way." Kiara wanted to take a shower but hated how filthy GQ allowed his bathroom to get. It was only out of absolute necessity when she peed in his toilet.

"I can take you out to dinner, if you'd prefer." He let out a long, noisy yawn, pulled on the tip of his penis, scratched his balls, and then rubbed his face. In that order. "You want to shower before you leave?"

"No, that's okay. I'd better get going. Plus, your bathroom has more bacteria growing in it than a Petri dish." She removed his t-shirt and bent over to pick up the clothes she left scattered on the floor.

GQ reached for her hand, pulling her close. "Will I see you after class tomorrow?"

"Sure. I still have a few more things to take care of for the trip, though. That is, if you don't mind tagging along with me to go shopping. We can hang out."

"Shopping? I had something more intimate in mind." He kissed her perky nipples, put his hand between her slender thighs and gently squeezed. She squirmed away when he slipped a finger inside.

"Oh really? I suppose I can stop by afterwards and we can have some more fun," she replied, amazed how quickly his erection returned. "But for now, I've got to go."

Kiara's phone vibrated again with a text message. This time she checked. The text was from Travis. There were also several missed calls from Travis and one from Ronnie. "Hey, I've really got to get going. I'll call you later." She quickly dressed and grabbed her bag.

GQ, realizing he'd have to take care of his arousal himself, walked her to the door and planted a big wet kiss on her lips. "All right, my Sweet K, go on home and study. I'll talk with you later. Just remember he'll be waiting for you." He pointed towards his erection, making in bob up and down.

Kiara gripped his penis and playfully swatted it down. She opened the apartment door at the exact moment GQ's neighbor was coming up the steps.

"All right, Sweet K, don't start nothing, you can't finish," he joked.

The elderly white woman gasped loudly upon seeing GQ standing naked at the door in all his glory. And yet, though appearing to be shocked by seeing her neighbor's genitals, she didn't avert her eyes.

Kiara and GQ both laughed as he stepped behind the door to cover himself. He called out, "Good afternoon, Mrs. Wheeler."

"Afternoon, Gerald. I see you're still up to your old tricks again. They seem to get younger every year." The woman shook her head in disapproval and continued along her way to her apartment. As she did so, she glanced backwards one more time hoping to sneak another peek. GQ obliged her curiosity by stepping from behind the door and exposing his enormous erection. The woman gripped her purse tightly. "Why I never!" she proclaimed.

Kiara pretended to disregard the woman's remarks about the younger women. "You are so bad! Look at you flashing all your stuff to your neighbors. Dude, you better go inside and put some clothes on before that old lady calls the police and tells them, 'Officers, this black Mandingo man flashed me his big 'ole black cock. I was so frightened I nearly fainted from shock. I took one look at it and wondered how I ever got along all those years with just my husband's teeny, weenie cocktail sausage.'" She mocked the woman using a fake southern accent.

"You are crazy, you know that. And you really need to work on your accent." He laughed still feeling the effects of the marijuana. "Now get out of here, but first give me another kiss. With your fine young self."

"See you later, *Gerald.*"

Once in the car, Kiara immediately called her father. *There must be something wrong because Daddy has been trying to reach me all day.* First she tried his work number. His voicemail kicked on with "You have reached the voicemail of…" She hung up and dialed his cell.

He picked up on the second ring. "Kiara, where have you been all day? I've been trying to reach you for hours."

"Sorry Daddy. I, uh, was studying and had my phone turned off," she lied. "What's wrong? Is everything all right?"

"Nothing is *wrong.* I got back in town yesterday and wanted to see you. That's all. You were the one who kept asking me when I was coming back."

"That's a relief. I thought something was wrong when I saw all your missed calls."

"What are you up to now?"

"I have to like study for my final. Can I stop by for dinner?"

Travis laughed, "Of course, you can stop by for dinner, but bring food with you because I haven't had time to shop."

"I'll pick up something from the Thai restaurant. Be there in about an hour."

Satisfied that her father was all right, she threw the car in reverse. Before she pulled away, she glanced briefly at GQ's apartment wondering how many other young women he had brought up there over the years. According to his neighbor, it must have been quite a few.

She knew that her involvement with GQ couldn't have been serious because they rarely went anywhere together. She hadn't met any of *his* friends, or his family, despite their being together for almost a year. Yet, because he had been—and still was an excellent teacher, both in and out of bed, she felt her relationship with thirty-five year old Gerald Quinn was fulfilling a purpose in her young life. So what if he was old? She just wanted to have a good time for as long as it lasted. And making love to GQ never left her unsatisfied like so many of her girlfriends complained guys their own age did.

Chapter Sixteen

"*C*armen, please tell Senor Hernandez, that it has been a pleasure doing business with him. And I'll get those changes made as quickly as possible tonight and will review the revisions with him tomorrow afternoon."

Carmen did as she was asked while Luis stood and shook hands with the rest of the Hernandez team.

She replied back to Luis, "He says you can brief him over lunch instead of here at the office. He's going to have his secretary reserve a private room at their family owned restaurant tomorrow at noon. The business card lists the address."

"*Gracias*, Senor Hernandez. I will see you tomorrow." Luis accepted the card.

Mr. Hernandez and his team listened while Carmen translated the instructions for lunch. After everyone was in agreement, the remainder of the team filed out from the conference room speaking in exuberant Spanish. Luis caught every other phrase and signaled to Carmen for her to pay attention. He would need her to fill him in later.

Despite the outcome of the meeting, Luis hadn't expected to spend another full day in San Diego. Yet, that was exactly what he had to do to seal the deal. So far, the company had approved all but two of his concept designs for their marketing campaign. It would take some tweaking and several calls to Julio to make the desired changes, but he was confident he could pull it off. They had agreed to meet over lunch to discuss the changes, and since the meeting could last for hours, it was best to plan on sticking around.

On the way to the car, Luis was full of praise for his employee. "Great job, Carmen. You really handled yourself well in there. I know it was probably intimidating being around a bunch of *Latino* men, but you held your own very well."

"Thank you, *Senor Duarte…*"

"Listen, after everything we've been through this afternoon, please call me Luis."

"Very well… Luis. I must admit it was different because I'm not used to attending high powered board meetings. And they spoke a different dialect of Spanish than I'm used to, so it was difficult for me to not get lost in the translation."

He nodded his empathy. "Well, I think you did great."

"Thanks," she replied, accepting the compliment. "What now?"

Luis knew he needed to get started on the revisions ASAP, but his growling stomach spoke up for his indecision.

"I haven't eaten all day and I'm starving," Carmen said.

"Yeah, me too. Tell you what. Let's go back to the hotel. I have a few calls to make; then we can get dinner. I have lots of work to do this evening, so it's going to be an early night for me. You okay hanging around on your own?" He opened the car door to let her in.

Carmen loved the attention from Luis. It felt nice to be in the company of a gentleman. She blurted out, "My husband never opens any kind of door for me. In fact, he rarely pays attention to me at all except for when the kids start to act up," she replied, testing the waters to see if he would flirt back.

"Then he is a foolish man." Luis let it go at that. He didn't want Carmen to get the wrong impression. His appreciation was limited to her administrative skills and nothing more.

* * *

Luis sat on the side of the bed. He removed his tie and then quenched his thirst with a bottle of cool water before calling Ronnie. As he hit her number on speed dial, he prepared himself for the argument that was surely to come.

"Luis, are you kidding me? You're going to spend another night down there? Why?" Ronnie tried her best to control her breathing. It was a stress reduction technique she learned from working at the center.

"Baby, first of all the meeting went really well, but there were a few items I need to change. I'm going to be working on these revisions for most of the evening. The Hernandez's want to meet tomorrow at lunch and I expect the meeting will last several hours. Maybe into early evening."

"So why can't you come home after the meeting is over? There's no need to spend another night." Normally, she hated whining of any kind, but in this situation, it seemed appropriate.

"Look, I cannot put myself on a clock with these guys. Chances are they will want to have a few drinks afterwards and I don't want to pull out just because you want me home."

Ronnie sucked on her teeth. "Fine," she said.

"I have to develop a good rapport with the owner—let them know I'm one of them. Anyway, it's a four hour drive to get home. Do you really want me on the road after I've been drinking?"

"No, I suppose not. Well, all right... Since you say it's necessary."

"Unfortunately, it is…"

"You promise no more extensions?"

"Yes, my love. I'll be home the day after tomorrow."

"What hotel are you staying at?"

"We're at the downtown Marriott. It's close to Hernandez's office."

Ronnie cringed at his reference to *we*. "Is Carmen going to this meeting as well?"

"Of course, she is. She's a great Spanish translator. Why?"

"Luis, don't play stupid with me. You know *why* I'm asking. I don't trust that woman. She looks like the type of woman who sleeps her way to the top and doesn't matter who she steps on to get there."

"Ronnie, she is my *employee*. I *pay* her salary. She *works* for me as my assistance. That is the only relationship I have with Carmen. Please, stop being so paranoid."

"Men are so fucking stupid," she muttered under her breath.

"I'm sorry, I missed what you said," replied Luis.

"I said for you to be careful around her. That woman is up to something. Mark my words…"

Luis humored her, "Okay, I'll watch my back."

"It's not your back I'm worried about. Call me before you go to sleep, so we can say goodnight."

"Okay, I will. By the way, how is Joie?"

"Joie?" she said. "Joie is fine. In fact, Joie is getting dressed to go on a date with Tomas this evening."

"Tomas? *My* cousin, Tomas?"

"One and the same. I tried to warn her, but she wouldn't listen. I honestly believe that Joie is a sadist as heart. Why else would she disregard my advice and go out with him?"

"C'mon Ronnie, Tomas isn't that bad. He tends to be immature at times, but deep down he's a good guy. I'm sure they'll have a great time together."

"I'll let you tell it. Anyway, my love, I don't want to keep you from your work. I miss you."

"Miss you, too. I'll call you in a few hours."

Ronnie ended the call and listened to Joie singing happily in the living room. Tomas was picking her up in less than an hour. She had to admit, she was thrilled to see her girl so excited. According to Joie, she hadn't been on a real date in too many months to count.

When she laid eyes on her friend, she thought Joie was a sight to behold. The black dress she wore hugged every curve and accentuated her shapely well-toned body. A heart shaped cutoff at the neckline showed off her ample breasts. Her short hair was styled in a funky cut that tapered down her neck and flared up on top. A plug of blue hair was stylishly woven into her bangs on one side.

"Oh my goodness, Joie! You look absolutely amazing!"

"Thank you. I brought this dress with me on the off chance you and I would go out somewhere fancy. Never imagined I'd be going on a date."

"Whatever you've been doing in the exercise department has paid off."

Joie twirled around and replied, "I've been doing this crazy new workout at least three times a week to get into shape."

Ronnie frowned when she asked, "You really like him, don't you?"

"Who? Tomas?"

"Yes, Tomas."

Joie shrugged and replied nonchalantly, "He's all right. I think he's sweet."

Ronnie groaned in frustration, "Girlfriend, don't get caught up with him. Please? He is not good with women *or* relationships with women."

"Will you please give the man a chance? How do you know he won't be different with me?"

Ronnie held up her hands in defeat. "You're right. I only know Tomas through Luis and the stupid shit he's told me over the years. Maybe he *is* a great guy and I haven't given him a chance to prove it."

"I know a dog when I see it." She hunched her shoulders. "I can't say I'm getting that vibe from Tomas. Look, I'm only here for a few days, anyway. How much trouble can I get into?"

"Okay. I'll leave it alone. You tell me how Tomas is after you've spent time with him."

Joie strode over to hug her friend. "Thanks. I hope you don't mind me leaving you alone tonight, especially with Luis being out of town."

"Don't worry about it. I have a date with a couple of movies on *Showtime* and a pint of chocolate-chip ice cream.

"Luis will be back before you know it. Tomorrow isn't very far away."

Ronnie dropped her gaze and picked at imaginary dirt under her fingernails.

"Wait a minute. He *is* coming back tomorrow, right?"

She shook her head. "Nope. I just got off the phone with Luis. He's staying an extra night."

"Ronnie? Are you serious? He's spending two days down there with Miss Thang?" Joie asked quietly, "You okay with this?"

"Hell no, I'm not okay with it, but this is a business trip and it involves an important client who can change everything for him. What am I supposed to do about it? Tell him to screw up this big deal because I am insecure?"

"No, you can't do that. You said you trusted him. I suppose this trip will put that trust to the test."

"It's just that this is the first time he's done something like this. I've never had a real reason to *not* trust him until now." Ronnie sighed loudly. "I've been through this shit with several men, but never expected Luis to trip."

Joie tried to reassure her, even though she suspected differently. "You don't know that. Maybe Miss Thang is just his assistant..."

She sighed. "I sure hope so."

Ronnie went to the front door upon seeing a car turn into the driveway. Florescent headlights poured an artificial blue through the living room curtains. A sleek black limousine parked in front of her house.

Because it was a little after dusk, it was difficult to see who was stepping outside the limo. She flipped on the porch light and peeked through the peephole. Ronnie asked incredulously, "Tomas? Is that you?"

He shouted through the closed door, "*Si*, Veronica. I am here to see Joie."

Tomas was pulling out all stops for this date. Ronnie opened the door and was greeted by a clean shaven, very attractive man carrying two dozen red roses. She stepped aside to let him in.

"*Buenos tardes*, Veronica. *Como esta?*" He handed her one of the bouquets of roses, while holding the other close to his chest.

For the first time in a long time, Ronnie was at a loss for words. The man who stood before her could have come straight from the runways of Paris. Tomas stood before her grinning from ear to ear upon seeing her reaction. He knew then that his mission of changing how she felt about him was halfway accomplished.

"Hey Tomas, are those for me?" asked Joie, gliding into the living room looking as if she had walked off the same catwalk.

"You are absolutely beautiful!" Tomas handed her the flowers and leaned forward to plant a kiss on her cheek.

Joie turned her face slightly, causing him to accidently graze her lips. She blushed. "Thank you, they're beautiful."

Ronnie watched the exchange between the couple, unable to control her thoughts. *Good Lord! What in the world has come over these two? They're behaving like teenagers on their first date.*

Tomas was caught off guard by Joie's appearance. He thought her to be absolutely, positively, breathtaking. He had seen beautiful women in his lifetime, but there was something more to Joie. She possessed an undefined quality—the *it* factor—a special uniqueness within her spirit that was unlike anyone he had come across before. And even before Tomas reached for the door handle with Joie on his arm, he suddenly realized he was gone long before his feet crossed the threshold.

* * *

On the way to her dad's house, Kiara stopped by the local Thai restaurant and purchased enough food to feed a small family. She hadn't eaten all day and was absolutely famished. The aroma of Pad Thai and lemon grass chicken wafted from the bag into her nostrils. She was tempted to dig into the container of lettuce wraps and wolf down each and every one, in a single bite. So fighting the urge to pull over and devour the food before she reached her destination, she pressed on.

Kiara opened the door to find stacks of unopened mail scattered about the floor. "Daddy, I'm home!" she cried out. With one foot, she pushed most of the letters aside and stepped over what remained.

Travis responded, "Okay. Be right there." He turned the television off and wheeled out to meet his daughter.

"Hey Daddy, what's up with the house? Did Lila like quit or something?" she asked, noting the disarray.

"No, I gave the maid some well-needed time off. I'll call her tomorrow to come in next week. Since you're here, can you gather the mail for me?"

"Yeah, right after I put the food out. I'm so hungry I can eat right through the paper bags."

"You are looking pretty thin," he noted.

She shrugged his comment off. "I'm fine. You want me to fix your plate?"

"Sure. Thanks." He watched Kiara move about the kitchen effortlessly retrieving dishes and utensils from their cabinets. For so long, this young woman had been the woman of the house. Yet now, he was about to lose her.

"How was your day, Daddy? Glad to be back at work?" she asked, sucking on a shrimp.

"My day went well. I think I found an RN to replace the one who's leaving."

"That's cool. When does she start?"

"She's coming down to check out the center next week. She's the lady I met in Sedona."

"Oh *really?* Is she hot?"

He chuckled. "As a matter-of-fact, she is. But that's not why I'm hiring her. She just happens to be one of the top nurses in the rehabilitation field. There are several other centers that would like to get their hands on her."

"Does that mean she is like off limits or something?" Kiara placed a forkful of the spicy noodles in her mouth while she fixed their plates.

"That's right. And I don't want to do anything to mess this up."

"Awww… I wanted you to find someone nice."

"I guess having someone special isn't in the cards for me," he sighed. "In other news, Ronnie told me about her engagement."

Kiara stopped serving the food and turned to face her father. "How do you feel about Ronnie marrying Luis?"

"I'm happy for her—for them. She deserves to be with someone like Luis. He's a "whole man" who can make her happy."

"Daddy, don't…" She hated when her father started talking like that. "You have so much to offer some lucky woman. Anyhow, I have a feeling you're going to meet someone special very soon."

"And how do you know that? You been reading my future again?" He smirked.

"No, but now that Ronnie is officially off the market, you can finally let her go. Make room for someone else to come into your life.

Kinda like you did when you met Janelle."

"Yeah, you're probably right."

"I know it hurts thinking about Janelle, but you gotta let go of the past to get on with your future."

He balked. "Is that right? What do you know about relationships?"

Kiara took a deep breath and decided that now was the perfect time to tell Travis about her and GQ. "I know you have to be dedicated and committed to one another to like make things work. Otherwise, you are basically like wasting each other's time."

"Darling daughter, are you trying to tell me that you are in a relationship?"

"As a matter of fact, I am." Kiara put down the food and concentrated on her father's questions.

"Well, what's his name? Maybe I've had him in one of my classes."

"He's not a student."

"That's okay. School isn't for everybody. So tell me, what does he do for a living?"

"Uh, he is very smart. Educated. Someone like you."

"Kiara, you're stalling. What's the boy's name?"

"Well… He's not exactly a *boy*."

"If he's not a boy, what is he?" Travis gasped sharply. "You're involved with a girl? Are you trying to tell me you're *gay*?"

"No, I'm not involved with a girl and I'm not gay."

He visibly relaxed. "Okay, then tell me who this person is? Why are you being so evasive?"

She sighed deeply and whispered. "Daddy, his name is GQ."

"*GQ*? What kind of a name is that?" he scoffed.

"It's not his name; those are his initials. His name is Gerald Quinn."

"That's a coincidence. He has the same name as the teacher who's going on the trip to Haiti with you." Travis stopped speaking when he saw the expression on Kiara's face.

She shook her head slowly and uttered, "Not a coincidence, Daddy. GQ *is* Gerald Quinn. Mr. Quinn is my boyfriend."

Chapter Seventeen

*L*uis felt awful about having to spend another night away from Ronnie, especially since they parted on the heels of an argument. Unfortunately, attending the meeting in San Diego to hopefully snag the account was the price he had to pay for the continued success of his business.

After a quick dinner with Carmen in the hotel's restaurant, Luis spent the rest of the night refining his presentation. He skyped Julio back at the office for assistance and they worked well into the night. Julio did what he could to help out; making suggestions and transferring files Luis requested. After they reached a point of completion, Luis transferred the samples over to the local Kinko's for printing. He would pick up the documents on the way to the meeting.

By the time Luis logged out of his laptop, it was well after four in the morning. His cell phone sat on the nightstand as a silent reminder that he needed to phone Ronnie. Instead of waking her, he decided to send a text. He picked up the phone and tried to turn it on. *Coño! My phone is dead. Now where did I leave that damn charger?* He searched every corner of his room but couldn't locate it. Exhausted, he gave up and fell into bed. "I'll just call her first thing when I wake up so she won't be worried."

*   *   *

Ronnie stayed awake for as long as she could, waiting for Luis' phone call. After surfing through endless channels of mindless television, she decided she had seen enough "not for prime-time dramas" to last her for weeks. When midnight rolled around and she hadn't heard from Luis, she dialed his cell phone. Her call went straight to voicemail so she left a message, "Luis, where are you? And what the hell are you doing? Call me."

After she completed her voicemail message, she heard the front door open. The voice on her home security system told her as much. It was Joie returning from her date with Tomas. Securing her robe around her expanding waistline, she went to see how things went.

"Hey lady, what are you still doing awake? You didn't have to wait up."

Ronnie noticed the happy glow radiating from Joie's face. "I wasn't waiting for you. I was waiting for Luis to call. He didn't, so I couldn't go to sleep."

Joie raised an eyebrow, but didn't utter a word. She knew better than to express her true feelings about a girlfriend's man. From prior experience, she knew that some women had an awful habit of allowing their girls to diss their man when they were angry, and then hold those same words against them once they got back together with their man.

"Anyway, forget about my problems. Tell me how your date went." Ronnie wanted to discuss anything but the troublesome thoughts that nagged at the corners of her mind.

Joie proclaimed, "Girl, I am so packing up my kids and moving out here to Santa Elena, California!"

"Oh really? It went that well, huh?"

"Um huh! Sho' did!"

"You didn't give him *any*, did you?" Ronnie laughed.

"He was a total gentleman, if you must know. Girl, he took me to this swanky restaurant up in the hills where they treated us like royalty. That dinner must have cost him a few hundred dollars. And that limousine! Oh my Gaaawd!" She held one hand to her chest and fanned her face with the other.

"Tomas De La Cruz did that for you?" Ronnie asked in disbelief.

"Yes, he did," Joie replied, smugly.

"And he didn't try to get in your panties?"

"No, he didn't."

"Hmmm, he must really like you. What did you put in his drink the other day?"

"I didn't put nothin' in his drink. He told me I was the most *real* woman he has ever been with. Said I was smart, funny and beautiful— traits he hasn't been able to find in any one woman."

"Is that right? He did all that without trying to get the cootchie?"

Joie nodded, pleased with herself.

"All this time I thought Tomas was all style and no substance. You mean to tell me he's not as shallow as I thought he was?"

"Apparently, you don't know him well at all. Did you know he invested in a commercial real estate venture a few weeks ago? Well, since then the value of the property he purchased has supposedly gone up like crazy. He said he's set to make some serious paper."

"Know what? I have no idea what Tomas does for a living. I always imagined some woman was taking care of him. You sure he wasn't just telling you what you wanted to hear?"

"I don't know what to say about that, but he wants to see me again tomorrow when he gets off work."

"I thought you came out here to visit me, not get your freak on with Luis' cousin. What kind of wild stuff do you guys have planned? Knowing the two of you, it is bound to be crazy." Ronnie smirked.

"I don't know yet. He said he was going to surprise me."

"Cool." Ronnie's attention drifted back to wondering where Luis was and why he didn't call.

"Do you mind if we pick this up in the morning?" Joie let out a long, loud yawn. "I am still jet-lagged. By the time my body catches up to Cali time, it's going to be time for me to leave."

"Sure. Go on to bed. I'm going to do the same. See you in the morning, Joie."

Before she retreated to her bedroom, Ronnie strode from room to room taking note of the tropical décor she had fallen in love with. She recalled the first day she set foot in the house—the day Luis rescued her from the roach infested apartment she rented sight unseen.

In the beginning, they couldn't get enough of each other and was content just to be in the other's presence. Regrettably, the once beautiful house had lost its luster as her doubts about Luis grew. She looked around the home filled with exquisite art and tasteful decorations. *How much more money did we need to live comfortably? When did all this stop being enough?*

When they first met, Luis had plans of returning to the Dominican Republic and opening a business. It used to be part of their daily conversation—a goal they both wanted to attain. Now, she felt she was losing him—and losing each other—to the trappings of success she fled from in Virginia.

Ronnie studied a picture they took during a balloon ride in Albuquerque a few years ago. "We used to be so happy, but that was before Luis' obsession with growing his business began to mess up our relationship. He must know the end is near. Why else would he leave me and go to San Diego with another woman? Why try to secure a million dollar deal that could hold him—us, here indefinitely?"

Both his dogs came in from outside after doing their business. Once they settled down into their beds, Ronnie secured the house and reset the alarm.

"Fuck it! I'm going to bed. I'll deal with this mess tomorrow morning. With or without Luis, I'm going to make it. I did it before and I can do it again." She had resigned herself to her fate even before she had a reason to.

*   *   *

Luis caught a few hours of fitful sleep before awakening to a morning that arrived much too soon. He quickly showered and went through a dry run of the presentation as he dressed. And noting the time, he used the hotel phone and punched in Carmen's room number. She picked up immediately.

"Hello?" she answered.

"Good morning, Carmen, I'll be downstairs in fifteen minutes. Bring your laptop so you can take notes over breakfast."

"I'm already up, dressed, and ready to go. See you in a few."

After he hung up the phone, Luis thought about calling Ronnie. He glanced at the time as he slipped his watch on his wrist. *I'm already running late and don't have enough time to explain why I didn't call last night.* He sighed wearily. *I'll just have to call her after the meeting.* He took one last look around the room to make certain he wasn't forgetting anything before pulling the door closed behind him.

"Luis, these documents are absolutely brilliant! I can't believe you made all these changes in just a few hours. Very impressive." Carmen surveyed the presentation including the samples of business cards, brochures, and marketing materials.

"Thanks. I just hope the Hernandez Group will also be impressed. Now, let's grab a bite to eat and review what we need to cover this afternoon," Luis instructed.

"Sure boss. Whatever you say," replied Carmen.

Luis eyed Carmen. "You look very nice today," he said, innocently.

Carmen pretended her clothing choice was no big deal. She didn't want him to know the many hours it took for her to decide upon the dress. Once she tried it on, the saleswoman assured her that she looked both professional, as well as extremely sexy.

She murmured softly, "This old thing. I've had this dress for years. It's been hanging in the back of my closet..."

They took a seat at a table away from other customers and a waitress brought over coffee, buttery croissants and fresh fruit. They nibbled on the food while reviewing every aspect of the presentation. Luis wanted every detail covered to ensure Mr. Hernandez proceeded with the deal. As he queried Carmen, he thought, *she is really bright. In spite of Ronnie's feelings about her, I think I made the right decision bringing Carmen. She sure did bring her A-game with her.*

* * *

Because Ronnie had stayed up so late waiting for Luis' call, it was almost noon by the time she awoke. Before she made her way to the kitchen, she checked her cell phone for missed calls. There were several from her mother, but none from Luis. She called his cell again and the call went straight to voicemail.

Joie entered the kitchen through the back door, stepping aside to let the two Boxers by. The dogs permitted her to pass only after sniffing her up and down to make sure she wasn't dangerous.

"Hey girl," Ronnie said.

Joie took one look at Ronnie's expression and said, "Let me guess. You still haven't heard from Luis?"

"Is it that obvious?"

"Only because you look like you haven't slept a wink. So I suppose the answer is no?"

"It's already after twelve. He's probably meeting with that company as we speak. I'll give him a few more hours before I really get pissed."

Joie joined Ronnie as she stood staring blankly into the refrigerator. "If you're waiting for those chicken wings to explain what's going on, you've got a long wait."

"I'm sorry... My thoughts are all over the place right now."

"I know... Let's do something fun to take your mind off Luis; like we used to do back in Virginia."

"Girl, you know I can't drink." She pulled out a carton of eggs and the remaining ingredients for a hearty omelet.

"We don't have to drink to have fun."

Ronnie looked at Joie as if she'd lost her mind. "When did we ever do anything that didn't involve drinking?"

Joie furrowed her brow. "Can you think of something fun to do that doesn't involve liquor?"

"Of course, I can. Don't you know that Santa Elena is a tourist's haven? People come from all around the world just to see the sparkling ocean, the historical missions, the exquisite vineyards... This is one of the most beautiful locations on the west coast. In fact, travel agents refer to Santa Elena as the American Riviera."

"Okay, you can be my tour guide and show me around Santa Elena. Give me the insider's look."

"You know what Joie? That sounds like fun. We'll leave right after we have breakfast. There's no use in me moping around here while Luis is down in San Diego having a good time."

"There ya go, sistah. That's the Veronica Pierce I know and love."

* * *

Luis and Carmen attended the noontime lunch meeting at Mr. Hernandez's family restaurant. Luis made the most of Carmen's translator skills, resulting in a remarkable presentation. Mr. Hernandez, a serious man who rarely smiled, was very impressed with Luis' dedication and willingness to implement the company's ideas into the campaign.

Finally, after a gut-busting meal consisting of five courses of Mexican food and several pitchers of beer and margaritas, the two companies sealed the deal and signed a two year agreement. By the time they were finished celebrating, it was well after six.

* * *

For the next several hours, Ronnie and Joie toured Santa Elena as if they were both visiting for the first time. They explored the world famous State Street teaming with visitors ready to drop loads of money on one-of-a-kind, locally made souvenirs. Joie did her part to support the locals by buying souvenirs for the twins and her parents.

Ronnie suggested they visit the beautiful and historical *Mission Santa Elena*. The women literally spent hours reading historical facts about how the Mission was founded by Spanish Franciscans in the late 1700's. They toured the still functioning church, fascinated by its architecture and gracious beauty. The adobe building with its many archways and terracotta roof had withstood numerous earthquakes over the centuries and looked like it could withstand even more.

The *Santa Elena County Courthouse* was next on the list. Strolling through the historical hallways, they marveled at the Spanish influenced architecture of the building and the scenic landscaping that included southern tropical Californian foliage.

Joie exclaimed, "Y'all must be rich out here. This don't look like any courthouse I've ever seen. You sure the state owns this property?"

"I know, right. It is amazing."

"I suppose going to court has a whole new meaning out here."

"Uh huh, and would you believe people get on a waiting list just to get married at the courthouse? They come from all over the world, not just California. Come on, I want to show you the *Sunken Garden* area. Lots of couples get married down there because it's so beautiful—like being in a botanical garden, but it's on the actual courthouse grounds. See all those people standing over there? They're waiting to be married."

"I can see why they want to be married here. You don't even have to bring flowers—they are already supplied by nature. Girl, I don't feel like I'm still in the United States!" Joie declared. "Santa Elena looks and feels more like what I'd imagine a Spanish villa to be."

"That's because of the heavy Spanish influence and later the Mexicans. I've never lived in a more beautiful city..." Ronnie pulled out her phone and checked her messages. Still nothing from Luis.

"Would you please put that phone away? I am having so much fun just hanging out with you. Please don't ruin our day by worrying about Luis. You said you trust him. So *trust* him."

"Yeah, you're right. But at this point, I should've heard from him by now. It isn't like him to not call. I'm starting to get worried..."

"I'll tell you what... When we get back to the house, we'll look up his hotel. It's possible his cell phone died and he simply wasn't able to call. It happens all the time with mine."

Ronnie chuckled at Luis' behavior. "You're right. If he forgot his cell phone, chances are good he also forgot the charger." Yet still, she was worried because her intuition told her something wasn't right.

* * *

"Carmen, can you please drive us back to the hotel? I think I had a bit too much to drink." Luis badly slurred his speech. Beads of perspiration gathered on his forehead. He also felt the first naggings of a headache coming on. "I'm in no condition to drive..."

"Where are your keys?" Despite her boss being drunk, he seemed to be in a very good mood. Perhaps, they could continue the celebration back at the hotel over a few more drinks. Just the two of them…

Luis opened the driver's door for Carmen. He handed her the keys, and then staggered clumsily over to the passenger's side.

"All right, this is how you start the car. Insert the key there. Put your foot on the brake and press this button." He noticed the cell phone charger sticking out of the outlet. Even in his drunken state, he had the presence of mind to think about charging up his cell phone. Luis patted down the pockets of his blazer looking for his phone. A few moments passed before he realized he had left it in the hotel, sitting on the nightstand, with a dead battery. He relaxed in the seat while Carmen drove to the hotel—grateful that the meeting was finally over.

"Are you going to be okay? You don't look so good," she remarked, as she pulled into the hotel's parking lot.

He held his stomach and groaned. "I don't feel so good. Must've been something I ate."

"I told you to slow down eating that so-called 'home-style Mexican food'. You don't know what they put into those dishes. *Just like Mama used to make*, my foot. No telling what you just put in your stomach… That's why I only stick to food I recognize, like chicken enchiladas."

"Ugh…" He groaned again, only this time much louder. "I'm going upstairs and try to sleep this off. We need to get back home tomorrow. First thing." He staggered trying to get out of the car.

"If you say so, but you don't look like you'll be going anywhere soon." *I know I'm not ready to go. I like it here. It is a well-needed vacation from home—from my family.* She frowned noticing how intensely Luis had started to perspire.

"C'mon, big boy. Let's get you up to your room before you start puking all over yourself."

He hoisted himself from the car and with Carmen's assistance, staggered to the lobby. "I'm probably going to need you to get anti-diarrhea medicine. If you're not sure what to get, you can ask the drugstore pharmacist what he recommends for food poisoning."

She draped Luis' arm across her shoulder, steadied him into the elevator and then down the hallway to his room.

"Where is your room key?" she asked, patting down his pockets; enjoying the close physical contact.

"That's all right, I can do it." He pushed her hands away and managed to pull the key card from his own pocket. The card found its mark in the slot causing the little light to turn green.

"You want me to come in?"

"No, no, I'll be fine. For now, I just need to rest."

"Okay, I'll leave, but only if you're sure you're going to be all right. I can stay if you need me..."

Though ill and slightly intoxicated, Luis was still very cognizant of his situation. Even in his current state, he understood how having Carmen Sanchez in his room, even if she *was* taking care of him, would appear. He did not want to go down that road.

"Thanks, I appreciate it. I'll be fine... Just need to sleep... I'll call you later." He felt the sour bile rise up his throat. Swallowing hard did nothing to alleviate the overwhelming urge to vomit. He gave in and rushed into the bathroom.

* * *

Ronnie pulled up to the house half expecting to find Luis' car parked in the driveway. "He should've been home by now. It's almost seven o'clock."

"Don't worry, girlfriend. I'm sure Luis is fine. What's the name of his hotel?" Joie asked, pulling out her *iPad*.

Ronnie unlocked the front door and went directly to check the answering machine. Just in case. "I think he told me he was staying at the Marriott in downtown San Diego..."

Joie's phone rang, interrupting their conversation. "Hey Tomas, how ya doing. Yeah, eight o'clock sounds perfect." She mouthed to Ronnie who it was on the other end. "Yeah, we had a great time today. No, we haven't heard from Luis. Have you? We're trying to pull up his hotel info right now... Okay, I will... See you soon. Bye."

Ronnie shot Joie a questioning look. "Anything?"

"He hasn't heard from Luis." Joie's disposition quickly changed to match Ronnie's. She used her stylus to tap through the screens.

"I can't believe this man has us calling up every friggin' hotel in San Diego."

"Damn, there are several Marriott hotels in downtown San Diego. Guess we'll just have to call each one until we locate the right one. You start from the top and I'll take the bottom."

"Thanks for helping out, girlfriend." Ronnie took a deep breath and pulled out her cell phone.

Joie dialed the toll-free number listed at the bottom of the list and waited patiently for someone to answer.

Ronnie selected the Marriott at the top of the list. No luck. She called two more hotels.

"Marriott San Diego, how may I help you today?" answered the clerk.

"I'm looking for a Mr. Luis Duarte. That's spelled D-u-a-r-t-e. He checked in a couple of days ago." Ronnie held her breath for the third time.

"Yes, we have a Luis Duarte. Would you like me to connect you to his room?"

"You mean he hasn't checked out?" Ronnie felt her blood pressure rise.

Joie stood next to Ronnie and placed her hand on her shoulder for support.

"No ma'am. We're showing he extended his stay for one night, but he hasn't checked out, yet. Would you like me to connect you?" the hotel clerk asked again.

"Yes, please." Ronnie held her breath praying he'd answer, hoping he wouldn't. For if he *were* still at the hotel, there was no reason for him not to have called. The phone rang several times before being picked up.

"Hello?" answered a woman's voice on the other end.

Ronnie listened without saying a word.

"Hellooo?" the woman asked again.

Caught off guard, Ronnie uttered, "Uh, I'm not sure I have the right room. I'm looking for Luis Duarte."

"You have the right room. He's in the shower. Can I take a message?"

"Who is this?" Ronnie.

"*This* is Carmen. Whom may I ask is calling?" She knew exactly who was on the other end—it was Luis' wife calling to check up on him.

Ronnie didn't respond. Instead, she calmly ended the call and threw her cell phone across the room, watching it hit the wall and break into several pieces. Just like the pieces her heart had broken into.

"What's going on? Who was on the phone?" asked Joie.

Ronnie wasn't able to answer due to the lump stuck in her throat. Images of the smirk on Carmen's face haunted her. She looked past Joie and whispered, "It was Carmen…"

Devastated with the realization of Carmen being in Luis' hotel room, she dropped her head in her hands and began weeping uncontrollably. Only this time it wasn't from pregnancy hormones. This time it was because unwillingly she had come full circle; returning to the awful place she had spent too many years getting out of. *What the hell happened? It was only a few days ago that my world was perfect.*

* * *

Several minutes later, after nothing remained in Luis' stomach to expel to the porcelain god, he exited the bathroom. Getting rid of the food seemed to have helped some, but he still wanted to lie down to rest. Wiping his face with a towel, Luis was shocked and surprised to find Carmen sitting on the bed with a sly smile spread across her face, replacing the bedside phone in its cradle.

* * *

Joie sat down beside Ronnie. "Oh, hell to the no! You ain't going out like this girlfriend. You might be pregnant and all but snap the fuck out of it! Where the hell is my girl? What happened to the Veronica Pierce who took her power back from assholes?"

"Joie, why would he do this to me?" Ronnie cried.

"You ain't got to take this shit! Some bitch up in your man's room? And she got the nerve to answer the phone, too? What the fuck? Ronnie, get dressed. We're gonna roll to San Diego." Joie plucked her cell from her bra where she kept it conveniently stored.

Ronnie wiped away the snot dripping from her nose with a dishtowel. She glanced at Joie. "You're right. This ain't no time for a pity party."

"Damn right, it ain't! Let's go find Luis' ass!"

Joie placed a single phone call to the one person who could help them both.

Tomas arrived within thirty minutes of Joie's phone call looking like some action hero from a cancelled television series. Dressed in a black leather jacket, black denim jeans, and a pair of black leather driving gloves, Tomas was ready for anything. And when Tomas opened his trunk to toss her overnight bags inside, Ronnie could have sworn she saw a leather cape in his trunk.

He too was worried about his cousin, because having a woman in his hotel room was totally out of character for Luis.

"Tomas, thanks for offering to drive us to San Diego," Ronnie said.

"Don't worry about it. After Joie told me what happened and I also couldn't get him on his cell, I realized I have to go check on him. Luis is *mi primo*—the only family I have here."

"Well, something is going on and I intend to find out what it is."

"I understand." He looked towards the house. "Did you get a chance to talk to him?"

"No, I only talked to that bitch, Carmen."

"Oh... Well, as soon as he finds out that you called, I bet he'll call you right back. Have you checked your voicemail?"

"I can't. I broke my cell phone. Threw it at the wall..."

"I see..." He was at a loss for words. "Is Joie almost ready?"

"Yeah, she's packing an overnight bag—just in case. She'll be out soon."

"I am sure there's nothing to worry about, Veronica. Luis just proposed to you, right?"

"So you heard?"

"He told me. In fact, he called me up before he asked you. That doesn't sound like a man who is going to cheat."

"I suppose you're right, but that still doesn't explain why Carmen was in his hotel room. *Or* why he hasn't called."

"There has to be a plausible explanation for all of this. I'm just saying to not jump to any conclusions."

Joie approached the car carrying a small overnight bag. "Okay, I'm ready. Y'all ready to roll?" she asked.

"I am if you are," replied Tomas as he put her bag in the trunk with the rest of their luggage. He made certain the ladies were securely comfortable before heading south on the 101.

Chapter Eighteen

"**W**ait just one minute young lady! I don't think I heard you correctly. Did you say you're dating Professor Quinn? Quinn from UC Santa Elena?" screamed Travis.

"Yes, Daddy. GQ and I have been dating on and off for about a year now." She scooped a healthy serving of pad Thai unto her plate.

"Jeez Kiara! The man is almost twice your age and he's notorious for screwing his students. Don't you know that?"

"I never heard anything about him being with other students, but it doesn't matter. We really like each other." She crossed her arms, pouting like a child.

Travis couldn't help but to laugh at the absurdity of the situation. "You are something else, you know that? You actually convinced me to let you go to Haiti knowing full well I would have disapproved if I'd known about you and Quinn. Since when did you start to lie to your old man, huh?"

"I didn't lie to you." She turned away from her father and faced the entrance hallway. Every fiber in her being told her to run from the house and end this conversation before it got any uglier.

"Really? Then why didn't you mention you two were involved when we first discussed this Haiti trip?" He angrily tossed the spoon in the sink. The clank of metal against metal reverberated throughout the house.

"I didn't mention him because I knew you would react this way," she said, rolling her eyes.

"Watch yourself, young lady!"

"Daddy, I am a grown woman. You can't keep treating me like a child!"

"Is that what this trip to Haiti is about? Are you trying to gain your independence from me by going to Haiti with Quinn?"

Kiara softened her tone. "Daddy, I'm sorry for not telling you about GQ earlier. You've done so much for me. Given me everything you have to give, but now it's time for me to start making my own decisions. It's time for me to grow up."

"You're a smart girl, so why are you being so stupid about Quinn? He is all wrong for you, baby."

"Explain to me why he's so wrong for me? We get along great."

"First of all, he's almost forty… He used to be your instructor, you're barely out of your teens, and he's only interested in you for one thing."

"Daddy, you're wrong. GQ really cares about me. He exposes me to new things… And he treats me like I'm an adult."

"Look sweetheart, I just don't want you to get hurt. I believe you're making the wrong decision about being in this relationship with this man. Trust me. I know how these guys operate." She was so much like her mother. Sweet, independent, trusting, and stubborn as hell.

"Daddy, if I am making the wrong decision, then let me. It's mine to make. I don't want to end up alone and bitter." Kiara wished she could take back the words as soon as she said them. Unfortunately, once they were released into the world it was too late. She had already given them power.

"You mean alone and bitter like me?" Travis stared in bewilderment at the young lady who stood before him. He almost didn't recognize Kiara. Tonight when he looked at his daughter, he didn't see the baby he brought home from the hospital over twenty years ago. The motherless little girl he raised alone, making so many mistakes along the way, had grown up in the blink of an eye. All the times when he was unsure of the decisions he made, he prayed that he wouldn't mess her up too much, because he didn't know anything about raising a child. And yet, here she stood tonight, before him, asserting her independence. He couldn't think of the right words to say to express how he felt inside. He knew anything he said would come out wrong.

"I didn't mean it that way, Daddy…"

"This discussion is over. And I forbid you to see Quinn again. Travis turned his wheelchair away from Kiara and towards his bedroom. "Lock up when you're done."

"Is that it? This discussion is over? And what if I disobey you? Then what?" She wished she had never asked the question.

Travis didn't answer because he was afraid of what he'd say. He continued down the hallway to his room and quietly shut the door.

Chapter Nineteen

*L*uis tossed the towel aside and focused his attention on Carmen sitting on his bed with her legs crossed. His stomach continued to lurch despite having nothing inside except watery mucus. "What are you still doing here? I thought you had already left."

"You didn't look so good, so I wanted to see how you were before I returned to my room. You were in the bathroom for quite awhile."

"Thanks for your concern. I'm feeling better since I got whatever it was out of my stomach." He shrugged his blazer off and tossed it on the chair.

Carmen didn't budge from her spot. On the contrary, she leaned back and made herself more comfortable. She noted Luis' color was off and his face was covered in perspiration. "Have you looked in the mirror lately? You look like *caca*."

He managed a smile. "I feel like shit, too. And who was that on the phone?"

"Hmm, what phone?" She feigned ignorance.

"The phone on the nightstand. I noticed you were hanging it up when I walked in."

"Oh, it was just the front desk. I called them asking where the nearest pharmacy was. They have one off the lobby."

"Thanks. I think I'm going to need some *Imodium* or something. Can you please ask them to send up a box?"

"Of course. Anything else?"

"Yes, if you have a cell phone charger I can borrow, that would be great."

"Um, I don't know if I brought mine. I'll check in my room."

"Thanks. What time is it anyway?"

"A little after eight."

"Damn! I don't know if I'm going to be able to shake this before tomorrow morning. The way I feel, I may not be able to drive home." But before he could do anything, he clutched his stomach and ran back to the bathroom.

Carmen allowed a mischievous smile to spread across her face. She retrieved Luis' room key from his blazer pocket. Even though she was going for medicine, she had no intention of leaving Luis alone tonight. And she sure as hell wasn't giving him a phone charger so he could call his wife.

She called out, "Luis, I've got your room key. I'm going out for your medicine. Be back in a minute!" *Yes, it is a new low for me to take advantage of a sick man. So what? He isn't married yet. As far as I'm concerned he is fair game.*

Luis vomited what little remained of his dinner into the toilet. And in the midst of retching, he heard the door close. *Great, she's gone. Now I can finally relax and get some rest.* Upon realizing how awful he smelled, he stripped down to nothing and got in the shower. Afterwards, he dried himself off and climbed into bed, exhausted and weary.

Before turning in, Luis used the hotel's phone to call Ronnie. The call went straight to her voicemail. "Sweetheart, it's me. I'm so sorry it has taken me so long to call. The meeting went well, but I ate something that is kicking my ass. I'm going to try to get out of here first thing tomorrow morning. Just didn't want you to worry. I love you and can't wait to see you." He placed the phone back on the base. After which, he passed out in a deep, soundless sleep.

In the meantime, Carmen perused the hotel pharmacy and picked up a package of *Imodium-D*. After confirming with the pharmacist that the medication was right for Luis' symptoms, she returned to her room to retrieve her overnight bag. Her cell phone charger was plugged in the wall, but she chose not to bring it. She took a quick shower and headed directly back to Luis' room. All told, she couldn't have been gone for more than thirty minutes.

Using Luis' room key, Carmen unlocked his door. All the lights were off. She tiptoed inside to find Luis in bed snoring lightly, dead to the world. Not to be dismayed, she removed all her clothes and slipped under the covers with him. Sighing contently, she snuggled up close and imagined Luis was her husband.

* * *

Tomas drove like a madman on a mission weaving in and out of traffic. He appeared to be fighting a case of road rage as he tried to pass a car cruising in the fast lane ten miles under the speed limit. As he swore under his breath in his native language, Joie attempted to keep him calm.

Ronnie relaxed in the back seat listening to a local jazz station. She blocked out Tomas and Joie's conversation, letting her mind wander back to Luis. Being on the verge of exhaustion, the rocking motion of the car quickly put her to sleep.

She dreamt. In her dream, Ronnie was watching Luis marry Carmen. She stood outside a church pounding on the door and screaming for someone to stop the wedding ceremony. Next she found herself inside the church, standing before the couple trying in vain to convince the preacher that Luis was marrying the wrong woman; only to have the entire church erupt in laughter. To add insult to injury, Luis told the ushers to throw her out. She also dreamt her baby was born, looking like Tomas dressed in black leather. The dream ended with her floating in a life raft with the face of her deceased ex-husband telling her to chill out.

Tomas followed the directions provided by the melodious voice of his GPS to locate the hotel. Joie had also drifted off about an hour earlier, leaving him on his own. Traffic was lighter than anticipated, allowing him to reach downtown San Diego in record time.

"Wake up ladies, we're here." He gently shook Joie's arm.

Joie awoke immediately, turning to wake her friend. "Wake up, sleeping beauty. We're here."

"Huh, where are we?" Ronnie shielded her eyes from the bright florescent lights.

"We're in San Diego at the downtown Marriott. Get up so we can go find Luis' ass."

Tomas interjected, "I'll let you out here and then I'll go find a parking space. Give me a few minutes."

Ronnie wiped the sleep from her eyes. "Okay. Just give me a moment to get my bearings. I was having a helluva nightmare."

"C'mon, I got ya, girlfriend."

Taking a deep breath to gather her strength, Ronnie got out of the car. With Joie at her side, she bravely approached the front desk. She prayed, "Lord, I know I haven't been calling on you much lately, but I need you right now. Please give me the strength to deal with whatever it is I may discover tonight."

A middle-aged black woman greeted them as if it were the middle of the day, instead of being after midnight. Her name tag indicated her name was Stephanie. "Welcome to the Marriott San Diego. What can I help you nice folks with?" she asked, displaying a genuine smile.

"Hi, I'm looking for my fiancée. His name is Luis Duarte. He checked in a couple days ago and I haven't been able to reach him on his cell phone. Can you please give me his room number so I can go check to make sure he's all right?"

"I'm sorry ma'am, but I can't give out that information. It's for the protection of our guests. You understand... However, I'd be more than happy to ring his room for you," she replied, keeping that same smile plastered across her face.

And that is when Joie decided to intervene. She leaned over the counter and whispered, "Stephanie, you don't seem to understand. Can I speak to you, sister to sister?"

The hotel clerk's smile began to fade as she studied the crazed looking woman on the other side of the counter. "Sure, what's going on?"

"I'm out here visiting my best friend." Joie tilted her head towards Ronnie. "She just found out she's pregnant."

"Well, congratulations! I was in my late thirties when I had my last one..."

"So you know what my girl is dealing with? Hormones and shit..." Stephanie shrugged. "It wasn't so bad."

"Anyway... She hasn't heard from her fiancé, Mr. Duarte, in several days and she's worried. We drove all the way from Santa Elena to check on him."

"I feel for you ladies. Really... I do... but I have to follow the hotel's policies. There are written procedures in place to protect our guest's safety."

"Um, Stephanie... look here... Her husband came down here with his secretary—his very *young* and very *beautiful* secretary," Joie added, letting that tidbit of information sink in.

Stephanie cleared her throat. She felt bad for the women who stood before her looking an absolute wreck. "Well, I suppose I can bend the rules and give you his room number. How do you spell his name?"

Ronnie replied, "D-u-a-r-t-e."

"Listen, I don't want no mess up in this hotel tonight." Her smile had altogether disappeared and was replaced with a grimace.

"We promise. We just want to make sure he's all right," Joie said.

"Just so we don't have any problems, I'm going to send a security guard up with you and one of you has to leave her driver's license with me." She typed in her computer and pulled up his info. "He's in room 815."

Ronnie pulled out her purse and driver's license. She placed the card on the counter and said, "Thank you."

"Good luck. I sincerely hope you don't find what you've come all the way down here for." After twenty odd years in the business, Stephanie had seen it all. Nothing new under the sun. Same shit just a different day.

The ladies were headed towards the elevator when Tomas finally joined them. The security guard followed closely behind.

"We cool? You have his room number?" asked Tomas.

"He's in room 815," replied Ronnie.

The big burly security guard eyed Tomas and the ladies closely. He placed his hand on his gun and glared at them. He wanted to make sure they respected his authority and understood he wasn't about to let no bullshit happen. Not under his watch, anyway.

"Ronnie, Joie. Please let me handle this," Tomas insisted.

The elevator delivered them to the eighth floor in less than a minute. In direct contrast with the cheerful décor of the hotel, the group's mood was gloomy. They each wondered how this would go down in just a few short minutes. Room 815 was the furthest room from the elevator. Ironically, it was also one of the hotel's nicest rooms because it was tucked away in a corner with a fantastic view of the ocean.

* * *

Inside the comfortable hotel room, Luis tossed and turned in his bed, unable to get comfortable. In his half awakened state, he dreamt he was at home in bed sleeping next to his woman. He caressed the warm, soft body he thought was Ronnie's, feeling the tingling sensation of his erection as it stiffened under the sheet. Still half asleep, he sighed in satisfaction at what he thought was his woman's reaction to his fingers exploring her body.

Carmen moaned in ecstasy, guiding Luis' hand between her thighs to her sweet spot. She maneuvered her ass closer so he could touch her more intimately. And wet with anticipation, she could hardly wait for Luis to enter her.

She whispered, "Oh Luis, I am so hot for you." She reached behind and wrapped her fingers around his penis gently stroking it, feeling it pulse in her hands.

Hearing the voice that wasn't Ronnie's, Luis woke up fully and jumped from the bed. He switched on the lamp. "What the hell?! Carmen, what are you doing in my room?! In my bed?!" He stood before her, totally exposed, with a throbbing erection he could barely contain.

Carmen tossed the remaining covers from the bed and spread her legs wide open exposing her delicacies. In the soft light emanating from the lamp, nothing was left to the imagination. She tilted her hips upwards inviting Luis to join her. "I know you want me. You know you want me. No one ever has to know. C'mon, what are you afraid of Luis?" Her fingers disappeared first in her mouth and then between her thighs.

Luis was hypnotized watching Carmen writhe under her self-induced pleasure. Totally nude, she was even more desirable than he ever imagined. His penis throbbed in agony as her glistening wetness was just a few feet away. Smelling her musky scent rise up towards his nostrils, he began to stroke himself, feeling torn by the age old nemeses between good against evil.

"Just... what... do... you... think... you're... doing?" he asked, weakly. He swallowed the excessive saliva gathering in his mouth and stepped closer to the bed. Observing Carmen's salacious attempt to bring herself over the top, he was very tempted to throw caution to the wind and literally dive right in. His eyes glazed over anticipating being inside her softness. Feeling her heat the right way. It felt as if his penis had taken over his brain.

"That's right, come on over. Tonight it is just me and you in this hotel room. Luis and Carmen. Let's just have a little bit of fun while we're here. C'mon, I can tell you're more than ready." She licked her honey from her fingers and sat up. She scooted to the side of the bed where Luis' feet were planted with indecision.

Luis' erect penis was inches from Carmen's face. She licked her lips and blew her hot breath on his erection, smiling in delight as she watched it bob up and down while he tried to catch his breath. When he didn't step back; she leaned forward and placed the tip of his penis in her mouth catching him by surprise. She gripped his ass and brought him completely to her, licking and sucking as if her life depended on it.

He gasped, closed his eyes, and moaned out loud from the sheer pleasure. Carmen was a master at bringing him to the edge and then pushing him back. She sucked, slurped, and stroked his member until Luis was close to losing his mind. He grabbed her hair and vigorously pumped into her mouth in ecstasy.

Carmen smiled inwardly realizing this man was now under her total control. She was in charge and Luis would do whatever she asked. Her every wish would be his job to fill—along with her every orifice. She felt his silent explosion come inside her mouth, along with the hot fluid trailing down her face. As he grunted one last time, she smiled when the last wave of his orgasm slowly drifted away.

Luis opened his eyes. Feeling as if he was having an out-of-body experience, he stared down at the top of Carmen's head where his hands rested. A quick glance at the clock on the table indicted it was 12:26. He gawked in amazement at the naked man pressing a woman's head to his genitals, realizing the reflection in the mirror belonged not to a stranger who was stupid enough to get caught up in a bad situation, but to him. *Oh my God... What have I done?* Luis stepped backwards away from Carmen. His previously engorged penis was now flaccid.

"Mmm, I see you really enjoyed that. Don't worry, there's more where that came from." She grinned, wiping her mouth with the bed sheets.

Luis returned to his senses. He grabbed the towel he tossed aside earlier to cover his nakedness and murmured, "Carmen, I am so sorry. This wasn't supposed to happen. You have to go."

"What's the matter? Didn't you enjoy the blow job? Did I do something wrong?" she asked, not fully comprehending the turn of events.

His tone became more firm. "Carmen, get dressed. This isn't going any further. In fact, you shouldn't be here at all." Luis felt his anger grow.

"Oh, so now you're trying to get all righteous on me? You weren't screaming for me to leave when I had your dick in my mouth a few seconds ago." She stood to face him.

"That should not have happened."

"Kinda late for regrets, don't you think? All right, I'll leave. Just give me a few minutes to clean up."

"I'm going to take a shower and I want you gone by the time I get out." He paused at the bathroom door. "What are you doing in my room anyway? How did you get in?"

"I went to get your medicine from the pharmacy; it's over there on the table. I let myself in with your room key. I *thought* this was what you wanted…" She ran her hands over her body.

"Hand over my room key and my car keys, please." Luis looked at her with disgust.

As requested, she tossed both items on the bed. "Hey Duarte, if you want me to keep this little encounter a secret, it's going to cost you." She added with a smug expression on her face.

He felt like bitch slapping her. "Are you serious? Look, you won't get a penny out of me. And if you say anything to anybody about this…"

"You'll what? Fire me?" She laughed. "Sweetheart, you need me! How else do you think this little deal of yours went down this afternoon? I'm guaranteed to be with your company for the next couple of years."

"What are you talking about?"

"Mr. Hernandez and his company, that's what. He was so impressed by me that he said he'd only do business with your company if I were part of the deal. Look at the terms closely when he sends it to your lawyer. There's a clause that lists me as one of the prime players."

"You sneaky, conniving, little bitch! You must be out of your fucking mind if you think I'm going to keep you on. Not after what you pulled tonight."

She smirked. "Is that right? You'll be changing your tune after you speak to Mr. Hernandez about me. We can discuss my bonus and a raise when we get back to the office."

"Who *are* you?" He looked at Carmen in utter contempt. And suddenly a wave of realization washed over him like someone had flipped a light switch on. "You set me up?"

"Oh, don't act like you didn't want it. I see how you've been looking at me. There isn't a man alive who wouldn't want to get some of this—including you."

"You are really pathetic if you believe all you're good for is a fuck. I feel sorry for you."

"Don't feel sorry for me, Duarte. You'd better start feeling sorry for yourself because I am getting paid!"

A loud knocking at the door ended their conversation in midsentence. They both froze, wondering who could be dropping by this time of night. Perhaps all the yelling woke up the people in the next room. The knocking continued. Luis crept to the door and pressed his eye against the peephole.

His heart literally stopped beating. Outside the door stood Tomas, Ronnie, Joie, and a huge Hispanic security guard.

Chapter Twenty

Kiara locked up after she left her father's house, leaving the uneaten Thai food sitting on the counter. Feeling totally distraught over their argument, her appetite had all but disappeared. Had this been any other night, they would be sitting on the couch eating takeout and watching some stupid television show that she and Travis would playfully rip apart. But not this evening. Tonight, she put the car in gear and drove aimlessly throughout town with no clear destination in mind.

While waiting for the light to change, she sent a quick text to GQ. *Need to talk. Call me.* The driver of the car behind her beeped his horn.

She hit the speed dial, ending up leaving a message on the voicemail. "Mom, please call me as soon as you can. Daddy and I just had like a really bad argument and I don't know what to do. I need to talk to you."

Back at the house, Travis shuddered when he heard the front door slam. He returned to the kitchen to find the mess from earlier. "What the hell am I supposed to do? Let her screw up her life? I raised her better than that."

The stillness of the house was deafening. Without Kiara or the maid piddling about, the spacious home now seemed entirely too large. Suddenly, he felt all alone. He wheeled himself from room to room, finally ending up in Kiara's. "Baby girl, you're all I have left. I can't sit idly by and let you ruin your life by screwing around with a middle aged sonofabitch. I've got to fix this…"

He retrieved his cell phone from where he kept it tucked away in his wheelchair. And just as he was about to call Kiara, the phone vibrated with an incoming call from a number he didn't recognize.

"Hello?" he answered.

"Hi, may I please speak with Travis Bradford?"

"Speaking."

"Mr. Bradford, my name is Monique. You don't know me, but I'm Trudy's granddaughter."

"Monique? You're the budding actress of the family, right?"

"That's right. Still waiting for my big break, though."

"Trudy has a picture of you on her desk. What can I do for you?"

"I'm sorry to be the bearer of bad news, but my Grandmother had a major stroke earlier today and was admitted to the Santa Elena hospital."

"That's awful! Is she going to be all right?"

"It's touch and go for now. We don't know much more than that."

"Is there anything I can do?"

"Just send up your prayers. That's about all anyone can do for now."

"Well, thanks for calling. I'll drop by the hospital tomorrow. Uh, I didn't realize she had family in the area."

"She doesn't. Mother and I drove up from Los Angeles when we got the call from the hospital; us being the next of kin and all. But she always considered you and the others at the center as her family."

"I see..." Trudy rarely talked about her family. He always thought they were estranged.

"As you probably already know, my grandmother is a very stubborn lady who doesn't take kindly to being told what to do. Mother wanted her to move down south to be closer to us, but she wouldn't hear of it. Said Los Angeles was too hedonistic for her tastes."

"Now *that* sounds like Trudy." He looked at the number on his display. "Is this a good number to call before I come out?"

"Yes, it's my cell." Monique paused. "Grandmother and I were very close and she often suggested that I should come up to meet you, but I never did because I was always so busy with acting gigs. She's very fond of you, you know.... She often told me we'd make a good couple."

Travis' interest was piqued. *I wonder why Trudy thought we would make a great couple.*

Monique noted his lack of response. It spoke volumes. "Anyway, Mr. Bradford, I look forward to meeting you tomorrow."

"Please call me Travis... And I look forward to meeting you, also. Just wish it was under better circumstances."

"Me too."

"Please give Trudy my love when you see her."

"I will. See you soon, Travis."

"Good-bye, Monique. And thanks again for calling."

"What a day…" After hanging up from Monique, Travis didn't have the emotional strength to deal with Kiara so, he put the food away and called it a night.

* * *

"Sweet K, your father will come around; just give him some time. In the meantime, you have a major exam to study for and I have several papers to grade." GQ cradled the cell phone with his shoulder while balancing his briefcase and a pile of folders in his hands.

"It's not like us to argue. Daddy has always like supported me in just about everything, so I don't understand why he doesn't want us to be together."

"He's your father. He probably doesn't want you to be with any man. I don't have children, but if I did, I'm sure I'd be the same way with my daughter. Don't worry about it because he will accept us. Eventually."

"Yeah, I guess you're right. Telling my father about my first real boyfriend wasn't supposed to be like this. Why do I feel so awful?" she asked the question more to herself than to GQ.

Kiara sat in her car, watching the brightest stars gradually appear in the evening sky, talking to GQ. As the sun began to set, she contemplated her life and her future; wondering if she was making the right decisions. From the corner of her eye, she watched surfers of various ages gather up their surf gear to call it a day. An older guy gave her the "hang loose" sign as he tied his surfboard unto the roof of a car parked next to hers. She smiled and returned the gesture, feeling much better afterwards.

Daylight waned when the sun parked its fiery mass on the horizon at the edge of the ocean. It momentarily skirted the water as if it wasn't certain it wanted to fully disappear—as if it had a choice. But just like it had for millions of years, the earth continued to rotate; leaving the sun behind so another young woman, in another part of the world, would have the chance to contemplate her future. So it was and so it shall be; forever and a day…

"Do you want me to speak to Travis?" he asked after a very long moment of silence had passed.

"No, that would only make things worse. We'll work it out. We always do…"

"If you want me to, I will…"

Kiara cut him off. "No thanks, GQ. Like you said, he'll come around soon."

"All right, well, I've got tons of work to do. I'll call you later."

"Okay. I'm headed home, now." The old surfer dude waved and tooted his horn as he took off. The remainder of the surfers left one-by-one as darkness gradually descended upon the beach.

By the time she ended up back at her dormitory, she had received a text from Travis. *Daddy loves you and we will work this out.* A happy smile erupted across her face as she felt the weight of her father's anger lift from her shoulders. She texted him back a simple smiley face, then bounced up to her room to study. All was right in the world again. At least for now.

Chapter Twenty-One

"*L*uis, if you're in there open up! It's me, Tomas." He pounded on the door again waiting for a response.

"Let me try," Ronnie insisted.

"Just stand back there with Joie and wait. I want to make sure he's cool. Give me a minute, okay?" He knocked again.

"Hold on a minute, *primo;* I've got to get dressed."

Luis told Carmen in hushed tones, "Gather your clothes and hide inside the bathroom. I can't let them know you're here."

"Why should *I* hide? They're not looking for *me*." She smirked.

Luis watched in amazement as the once beautiful Carmen seemed to morph into a creature resembling a snake. Her full pouty lips were now just a slit in her face allowing a long, forked tongue to protrude making hissing sounds. And all traces of a Spanish accent had all but disappeared only to be replaced by *hoodrat* speak.

"Look, if its money you want, then you'll get money, but I can't talk about it now. Will you please just get in there?"

"Fine… But hiding me in a toilet is *really* going to cost you," she replied as she gathered her clothes in her arms.

"Luis, I've got Veronica and Joie with me. So make sure you're decent before you open the door." Tomas turned and smiled at the ladies.

"I'll bet that muthafucka probably hidin' a bitch up in there," the security guard told the ladies.

"Who asked you? You're supposed to be here for our safety, not to give us your opinion," replied Joie.

"I'm just sayin' that homeboy shoulda opened the door by now. That muthafuckin' room ain't *that* big."

"Shut the fuck up!" Ronnie told the guard. She pushed Tomas back and pounded on the door.

"Luis, open this goddamn door! Now!"

Luis checked to make sure Carmen's clothes were nowhere in sight. He pulled on a pair of pants and then opened the door.

"Hey… What a surprise! What are you guys doing down here?" He yawned noisily, pretending to be just waking up.

Ronnie pushed past Luis and surveyed the room, looking for any clues of a woman. "Why did it take you so long to open the door?"

He snickered nervously and said, "It *is* after midnight. I was asleep."

"We came down here to check on you, *primo*. See if you're okay. Nobody has heard from you in days." Tomas looked around the room. His eyes settled upon a woman's overnight bag sitting in the open closet.

"Yeah, sorry about that. My cell phone died and I didn't bring the charger with me. Plus, I got food poisoning earlier today and was sick as a dog most of the evening."

"Why didn't you use the hotel phone near the bed? I know *that* damn phone works because I called you on it." Ronnie narrowed her eyes at Luis.

"You did? When? I didn't get any message that you called."

"Oh really? You didn't get the message? You mean *Carmen* didn't tell you I called?" asked Ronnie. She stood facing Luis with her arms crossed tightly over her chest.

While Ronnie gave Luis the third degree, Joie also surveyed the room, noting the box of *Imodium-D* on the counter. Nothing else seemed amiss in the room. Her eyes traveled to the partially open closet immediately recognizing the intertwined initials on an overnight bag that only a woman would carry. She and Tomas saw the bag at the same time. Their eyes locked; each wondering what to do. What to say. Joie noted the light coming from underneath the closed bathroom door. So did Tomas. So did the security guard.

"What do you mean you spoke to Carmen?" asked Luis. Unfortunately, there was no way possible to explain to Ronnie why that woman had answered his phone.

"I spoke to her while you were in the shower. Do you care to elaborate on that *Senor* Duarte?" Ronnie's hands made their way to her hips.

"Baby, don't get yourself overly excited. Stress isn't good for someone in your condition. How about I get my things and we can all leave together. You can ride back with me and Joie can ride with Tomas." He began throwing his clothes in the suitcase.

Ronnie's stance softened. You'd really drive back home with me tonight?"

"Sure, baby. Of course. We can leave right now if you'd like." Luis went to the closet and retrieved his suitcase, pushing Carmen's bag out of sight with his foot. He then ran around the hotel room, stuffing his suitcase full of his belongings. Afterwards, he wrapped his arm around Ronnie's waist and pushed her towards the door.

Suddenly the bathroom door burst open and Carmen came charging out half dressed and screaming, "Wait just a minute! You think that you're just going to leave me down here without a way to get back home?"

"Oh shit! I knew that was gonna happen! Told y'all he had some bitch up in here! Damn… She a fine one, too." The security guard licked his lips as if Carmen was a slab of baby back ribs.

"What the hell is that bitch doing up in here, Luis?!" Ronnie shouted, feeling as if her world had collapsed upon itself.

"Uh, uh, uh…" Luis stuttered. "Sweetheart, it's not what it looks like. Please, let me explain…"

Before she realized what she was doing, Ronnie hauled back and slapped Luis' face as hard as she could. She turned to do the same to Carmen, but changed her mind. It was Luis she was angry at because he was her man. Carmen was nothing but an opportunistic 'ho.

She hissed at Carmen, "I am not going to waste my time or energy beating the shit out of you. It's sluts like you who fuck other women's men… You are the worst kind… You don't give a damn about your life, so you're willing to fuck up everybody else's. Bitch, as far as I'm concerned, you can go straight to hell."

Carmen didn't know what to say. She had never been confronted by the wife or girlfriend before. Never looked them directly in the eye to see the damage she caused. Feeling Ronnie's wrath, the decent part that still remained, caused her to drop her head in shame.

Luis stood there staring at Ronnie as if his tongue had mysteriously disappeared from his mouth. He covered his cheek, feeling the sting from her angry slap. His brain seemed to shut down, as if to protect itself from the ass whipping that was surely to come. And like an imbecile he could only spew out meaningless words of apology. "Baby, it's not what you think. I'm sorry. She doesn't mean anything to me. Please, let me explain…"

Ronnie was furious on the inside, but somehow managed to portray a controlled calm exterior. She quietly spat out, "Fuck you, Luis. And fuck you too, Carmen. C'mon Joie, let's go. There's nothing left to see here."

Luis stepped towards his fiancée and shouted, "Ronnie, please come back! Let me explain. It's not what you think."

Unwilling to hear any of his lame excuses, Ronnie stormed from the room, giving him the middle finger on the way out. Joie followed closely behind.

Luis turned to Carmen. With eyes narrowed, his jaw clenched, and his fists balled up at his sides, he whispered, "Get... the hell... away... from me."

Carmen took one look at Luis' angry expression and grabbed her bag from the closet. "I'll find my own way back," she replied, grabbing onto the security guard for protection, before running from the room.

Tomas eyed Luis. Until now, he hadn't said a word. The situation seemed to speak for itself. He asked, "*Primo?* Why?"

"Man, that bitch set me up."

"Just please tell me you didn't hit that," he pleaded.

"Well, not exactly."

"Not exactly? How much exactly?" asked Tomas.

Luis stuck his finger inside his cheek. "Man, I really fucked up this time, didn't I?"

"Yeah, dude. I think you did."

"You know that I would never do anything to intentionally hurt Ronnie. Carmen is not who you think she is. She is a fucking, manipulative, lying, back stabbing bitch."

"If that's true, then don't let Veronica go this easily. Tell her what happened, dude. She's a smart lady."

"At the moment, I don't think she's trying to hear anything I have to say."

"Hey, I've got to go. They're waiting for me..." Tomas slowly backed from the room.

"Yeah, all right. I'm going to get the hell out of here, too. Don't know where I'll be staying. You got a couch I can chill out on until me and Ronnie can get this straightened out?"

"*Mi casa es su casa.* I'll leave the side door open for you."

"Thanks, man. And drive safely. You have the mother of my unborn child in your hands." Luis wearily ran his hands over his head and sighed deeply. "This isn't exactly how we planned to..."

"I already know."

"You do? How?"

"Joie can't exactly keep a secret. Now get home so you can get this mess straightened out."

"Thanks, Tomas. See you in a few hours."

Ronnie was absolutely beside herself and sobbing uncontrollably once she made it down to the lobby. The brave façade she put on in front of Luis came crashing down. Joie tried in vain to console her, but at the moment, she was inconsolable.

Stephanie handed back her license, sympathetically shaking her head. "I see she found him."

"Yeah, we found him all right," replied Joie. "Thanks."

"You're welcome." She hesitated before adding, "Ladies, let me share this with you. Sometimes what you see with your eyes isn't exactly the entire picture. You must look deeply within yourself to find the answers you seek. Whatever you think may have happened up there... Just give the man a chance to explain. I've been in this business long enough to know that *seeing* isn't always *believing*."

Ronnie listened to the woman and took her words in. The little bit of worldly wisdom was enough to calm her. She and Joie stepped outside to wait for Tomas.

"Life can be a bitch, huh?" Joie offered Ronnie another tissue. "What gets me is Luis had the nerve to sleep with his secretary. How fucking cliché is that?"

"Girl, I can't believe Luis cheated on me."

"Umph, umph, umph. It's a damn shame is what it is..."

"I guess he's just a man after all, prone to the same fuckups as every other man in this messed up world." Ronnie wiped her nose with her sleeve before accepting the tissue.

"Hold on a minute. I'm not trying to defend this man, but from everything you've told me about Luis, this don't sound like his M.O."

A nagging suspicion tugged at her consciousness. Ronnie glanced back towards the hotel. "Joie, something ain't right here. I don't know what it is, but I can feel it."

"Does this have anything to do with what *Miss Oracle* told you?"

"What in the world are you talking about?"

"Stephanie... The hotel clerk..."

Ronnie shrugged. "And...?"

"Don't you remember that black woman who played *The Oracle* in *The Matrix*? The light-skinned woman with the wedge cut curl..."

"Oh yeah, she did kinda look like her." In spite of herself, Ronnie chuckled out loud.

"Sounded like her, too. You sure it *wasn't* her?" Joie laughed.

"Could have been, and what she said did make a lot of sense."

The women let the lighthearted conversation momentarily lift their spirits, because at this point, any little distraction was welcomed.

Ronnie said, "Oh good, here comes Tomas. I can't wait to get out of here." The cool night air and the run in with Luis chilled her to the bone. She pulled the light sweater tighter to ward off the shivers.

"You ladies ready to go?" he asked.

"We're ready." They replied in unison.

"Are you going to be all right, Veronica?" He tenderly touched her arm.

"Yeah, Tomas, I'm going to be just fine."

"In spite of what just happened up there, he really does love you."

"Look, I know Luis is your cousin and all, and y'all stick up for each other, but right now, I am *not* trying to hear how much Luis loves me. Not after what I just saw."

"He's driving back to Santa Elena tonight and asked to sleep on my couch. I just wanted you to know that."

"Okay. Now let's go before you get too tired to drive us back home."

*   *   *

Luis sat alone in his hotel room contemplating the night's events. Good thing there wasn't any liquor in the room. Otherwise, he would have ended up being just another man looking for answers in the bottom of a bottle. This business trip to San Diego was supposed to make life better for him and Ronnie—for their baby. Not make it worse. Getting the Hernandez account was like hitting the lottery, but if what Carmen said about being a crucial element of the deal were true; the price to keep it was much too high.

He reflected upon Ronnie and the plans they made when they first got together. His dream was to return to the Dominican Republic and renovate that old hillside villa; settle down and raise a family, and open a graphics design agency in Santo Domingo.

To Ronnie's credit, she fully embraced and supported his dreams, focusing on a life filled with passion. They called it *living in the offbeat*. But he had fucked it up royally by putting on blinders—getting tunnel vision; trying to chase after the all mighty dollar. Ronnie had warned him about Carmen and told him to be careful. He unwisely dismissed her concerns as those of a jealous female.

Staring at his reflection in the mirror, Luis had an epiphany. Over the past three years, while he was busily chasing down clients to build his business, he had slowly lost himself, his woman, his unborn child, and the life he had always dreamt of. He knew without a doubt that if he continued down this path, he would end up living a life filled with nothing but regrets. Hell, they hadn't even made it back to the DR.

In a matter of minutes, he had possibly thrown it all away over a piece of ass. Letting Carmen get to him had been a huge mistake, of which he would pay dearly in more ways than one. He had let his guard down, believing Carmen was the real deal when she was nothing more than another gold digger.

"When did I forget what I was living for? Since when does wealth become the yardstick I measure myself by? I used to tell everyone who listened that living well isn't about getting more things—it' s about being surrounded by family. Well, I don't want to be "that guy" living in a mansion filled with expensive toys—alone and depressed. In Santa Elena, I see more miserable millionaires than I do happy ones. The time has come for me to fix this situation and I know exactly what I need to do."

Luis retrieved his toiletries from the bathroom. He tossed the box of *Imodium-D* in the trash, finished packing his clothes, and made his way down to the lobby to settle his final bill.

"Good evening sir, how can I help you?" asked the pleasant looking older black woman standing behind the counter.

He read her name tag. "Hi Stephanie. I'd like to check out."

"Certainly sir. What room?" she asked, still displaying that helpful, friendly smile.

"815," he replied.

Stephanie's demeanor changed in an instant as she typed in his information. She narrowed her eyes and smirked. "So, *you're* Mr. Duarte?"

"Yes, that's right."

"Humph!" she replied loudly, rolling her eyes.

"Is there something wrong?"

"Sign here." She slammed the pen on the counter and pushed the bill at him.

"All right." Luis signed her copy and took his receipt.

"I hope your stay was a pleasant one. Please keep us in mind the next time you visit San Diego," Stephanie said in a cold, robotic voice.

"Thank you. I will."

"Humph!" she replied again then muttered under her breath, "No good pretty-boy son-of-a-bitch."

"Uh, did you say something?" asked Luis, puzzled by the woman's chilly reception.

"Nope. Didn't say a word. Drive safely, sir." And she turned away and went into the back room.

He shook his head, remarking, "Hmmm, must not be my day to deal with women." Luis picked up his bag and headed to his car. As he drove through downtown headed for the freeway, he passed by Mr. Hernandez's family restaurant. With a grimace on his face and a bad feeling in the pit of his stomach, he signaled for a left turn, and merged in the light traffic headed north.

Chapter Twenty-Two

*I*n spite of his text to Kiara indicating otherwise, he was unable to get the situation with his daughter out of his mind. *That girl is so stubborn—but she's too young to understand that what she's doing isn't good for her. I'll just have to handle that situation later, but right now its first things first.* He dialed Monique's number. It rang several times before she picked up.

"Hello?" she answered out of breath.

"Hi Monique, its Travis, I hope I didn't catch you at a bad time."

"Good morning, Travis. I was just rounding up my kids to take to a babysitter so I could visit Grandmother. Being a single mom is a pain sometimes."

"You have children?"

"Yep. Two boys and a girl, and believe me; they are a handful."

Travis didn't ask about the whereabouts of the father, although he was curious. "I won't hold you then. I just wanted to know if this is a good time to visit Trudy. I wanted to drop in before I went to work."

"Visiting hours are nine to eleven. So you should be okay if you wait about half an hour."

"I'll do that. Will I see you there?"

"If I can get these kids dressed and in the car, I'll be there by nine thirty."

"Great. See you then."

"Bye." She hung up.

She has three children? And yet somehow Trudy thought Monique and I would make a great couple? No, thank you. I don't care how attractive Monique is, I haven't the slightest inclination to be around three of anyone's kids.

After he hung up from Monique, Travis called Ronnie next.

"Hello?"

"Hi Ronnie, did I wake you?"

"Hey Travis." She checked the clock on the end table. "No, you didn't wake me," she lied. "I was just getting out of the shower. What's up?"

"How are you?"

"I'm fine."

"Good. Well, the reason I'm calling is to let you know Trudy had a major stroke yesterday and was admitted to the Santa Elena hospital."

Ronnie sat straight up in her bed. "Oh no! Is she okay?"

"I don't know. I'm on my way over to visit her this morning. I just thought I'd give you a call and let you know."

"Well, thanks for the call." She rubbed the sleep from her eyes. It was eight thirty.

"You're welcome. I'm sure she'd be thrilled if you stopped by to see her."

"Yeah, I'll get dressed and get right over there." She turned over to tell Luis the news when the events from last night hit her like a ton of bricks. Of course, he wasn't there.

"Not to change the subject, but when are you coming back to work?"

"About that… Uh, we need to talk."

"Maybe I'll see you at the hospital?" said Travis.

"Yeah, yeah, sure. Okay… Just let me get dressed and I'll be over."

Ronnie managed to drag herself into the bathroom. It was well after six by the time they made it back from San Diego and with less than three hours of sleep, she was absolutely exhausted. The last thing she wanted to do was work, but since Trudy was in the hospital, her being in the office was more important than ever. After she showered, she trudged outside to the guest cottage.

"Joie? It's me. Hey Joie, wake up!" She shouted through the front door.

"Hold up, I'm coming…" The swish, swish, swishing sound of Joie's house slippers came down the hallway. "What's up girl? Why aren't you still in bed?"

"Is this what you look like first thing in the morning?" Ronnie laughed.

"Forget you, heifer. You don't look so hot yourself." Joie yawned. "Why are you up this early?"

"Travis just called. My coworker, Trudy, is in the hospital. I'm on my way over to see her and will probably go on into the office for a few hours."

"Sorry to hear about Trudy, but are you sure you should be going anywhere? You know you need your rest, especially now. And considering what happened last night, I would think you'd want to stay home and de-stress."

"Staying home isn't going to make me feel any better. Plus, Travis doesn't know I'm expecting. I haven't told him yet."

"So tell him. He's bound to find out sooner or later. There aren't too many women around who can pull off a full nine month pregnancy in secrecy."

"Anyway… Are you going to be all right staying here by yourself?"

"I'm sure I can find something to get into. Tomas has today and the rest of the weekend off. Maybe we'll hang out together."

"Suit yourself." Ronnie opened her mouth and let out an extended yawn. "Make yourself at home. The fridge is fully stocked and you know where everything else is. I don't expect Luis will be coming home anytime soon."

"Girlfriend, everything is going to work out the way it's supposed to. Ain't that what you used to tell me when I went through my stuff?"

"Easier to give advice than it is to take it. I just can't get the thought of Luis fucking Carmen out of my mind. His hands touching her body the way he touched mine." She shivered, but not from the cold.

"Now wait a minute Ronnie. Don't go jumping to conclusions. You really don't know what happened."

"Why are you so quick to jump to Luis' defense? You're supposed to be on my side."

"Because *I* know what it feels like to fuck up. I know what it feels like to not be forgiven and having to spend the rest of your life paying for a stupid mistake. To be judged. When I told Cedric about my affair, that shit devastated him and he couldn't forgive me. He didn't even give me a chance to explain myself."

"Well, it *was* a long term affair. *And* it produced two children."

"Damn it Ronnie! You don't have to keep rubbing my face in it. I know I fucked up, but I have to keep on living. As much as I love Maya and Trey, I will regret having that affair for the rest of my life. I messed up a perfectly good family to satisfy my own selfish needs."

"Two families… But who's counting?"

Joie smacked her lips, rolled her eyes, and then crossed her arms over her chest. "You ain't heard a word I said, have you?"

"So your point is that I should forget what Luis did and welcome him back with open arms? Did you really expect Cedric to take you back after what you did?"

Joie chose to ignore her jabs. "Listen, all I'm saying is to give Luis an opportunity to explain. You saw that bitch Carmen. You suspected she was up to something even when he didn't."

"You're right. However, nothing he says can ever justify why he cheated on me. He's just like Derek's lying-cheating-good-for-nothing-ass. God rest his soul," she added as an afterthought.

Joie pretended the zinger didn't hit home, even though she flinched at the reference to Derek's cheating. "Girl, get over it. The man is human and we all make mistakes. Look at it this way... You get a skank who looks like that offering up her cootchie to a man? Well, chances are they're going to take it. Maybe Luis did, maybe he didn't. But you won't know if you don't talk to him."

"I get what you're saying Joie and maybe I'll get to that place of forgiveness, but right now... Let's just say I have a lot of praying to do first." She started towards the door.

"I suppose you'll handle this situation the best way you know how."

"That's the only way I can... One day at a time, you know."

"I hope you don't plan on staying out all day. You look awful." She referred to the dark circles forming under Ronnie's eyes.

"Can't look any worse than I feel... If you need me, call my work number."

"Your work number?"

"Yeah, I forgot that I threw my cell phone against the wall last night. I'm going to get a replacement later today. I'll see you later."

* * *

Travis drove himself to the hospital in his modified custom van. The vehicle was a recent purchase that afforded him increased mobility and less dependence on his car service. To his annoyance, all the designated handicap spaces were already taken, so he ended up circling the parking lot several times before he found an open spot near the entrance.

The nurses at the station pointed him in the direction of Trudy's room. Because she was no longer considered to be in critical condition, she had been moved to a semi-private room with a view facing the courtyard filled with tall fan palm trees.

He wheeled himself in and observed a little old woman lying in bed, drooling from one side of her mouth. He had to look twice to make sure it was Trudy.

"Hi Trudy, it's me, Travis."

"T-T-Travis? What… are you… d-d-doing here?" she asked, using slurred, broken speech. She wanted to raise her hand, but her body didn't respond to her brain's commands.

"Monique called and told me what happened."

"Who?"

"Monique. Your granddaughter."

"Oh. Monique… Is she here?" Trudy looked around the room, her eyes glazed over in confusion. More drool leaked from her partially open mouth. The right side of her face sagged, resembling an overly ripened cantaloupe.

"No, she isn't here, yet. She's going to stop by later this morning," Travis explained.

"Oh good." She closed her eyes and began to snore lightly.

Travis felt sorry for Trudy lying in the bed barely able to speak. She had divorced her last husband several years ago because she declared him to be an old "fuddy duddy". Now she was simply alone. An old woman left to rely upon a daughter who was concerned primarily with getting the latest plastic surgery and a much too busy granddaughter— both who lived hours away in L.A.

Lost deep in his thoughts, a noise at the door startled Travis causing him to turn around.

A pretty woman, dressed in a pink ballerina's costume floated into the room, speaking a mile a minute on her cell phone, while balancing a large plant on her hip. She absentmindedly handed the plant to Travis, continuing her conversation.

"I promise I'll be there. Twenty minutes. Got it. No, I won't be late. I do realize how big this audition is. Yes, I will. I'm at the hospital right now. Okay. Good-bye mother."

She took a deep breath and gawked at Travis, "Ugh! That woman drives me positively insane. It's always, Monique do this. Monique do that. Remember such and such. Blah, blah, blah…"

Travis watched in amusement as the animated young woman flitted around the small room like a caged butterfly. Her hair was swept upwards into a lopsided bun and she wore sparkly ballerina slippers on her feet. It was obvious she was having a stressful morning.

"I'm sorry. Where are my manners? You must be Travis."

"That's right. Monique, I presume?" He pushed the plant back at her.

"The one and only," she replied and curtsied clumsily. "How long has she been out?"

She accepted the plant and placed it on the windowsill, alongside several other floral arrangements. She stopped buzzing around long enough to go to her grandmother's bedside where she bent over and kissed Trudy's forehead.

"Just a few minutes…"

"Shoot. That means I won't be here when she wakes up."

"I'm sure she'll understand."

"Did she say anything? How did she sound? Was she looking for me or my mother?"

Travis wasn't quite sure how much of his concerns he should relay so he simply said, "She sounds good. And, she did ask if you were here."

"I really wanted to see her this morning." She checked her cell phone. "I have an audition I have to be at in fifteen minutes."

"Ah… Now I understand the getup."

Monique stared at Travis and replied with a deadpan expression, "What 'getup'? My costume is in the car."

Travis blushed in embarrassment. He stuttered, "I-I-I'm sorry. I didn't mean… I love your outfit… In fact, pink is my favorite color."

Monique let out a sly smile then burst into laughter. "I'm sorry, Travis. That was mean. I couldn't help it because you walked right into it. Actually, I wore this outfit because Grandmother would've gotten a kick out of it. She loved taking me to the ballet."

Travis was amused at her wry sense of humor.

"This is also what I'm wearing to the casting call for a new comedy they're opening up in downtown Santa Elena. Mother found out about it and advised me to get my butt over there, especially since I'll be hanging out here for a while to help out."

"You got me good. Trudy didn't tell me you were a comedian."

"That's probably because she doesn't know."

"You mentioned your mother. How is she taking this?"

"My mother? She's fine. As long as I'm around, she knows grandmother will be okay."

"That's fortunate for all of you, then."

"Yeah, grandmother says I was just like her when she was my age—a free spirit." She turned to watch Trudy. "My mother believes I'm still "trying to find myself"."

Travis studied Monique closely. She was very pretty and in her late 20's or maybe early 30's. Her body was shapely, petite, and physically strong. Her hair was a rich blend of copper and auburn, much like the leaves on an autumn tree. And she had an energetic way of moving that left him wondering if she had ADHD as a child.

"One thing I've discovered is you'll never find yourself if you stop looking."

Monique stopped fidgeting and took a good look at Travis for the first time since she entered the room. *He sure is a very handsome guy. Charming too. Too bad he's in a wheelchair or I'd ask him to go hiking in the hills.*

Trudy stirred in the bed and awoke, appearing to be confused. Her rheumy eyes searched the room for anything that looked familiar. Something to help tell her where she was. "Who is that over there? Monique? Is that you dear?" she slurred, still half asleep.

"Yes grandmother, it's me. How are you?" she asked, moving closer to hear her soft voice.

"I'm fine, but what are you doing in that awful tutu?" Trudy managed a smile.

Monique went to the middle of the small room, did a quick twirl and another curtsy. "Does this meet your fancy, madam?"

"Yea!" Trudy gave what was supposed to be a brief applause using her good hand and fell back asleep with a smile on her face.

Monique heard the difficulty Trudy had with her speech and even noticed the slackness of her face. But she didn't let on to Trudy how much it disturbed her. She planned to speak to the doctors about her grandmother's condition as soon as the audition was over.

"That was wonderful! See, you did get a chance to see Trudy this morning after all. Maybe you'll even make it to your audition on time." Travis added pointing to the wall clock.

"I'm worried. Grandmother doesn't seem at all like herself. She looks so…old." Monique glanced at the shell of the once energetic woman, now lying motionless in bed.

"Give her some time. She's been through a lot." Travis offered up his encouragement.

She checked the time. "I've got to get out of here. Hey Travis, it was great finally meeting you. Grandmother was right. You are sweet. Well, I'd stick around if I didn't have to get going."

Travis knew he only had one chance to get this right. "Monique, would you like to meet for coffee or a drink sometime."

"Sure," she replied. "When?"

"You free later on today?"

"If I can find a babysitter, I am. Mother is supposed to drop by later, but she can be so unreliable at times. Call me and I'll let you know."

"Okay. I will. And good luck. Break a leg."

"Thanks. And don't forget to call." She left the room in the same manner as she came.

The nurses directed Ronnie towards Trudy's room. She purchased a floral arrangement from the hospital's florist shop before coming up. As she was about to enter the room, a petite woman dressed as a ballerina ran past her, almost knocking her down.

"Who, I mean, *what* was that?" Ronnie pressed up against the wall.

"Hi Ronnie. *That* was Monique, Trudy's granddaughter."

"I didn't know Trudy had a granddaughter. In fact, I didn't know Trudy had children at all. Dang, I guess I really don't know much about her," she whispered.

"Well, she does and that woman was one of them."

Ronnie leaned over Trudy to study her face. She stroked her hand and caressed her cheek. Noticing the drool running down her face, she plucked a tissue from a box on the nightstand and carefully wiped away the saliva. Turning her head towards Travis, she whispered, "How is she?"

Travis didn't want to chance speaking in front of Trudy, just in case she was awake. He motioned for Ronnie to follow him out to the hallway.

"Trudy's speech is pretty bad. I can barely understand her. She recognized me and Monique, however, it took a while and she fades in and out. She's lost most of the use of her right side, too. I am not a doctor, but from what I've seen in some of our clients I think she's going to need major rehabilitation before she gets back to normal. *If* she gets back to normal."

"That's too bad. I wanted her to stop working, but not like this." She sighed and returned to Trudy's bedside.

Travis followed Ronnie, noting the weariness that Ronnie wore like a too tight pair of pantyhose. "Hey, what's going on with you? You look really tired."

"I had a late night, but I'll be fine." She quickly changed the subject. "What happened between you and Kiara? She left a pretty emotional message on my voicemail last night. I tried calling her back this morning, but the calls go straight to her voicemail."

"I'm not surprised she called you. We got into it about her seeing Quinn."

"Oh… I see. Look Travis, I know it's going to be difficult for you, but you've got to let her grow up. Let her make her own decisions."

Travis held his hand up. "Don't. You do not know this man like I do, so please don't tell me that I'm being overprotective."

"So clue me in. What do you know about him?"

"Other than him being almost twice her age, he has a reputation at the university for dating young female students. He usually works his way through several girls by the end of the school year. Unfortunately, because of the charitable work that he does and the financial donors he brings to the school, the administration tends to look the other way."

"What? And Kiara doesn't know this?"

"Yeah, I told her, but said she doesn't believe me."

"Of course, she doesn't. So what do we do? She's going to Haiti next week. With him." Ronnie inhaled, exhaled, inhaled, exhaled…

"I'm going to speak directly with Quinn and tell him to stop seeing Kiara. It's obvious talking to *her* won't do any good."

"Unfortunately, you're right. She's very headstrong."

"That she is. I wonder where she got that from."

"What do you mean? I'm not that bad, am I?"

"When you get an idea in your head you become unbearable. It doesn't matter what anyone tells you because as far as you're concerned, you're right and everyone else is wrong."

She crossed her arms and thought about what he said, "Am I *really* that bad?"

"At times, you can be."

"Ouch."

The nurse entered Trudy's room to adjust the meds and check her vitals, after which she entered the results into an electronic keypad. As she was about to leave, she told them, "Trudy really needs her rest now. Maybe you two can come back later today. The next visiting hours are from five to seven."

"Okay, thanks," Ronnie replied.

"I need to get to the office anyway. We have a new RN showing up this morning to tour the center and I have to make sure she's given the royal treatment. What about you? Are you coming to work today?"

Feeling a wave of exhaustion overtake her, Ronnie dropped her head into her hands and closed her eyes. "Sure. I can come in for a few hours."

"Look Ronnie, I can see something is going on with you. If you need more time, let me know. I can hire a temp until we can make more permanent arrangements."

"No, it's no problem. I can come in and work half days for a while." *Plus, it'll help keep my mind off my troubles with Luis.*

"Very well, I'll see you at the center."

Chapter Twenty-Three

*K*iara stayed up practically all night, sucking down cup after cup of black coffee while she crammed for finals. And early the next morning, after almost oversleeping, she arrived with just enough time to take her last exam. After she handed in her final paper, she sent a text to GQ. *Finals were breeze. Free rest of day. We on 4 later?*

He responded back, *Must finish grading. Will c u this evening.*

She dialed Ronnie's number. "Still no answer. Dang, everybody must be like really busy this morning. Guess I'll go back to my dorm and pack for my trip."

* * *

"Kaylee, please see that Miss Moore gets everything she needs while she is here. In about an hour or so, the head nurse will take her on a personal tour of the center and show her the physical therapy facility, as well the patients' personal quarters. If she has any questions you all can't answer, be sure and give me a call."

"Sure, Travis. We'll make sure Miss Moore is well taken care of."

"Thanks. We want to make sure she's comfortable with her decision if she accepts the position."

"I understand."

"I have a good feeling about her. I think she'll fit in fine here."

"Hey Travis, when is Kiara leaving for Haiti? I think what she's doing is so cool. Wish I could go with her."

"I wish you were able to go, too. To answer your question, she's leaving in just a few days. That reminds me, I need to stop by the university. Would you check my calendar, please? Do I have anything urgent going on today?"

Kaylee pulled up his schedule, reviewed appointments and said, "Except for Miss Moore's tour, the rest of your day is open."

"Great. Block off my schedule for the remainder of the day. Oh, I almost forgot to tell you, Ronnie will be coming in later to fill in for Trudy."

"How is Trudy?"

"She'll be fine, but I don't think she'll be able to return to work anytime soon, if at all."

"That's too bad. Trudy is like a grandmother to me."

"I think we all feel that way about Trudy, but she needs to relax and probably retire soon."

Kaylee nodded.

"I need for you to put in a request at the temp agency for an experienced administrative assistant. Let them know we need someone ASAP because Ronnie is also thinking about cutting her hours."

"All right boss. Consider it done."

* * *

Ronnie arrived at the center just in time to see a red convertible backing into a visitor's parking spot. The driver of the sports car was a blonde who sported a cool pair of expensive shades and looked as if she had just stepped out of *Shape* magazine. *She looks very familiar.* Ronnie thought, unabashedly staring at the woman.

Rachel retrieved her briefcase from the convertible's tiny trunk. From the corner of her eye, she noticed a plump black woman staring at her. She was about to ask what her problem was until she recognized her old colleague. "Veronica Pierce? Is that you?"

"Rachel Moore? I thought that was you. What in the world are you doing way out here?"

"I'm here to interview for an RN position."

"*You're* the RN Travis told me about? That's wonderful!"

Rachel furrowed her brow. "What are *you* doing here? The last time I saw you, you were well on your way to leading that sports recruiting agency back in Virginia."

"Long story short, I moved out here to reunite with my daughter, Kiara. She's completing her third year at UCSE. Travis needed someone to work here and I needed a job. He offered and I accepted."

"Really?" She crossed her long tanned arms. "You know Travis Bradford personally?"

"Yeah, I've known Travis for years."

"Well, I only just met him a couple of weeks ago when he was on vacation at the resort in Sedona. He seemed like a really good guy and from what I read on the internet, this center is awesome."

"Yes he is *and* this is a great rehabilitation center. C'mon, I'll take you to his office." Ronnie led the way.

Rachel strode alongside Ronnie. "My boyfriend and I have been thinking about moving to California for some time now. We decided it would be good to put a few miles between us and my parents. They never liked him, so they have been trying to pawn me off on every eligible bachelor they lay eyes on. In fact, that's how I met Travis." She laughed.

"You don't say? Your parents introduced you to Travis? Did they know he was looking for an RN at the time?"

"Heck no! They only knew that he was a successful, handsome, eligible bachelor. He found out what I did over dinner one night. My mother just happened to "conveniently" invite us both to the same meal." She laughed again.

"Your parents tried to set you up with Travis because they didn't approve of your boyfriend, huh?" *That sounds familiar.* "What made you decide to come here?"

"After Travis and I recognized that we were the victims of my parent's scheming, we ditched them and got to talking about our personal goals. He described the center and what you guys are doing to help those with spinal cord injuries. It's my specialty, so I was very interested."

Even though Ronnie didn't believe in mere coincidence, she responded with, "Life is full of little coincidences, isn't it?"

Rachel cocked her head to the side. "That's enough about me. I know what you said earlier, but what are you *really* doing here? I can't imagine they have a need for a sports agent consultant."

"To tell you the truth, I got fed up living in Virginia, became disillusioned with my job, and with what I was doing with my life. Or not doing... Anyway, one day I decided to put my house up for sale, packed up my car, and drove cross country to Santa Elena. Like I said, my daughter goes to school at UCSE so I decided to stick around. I'm now engaged to a wonderful man." As she spoke the last sentence, she realized how accustomed she had grown to being Luis' fiancée. She twisted the engagement ring around her finger, wondering for how much longer it would be true.

"Good for you. From what I've seen so far, I think I'm going to like it here."

"Well, here we are." Ronnie stopped outside Travis' office and knocked loudly.

"Will you be around after we've finished with the interview?" Rachel asked.

"Probably not… I'm only working half days now and my girlfriend is in town visiting. I promised her we'd get together later."

"I understand. Well, if everything goes well today, you'll see a lot more of me."

"Come in," Travis called out.

"Hey Travis, I brought Rachel by," Ronnie replied, pushing the door open slightly.

"Great. Bring her in."

Ronnie stepped aside, allowing Rachel to enter. She remained for just a moment to say hello.

"Miss Moore, I see you made it. How was your trip?" asked Travis.

"My trip was fine. Got here last night." She tilted her head towards Ronnie and said to Travis, "Want to hear something funny?"

"Sure," he replied.

"We know each other." Rachel pointed from Ronnie to herself.

"You don't say," remarked Travis.

"Uh, huh. Veronica and I worked together on a couple of cases several years ago. We were just catching up."

Travis smiled, unsure of how much detail Ronnie had gone into about their relationship. He was a very private person who didn't want his potential new employee knowing more about his personal life than he was willing to share. "It's a small world." He decided to put it out there, so there would be no misunderstandings later on. "Did Ronnie tell you about our daughter, Kiara?"

Rachel stared at Veronica with a puzzled expression. "*Your* daughter? Um, not really. She said she came out here to reunite with *her* daughter. You and Ronnie were married?"

"Not married, but involved. Anyway, what's really important is that our daughter, Kiara, has both parents back in her life again."

Ronnie nodded in agreement. *Travis, you never disappoint me. You always were an honorable man who believes in setting the record straight from the get-go.*

"I think that's wonderful." Rachel gave Veronica a friendly shove. "I didn't even know you had a child back then."

"Like I said, it's a long story." She slowly backed out of the room. "Well, I'll let you two get back to business. I've got lots of work to do and not much time to get it done. Rachel, we'll talk later. I hope you accept the position. It's a fantastic center and truly a great place to work. Travis, you made a good choice with Rachel."

"Thanks Veronica. See you later." Rachel took a seat to begin the interview process.

After taking several minutes to confirm that his initial impression was spot on, he called his head nurse in to give Rachel a tour of the center.

While Rachel stepped out to use the restroom, he gave instructions to the RN she would eventually replace. "Please see that Miss Moore gets the full tour and has a good idea of what her duties will be if she accepts this position. You know I hate to lose you and you will be difficult to replace, but I certainly understand you wanting to move on."

The RN replied, "Don't worry Mr. Bradford, I'll show her the good, the bad, and the ugly about being head nurse here. If she comes back to accept, then you'll know she is right for the job. If not, better to know now than later."

Two hours later, Rachel returned to Travis' office beaming. "Oh my goodness, Travis! This center is amazing! When do I start?"

Travis replied with a huge grin, "How does two weeks sound?"

"Three would probably be better."

"All right, three it is."

"Perfect, that'll give us enough time to quit our jobs, pack our things, and relocate. Since we've already discussed my salary, I think we're good."

He offered his hand. "Welcome aboard, Miss Moore. I'm so pleased you'll be working with us. I'll have Kaylee send over the applicable documents first thing tomorrow morning."

"Please, call me Rachel." She accepted his handshake. "Thank you so much for this wonderful opportunity, Mr. Bradford."

"You are most welcome, and you can call me Travis."

"Travis, it is. Well, is there anything else you need before I head out?"

"I can't think of anything at the moment, but I'll be in touch. You're going to love Santa Elena. It's a beautiful place to live and there are so many things to do."

"From what I've seen already, I think you're right. We're spending the weekend downtown to get a feel for the city."

"The staff and employees are a close-knit group—almost like family."

Travis watched Rachel gather her things and his curiosity got the better of him. "Rachel, can I ask you something?"

"Sure, what is it?"

"You mentioned you were moving here with someone?"

"Yes, my boyfriend and I have thought about moving out this way for a while now. Why?"

"Well, it's just that your parents never mentioned you were in a relationship—committed or otherwise, not that it's any of my business. But why would they try to fix you up with someone when you were already attached?"

"I hope my having a boyfriend isn't going to be a problem." She paused, wondering where the conversation was headed.

"No, of course it's not. I was just curious, that's all. It just seems strange that your parents would introduce us knowing you were with someone already."

"Travis, can I be perfectly honest with you?"

"Of course… In fact, I prefer honesty."

She chuckled, "So do I. Well, my parents don't particularly care for my boyfriend because he's black. It doesn't matter to them that he is a very successful attorney with his own practice. Nor, does it matter that we've been together for years."

Travis shook his head. "You would think that at some point, race would no longer be important…"

"One would think, but whenever my parents meet a single, eligible, *white* bachelor, they automatically try to fix me up. It is so annoying and I've asked them to not do it, yet they persist. The night we met, I had no idea you would be at dinner."

"Oh, I see…"

"Is this going to be a problem? Because if it is…"

"Of course not. It won't be a problem at all. It is none of my business who you're involved with, I was just curious because your parents never mentioned him. Now, I know why."

"You know the old adage, 'You can choose your friends, but you can't choose your family'."

"Yes, I know it well." *Unfortunately, I know it all too well*, he thought, remembering how he and Ronnie were torn apart by her parent's intolerance.

"Anything else before I head out?" she asked, relieved he finally brought up the only issue that had bothered her since she considered taking the position.

"No, nothing else."

"Okay, well, I'll see you next month."

"Have a great weekend. And make sure you stop by the chamber of commerce. They have lots of suggestions for great spots to visit."

"Thanks, I'll do that." Rachel glided out of Travis' office, secure in the belief that she had made the right decision.

Travis was also relieved that the air had been cleared of any potential misunderstandings. Now he could work with Rachel Moore with a clear conscience of having hired her for the right reasons—that being her qualifications and experience.

He slowly exhaled thinking about Kiara and Quinn. Then he pulled up the university's website and dialed the cultural anthropology department. "Let the fun begin…"

"You have reached the University of California, Santa Elena campus. How may I direct your call?" asked the live attendant on the other end.

"Professor Gerald Quinn, please."

"One moment, please." She clicked off and returned moments later. "Please hold and I'll connect you."

"Thank you," replied Travis.

The phone rang several times and just when Travis was about to hang up, a man's voice on the other end answered.

"Hello?"

"Professor Quinn?"

"No, this is Lyle, his teacher's assistant. Hold on a minute and I'll get him. Whom should I say is calling?" the young man asked.

"Travis Bradford."

"Okay, hold on." He placed the call on hold.

Travis held on, listening to the DJ announce what was going on around town via the local university's radio station. He was embarrassed to realize he hadn't even known the university ran a radio station.

Several minutes later, an older man's voice answered, "This is Quinn."

"Professor Quinn. My name is Travis Bradford. I don't know if you remember meeting me, but I taught a few seminars at UCSE last summer. A mutual friend introduced us…"

"Travis, of course I remember you. How's it going?"

"Fine…" He paused to gather his thoughts. "Look Quinn, I'm not going to beat-around-the-bush with small talk. I called you because I need to talk to you about my daughter, Kiara. Can we meet somewhere for coffee or a drink?"

GQ held the phone in his hand searching for the right words. Even though he had expected the call from Travis, he was still caught off guard. "This is about Kiara? Sure… Of course. Where would you like to meet?"

"How about *Joe's Place*? It's the tavern at the corner of Alpaca and Zuniga Street. The wall facing the corner has a painted mural dedicated to local indie bands. You can't miss it. Can you be there in an hour?"

"I know where it is. We were just finishing up here. I'll see you there."

"Quinn, don't tell Kiara we're meeting. She doesn't need to know about this."

"As you wish. I'll see you in an hour."

Chapter Twenty-Four

After spending the night on Tomas' uncomfortable couch, Luis' entire body ached. "Yo man, you got any aspirin? My head is pounding like there's no tomorrow."

"Check the medicine cabinet," he replied stepping out of the shower, dripping wet.

Luis threw a towel at him. "Man, put a towel over that thing! I don't want to see you strutting around in the nude."

"Hey, this is the way I walk around my place—totally free and totally naked."

Luis checked the medicine cabinet for anything that resembled a pain reliever. He picked up a small bottle and asked, "What is this? Is this some new brand of aspirin?"

"What does it say on the bottle?"

"*Pamprin*. It's supposed to be a pain reliever, so I guess it'll work. What do you think?"

Tomas laughed. "I don't know. One of my ladies left those here months ago. It's supposed to relieve menstrual cramps."

Luis read the tiny print instructions. "If it's strong enough to take care of cramps, it should be strong enough to end this headache."

"Okay dude, but don't come crying to me when you start sprouting breasts."

"Right... Um, I don't think it works that way. You got any bottled water?"

"Here ya go. Catch."

Tomas smelled as if he had dumped an entire bottle of cologne over his head. Luis opened a window to release the overpowering scent.

"Where are you off to? Got another hot date with one of your 'ladies'?" Luis asked, fanning the air.

"No *primo*, I am going out with Joie. We're spending the afternoon together. I'm taking her up in the hills to Ojai where the air is clean and the people are friendly."

"Joie? Ronnie's friend, Joie?" Luis swallowed two *Pamprin*, almost choking on the water.

"Yes. So?"

"I think you might have overlooked the part about she's only out here visiting. The woman lives thousands of miles away on the other side of the country."

"I don't seem to recall you letting thousands of miles stop you from seeing Veronica."

"No, I didn't, but that was different."

"What was so different about it?"

"Ronnie was a normal person. Joie is something else entirely... I'm not really sure what to say about Joie."

"My point exactly. That is what's so fascinating about her. Joie is smart, funny and sexy as hell without even trying to be."

"Uh, you do know she has a couple of kids."

"Kids?" Tomas stopped dead in his tracks at the mention of children. He furrowed his brow. "Come to think of it, Joie never mentioned she has children. How many?"

"See. You don't know her as well as you think you do. I believe Ronnie told me she has a set of twins. Looks like you guys should talk more about the significant things if you're really interested in each other."

"Twins, huh?" He returned to getting dressed.

"Still interested since you know she has kids?"

"Is the father in the picture?"

"I don't believe so. Does it make a difference?"

"Damn straight it does. If there is a man around, then he will make nothing but trouble for the next dude involved with raising his children. If there isn't a daddy in the picture, the children will have only one father figure to listen to. That, my cousin, makes things a whole lot simpler."

"You're considering raising her children, now? Isn't that a bit premature?"

"I am telling you, *primo*; there is something about this woman that intrigues me. She makes me want to know everything about her. Makes me want to spend every free moment in her presence."

"Tomas, you never fail to surprise me. I thought you were a hard-core bachelor, but it sounds like Joie has gotten your nose wide open."

He chuckled, "Now I know how you felt when you first met Veronica. I get it. You would have gone to hell and back just to be with her..."

Luis diverted his eyes and walked into the other room.

"Hey, I'm sorry..."

"It's not your fault. I've got to fix this mess I've made. I love Ronnie, that's all there is to it. And now that she's pregnant…"

"What are you going to do?"

"I don't know. I've tried calling, but she won't take any of my calls."

"Give her time. It's only been a day. She's still angry with you."

"You're right." Luis ran his hands over his face, feeling a days worth of beard growth. "I need a favor."

"Sure. What is it?"

"I need to get into the house to get my clothes, toiletries and such. When you see her, can you please ask her to call me?"

"Don't sweat it; I'm sure she'll come around."

"I hope you're right. The problem is I know Ronnie and she can be as stubborn as they come. And if she doesn't come around soon, I'm going to have to look for a place to stay. This damn couch is killing my back."

* * *

This time, Travis used his car service, rather than drive himself to meet Quinn. He arrived at *Joe's Place* minutes before GQ and requested a table near the back for privacy. He glanced around the room at the other customers. Some sipped on coffee, while others who seemed to need it, downed shots of liquor. *I suppose it is five o'clock somewhere…*

GQ swaggered into the bar, strutting in as if he owned the world and everything in it. Upon recognizing several of the patrons, some were ex-students; he stopped and spoke with each and every one before making his way to Travis.

"Travis, my man. How have you been?" he asked, taking the opposite chair. He held up his fist for a dap.

To be polite, Travis completed the motion. However, instead of dapping Quinn's fist, he wanted to connect his fist with the man's jaw. "I'm doing fine."

"Taught any new seminars lately? The summer sessions will begin in a couple of weeks and the university can always use good instructors. The pay isn't bad either."

"Quinn, I am not here to catch up with you or to discuss work as if we were a couple of friendly colleagues. I simply want to know what your intentions are for my daughter."

"Intentions?" He laughed. "Man, look… The only *intentions* I have for Kiara is to make sure she has a good time and remains safe while in Haiti. What exactly are you asking?"

"I know about your reputation around campus. Everyone knows. I'm speaking to you as a concerned father, that's all."

GQ lit a cigarette and took a long drag, "And what reputation is that, Travis?"

"I've heard rumors that you like to date your students—young girls barely in their twenties. A new one every semester is what I've heard."

"Is that right? Well, let me tell you something…" GQ leaned forward, blowing smoke from the side of his mouth and away from Travis' face. "I don't give a rat's ass about rumors."

The waiter interrupted their conversation, "Excuse me gentleman, can I get you something from the bar?"

"I'll have a cup of coffee," replied Travis, without taking his eyes off Quinn. "Black."

Quinn sat upright. "Bring me the same, please."

"Two cups of black coffee coming right up."

Travis narrowed his eyes and whispered loudly, "Listen Quinn, like I said, I am speaking to you as a father."

"Go on."

"I truly don't give a damn what you do in your personal life with other consenting adults."

"The operative word is *consenting* adults, my friend."

"Kiara is legally an adult, but she's still very young and impressionable. She looks up to you because you were her teacher. In my opinion, and the opinion of many other teachers, you should not be violating her trust, or the trust of any of these other young girls."

"I see." He puffed on the cigarette until all that remained was the brown filter tip.

"No, I don't think you do. So, let me be frank with you. We're almost the same age and Kiara is *my* daughter. I want you to leave her alone."

"Look, man… All the students I deal with are adults. It's not like I'm forcing her *or* any of the other young ladies to be with me. Can I help it if I have a certain charisma with the ladies?"

"Quinn, don't you get it? Every year you get older, but the freshmen and sophomore students you "date" are always going to be 19 and 20. As a matter of ethics, don't you think the time has come to leave these young girls alone?"

GQ leaned back in his chair. "Why should you care who I'm sleeping with?"

"Jeez, man! You're almost twice my daughter's age *and* you were her teacher for Chrissakes! Don't you have any sense of morality?"

"These girls are with me because they want to be. I don't force myself on anyone." He protested.

"That may be true, but what do you think the Dean would say if he knew you were fucking half the student population? News about one of the university's most popular teacher's being involved with students probably won't go over so well."

GQ lit another smoke, this time he blew the smoke directly at Travis. "It that a threat?"

"No." Travis relaxed, feeling he was making progress. "I'm just telling you what I've heard."

"Ain't that a bitch? My sex life is fodder for the campus rumor mill?"

"Like I said, I don't care who you're sleeping with. But maybe *you* should."

The waiter brought over their coffee. "Is there anything else I can get for you gentlemen?" he asked.

"No, thank you," Travis replied for them both.

The young man placed the bill on the table, leaving the two men to their intense discussion.

"Kiara doesn't know that I've spoken to you and I hope you let it stay that way. As her father, I only want what's best for her. When she told me about this trip to Haiti, the only reason I was willing to let her go was because you were chaperoning the group. You are a great teacher. I know that from the rumors, also."

"I get that you're trying to protect Kiara. In fact, she mentions your over-protectiveness quite often." GQ sipped the hot coffee.

Travis smiled inwardly at Kiara's acknowledgement of his parenting tactics.

"So you're cool with her going down there with me?" GQ eyed Travis intensely.

"Volunteering to help out in Haiti? Yes. Her involvement with you? No."

"Travis, you did a great job raising Kiara." He inhaled the last of the cigarette and snuffed the butt in the ashtray. He glanced at the other patrons in the bar, noting a haggard looking woman perched at the end of the bar, tossing down shots of tequila. Succumbing to Travis' request, he acquiesced. "Okay, I'll break it off."

Travis exhaled his relief. "Do it right way, but please let her down gently. She shouldn't have her heart broken in the process."

"I know how to handle this. If I tell her now, she may not want to go to Haiti. You *do* want her to go?"

He pondered Quinn's concern. "All right... I'll let you do it on your terms, just as long as you do it soon."

"You have my word."

"Thank you."

"Humph! I was going to break it off anyway. She was starting to get a little too clingy," he replied smugly. GQ took one last sip of his coffee, threw a twenty on the table, and swaggered towards the door.

Travis murmured under his breath, "Arrogant asshole. What could my daughter possibly see in someone like him?"

Chapter Twenty-Five

At the Santa Elena International Airport, Ronnie walked Joie as far as she was allowed per the security restrictions. They stopped outside the security gate and hugged each other while a bored TSA agent looked on.

"Joie, even though we really didn't get to hang as much as I wanted to, I am so happy you were able to come out and visit."

A man's voice boomed over the airport's intercom system. "May I have your attention please? The passenger who left her handbag at the Southwest Airlines check in counter, please come to the security gate to claim it."

Joie double-checked her bags to make sure she hadn't left her purse by accident. "I wished I could have stayed longer, but I've got to get home to the kids. *Skyping* just ain't working no more. The twins miss their mommy and I miss them."

"I know you do. I can't wait to see them again. It's been so long, they probably won't even recognize me."

"They are growing up fast," she added. "Girl, I'm sorry about you and Luis. I really do hope you guys are able to work this out."

"Thanks. *This* has been our biggest challenge so far, so I don't know…"

"I know it's hard, but try to find it in your heart to forgive Luis. He really loves you."

"That's what everybody keeps telling me. What keeps bothering me is, if he loved me so much, he wouldn't have been messing around on me."

"All I'm saying is people make mistakes."

"I know they do. We all do. But honestly, once a man cheats on you, can you ever really trust him again?"

"That is the one question that only you can answer, girlfriend."

"Enough about me and my problems. What about you and Tomas? You guys make any plans to get together after you return home?"

"As a matter of fact, he's coming out to visit in two weeks. I'm going to show him around Hampton Roads and let him compare notes with So Cal. Santa Elena is beautiful and everythang, but it don't have none of that East coast *flava*."

"Maybe that's what I've been missing out here—the edginess of the east coast peeps. I suppose the beautiful scenery and temperate climate makes people too chilled out. Anyway, you'd better get going so you don't miss your plane."

"You gonna to be all right?"

Ronnie sighed, "I'll be fine. Other than the situation with me and Luis, I'm cool. The doctor gave me a clean bill of health and informed me that my pregnancy is going great for someone of my age."

"I know that was a relief to hear. What about Kiara?"

"She'll be headed to Haiti first thing tomorrow morning. Travis is having a small get-together at the house this evening to send her off and I'm supposed to be baking her favorite cake when I get home." She checked her watch.

"Wish her good luck for me." Joie embraced her friend. "I will miss you, Veronica Pierce. Take care of yourself and my unborn Godchild."

Ronnie laughed, "Oh, so you just know I'm going to make you the Godmother, huh?"

Joie pouted. "In spite of all we've been through, we have always had each other's back. And that sentiment extends to our children. So, of course, I expect you to name me as the Godmother."

"Girl, I'm just messing with you. I wouldn't have it any other way. Now get going."

"I'll see you soon, girl. And call me if you need anything." Hearing the announcement for her flight, Joie headed towards the security gate holding her boarding pass and driver's license in one hand. She waved at Ronnie with the other. And before handing her documents to the agent, Joie shouted out, "Keep the faith sister, everything is going to be fine!"

"I will. Have a safe flight and call me when you get home."

As she returned to the short term parking lot, Ronnie passed by a patch of decorative landscaping covered by exotic flowers native to California. A pair of purple butterflies flitted past her and landed on a *bird of paradise* flower.

"It's been years since the last time I spotted a purple butterfly and now they seem to be everywhere. Maybe I didn't need to see them until now, but I know why they're here. *A simple reminder of God's love.* I need it more now than ever…" And with a huge smile on her face, Ronnie got in her car and headed home.

*   *   *

"Daddy, did you call the caterer to confirm their arrival time at four?" Kiara tightened the towel around her damp hair. She continuously checked her iPhone every few minutes for updates on people either confirming or canceling their RSVP to her going away party.

"Yes, they'll be here at four. I hope you didn't add anyone else to the guest list. Fifty people should be more than enough."

"Half the people coming are *your* friends so don't blame me for the large number."

He laughed. "Can I help it if I'm proud of my little girl and want to show her off one last time?"

"Daddy, I'm not a little girl anymore. When are you going to stop referring to me that way?"

"I don't know. Possibly when you have children of your own."

"Whatever... Did you remember to call Mom to see when she'll be here? She's bringing my favorite 7up cake."

"No, sorry. I haven't had time." Travis wheeled into the kitchen wearing a worn out sweat shirt and matching pants.

"I'll call her." She glanced at her father's unkempt appearance. "You're not wearing that, are you?"

"What's wrong with how I'm dressed? You should be happy that I'm wearing pants today." He kidded.

"Daddy, that is not funny."

"Of course, I'm going to change. I promise I won't embarrass you in front of your friends."

"Thank you. Hey, are you like still okay with GQ coming to the house?"

"Uh, sure... Why?"

"No reason. Just checking. He mentioned that the two of you met for coffee."

"Did he now?" Travis wondered how much of their conversation he had shared with Kiara.

"Yeah. He said you men had a like heart to heart talk and you told him to watch out for me in Port-au-Prince. Said you went all Rambo and shit on him."

"Watch your language, young lady," he warned. "That's right. I asked him to keep an eye out for you."

"Will you ever stop worrying about me?"

"Nope. Don't believe I will ever *not* worry about you."

"Why? Aren't I becoming more responsible?"

"Yes dear, you are. But being a parent is like putting your heart outside your body and watching it walk away. I will always worry about you and want the best for you. You're my daughter and I will always love you—no matter how old you get."

"Aw, Daddy. I love you, too. Now go get dressed before our guests starts to show up."

"I feel sorry for the man who marries you," he teased. "You sure are bossy."

Kiara ripped the damp towel from around her head and playfully tossed it at her father.

"Hey watch it! You want me to put clothes on or not?"

Kiara stuck out her tongue and headed to her bedroom to change. She felt on top of the world and nothing was going to bring her mood down today.

* * *

Ronnie had just enough time after returning from the airport to bake the cake and get dressed before heading over to Kiara's going away party.

Once the cake was in the oven, she headed to the guest house. Luis had hired a maid service that came in once a week to clean, but she wanted to at least strip the dirty linens from the bed. She entered the apartment and headed to the bedroom only to discover that Joie had already stripped the bed and tossed them in the hamper along with the dirty towels.

As she was about to leave, the partially opened office door caught her attention. A stack of books at least a foot high was piled atop the small desk. The original covers were replaced with jackets listing V.I. Pierce as the author. Scrolling across the computer screen in large white letters were the words, *"Just do it! Sit down and write for heaven's sake."*

"Joie, you know exactly what to do to cheer me up." She smiled at the gesture and returned to the main house with a lighter heart.

She gasped out loud after she opened the kitchen door. "Luis, what the hell are you doing here?"

"I'm sorry. I didn't mean to frighten you. I just stopped by to get a few of my things."

"Why didn't you call first?"

"I rang the doorbell. I even called your cell phone and the house phone. When I didn't get an answer, I assumed you weren't home."

She swallowed the lump stuck in her throat, trying to catch her breath. It *was* still his house, after all. "I just got back from taking Joie to the airport. Go on and get what you need. I'll be leaving in a few minutes anyway. Travis is throwing Kiara a going away party today."

"I know. We ran into each other a few days ago. He asked if *we* were coming. Obviously, he doesn't know about our separation."

Ronnie crossed her arms and looked up towards the ceiling. She sighed heavily, cut her eyes down at him and asked, "And what did you tell him?"

"I told him I probably wouldn't be able to make it."

"That *is* a true statement." She pursed her lips together and started sucking her teeth.

Once she began acting this way, Luis knew she wouldn't hear anything else he had to say, so he made it quick.

"Look, I can come back after you leave."

"Yeah, that would be a good idea."

"Do me a favor and give this card to Kiara. It's the contact information for my cousin who lives in Port-au-Prince, Haiti. I've already spoken to him and asked him to be on the lookout for her… Just in case she needs anything."

Ronnie took the card and sucked at her teeth even more, if that were possible. "Thanks, I'll make sure *my daughter* gets it."

"Right… Well, I'll drop by after you leave. Is an hour from now good?"

"Sure."

The oven timer went off and she removed the cake from the oven, sitting it on the counter to cool. She went about her business as if he weren't there.

Seeing that Ronnie was now ignoring him, Luis decided it was time to leave. He almost made it to the door without saying another word, but he couldn't help himself. "Sweetheart, I am so sorry for hurting you. You and the baby mean more to me than life itself. Is there anything I can do to make this right?"

"Okay, you wanna make this right, huh? Answer me this… Did you and that bitch spend the night together in that hotel room?" she asked, slamming the box of confectioner's sugar on the counter. The white powdery contents floated into the air like dust.

He dropped his head. "Yes, but…it's not what you think. Baby, let me explain."

"Guess that answers my question. Goodbye, Luis." And she went into the bedroom slamming the door behind her.

Ronnie didn't leave the bedroom until she heard the front door slam and Luis' car back out the driveway. Funny thing was, in that moment, when Luis stood before her, she wanted to throw her arms around him and forgive his trespasses against her. Yet, at the same time, she wanted nothing more than to beat the shit out of him. She loved him so, but the wounds from the betrayal had cut deep.

"Luis Eduardo Duarte, I truly don't know how *or* if we can get past this. You promised me you'd love me forever. Forever ain't here yet, so when did you stop?" She spoke to the walls that had witnessed the special love they shared. This time when the tears began to flow, she let them.

*   *   *

"Ronnie, I'm so glad you could make it. Where's Luis?" Travis asked, looking past her.

"Um, he couldn't make it. Said he needed to put the final touches on some project he's working on."

"Oh, that's a shame. I was looking forward to seeing him again. Did he tell you I ran into him at the bookstore? He was carrying an armful of books he said he was buying for you—a bunch of those expensive hardcover books with the removable covers. I asked him if you were doing some kind of research and he told me you were finally going to pursue something you've dreamt of for years. I didn't know you had time to read like that."

What the…? So it was Luis and not Joie who fixed up the office with all of those books? Put that message on the screen encouraging me to write? Well, I'll be… She recovered from her shock and replied, "Actually, it's only been recently that I've had time to read."

"Well, anyway, c'mon in. Kiara's out back. And you can put that cake she's been talking about all day in the kitchen."

Ronnie laughed good-naturedly. "As soon as I told her I was baking this 7up cake, she's been blowing up my phone to make sure I didn't change my mind." She studied him closely. "You look different. Did you cut your hair?"

"Yeah, I'm trying to go for a younger look. Kiara has recently started referring to me as the 'old man'."

"I like the new style—it looks good on you. And you are far from old, because if you *are* old, what does that make me? Considering we are the same age..."

"Ronnie, you look great, too. You really do. In fact, you're glowing."

"Thanks."

"That Luis sure is one lucky guy. When we were in the bookstore, I congratulated him on your upcoming marriage and he was so overcome with emotion, he practically tripped over his feet trying to get out of there."

"That's Luis for you. He's not one to wear his emotions on his sleeve."

"I understand. Anyway, like I said. Congratulations!"

At that very moment, GQ seemed to appear out of nowhere. Overhearing only the last part of the conversation, he placed his hand on Ronnie's shoulder and asked, "I assume it is okay to openly offer my congratulations on the baby?"

"Baby?" Travis asked, looking from GQ to Ronnie and back again. "You're p-p-pregnant?!"

Ronnie glared at GQ willing him to disappear into the depths of the earth. Hearing his untimely outburst, she trembled with anger, all the while holding on to that cake.

GQ turned to face Ronnie upon realizing his blunder. "I'm in big trouble, right?" he uttered. "Hey, I'm sorry. I thought you were talking about your baby. Kiara told me you were keeping it a secret until the doctor gave you the okay. When I heard Travis offer his congratulations, I naturally assumed..."

"Is it true? You're really going to have a baby?" asked Travis.

Kiara chose that moment to bound towards the group; full of abundant youthful energy she seemed to possess so much of. She addressed Ronnie and GQ. "I'm so glad you guys are here. We were just about to start opening the gifts I'm taking with me to give to the orphans."

Ronnie glared at Quinn. Through clenched teeth she said, "Travis, I wanted to tell you. I was going to tell you... I, uh, was just waiting for the right time."

Kiara watched the unspoken emotions emanating from her parents. They both appeared distressed. She watched GQ rub his face as if he were also deeply troubled. "What's wrong? Why are you guys like acting so weird?"

"Why didn't you tell me Ronnie was going to have a baby?" Travis questioned Kiara, as if she were the enemy.

"Daddy, it wasn't for me to tell. I only found out by accident because of her big mouthed friend, Joie."

"Watch your mouth, young lady," Ronnie reprimanded Kiara.

"Dang! Why are you guys jumping on me?" She latched unto GQ's arm. "C'mon, let's go. We'll let them straighten this out."

GQ felt awful about his careless blunder. He turned to Travis and said, "I'm sorry. I thought you knew…"

Travis ignored GQ's apology. "Kiara, please take the cake to the kitchen. I want to talk to your mother. Privately."

"Okay. But don't you guys start fighting. I don't want anything to like ruin my last night here."

"Ronnie, do you have a moment?" Travis switched on his wheelchair and motioned for her to follow.

She trailed closely behind, listening to the quiet hum of the motor, curious about Travis' state of mind and where he was taking her. He followed a path through the trees. They ended up in the same clearing overlooking the ocean that Kiara had taken Ronnie to so many years ago.

"Travis, what are we doing here?"

"You and I have known each other for over twenty years. Back then, we were in a committed relationship. And today we're not only good friends, but we are the parents of a grown daughter."

"True. And…"

"It's time to define what *this* is."

"What do you mean—*this*?"

He sighed, "Do you remember when we first met? When we used to talk around important issues to avoid hurting the other's feelings? We would say everything except what we truly meant."

"Uh huh, you used to always call me out when I did that. You used to tell me to spit it out because it was easier to deal with shit when it wasn't covered in honey."

"That's right. We promised each other we would always be honest with one another, no matter what."

"Yeah, I remember. Guess I failed miserably there, too, huh?"

"I suppose we both did. Since we're now adults, we should be able to be honest with one another."

"Okay…"

"Ronnie, I've been holding on to something I should have shared with you when you first moved to Santa Elena."

"Look, if you're going to say what I think you're going to say… It's too late for us to get back together. That ship sailed long ago."

"If that is true, why are you having such a terrible time leveling with me? Why hide your engagement with Luis? And why did you feel the need to break the news about your being pregnant to me gently? What the hell is going on?"

Ronnie used the tip of her shoe to pry a rock free from the sandy gravel. The wasted motion was an attempt to help her process Travis' unrelenting questions. The rock was wedged in too tight; it didn't budge and her mind didn't clear. She shook her head trying to find a logical explanation for his very logical questions.

"It's complicated, Travis. I fell in love with Luis during my trip out here. I wasn't looking to get involved with anyone. It just sorta happened."

"Timing is everything, isn't it? Especially, when it's bad timing." He smirked.

"You said a mouthful."

"In all seriousness, weren't you ever curious about me?"

"All the time I was pregnant, I fantasized about what it would be like for us to be a family. And after I gave birth, I wanted nothing more than to be with you, but I listened to my mother and gave up my baby—our baby." She sighed again. "Anyway, after several years had passed, I resigned myself to the fact that you had probably moved on with your life."

"Except I couldn't because I was raising *our* daughter who reminded me of *you* every time I looked at her. I didn't have the luxury of moving on with my life. Kiara was a constant reminder of the love we shared and the love you so casually threw away."

She flinched at his honesty. "I often thought about you over the years, wondering where you were and how your life was going. I remember the day Lexi came to my house and told me you had raised Kiara from a baby…."

Travis turned and rested his eyes on a couple of seagulls playing in the surf. He wondered if they were the type of birds that paired for life.

"Look… I get that you're still angry with me. Don't you know that if I could turn back the clock to that awful day I left my baby in that hospital, I would? Each and every day of my life, I've regretted that decision."

"And what about me? Did you regret walking away from me? Turning your back on us? Throwing away the chance for us to have been a real family? Did you ever regret any of that?"

"Yes, Travis, I did. You want to know something?"

"What."

"For years, I blamed my parents for ruining my life; then it occurred to me that I was to blame for how my life turned out. It was my decision to leave you, not theirs."

"I was so ticked off when I received that letter asking me to give up our child. You have no idea how angry I was with you, Ronnie."

"I used to daydream about what it would have been like to be a real family—you and I together, raising *our* daughter. I remember we used to be so happy and to this day, I regret having walked out on you *and* Kiara, but what's done is done and we will never know how it would have turned out."

"You're right, we won't. No good ever comes from trying to live in the past."

Ronnie took a deep breath. She explained, "When I married Derek, I thought he and I would have children of our own and become like those families you see on television. Subconsciously, I was trying to replace what *we* were supposed to have by marrying another man. Since I couldn't have the family I was supposed to have, I tried making a family work with someone I shouldn't have."

"Considering where you are now, I can see that didn't work."

"No, it didn't. Derek and I didn't have any children because he already had kids from previous relationships. And you know what? After awhile, I used to resent taking care of his kids because they treated me worse than a stranger. For eleven years, I cooked, cleaned, and chauffeured those children back and forth to afterschool activities. Even took a class so I would be better equipped to help them with homework. You name it, I did it. I willingly threw myself into the role of being their mother."

"Wow! Seems like you took on quite a lot."

"I suppose I did, but you know what? At the end of the day, they already had mothers and I was just a poor substitute. After Derek and I divorced, do you think any of those kids ever sent me a Mother's Day card? Or even called to see how I was doing?"

"Did they?"

"Nope, because as far as they were concerned, I was nobody. None of his kids appreciated what I did for them for all those years. And the many times I spent wiping their snotty little noses, I was thinking about the baby I gave up. I should have been taking care of my own child instead of someone else's." She swiped away the tears from memories long past.

"Ronnie, I'm sorry. I cannot imagine not having Kiara in my life. When that hospital called and said you had left her there, I was willing to give up everything just to get her back."

"To this very day, I wish I had been as unselfish as you. I ended up paying for my mistakes by getting stuck with Derek. God has a plan, a purpose, *and* a sense of humor. And if you want to see all three, try to plan out your life. It never works out the way you think it will."

He nodded in agreement. "Whatever happened to your ex and his children?"

"My ex?" She chuckled. "He ended up fathering a few more kids before he was done. Even married the woman he got pregnant and left me for. What happened to his children? I'm not sure. I suppose they're all still in Virginia. Like I said, I was a nobody to them."

"That must have been tough."

"It was… He died shortly before I left Virginia."

"Seriously?"

"Yeah, he died unexpectedly following a short illness. Thank goodness, I forgave Derek years before he passed. God rest his soul. I discovered life is too short and much too precious to hold a spirit of unforgiveness in your heart."

"You forgave him, huh? That must have taken some work."

"You don't know the half of it. I figure I must have done something right for Kiara to have found me. God helped me to set things straight during all those years I was without her. And as much as I'd like to think that time with Derek was wasted… Well, let me put it this way. I learned the hard way that my life ain't always about me."

Travis nodded his understanding.

"So, as you can see, my life has been filled with many regrets. I wish I could take back the pain I inflicted upon you—on my child. Saying I'm sorry doesn't seem to be enough, but I am. I am so sorry."

"I accept your apology."

"Thank you. I know it's not much and we can never regain that lost time…"

"You know, for years Kiara asked about you, but I didn't know what to tell her. It was her idea to locate you, and she and Lexi did all the work. I only found out after the fact. We were both so excited to discover you were coming out here to meet her."

Ronnie smiled fondly at the memories from three years past.

"I'll admit there was a part of me that wanted us to pick up where we left off. See if we could reignite that passion we had."

"We were just kids back then."

"Like I said, I never had the chance to totally move on. I thought I had when Janelle and I were married, but even that turned into a tragedy. And then you showed up out of the blue… I never expected those old feelings to resurface."

"Travis, I love Luis, but I also never stopped loving you. You were my first true love. In fact, you were the only man I had ever loved until I met Luis. You raised our daughter and sacrificed so much of yourself to make sure she turned into the wonderful young woman she is today. Not to mention what you have done by overcoming your disability to create this magnificent center… I am so proud of you."

"Fine, I overcame my disability and you're proud of me," he said flatly, sighing in frustration. "Can I ask you a question? And I want your total honesty."

"Sure. What is it?"

"Did my being white have anything to do with your leaving me?"

"Of course not! You know me better than that; I loved you for who you were. It was my youth, my parent's influence, and life that interfered with our relationship. *You* did nothing wrong—nothing at all. And the color of your skin was never a factor for me. You asked me why I was hesitant to tell you about me and Luis. It's because there is a part of me that still loves you. That will always be true, but you have to know that our time has passed."

And that's when he finally smiled. "That is all I ever wanted to know. I love you, too, Ronnie. Always have, always will. You gave life to our child and I shall always love you for that. As far as you and Luis are concerned, I hope you two find all the happiness you deserve and more. I pray that the little baby you're carrying inside grows up knowing and loving both parents."

"Thanks." She paused. "Hey, since we're being totally honest with one other, can I ask you a kinda personal question?"

"Shoot."

"You don't have to answer if you feel uncomfortable."

"Woman, just ask me…"

"Uh, with the accident and all… I've always wondered… Does your equipment still work? I'm just asking out of curiosity."

He looked at Ronnie first with a smile and then he laughed out loud. "Veronica Pierce? Now what kind of a question is that to ask a man in a wheelchair?"

"Well, does it?"

"Considering I am a paraplegic, thankfully, I am still able to have an active sex life. You'd be amazed how imaginative a wheelchair bound man can be when it comes to intimacy. So, to answer your question… Yes, my *equipment* works just fine when I have the opportunity to use it. Why? Do you want to check it out for yourself?" A devilish grin tugged at the corners of his mouth.

"No, I don't want to 'check it out'. Although for your sake, I am happy to hear you can still get your groove on. From what I remember, you were truly blessed in that department."

"You are something else." He joined in her laughter.

When the laughter finally subsided, they looked at one another with a newfound appreciation and respect. Ronnie's confession had finally allowed her to let the walls down, exposing the main reason for her reluctance in marrying Luis. On a deeper level she had punished herself because she felt guilty about Travis' accident, how he had singlehandedly raised Kiara, and her absence in both of their lives.

Travis realized he had been stuck in the past waiting for Ronnie to open her eyes and see how much he loved her still. Without knowing it, they were both waiting on the other before they could truly move on with their lives.

Ronnie stooped down to Travis and threw her arms around his neck. She nestled her head on his chest, listening to his strong steady heartbeat, and they both cried the tears they had kept pent up inside for too long. And in that little clearing overlooking the ocean, Travis and Ronnie consoled one another and grieved for the life they would never have together.

"Friends?" asked Ronnie looking up, trying to dry her tears.

"Through thick and thin," replied Travis. As if on cue, he produced a handkerchief and gently dabbed her tears away.

The sound of rustling leaves drew their attention to the path. Kiara bounded through the trees and into the clearing, out of breath from running. They both looked up at their daughter and smiled.

"There you two are. I've been looking for you guys all other the place. You guys okay" she asked, catching weird vibes coming from them both.

"We're fine. We were just catching up. What's going on?" Travis replied.

"This lady… I think she said her name was Monique, is looking for you. She said you invited her."

Travis slapped his forehead. "Jeez! I forgot I invited her. Where is she?"

"*She's* in the backyard telling my friends about some Broadway play she like performed in. She seems like a very interesting lady."

Ronnie butted in, "I think we've covered everything, right, Travis?"

He nodded, "Yeah, we're good. Wanna head back to the party now?"

"Okay, lead the way."

She and Kiara followed Travis. Ronnie sighed inwardly as they walked quietly—each one lost in their own private thoughts, back to the house. Only the soft whir of his motorized wheelchair and birds singing in the trees broke the silence. *This is so nice. Just the three of us on a nature walk. This is how my life was supposed to turn out. How it would have been had I not been so damn selfish.…* After walking another half mile or so, the spell was broken; they were back at the house filled with people arriving for Kiara's going away party.

Kiara pointed to Monique. "See, that's her over there."

Travis smiled at Ronnie. "Would you please excuse me? I invited her, so I feel obligated to make sure she's comfortable."

"Daddy, I don't think you have to worry about that. Monique seems to feel quite at home already. She even brought her bratty kids with her and they have been running all over the place," she told him, rolling her eyes in annoyance.

"Is that right? I seem to remember you were also quite a handful when you were their age. Or are you too old to remember that?"

"Whatever. I just wish they'd like stop throwing water balloons all over the place. They've already hit my friends several times," she complained.

"Relax. I'm sure your friends all have little brothers and sisters who do the same thing."

"None of *my* friends brought their brothers or sisters with them, did they?"

Ronnie interrupted the banter between father and daughter. "I was leaving anyway. I just wanted to stop by for a few minutes to drop off the cake. I'm really beat."

"Mom, I am so glad you stopped by and thank you so much for baking my favorite cake. I sure will miss your cooking."

"You're very welcome and it was my pleasure."

"Will you be at the airport tomorrow morning?"

"Of course, I'll be there. I wouldn't miss seeing you off for anything." She hugged her woman-child tightly, missing her already. "What time are you leaving?"

"Our flight leaves at six o'clock."

"That early, huh? All right, I'll be there. I almost forgot; Luis gave me this card to give to you. It contains his cousin's information. He's a doctor in Port-au-Prince and Luis asked him to keep an eye out for you."

"You guys worry too much about me." She took the card and tucked it inside her bra. "I'll hold on to it just in case I need it," she replied, glancing over at GQ who seemed to be engrossed in a private conversation with an attractive young woman. "Well, I'd better get back to my guests. I'll see you later."

"See you in the morning." Ronnie's gaze connected with Travis' as they watched Kiara stroll over to GQ. Her casual gait was more womanly than childish—full of self-assurance and confidence. On the other hand, GQ's relaxed stance changed as he shifted his focus from the young lady to Kiara.

"What's going on with them?"

"I told GQ to break it off with Kiara after they get to Haiti."

"What did he say?"

"The arrogant bastard told me he was going to break up with Kiara anyway. Apparently, she was getting a little too 'clingy' for him."

"Why did you ask him to wait? Why not do it now and just get it over with?"

"If he broke up with her now she probably wouldn't want to go to Haiti. I don't want to ruin that part of this for her. Thought it would be best if he waited."

"Uh, don't be so sure about that. I saw how excited Kiara is about this trip and it's not all about being with GQ."

"Really?"

"She honestly believes she can make a difference in those people's lives. I think she would have gone regardless of him."

"I hope you're right."

"Travis, for someone who has been around Kiara all her life, sometimes I think you don't know her at all. That child is not going to go into some deep depression because of Gerald Quinn ending their relationship. I got the impression she was getting bored with him, as well."

"Women! I'll never figure you guys out." He observed Monique headed their way. "Hold on a moment, I want to introduce you to my new friend."

Ronnie recognized the woman from the hospital. *That's that woman who was dressed in that outrageous tutu who almost knocked me down.*

"Travis, there you are."

Monique was dressed in a very pretty silk top and knee length shorts. She carried a bottle of beer in one hand and a plastic grocery bag filled with water balloons in the other. Three small children trailed closely behind.

Travis' face lit up at the sight of Monique. "I'm glad you could make it. Ronnie, this is Monique, Trudy's granddaughter, and her children. Monique, this is Ronnie—Kiara's mother."

"Pleased to meet you."

One of the boys ran up to Monique and took away the bag of water balloons. He pulled out a blue balloon and threw it at his sister, soaking her sundress. The little girl retaliated by throwing two red ones, making a direct hit on her brother's back.

"Nice to meet you, too." Ronnie glanced over at the kids chasing each other around the yard. "How old are they?"

"My daughter is eight and the boys are five and six."

"They sure do have a lot of energy."

"Yep, and there's never a dull moment in my house. That's why I love outdoor parties. My kids can burn off all that energy and I can keep an eye on them at the same time."

"Is your husband here, also?" Ronnie asked, being nosey.

"No husband. He took off for good shortly after he returned from Iraq. I lovingly refer to my kids as "war babies" because I got pregnant every time he came home from a deployment. I hope his aim with a gun was as good as his sperm's were with my eggs."

"I'm sorry. I didn't know…"

"That's all right. My ex wasn't a bad guy, but he came back with so many unresolved issues from the war that it was probably best for him to leave. He sends the kids birthday cards, Christmas gifts, etc., but that's about the only contact we've had from him in years." She shrugged.

Ronnie watched the children throw the balloons at each other. "It must be difficult raising three children on your own. How do you do it?"

"We make due and my mother helps out quite a bit. Since Trudy got sick, me and the kids have temporarily moved in to keep an eye on her. They love it here in Santa Elena and so do I."

"How is Trudy? Didn't they move her to an assisted living center?"

"She's doing much better, thanks for asking. In fact, we brought her home a couple of weeks ago because she prefers being surrounded by her own things."

"That's great!"

"Yeah… Me and the kids living with her is working out very well. She loves having them in the house. Says all that activity helps to keep her young."

"Please give her my love when you see her."

"I will," she replied.

Ronnie took notice of Kiara across the yard. She stood with a small group of her friends laughing and having a good time, listening to music blare through the outdoor speakers. GQ was nowhere to be seen. The caterer had arrived on time and one of Travis' friends manned the grill. The strong aroma of grilled ribs, burgers, and hotdogs permeated the air. Usually she loved barbecue, but ever since she found out she was pregnant, the smell of charred meat turned her stomach.

"Hey you guys! Don't go too far! Remember, if you can't see me, I can't see you!" Monique shouted at her kids.

Up until then, Travis sat idly by casually listening to the women's conversation. He didn't know anything about the whereabouts of Monique's children's' father and hadn't felt comfortable asking. Also, up until that moment, he really hadn't cared. Watching her kids play, Travis suddenly realized how much he missed that noise.

"I would offer you a drink, but I see you've already made yourself at home. How long have you been here?" Travis said.

"Not very long. I was just telling Kiara's friends how difficult and un-glamorous it is to be an actress on Broadway. Of course, they didn't believe me. To them it was just 'sweet'." She laughed.

Ronnie's interest was piqued by Monique's history. She decided to stick around a few minutes little longer. "New York City? Broadway? I must admit, being an actress does sound very interesting. I bet you have a million stories to tell about what went on behind those curtains."

"Oh yeah! You know I do, girl. Don't get me wrong, acting on Broadway *was* exciting. I just didn't want these young girls to get any ideas about acting at least until they finished college. I didn't finish and look where it got me."

"You seem to be doing okay."

"I could be doing better."

"We *all* could be doing better. I'm just saying."

Monique grinned. "Touché."

"You're cool people. We should get together sometime."

"Just say when. Until I find a job, I have nothing but time on my hands."

"What kind of job are you looking for?" Ronnie asked.

"I can do practically anything. I'm a jack of all trades," she joked.

"I'll keep my ears open. Well, I've got to do. You guys have a good time and I'll see you tomorrow." Ronnie affectionately touched Travis's shoulder.

"Thanks again for stopping by. See you tomorrow," added Travis.

Chapter Twenty-Six

*R*onnie stared blankly at the picture of the Grand Canyon before ripping it off to get to the next month. The calendar displayed twelve scenic pictures from various national state parks. She and Luis chose that particular calendar because they vowed to visit each and every park in less than a year. She held the picture of the Grand Canyon, the month of August, in her hand. The *Half Dome* from Yosemite National Park was featured for September. So far, they hadn't visited any. She balled up the paper and tossed it in the trashcan.

Life goes on as it always does; not stopping because of a failed relationship, a child who moves far away, or even feeling a baby growing inside my body. It's been three months since Luis moved out and just as long since Kiara went to Haiti. I don't know what to do with myself, but I do know I can't continue on like this.

She picked up the phone and began punching in numbers to connect with the one person who always understood her angst. Her mother answered on the first ring.

"Hi Mama."

"Well, it's about time you called to check up on your mother. How long has it been, anyway?"

"It's been awhile. I've been pretty busy lately and unfortunately let time get away from me. Anyway, do you have a few minutes to talk?"

"Child, all I got is time."

"I won't keep you long. I just needed to hear your voice, Mama."

"That's fine. So tell me, how is my granddaughter?"

"Kiara is great. Actually, she's in Haiti for the summer."

"What in the world is she doing down there?"

"She's been there for several months already and is supposed to return in a couple of weeks. *Your* granddaughter decided she wanted to volunteer to help rebuild the country after that earthquake. She and a group of students from her school went down to Port-au-Prince to volunteer."

"Bless her heart! That child has a heart of gold, just like her grandfather."

"Yes, she does. I am so proud of her."

"Send me her address. I'll put a few things in a box to send down there. Maybe I can get the church to donate some money to help out. I hear them folks got a long way to go before that country gets right again."

"That's a good idea. I'll text you her mailing address as soon as we hang up."

"So how are you and Luis doing?"

"Uh, that's one of the reason's I'm calling… Mama, I've got some good news and some bad news. Which do you want to hear first?"

"You know me. I always say get the bad mess out of the way so you can appreciate the good."

"Okay. First the bad news; me and Luis are taking a break from each other for a little while."

"Aw baby, I'm sorry to hear that. How long of a break are you talking about?"

"It's going on three months. That's one of the reasons I hadn't called. I've been trying to figure out what I'm going to do."

"Oh… What did he do? Is there a woman involved?"

Ronnie almost regretted telling her mother because she didn't want her to think she had made another bad choice of men. "What makes you think he did anything? Why couldn't we just be taking a break?"

"Because don't no woman let a handsome, successful man like Luis go unless he done did something wrong. Did he cheat on you?"

Ronnie wanted to lie—to keep Luis from being the stereotypical brother who couldn't keep his dick in his pants. "I don't know if he technically cheated or not, but let's just say I caught him in a compromising position."

"And what exactly do you call a 'compromising position'?"

"I really don't want to go into specifics. Let's just say I have good reason to not trust him."

"That means it *is* some woman. Have you talked to him about it, yet?"

"No, there's really nothing to talk about."

"Is that so? How in the world do you expect to get to the bottom of what happened if y'all don't talk?"

"To tell you the truth, I was too busy being angry to think about how we're going to get past this. *If* we can get past this."

"Child, pick up that phone and call that man. Tell him to get his butt over to the house so you two can talk. What you two have is too good to throw away over some foolishness."

"How would you know?"

"I just do."

"Please, Mama, I need for you to be upfront with me, especially now." Ronnie heard the pregnant pause on the other end, realizing whatever her mother was about to say must be difficult.

"I *know* because me and your father went through episodes of infidelity ourselves. I could have put him out and ended the marriage, but we loved each other. He admitted his mistakes and we worked through them. In the end, we both decided being together was more important than letting some foolish mess break us up."

Ronnie gasped in surprise. "Daddy cheated on you?"

"All I'm saying is your father was no saint. Neither was I, for that matter."

"Mama? Are you saying Daddy...? That you...?"

Dianna quickly changed the subject. She and Vernon had made a pact to never speak of their indiscretions, vowing to keep them buried in the past where they belonged. "Enough about me child. What is your good news?"

"Uh, uh, I almost forget what I wanted to tell you," Ronnie tried to regain her composure.

"Spit it out, girl. I'm dying of suspense."

Still surprised by her mother's revelations, she muttered, "Okay, here goes. I...uh... We're... Luis and I... Oh, to heck with it! I'm pregnant, Mama, We're going to have a baby!"

"Say what? You're pregnant? Seriously?"

"Yeah, I found out a few months ago, but I think you already suspected it before I knew it myself—that time when I thought I had the flu."

Dianna said, "You're that far along and you're just now telling me?"

"I have a lot going on and I just wanted to make sure the baby was going to be okay. I *am* what they call an 'older mother'. Oh, and Luis proposed." She added as an afterthought.

"Wait a minute... Did just you say Luis proposed?"

"Yes. He asked me to marry him the night before I found out I was carrying his child."

"You know what this means, don't you?"

"What?"

"It means that Luis loves you enough to want you as his wife. And whatever happened to break the two of you up... Veronica, let me put it this way; no man is going to ask a woman to marry him, find out he's going to be a daddy, and then go out and screw a whore to celebrate."

Ronnie was surprised by her mother's colorful language. "I know he loves me, but he disrespected me, Mama. I can't just let that go like it was nothing."

"I'm not saying to forget it like it was nothing. Eventually, you will have to forgive him."

"I know…"

"Luis *needed* to feel the sting of knowing what life is like without you, whether he did anything or not. This way, he will appreciate you even more when you take him back."

"Daddy didn't have a chance with you, did he? You are something else, you know that?"

"Vernon, God rest his soul, knew what he had in me. That's why we stayed together so long."

"Mama, all I ever wanted was to have what you and daddy had. I thought I had found my lifelong partner in Luis."

"You most likely have. And if you have, I'd advise you to hang on to it because you may only meet that person once in a lifetime. Vernon was mine. That's why I never got remarried."

"Mama, what if Luis is *my* once in a lifetime person?" Ronnie thought about how lonely her mother must've been after her daddy died. "How do you know so much about relationships?"

"When you get to be as old as I am, you will have experienced enough life to pass on some important lessons to your daughter. *Lesson one:* Don't let no hussy break up your home, chile."

"I do have half a mind to confront the conniving little bitch."

"If you know who she is, why don't you? If the little tramp was woman enough to mess with your man, she should be woman enough to deal with you."

"I can't stand the thought of being in the same room with that bitch, much less speaking to her."

"Don't you dare stand idly by and let some woman take what's yours. You are a Pierce woman."

"What am I supposed to do?" she asked.

"It's not just about you anymore, sweetheart. You are carrying that man's child and the least you can do is give him another chance."

"I cannot be with a man I can't trust."

"Remember all that talk about forgiveness you used to preach to me? Well, maybe it's time you started practicing what you've preached to everyone else. Forgiving isn't only done when it's convenient."

Ronnie held the phone away from her ear, very tempted to hang up on the truth her mother had so profoundly delivered. Just as she was about to start protesting about how her situation was different, the doorbell rang.

"I've got to go. Somebody's at the door."

"I hope you take heed to what I've told you. Stop being so doggone stubborn and take care of your business. Oh, I almost forgot to tell you the local good news. It'll only take a minute."

The doorbell rang again. "Okay, what is it?" She started towards the door.

"Remember that local group of five young men you were going on and on about? They call themselves *The Kamals*? Well, my friend Olevia told me that they were picked up by a major record label and will be touring the country soon. Supposed to be on that late night show with that funny-looking man... What's his name? Never mind, I can't think of it right now. Yes siree, those young men are on their way to the top. And that lead singer can really play that guitar."

"That's good news! I knew there was something special about *The Kamals* the first time I saw them perform."

"Only goes to show you that persistence pays off. Slow and steady wins the race. Of course, being talented also helps," Dianna said.

The doorbell rang again.

"Sorry to cut you off, Mama, but I've really got to go. I'll call you later. I love you. Bye."

Ronnie peeked through the curtains and saw a deliveryman standing there balancing two huge vases filled with roses. One dozen red; the other white. The expression he wore on his face indicated he was in a hurry.

"Delivery for Miss Veronica Pierce," said the driver when she opened the door.

"These are for me? They're gorgeous!" she exclaimed.

"Sign here ma'am." The driver thrust a clipboard towards her hands.

"Thank you." She took the flowers in her arms and tried to push the door closed with her foot.

"Just a minute, ma'am. I have a couple more vases for you in the van."

Ronnie placed the flowers on the hallway table and waited for the deliveryman to return. The fragrance wafting from the flowers was heady and sweet. She leaned over and inhaled.

The deliveryman returned with two more colorful floral arrangements. "These vases are a bit heavier. Where do you want them?"

"That table over there is fine." She pointed to the coffee table in the living room.

After the deliveryman left, she plucked the card from the first bouquet of red roses. She immediately recognized Luis' writing. The card read: *To the love of my life, I love you now and I always will.*

With her mother's advice fresh on her mind and the scent of Luis' roses permeating throughout the house, she began to miss her man with a fervor she couldn't control. *I can't take this anymore. I've got to fix this mess—one way or the other.*

Ronnie called the one person who could help her get to the bottom of this mess in no time flat. "Hi Tomas."

"Veronica? What a pleasant surprise," he stated.

"Do you have a few minutes to talk?"

"*Sí*, hold on a moment. I will step outside."

She heard the background noise of wherever it was he worked. After a minute or so, he came back on the line.

"What's going on? Are you all right?" he asked with concern.

"I'm fine. No, I'm not… Look Tomas, I need your help." She took a deep breath to help steady her nerves.

"Of course, what can I do for you?"

"Didn't you tell me you recommended that woman to Luis? That Carmen bitch?"

"I did, but I had no idea she would come on to my cousin, considering she's married with children."

"I'm not blaming you."

"How can I help?" He nodded at his coworkers as they headed out to lunch.

"I want to talk to that woman face-to-face. I need to find out for myself what happened in that hotel room."

"Have you spoken to my cousin about this yet?"

"No. I want to hear what happened directly from that skank's mouth. It's not like I don't trust Luis, but him being a man, I don't think I'm going to get the absolute truth out of him. He'll leave something out of his story."

"That does not sound like trust to me." He sighed. "So what specifically do you want me to do?"

"I want you to arrange a meeting between us."

"You want *me* to arrange a meeting with Carmen?"

"Who better?" Repeating her mother's words, she said, "If that 'ho was woman enough to mess with my man, she should be woman enough to deal with me."

"I understand. I'll see what I can do. Let me call you back in a minute."

"Thanks." She tossed the cell phone on the couch.

Ronnie wandered around the house going from room to room, stressing over what she would say if Tomas was able to arrange a meeting. She slipped one of Luis' favorite *merengue* CDs into the stereo. While the music played on, she listened to the sliver of silence that resided in the offbeat. In that miniscule place between each note resided an indescribable state of joy. It was what she missed in her life. At one time she and Luis had it; and now she would do anything to get it back. Hearing laughter in the background of one of the songs, she felt as if years had passed since they played any music and longer still since they had danced together.

Her cell phone rang. She took a deep breath before she answered.

Tomas said, "She agreed to meet, but only if there is no drama involved."

"Okay. What time?"

"I can pick you up after I get off work—around four. And I will be with you to keep things civil because her children will be home."

"C'mon... It's not like I plan on shooting the bitch. I just want to talk to her."

He wanted to tell her that her plans of "just talking" could go south very quickly, especially when two hot-tempered women were fighting over a man. Instead he said, "Got it. I'll see you later this afternoon."

"Thanks, Tomas. I really appreciate this."

* * *

Tomas showed up right on time, dressed to the nines in an expensive suit, looking very debonair. He stepped out of a luxury car Ronnie had not seen before.

"You sure you want to do this?" he asked when Ronnie opened the door.

"Not really, but I need to hear both sides of the story. I need to know that Luis is telling me the truth when I finally talk to him. C'mon in." Ronnie went to the kitchen for her purse.

"How do you know she's planning on telling the truth?" Tomas noted the numerous flower arrangements and smiled. Luis told him he was going to get his woman back, so the phone call from Veronica was not a surprise. *Looks like he's finally making his move.*

"I'm willing to take that chance."

"I suppose she has nothing to lose, so why not tell the truth?"

"What do you mean 'she has nothing to lose'?" Ronnie went to the security box and punched in the code to set the alarm. The thirty-second countdown to leave began to chirp.

Tomas followed her to the front door and explained, "Luis fired her months ago. And once her husband found out what she did, he kicked her out of the house."

"Oh… I didn't know Luis fired her. You sure about that?" She pulled the door closed behind them and made sure it was secure. Now that she was a single woman living alone, she took every possible security precaution.

"Look, it's not too late for you to change your mind. I can take you to see Luis, instead."

"C'mon, let's get this over with." She eyed Tomas from head to toe as she followed him to his car. "You look really nice, today. Where *do* you work, anyway?"

"I am a realtor. I thought you knew."

"*You're* a realtor?"

"Yes, I am."

"Wow! I would never have guessed you sold houses for a living. By the looks of things, you must be pretty good at it."

"I occasionally sell private property, if the price is right. However, I primarily specialize in commercial business properties. And I do all right."

"Color me impressed!" She raised her brow and smiled.

Tomas pulled up to a nondescript, multiplex unit consisting of eight apartments. The two story unit was located on the lower east side, next to a small shopping center, which housed the health food store where Carmen now worked. Several teenagers were gathered in the parking lot, lighting up cigarettes and sipping from beer cans hidden in brown paper bags. They casually tossed the empties on the ground next to a swing set.

Carmen stepped outside when she saw Tomas' car pull up. She turned and yelled to her kids, "You guys stay inside, I'll be right back. I'm going to talk to these nice people for a minute."

Ronnie took in Carmen's living conditions, almost feeling sorry for her. "Is that what she wears to work, nowadays? She sure looks a lot different dressed in that Hawaiian shirt and khaki pants. Don't look so sexy now, do you Miss Thang?" Ronnie murmured under her breath.

Tomas parked facing the street. "How do you want to do this?"

Ronnie surveyed the area. She definitely didn't want to go inside. It wasn't that type of a visit. "There's nobody around 'cept those kids. They're not interested in us. We can talk outside your car."

Carmen walked towards the car, immediately recognizing Tomas. She turned her focus on the woman who was the reason for the impromptu visit. It was Luis' fiancée. Suddenly the urge to return to her apartment caused her feet to become still. The idea of having Luis' woman confront her in front of her kids didn't seem like such a good idea after all. *What if this lady is a lunatic? More importantly, what if she has a gun?*

"It's all right, Carmen. We just want to talk. Isn't that right, Veronica?" interjected Tomas upon seeing the hesitancy on Carmen's part.

"That's right. I just want to ask you a few questions."

Carmen said in a loud voice, "What do you want to know?"

"I can shout out my questions so everyone can hear, including your kids, or you can come closer and we can have a decent conversation like two mature adults. Your choice."

Carmen exhaled her annoyance and came closer, stopping within a couple of feet. She crossed her arms protectively across her chest and looked up towards the sky. Her jaw muscles clenched tightly together and she narrowed her eyes.

Ronnie looked past her and noticed her three small children, two girls and a boy, ranging in ages from ten to three, peeking out the door—watching the scene unfold before their eyes.

"You have beautiful children." Ronnie said, meaning it.

Carmen turned and yelled, "I told you guys to stay inside. Maria, close that door. Now!" Then she refocused on Ronnie. She sneered, "What do you want?"

Ronnie looked at Carmen and wanted to say *Bitch! You got the fucking nerve to be pissed at me?! I should wipe that smug expression off your damn face with the bottom of my shoe.* Instead, she replied in as calm a voice as she could muster, "I want to know what happened in that hotel room in San Diego. Why were you in Luis' room that night?"

"Why don't you ask him? Why are you coming to me with this *bullshit?*"

"Because *I* am asking *you*, that's why."

"You know he fired me, right? He could have kept that million dollar contract if he had kept me on. But no, his self righteous ass told me to pack my things and leave. Just like that." She snapped her fingers.

Ronnie turned to Tomas for confirmation. *He really did fire her!*

"He didn't tell you that he turned down the Hernandez deal? What a fuckin' chump! All Duarte had to do was keep me on as his assistant, like I had Hernandez include in the contract, and he would be a rich man today. Things would have turned out fine if his dumb ass would've just played along and kept his big mouth shut!" She looked down at her clothes. "And I wouldn't be stuck dressing like some fool who just stepped off of some fuckin' beach."

Ronnie looked at Tomas again. She threw up her hands and said, "Know what? This was a bad idea. Let's go. I don't need to hear anything else from her."

"I thought you wanted to know what happened between me and Duarte." Carmen became even more emboldened, placing her hands on her voluptuous hips.

Ronnie shook her head. "I changed my mind."

Carmen narrowed her eyes and licked her lips, "You sure you don't want to know, mama?"

"Don't get it twisted, sister. The only reason I'm leaving is because what you have to say don't mean shit to me."

Carmen rolled her eyes.

Ronnie looked past Carmen. The oldest girl stood in the doorway wiping the younger one's nose. The little boy was crying for his mother. Suddenly she said, "Let's go, Tomas."

Tomas opened the door for Ronnie before jumping into the driver's seat. He was dismayed at the entire sad situation.

"Tell your husband or whatever the fuck he is, that he still owes me that bonus check. I did my part getting the Hernandez's to sign and it wasn't my fault he backed out. We had a deal!" she shouted out, watching the car pull away. "Duarte hasn't heard the last of me! You make sure you tell him that!"

Ronnie glanced back at Carmen standing in the parking lot shouting like a madwoman. Her children peeked through the curtains taking it all in. The teenagers seemed to get a kick out of their neighbor's behavior. One of the boys, filled with liquid courage, grabbed his crouch and sauntered towards Carmen. She swore at the man-child, pushed the boy away, and returned to her children.

Once they turned the corner, Ronnie tensed up more. The entire scene left her seething as she imagined Luis with Carmen. "Did you hear that bitch? She played Luis like a fuckin' violin trying to set herself up with some cash. And it sounds like he fell for it. You men are so fucking stupid when it comes to a little pussy."

Tomas flinched. He had never heard Veronica swear so vehemently. "What made you change your mind?" he asked when they were a couple of blocks away.

"I realized that no matter what happened in that hotel room, I didn't want to hear the sordid details coming from that woman's nasty mouth. Did you get a look at her? She's pathetic. I've known women like her all my life. They'll do practically anything to get what they want. Doesn't matter who they hurt in the process. Now look at her. Obviously, her little plan to secure her future backfired on her ass."

"Yeah, her scheme exploded right in her face. It is a shame about her and the kids, though. Her husband put them out and now she's raising them on her own."

"Serves her right. Nobody put a gun to her head and told her to seduce my man."

"No one put a gun to Luis' head, either."

"Whose side are you on, anyway?"

"I'm just saying it takes two to tango. Whatever was done by one; was done by both."

"Excuse me? I would think you'd take your cousin's side."

"I am not taking anyone's side. It's just that a whole lot of lives were affected and it is not all Carmen's fault. You being a woman, I'm surprised you're laying it all at her feet."

"You're right, Tomas. None of this mess would have happened without his consent." She blew off the remaining traces of her anger. "Okay, that's enough about that woman. I think I've wasted enough precious moments of my life talking about her, so I'm going to change the subject."

"Okay with me." Tomas stopped at a crosswalk and waited for a group of kids to cross the street.

"You heard from my girl lately?"

"Who, Joie?"

"Yes, Joie."

"As a matter of fact, I am going back out there again this weekend. She made reservations at a bed-and-breakfast in the Northern Virginian countryside. Supposed to be around Charlottesville. You know the area?"

"Charlottesville, Virginia? Yes, I do. It's really nice up there." She and Derek had spent many a weekend in Charlottesville—before their marriage turned sour.

"It will be my first time at a B&B." He chuckled.

"Come to think of it, I haven't spoken to Joie since after she left here. So, how many times have you been out there to visit my friend?"

"This will be my third weekend in two months."

"You guys must have really hit it off."

"I suppose we did."

"Know what?"

"What's that, Veronica?" Tomas turned his head slightly to focus on her.

"I think I had you all wrong. I used to think all you wanted out of life was to chase women in short skirts and get as much cootchie as possible. I also thought you didn't like me because I came here and took your running partner away from you."

"Part of what you say is true." He laughed. "Why did you think I didn't like you?"

"Because whenever Luis and I were together, it felt like you were trying to sabotage our relationship by bringing around a bunch of hoochie mamas."

"I did do that, huh?"

"Yes, more times than you probably realized."

"Veronica, I will admit I did not think you two would last this long. Luis was my road dawg and I suppose I was slightly envious that he had someone in his life who meant so much to him."

"You don't feel that way anymore?" She toyed with her cell phone, glancing at the stored images of her and Luis.

"The day my cousin told me he was going to propose to you, I decided it was time to give you guys my blessing. Veronica, you are the best thing that has ever happened to Luis and he damn well knows it."

"Thanks, Tomas. That means a lot to me." She reached over and patted his hand. "So what else have you been up to besides flying out east to visit Joie?"

"Since you asked… A few months ago, I invested in a real estate deal. I bought up several acres of agricultural land outside of town— rumors are that the land is speculated to be developed soon. When the time comes to sell, I will make a small fortune and reinvest in more. I want to retire by the time I am fifty."

"That is really cool, Tomas. I had no idea you had such lofty life ambitions."

"Luis isn't the only smart man in this family. And now that I have found a woman like Joie, perhaps, I too will finally settle down."

Ronnie blinked several times upon hearing his declaration, trying to determine if she heard him correctly. She stared at Tomas as if an alien had arrived from a distant planet and taken over his body. Totally out of character from his playboy persona, he seemed totally smitten with her sometimes raunchy friend. She pondered the possibility of Tomas being with Joie on a permanent basis and came to the conclusion that there were worse people either one could've ended up with.

"Where to now?" asked Tomas.

Gazing at a picture of her and Luis hugged up underneath an umbrella, taken by a stranger a couple years ago while they were in Seattle, she felt her heart melt. "Can you please take me to see my fiancée? I think it's time we cleared up this mess."

"I'd be more than happy to." Tomas did a quick u-turn and headed in the opposite direction.

* * *

Tomas pulled up in front of a Spanish-styled apartment building with signs touting "luxury executive apartment for short or long term lease". The building, as well as the neighborhood, was in sharp contrast to the dump where Carmen and her children lived. As soon as Tomas turned into the parking lot, Ronnie recognized their Jeep sitting in a reserved parking spot out front.

"Is this where Luis lives now?"

"Yes. He couldn't stand more than a week of sleeping on my sofa. It's actually pretty nice here. Come on, I'll walk you to the door."

Ronnie felt her heart beating strongly inside her chest as Tomas rang the doorbell. She wiped her palms, slick with nervous perspiration, on her dress. When no one answered, Tomas pounded on the door and shouted out, "*Primo*, it's me. Open up!"

"Give me a moment to get to the door, would ya?"

When she heard the sound of Luis' voice coming from the other side, her heart skipped a beat. And when he opened the door and their eyes locked, it felt as if her heart stopped beating. Within those few seconds, the past anguish-filled months, had all but disappeared upon seeing the love that still remained in his eyes. It was as if time had stood still in anticipation of this moment awaiting their reunion.

"Hey man, look who I brought with me."

"Ronnie…"

"Hi Luis. Can I come in?"

"Sure. I was just about to order dinner." He shot Tomas a questioning look, quickly followed with one filled with gratitude.

Tomas tilted his head and nodded.

Luis said to Ronnie, "You look great."

"Thanks," she uttered. "So do you."

"Can I get you something to drink?"

"Water would be nice." She surveyed the one bedroom apartment, noting how clean Luis kept it.

He retrieved a bottle of water from the compact refrigerator, poured it into a glass, and handed it to Ronnie. His hand accidently grazed hers, feeling her warmth. While his hand lingered there for only a moment, thoughts of pulling her tightly into his arms made his head swim.

"I guess I'll leave you two alone now." Tomas turned to leave. "Veronica, you going to be all right? I can hang around if you need me to."

Luis responded with a strained smile. "Thanks, cousin, Ronnie is perfectly safe with me." *Since when did they get to be so tight?*

"He's right. I'll be fine."

"I'm just a phone call away if you need anything." Tomas paused at the door trying to gauge whether or not it was smart to leave the two alone.

"Tomas, it's okay. I'll see you later." She wasn't so convinced herself, but didn't want to make the tense situation any worse.

"Later, cuz." Luis slammed the door behind him.

"Don't be upset with Tomas. I'm the one who dragged him out here. He was just helping out, that's all."

"I know. It's just that I hate to have him so involved in our private life."

"I don't think we have to worry about Tomas. He's too wrapped up in Joie to worry about our problems."

"Is that right?" Luis stared at Ronnie, fighting back an almost irresistible urge to take her in his arms.

"Yeah, he and Joie seem to be working on a long distance relationship."

"Good for them." He cleared his work from the sofa and said, "Have a seat."

"Thank you for the flowers. They were beautiful."

"You're quite welcome." Luis joined her on the sofa.

Now that the idle chitchat was over, the moment of silence turned into an awkward pause filled with unspoken questions neither wanted the other to ask. Both realized that whatever words expressed in the next few moments, would either permanently cement or finally destroy the relationship they worked so hard to obtain.

Luis sat on the sofa, half facing Ronnie, with his fingers interlaced. He broke the ice and spoke first, "How is the baby doing?"

"The doctor says my pregnancy is going well. No problems at all. In fact, since I'm around five months, I can get an ultrasound anytime I want."

"That's wonderful news." Hearing the update on his unborn child was exciting. He pushed down the emotional lump stuck in his throat.

"Yeah, I'm actually starting to show. Wanna see?" She stood and smoothed down her dress.

"Would you look at that?" He touched her stomach and grinned.

All of a sudden, Ronnie took one step back and said, "Luis, I came over here for a reason. I'm tired of living like this, not knowing where we stand. Not knowing whether or not we're still…us."

He sighed in relief, "I'm glad you did stop by. Finally. After you refused to take any of my calls or return my voicemails, I understood you would be the one who had to make the first move. So, I've been waiting patiently for you to come to me."

"I admit I didn't want to hear anything you had to say. After that night, I was so upset."

"I understand…" He ran his hands over his face.

Ronnie faced him, anxiously wringing her hands. "I've had time to think about it and I need to know what happened. It's the only way we can move forward."

Luis exhaled in quiet resignation. "All right. Come sit down." He patted the space beside himself. "I'm going to tell you everything that happened. Then you can decide on if you will forgive me. After which, we can move on or move forward."

"You promise to tell the truth? No lying or holding back details because you think I can't handle it, okay? I don't want to hear half-truths with missing details because that's still considered lying."

"I promise. Only the truth."

For the next two hours, Luis told Ronnie about how Carmen came to work for him and why he hired her. He explained that he had gotten so caught up into securing more business for *Duarte Graphics* that he lost sight of what was important. He told her about the Hernandez account and how important it was. Explained the need for a return trip to San Diego.

Ronnie sat quietly listening to Luis' explanation flipping back and forth between being angry and hurt. She processed his words, watching for signs of deceit. She saw none.

Luis went over the events that happened while he was in San Diego. Told her about the meetings with the Hernandez group and how he ended up with food poisoning from having lunch at the Mexican restaurant. Lastly, as painful and embarrassing as it was, he told her what happened in that hotel room with Carmen. As promised, he left out none of the sordid details.

When he finally got to the part about him and Carmen's sexual escapade, try as she might, Ronnie could no longer hold her tongue.

She jumped from the couch and backed away from him, spitting out her words in disgust.

"You're telling me that bitch was laid up in bed with you totally naked *and* you put your dick in her mouth? Let her suck on you until you came? What the fuck, Luis?! You're telling me you couldn't control where you put your own fuckin' dick?!"

Ashamed of his actions, he dropped his head and accepted her angry outburst, flinching with each word that came from her mouth as if they were cuts from a sharp knife. "Baby, I...I shouldn't have let it happen. Once I woke up and realized she had snuck into my room—into my bed, I should have kicked her out."

"Why the fuck didn't you?" Hot, angry tears streamed down her face.

"I...I...don't...know. It happened so fast, but it also felt like it was happening in slow motion. It was over before I realized it."

Ronnie crossed her arms over her chest and glared at him. "Did you fuck her?"

Luis recalled the explicit image of Carmen lying naked in the bed, fully exposing all she had to offer. Teasing him to take her. And for the briefest of moments back in that hotel room, he had considered it—wanting her so badly he was about to burst. But he didn't feel Ronnie needed to know that part. So he said quietly, "No. No I didn't."

"Did you want to?"

Now why did she have to ask me that? Luis hung his head feeling more miserable than he had at any other time in his life. He couldn't lie because he promised to tell the truth. "I am just a man, Ronnie..." He barely whispered.

She flung the glass of water across the room, barely missing his head. It bounced against the wall and shattered into a thousand pieces.

Reflexively, he covered his face and ducked.

As if she were possessed, Ronnie kicked over the end table, sending his phone and several take-out menus scattering across the floor. Her eyes narrowed and her nostrils flared, turning her into someone he no longer recognized. She picked up his laptop and held it over her head, with every intention of watching it connect with his face.

"Fuck you, Luis! Fuck you and your fuckin' whore! I hate your ass! You're just like all the rest of these asshole men running around with your damn dick in your hand, ready to stick it in any bitch's pussy who throws it up in your face. You think you did me a favor by trying to come home?" Reconsidering thoughts of killing Luis, she lowered the laptop to her waist and let it slip from her hand to the floor. She was angry, but she wasn't crazy.

Luis rose from his position on the sofa. He stepped towards Ronnie and explained, "I thought about it, but I didn't because I love you and only you. As soon as I realized what I'd done—what I was about to do, I knew I had already ruined what we had. You say you hate me? Well, I hate me also. She wasn't worth it then and isn't worth it now and if I could take back that night, I would a thousand times over. Baby, please, please, please forgive me!" With tears spilling from his eyes, he stretched out his arms towards her.

The sight of Luis begging for forgiveness filled Ronnie with deep seated resentment and rage. She charged him and began pounding his chest with her fists. He caught her arms, trying his best to subdue her.

She screamed, "Forgive you? Why should I forgive you? You told me you'd love me forever! You promised you would never cheat on me! I hate you! I hate you so much!"

"Don't say that…" he whimpered. He tried to touch her hand.

"Get away from me! Me and the baby are going to be fine without you. I don't need or want your lying, cheating ass in our lives! Get offa me and leave me alone!" She sobbed hysterically, trying in vain to push his hands away.

Luis gripped her tightly. He cried out, "Baby, I love you, so much! I fucked up this time and I know it. I can't live without you! I'm sorry. Please, baby, forgive me." He released her and dropped to his knees in defeat.

She backed up, chest heaving from sheer exhaustion. "Why? Why should I forgive you, Luis?"

He looked up at the woman he loved with all his heart. "Because we are meant to be together."

"Really? Is that the best you can do?"

"I have been miserable without you, baby. I love you and I'm sorry. I was stupid and I should've listened to you. Ronnie please…"

"You made the decision to hire that 'ho. I knew she was trouble the moment I laid eyes on her. Why couldn't you see it, too?" She turned her back to him.

He rose from the floor and approached her, stopping a foot away. "I don't expect you to make this easy for me. Damn it, Ronnie! I'm not infallible. Everyone makes mistakes. Even me."

Tears flowed freely down her face, settling on the bulge in her dress. She hiccupped with raw emotion. "Why did you take her to San Diego with you, Luis? Were you so blinded by her beauty that you couldn't think straight? Is that the kind of woman you want? What's wrong with me?"

He tenderly placed his hands on her shoulders. When she flinched, he removed them. "Nothing is wrong with you, sweetheart. You are perfect. I'm the one who did wrong. And no, I wasn't blinded by her *beauty*. That is so far from the truth it isn't even funny. I was blinded by the thought of success—of getting a million dollar contract from the Hernandez Group. The only reason I took her with me is because she spoke Spanish fluently. That is the *only* reason."

The emotional upheaval took its toll on Ronnie. Turning to face Luis, she backed against the wall, then slowly sank down to the floor in total exhaustion. She lowered her head and tried to shake the images of Luis and Carmen from her mind.

He dropped to his knees in front of her. "I don't know what happened to us. We got off track somewhere and slowly started drifting apart. This isn't the life we spoke about when we first started dating. Remember when I used to dream about starting my business in Santo Domingo? And you wanted to write your novel?"

She turned her head from Luis, as she still couldn't stand the sight of him or the sound of his voice. *I wish he would shut the fuck up and just leave me alone. I knew I should've driven myself over here. Now I'm stuck like Chuck.*

"Remember when we drove cross-country from Virginia to California and how we turned the many trials and tribulations we faced along the way into something positive? You were so focused on Kiara that you didn't even see that *we* were falling in love. But that was okay because I understood what was going on."

For a split second while remembering that wonderful time, she almost let out a smile.

"Meeting your daughter for the first time only happens once in a lifetime. I got that."

Ronnie crossed her arms and cut her eyes at Luis. "Meeting my daughter and you getting a blow job from your secretary aren't even close. You can do better than that, can't you?"

"I am not making a comparison. What I'm trying to explain is how a person can get so side-tracked by what's in front of them that they lose sight of what's happening around them. It's like getting tunnel vision. The reason I wasn't able to see Carmen Sanchez for who she really was is because I was too focused on snagging that huge Hernandez deal. Funny thing though, after I had it all in my hands, I discovered it wasn't what I wanted after all."

She propped herself up sideways and looked at Luis with a puzzled expression, "What do you mean? That deal was all you talked about for months." She wiped her nose with her arm.

"Hold on. Let me get you a tissue." He hurried to the bathroom and removed the roll of toilet paper from its holder. He handed it to her, joining her on the floor.

"Thanks." She wiped her runny nose.

"You're right, it was. A few days after I got back from San Diego, I returned to the office to review the details of the agreement with my attorney. He pointed out that somehow Carmen had finagled her way into being written into the terms of the deal. In order to do business with Hernandez, I had to agree to keep her on as my assistant in all matters involving them. I don't know what she did or what promises she made, but somehow she managed to make herself part of the deal."

Ronnie smirked. "Hmph, if she wasn't such a conniving little bitch, I *might* be impressed. So how in the hell are you going to work with her?"

"I'm not. The deal is off. I tore up the contract."

"What do you mean, you 'tore up the contract'?"

"After I had the papers in hand, I discovered I couldn't do it. After what happened in San Diego, I fired Carmen when I got back to work. If keeping her on as my assistant was the price I had to pay, I did not want, nor could I afford the Hernandez job. It wasn't worth losing you over. I called up Senor Hernandez and explained I wasn't able to comply with his terms."

Ronnie was finally able to catch her breath again. She asked, "If I hadn't shown up in San Diego, would you have accepted the contract and continued to let that bitch work with you?"

He shook his head and took her hands in his. "Sweetheart, let me explain something to you. For years, I have been going through the motions of trying to build my business here, in Santa Elena, but it's not what I *want* to do. Not where I want to be. And from what I remember, it's not what *we* wanted to do, either. So over the last couple of months, I've been very busy trying to put a few deals in motion."

"Oh yeah, what kind of *deals?*" Ronnie asked sarcastically. She pulled her hands away, still unable to connect with him.

Luis was not deterred by her cynicism. "When we first became a couple, we spoke of what we wanted to accomplish in life. Unfortunately, we allowed life to sidetrack our hopes and dreams."

Ronnie's interest was piqued. The thoughts he now expressed were the exact ones she had, earlier. "Go on, I'm listening."

"I have been working on turning the managerial aspects of the California location over to Julio because I have started the paperwork to open an office in Santo Domingo. I'm still working out the final details, but it should be fully operational within the next few months."

Ronnie leaned forward and stared wide-eyed in disbelief at Luis. "Um, say that again. Are you telling me that you're moving to Santo Domingo? The *city* of *Santo Domingo* in the Dominican Republic?"

Luis grasped her hands in his. This time she didn't pull back. "Only if you'll join me. I can only do this with you by my side. I love you so very much. I want to spend the rest of my life with you and our child loving each other in the offbeat of life. What do you say? Will you stick with me?"

Chapter Twenty-Seven

"*H*i Daddy, sorry it's taken so long for me to call. Phone service is still pretty awful down here and we're lucky if we can get a call out once a month. Most Haitians have to stand in line at the local government office to use the phone."

"Kiara, I was starting to get worried. It's been over a month since I last heard from you."

"Sorry for worrying you."

"At least now I know why the phone number you gave me doesn't work. Did you get the package I sent?"

"Yes, and also the one from Grandmama Pierce's church. Please tell Mom to thank her for me. I'll try to get a call out to her soon as I can."

"So how's it going?"

"I don't like know where to begin. I rarely have time to sleep because I have been so busy. There is so much to do here, it seems like we're barely making a dent."

"Real progress doesn't happen overnight. Significant change comes slowly, especially to a country that was third world poor to begin with."

"Daddy, the earthquake was like years ago, right? Well, when you look around the city, it looks like it just happened yesterday. There are still lots of dilapidated buildings that are unsafe, yet remain standing. Half the city is still in ruins. It's been years, but thousands of people in Port-au-Prince are still living in tents donated by the Red Cross."

Travis was dismayed by what Kiara told him. "What about you and the other volunteers? How are the living conditions for you guys? You getting enough to eat?"

"Volunteers live like royalty compared to most of the locals. Me and a few other girls are assigned to teach students ranging in age from four to ten, so we're living four to a room in an old school on the outskirts of the city. I've even started to pick up a few Haitian words. All in all, daddy, where I live isn't bad considering how and where our students live. And I think I've lost about twenty pounds since I've arrived."

"I see..." He tried to imagine his spoiled, pampered child having to live in such austere conditions. She seemed to be taking it in stride, though.

"I have learned so much since I've been in Haiti. We Americans have it so good and don't even realize it. Some of these children have lost their entire families and are living wherever they can find a place to rest their heads. If it weren't for the school, many would go for days without having a decent nutritional meal."

"Sounds like you have your hands full. I hope it's not too overwhelming."

"I haven't even begun to tell you the worst things I've seen. Did you know that some mothers carry their dead babies around in their arms for like days because they don't know where to bury them? It's heartbreaking…"

"Kiara, I had no idea conditions were so bad there."

"Neither did I. Nor does most of the world when you get right down to it. I don't know where all those billions of dollars went, but it looks like it didn't make it down to the people. After the fundraising telethons ended, and all the celebrities moved on to their next causes, it seemed like the world forgot about Haiti."

"For what it's worth, I think it's great what you're doing. Your contribution may not make a significant dent in the big scheme of things, but if you touch at least one child's life in a positive way, it will all be worth it."

"Thanks, Daddy. That's why I'm here. Hey, can you do me a favor?"

"Sure baby, what is it?"

"Can you ask Mom to resend Luis' cousin's information? I think she told me he was a doctor."

"Sure. Are you okay?"

"I cut my arm on an exposed nail. Luckily, I got my tetanus shot before I left, but to be on the safe side, I want to treat it before it like gets infected. Diseases are rampant and believe it or not, the Red Cross doctors have a really tough time getting medicine even for volunteers. Antibiotics are especially hard to come by."

"I'll call her as soon as we're off the phone. Can't Quinn help you get treatment? Isn't he supposed to be watching out for you volunteers?"

She laughed sarcastically. "Professor Quinn? Daddy, GQ dumped me as soon as we got here. He headed back to the states last month and took one of the other female students with him. So, I suppose what you told me about his weakness for young women was true."

At least Quinn kept his word. "Baby, I'm sorry."

"Don't be. I was like getting tired of him, anyway."

"Still, I thought he was supposed to remain with your group the entire time. Where did he go?" Travis felt his anger rise.

"GQ stayed with us for a month before returning to the states to raise more funds. It's okay and I am not upset. I'm actually glad he left. His being here was beginning to be a big distraction. Anyway, the missionary charity we're working with takes pretty good care of us."

"As long as you are doing okay… Anyway, summer is almost up and you'll be returning home next week, right?"

"That's one of the reasons I needed to speak with you. Several of us volunteers are thinking about sticking around here a bit longer—probably until the beginning of next year."

"What? Did you say next year? Kiara, this "volunteering thing" was supposed to be only for the summer. It was a project, not a life choice."

"This may have started out as just a project, but it's much more than that now. I'm already ahead in credits so skipping one semester of school won't kill me. Anyhow, there are a lot more important things in this world than my missing out on a few months of school."

"Kiara, we agreed…"

"But Daddy, you don't know what it's like down here. The Haitian people need our help. The children need *my* help."

Travis realized arguing with Kiara would be of no use. "I'd prefer if you came home next week, like we discussed."

"I'm only talking about staying here for another four months. Look I've got to go. Someone else needs to use the phone. Don't forget to have Mom get in touch with Luis' cousin."

"Kiara, wait…"

"I love you, Daddy. I'll call you soon."

"Kiara? Kiara?!" he shouted into the phone. The next sound Travis heard was a monotonous dial tone.

"Damn it!" In frustration, Travis flung his cell phone across the room.

Monique came running into the room with a frightened expression displayed across her face. She stopped in the doorway and stared. "Travis? Are you all right?"

"Yes, I'm fine. I didn't mean scare you. I just got off the phone with Kiara. That girl frustrates me so much."

Monique held her chest trying to still her racing heartbeat. "What did she do?"

"*She* has decided to stay in Haiti for a few more months. That's what!"

"Is that all? You make it sound like she decided to move there for good."

With signs of anguish written all over his face, he asked, "I suppose you think I'm overreacting."

"Maybe just a little bit." She walked behind Travis and massaged the knots from his neck muscles. "Look at it this way; Kiara is doing something worthwhile with her life. It's not like she quit school to sell drugs. The young lady is volunteering to help people who are in need—people who are dying in the streets because of poverty and disease. She's a good kid and has plenty of time to finish school."

He pulled her arms downwards until her face touched his. "You're right, she is a good kid and I may have *slightly* overacted."

Monique kissed his scruffy cheek. "Worry comes with the territory of being a parent."

"I am worried *and* concerned about her. She mentioned something about trying to prevent a cut from getting infected. She asked me to get Luis' cousins info, but I don't have a way to get it to her."

"I'm sure she'll be fine. Now, how about we get going? The movie starts in less than half an hour."

"Yeah, you're right. Just let me make one phone call and I'll be right there. What time did you tell the babysitter you'd be home?"

"I told *my mother* not to wait up for me. She's staying overnight with the kids, so we have the entire evening to ourselves." Monique purred.

"Perfect," Travis replied, before wincing in embarrassment, "One more thing… Can you please hand me my phone?"

Monique searched the room and spotted it. She retrieved the phone from where it skidded across the floor. "Looks like the screen is broken. Here ya go."

"Thanks." He took the phone. "You're right, the screen is cracked, but it's still usable. Guess I'll have to get a replacement tomorrow."

"I'll wait in the living room," Monique whispered.

* * *

Luis shouted from the bedroom, "Ronnie, your cell phone is ringing. You want me to get it?"

"Yes, please. I'm dripping wet."

Luis grabbed her phone from the dresser. "Hello?"

"May I please speak to Ronnie?"

"Who's calling?"

"Hi Luis, it's Travis."

"Hey Travis, I didn't recognize your voice. Ronnie can't come to the phone right now. Can I have her call you back?"

"Actually, it's you I need to speak to."

"What's up?"

"Kiara has decided she wants to hang around Port-au-Prince a little while longer—until the beginning of next year. She also needs to see a doctor to have a cut treated before it gets infected. So she asked me to get your cousin's information again. The problem is I haven't had much luck getting in contact with her. Their phone systems apparently aren't very reliable."

"No worries, man. I'll give him a call and ask him to look her up. Do you know which camp she's working in? Or the name of the charity she's with?"

"Not really, but it's something to do with missionaries. I believe she indicated the camp is on the outskirts of the city and she's volunteering to teach elementary school kids."

"Her being an American, she shouldn't be too hard to find. My cousin is familiar with most of the charities and missionaries scattered around Port-au-Prince. I'll have him call me with an update as soon as he finds Kiara."

"Thanks Luis, I appreciate you doing this."

"No worries. How is life treating you these days?"

"Other than my daughter's ongoing drama, life is good, man. I have no complaints. How about you?"

"Life couldn't get any better. I got my lady by my side, I'm going to be a father soon, and my business is expanding in ways I have only dreamt possible," Luis replied, watching the love of his life dance around naked, showing off her expanding waistline.

"That's great, Luis. Tell Ronnie I said hello and Kiara should be calling her soon."

"Will do. Take it easy, man. Later."

"Who was that?" asked Ronnie, coming from the bathroom with a towel wrapped around her body.

"It was Travis. He wants me get in contact with my cousin down there and have him look up Kiara. Apparently, she wants to see a doctor."

"What's going on? Is she okay?"

"She told him she cut her arm and needs medicine to treat it. I think I'll give my cousin, Fernando Doucet, a call first thing tomorrow morning and ask him to track her down. There's no telling what kind of diseases she's been exposed to down there."

"Luis, she's been gone for almost over three months. I miss her so much. I can barely wait to see her in a few weeks. She's going to be so surprised to see how fat I've gotten."

"Uh, that's another thing, sweetheart. Travis told me that Kiara volunteered to stay a while longer."

"What? Why? For how long?"

"He didn't say exactly, but the way it looks, we'll be living in Santo Domingo long before she returns to Santa Elena."

Ronnie took a seat on the bed. She slathered an outrageously expensive moisturizer—whose claim to fame was preventing stretch marks—all over her growing stomach. Luis took the bottle and rubbed the lotion on her back.

"I honestly don't know how I feel about Kiara staying longer. Of course, I want her at home where I know she is safe. On the other hand, I am so proud of what she's doing down there."

"Nothing wrong with how you feel. Haiti can be dangerous for even its own people, let alone someone who isn't from there."

She nervously chewed on her bottom lip. "Travis must be beside himself. Sometimes I think that child does these things just to get a rise out of us."

"He did seem upset, or should I say…worried."

"I wonder why she would do such a thing. And I can't even call her because she doesn't have a phone."

"I'm sure she will be fine."

"You're probably right. It's just that I was looking so forward to telling her about our moving to Santo Domingo. I wanted to speak to her face-to-face, not over the phone."

"Don't stress about it; we'll figure something out."

"Luis, are we making the right decision about moving to the Dominican Republic so soon before the baby will be born? I know we used to talk about doing it, but that was before I found out I was pregnant."

Luis enveloped her in his arms. "Yes, we are making the right decision."

"I'm still not sold on giving birth to my child in a Santo Domingo hospital. Is it safe? How about sanitary? What if something goes wrong? Are they equipped to deal with emergencies?"

Luis patiently waited out her barrage of anxious questions before responding. "Women give birth in Santo Domingo hospitals every day. You'll be fine, and so will our baby."

"Yes, but how many women over forty-years old give birth in Santo Domingo every day?"

"Probably more than you realize."

"Well, I'd still like to have my gynecologist recommend a reputable OB/GYN doctor there—preferably one fluent in English."

"I'll tell you what; I'll take you with me next month so we can take a look at various hospitals. I need to check on the progress of the new office, anyway. If we don't feel the hospitals are up to par, we can delay the move and you can have the baby here in the states."

"Okay. That solves that problem, but what about Kiara? I just don't want her to think I'm abandoning her. Again. Our moving to the DR is going to change everything between us. I wanted to speak to her face-to-face and explain."

"Darling, Kiara is growing up. Eventually, she will spread her wings and leave the nest to embark on her own life. Just look at her now; for all we know, she may just remain in Haiti for the unforeseeable future."

"Port-au-Prince *is* closer to Santo Domingo than California, but I still can't imagine her living there full time. Not my bourgeois child," replied Ronnie, matter-of-factly.

"If she is anything like you or Travis, the Haitians had better watch out. Once that young lady makes her mind up, there is no stopping her. Now come on to bed. We have a busy morning with your doctor's appointment and all."

"We also have another counseling session tomorrow afternoon." She slipped under the covers and snuggled closer.

"Baby, I'm so happy you suggested counseling. I think it helped us out so much."

"Me too. I admit discussing our problems with a stranger was difficult, but after getting through the first session, I realized we needed to really talk about our issues. I was just happy we were able to find someone so quickly."

Luis chuckled. "Well, one thing I quickly learned is how much I value my privacy. This character had us talking about everything from how we met to how frequently we make love. Talk about being intrusive."

"You're right. He didn't want us to hold anything back and I found out that even though we talk all the time, we don't communicate very well. Even couples who have been together for a while can be taught how to be better communicators."

"I'm happy you decided to stay with me. I couldn't bear to live my life with the thought of losing you. I wouldn't want to live a life filled with regrets because of my stupidity."

Ronnie sighed in contentment. "I know what you mean about living with regrets. It's definitely not the way to go if you can help it. Anyhow, *we* are worth fighting for and if it means we have to share our personal business with a stranger, then so be it."

"How did you locate this therapist anyway?"

"He was recommended by Rachel Moore, that new RN Travis hired. Remember I told you about running into her a few months back? Anyway, somehow Rachel found out we were having problems and she discretely recommended him. You know how people gossip."

"Don't I know it. For weeks, my workers ended their conversations whenever I was around."

"Gossip—the fuel for a boring workplace."

He laughed. "So everything is working out at the center with you being gone?"

"Didn't I tell you?"

"Tell me what?"

"Travis brought in a temp until he can hire a full-time replacement for me and Trudy."

"Good for him."

"And Rachel is working out great as the head nurse. All the positions are now covered. So now we can all breathe easier because the *J. Bradford Rehabilitative Center* is once again running like clockwork."

"Speaking of breathing easier, the next time you're feeling upset or angry with me, please let me know. I think it's much easier to address a problem early on than let it sit."

"You're right. I always did have the tendency to keep things that upset me inside, rather than talking about them."

"Well, if we want to keep our marriage running like clockwork, we have to keep the lines of communication open."

"I'll keep working on it."

"I have to admit I thought everything was cool between us. I never imagined you were unhappy. I suppose my being a man; I tend to overlook the small things that may irritate you. Like I had no idea that my throwing wet towels in the dirty clothes hamper irritated you so much. Why didn't you ever say anything to me about it?"

"I didn't say anything because I didn't want to nitpick over silly stuff."

"I'm sure there are things I do that irritate you too."

"Well, now that you mention it…"

Ronnie hit him with a pillow. "Watch it! Don't say something you're going to regret later," she teased.

"I was just going to say that nothing about you irritates me. I love you and I love that little baby you're carrying inside."

"I'm so excited. I hope it's a little boy."

"A boy *or* girl is fine with me, but if it's a girl, I hope she looks just like her beautiful mother."

"And if it's a boy, I hope he looks just like his handsome papa."

"I love you, baby." Luis turned off the bedside lamp.

"I love you, too."

Ronnie fell fast asleep snuggled in Luis' arms. Content in the knowledge that they were finally going to start living the life they spent so much time discussing.

* * *

Luis checked his watch. "Ronnie, it's already after nine. Let's go! You know Dr. Chung hates late-shows."

"I'm coming! I had to pee again." She looked down at her huge stomach, curious as to what news the doctor would provide today.

"How many times in one hour are you going to use the bathroom?"

"I don't know. As many times as it takes, I suppose. I swear my bladder must be the size of a walnut; I'm going every fifteen minutes." She padded into the living room with a huge smile on her face. "Okay, papi, I'm ready. Let's go."

They arrived at the doctor's office with a couple of minutes to spare. Ronnie checked in with the receptionist. Minutes later, a male nurse's assistant, who seemed to be totally out of place in an OB/GYN office, called her back.

"How are we doing today, Miss Pierce," he asked, in an overly effeminate manner.

Oh… He's gay. For a minute, I thought he might be one of the perverts who like working in gynecologist's office so they can look at women's private parts all day long. "We're fine, thanks for asking."

"Good to hear. I'm going to check your weight and blood pressure, then I'll need you to get undressed and slip into this gown. You can keep your underwear on and you'll want to have a full bladder for the ultrasound."

"Shoot! I just went; you got any water?"

"I'll get you a bottle. And don't worry, this happens all the time. Be right back."

"Can you please bring my fiancée back with you? I want him to be here for this."

The assistant's eyes glazed over. "Is he the good looking gentleman sitting by the window? Tall, athletic, beautiful dark skin, wavy hair, piercing black eyes? With a nice …." He snapped out of it upon noticing Ronnie's annoyed reaction.

She nodded, slightly disturbed by how well he seemed to have checked Luis out.

"Lucky you. I'll be right back with him and your water."

"Thanks," she replied.

After downing two bottles of water, Ronnie's bladder was completely full. "Oh man, I have got to pee so bad! Can you check and see what's taking them so long." She squirmed on the examination table.

"Sure thing," Luis replied.

As soon as he stood up, someone knocked on the door. "You ready?" asked the ultrasound technician, poking her head around the door.

"Yes, and can you please hurry up? I've really got to go."

"This is going to take about thirty minutes."

"I don't think I can wait that long."

"You'd be surprised how many women are able to hold it once they get a good glimpse of their baby." The young woman washed her hands and went about prepping Ronnie for the ultrasound.

Ronnie squeezed Luis' hand tightly to relieve some of the pressure. Unfortunately, it didn't work.

"Okay. Lie back. I'm going to squeeze this gel over your tummy. It's going to be cold, but that will pass."

The cool gel caused Ronnie to jump.

"Relax; you're going to be fine." She fiddled with the touch screen. "I'm going to take several pictures to see how your baby is doing. If you have any questions, please feel free to ask. I'm not supposed to give you any medical opinions, but I can answer your questions about the procedure itself."

"I understand." She looked at the images on the screen. "Is that my baby?"

The technician nodded and continued with the exam.

"Look, Luis, I can see the baby's face."

Luis squeezed Ronnie's hand; his eyes misting over. "Would you look at that? I think he's sucking his thumb."

"Would you and Mr. Pierce like to know the sex of your child?" asked the technician.

"You can tell us that?" Ronnie overlooked the incorrect reference addressing Luis as "Mr. Pierce".

"Only if you want to know. It's really up to you."

"Luis?"

Luis was too overwhelmed with emotion to speak, so he merely nodded.

"Yes, please tell us. Are we having a boy or a girl?"

The ultrasound technician stood with a confused look on her face, "Hmm, that's strange…" She moved the wand to another angle and took several more pictures. "That's…interesting," she murmured to herself.

"What is it? Is something wrong with the baby?" Ronnie looked to Luis for answers. He looked to the tech.

"I'm picking up two separate heartbeats. Give me one moment…"

The technician picked up Ronnie's chart, reviewed it, and scribbled down a few notes before putting it down. She then pressed the wand so deeply into Ronnie's side, she felt as if she were going to pee right there on the table.

"Yep, there you are, you little booger…hiding behind your big sis, huh?"

Ronnie looked at Luis. Luis looked at Ronnie. They both looked at the technician.

"Congratulations, folks. You're having twins. A boy *and* a girl."

"What? Are you sure?" Ronnie asked.

"Here, let me show you. This image right here is your daughter and that there is your son." She continued gliding that wand over Ronnie's stomach, stopping every few seconds to take more pictures.

"Oh my God, Luis! We're having twins," she whispered softly as tears of joy rolled down her face.

Luis appeared to be in shock, for he sat motionless, staring at the wall.

"Well, that's it for me." The woman wiped down Ronnie's stomach. "Now, that wasn't too bad now, was it? And I bet you forgot about having to use the restroom."

Ronnie was so overflowing with joy; she reached up to hug the technician. She didn't say a word, just wrapped her arms around that lady's neck.

"You're very welcome, dear," the technician whispered back. Being used to those reactions from expectant mothers, she briefly returned Ronnie's hug before pushing her away. "See, that wasn't as bad as you thought it was going to be, was it?"

"No, actually, it wasn't," she replied.

"I'll get these images to the doc right away."

"Uh, where's the nearest toilet I can use?"

"You can use the adjoining restroom over there. Afterwards, if you have a seat in the waiting room, Dr. Chung will be with you shortly to discuss your course forward. Once again, congratulations! And you guys have a nice day."

The technician quickly washed her hands and retreated out the door, providing the expectant couple with privacy.

Ronnie looked over to Luis who had tears forming in his eyes. Seeing Luis like that touched her deeply, and in that moment, she realized the depth of his love was infinite and true.

After they both took a few minutes to let the news sink in, Ronnie got dressed and headed straight to the restroom. Luis returned to the waiting room and picked up a well-worn magazine while he waited for Ronnie. He eyed the other men waiting for their women. Some appeared excited, others sad, while several looked like they preferred to be anywhere but where they were.

Ronnie plopped down in an empty chair beside Luis. "At least now I know why I've gotten so fat." She exhaled slowly. "Twins? Who'd have thought... I don't have any twins in my family, how about you?"

"Not that I know of. Incredible... I'm going to be the father of twins..." He stared blankly ahead, allowing the reality of the words to slowly sink in.

After thirty or so minutes had passed, the same male nurse's assistant came for them. "Miss Pierce, sir, please follow me." He pointed to an office. "Please wait there. Dr. Chung will be with you shortly."

The couple took a seat on a plush loveseat inside Dr. Chung's office. Over her desk was a huge corkboard filled with pictures of babies—babies she had delivered over the course of her career. A plastic womb, cut in half to display an upside down baby entrapped in the birth canal, sat prominently on her desk. A plant that desperately needed watering teetered precariously on the narrow windowsill. Scanning the room, neither one spoke. They just waited for the doctor to show.

Dr. Chung walked into the room holding the results of the ultrasound. "Good morning, Miss Pierce. I see you've brought Mr. Pierce along with you, today. Hi, I am Dr. Chung." She outstretched her free hand towards him.

Ronnie interrupted. "Uh, Dr. Chung... This is my fiancé, Luis Duarte."

"Oh, I'm so sorry for the mix-up. I stand corrected... Mr. Duarte, I am pleased to meet you." She shook Luis' hand before taking a seat at her desk.

"No problem..."

"The ultrasound has confirmed my suspicions that you are carrying twins. Also, all the tests have come back normal and the ultrasound indicates the babies are progressing quite well." She peered over her bifocals and studied the couple. "Is this news pleasing to you?"

"Yes, yes, of course it is. We're just still a bit numb from the news, that's all. I had no idea I was carrying twins."

"I see. Because you are an older mother, I want to monitor you very closely to make sure you don't develop complications later. Most likely, towards the last four weeks of your pregnancy, I'll suggest total bed rest to ward off a premature delivery. Other than that, you should continue doing what you're doing."

"Uh, Dr. Chung, I'm—I mean...*we* are planning on moving to the Dominican Republic in a few weeks. I was considering having my baby there."

She removed her glasses, placing them on her desk. Giving her full attention to the couple, she explained, "Being an older mother puts you and your babies at a higher risk of complications. Is it possible to delay this move until after the babies are born?"

"That is a consideration, but we really wanted to get there sooner, rather than later," added Luis.

"I see... Of course, the decision is entirely up to you. You said you're considering traveling within the next few weeks?"

"Yes, give or take a week." Ronnie's bladder begged to be emptied again.

"Considering your overall health and the stage of pregnancy you're in, you should be fine to travel, but I wouldn't push it past the seven month point. Do you have an obstetrician and a pediatrician in mind down there?"

"No, I wanted to know if you know anything about Dominican hospitals and if you could refer me to a good doctor."

She placed a finger to her temple. "I don't know any doctors in the DR, but I can check into it and get back with you."

Luis chimed in, "Thank you, Dr. Chung. My fiancée is very worried about the overall safety of the hospitals down there. It has been so long since I have lived in the DR, I cannot speak to how the conditions are."

"I understand. I can make a few phone calls and have my nurse call you with my recommendations."

"That will be wonderful. Thank you."

She perched her glasses on the tip of her nose, peering over the lenses. "Do either of you have any other questions?"

"No, I think that takes care of it." Ronnie stood to leave. Her bladder was about to open the flood gate.

"Oh, I almost forgot to ask. Have you considered having an amniocentesis procedure? You're at the right stage to have one performed. It will reveal any abnormalities that may possibly exist with…"

Luis cut her off. "We don't want the test. We have already discussed this and decided that no matter what God chooses to bless us with, we are going to love our babies. Regardless of their condition."

"Is this your view also, Miss Pierce? No disrespect, Mr. Duarte, but Miss Pierce is the mother and the decision is hers to make. And for the record, I need to have her response in both oral and written form."

"He's correct. I don't want the procedure. I'm going to love my children no matter how they turn out." She rubbed her stomach, feeling an almost imperceptible fluttering sensation.

"Very well. I'll have my nurse contact you with that information we discussed. Please schedule one last appointment before you leave. I want to do one final checkup before clearing you to fly. We want to make sure those precious little darlings arrive safe and sound."

"Thanks again, Dr. Chung. I'll do that," Ronnie responded.

Within the private confines of their car, and with the unexpected news about their babies health tucked safely away in their minds, Ronnie and Luis processed the information in their own unique way. Ronnie hummed softly, all the while gently rubbing her stomach, hopefully relaxing her little ones. Luis allowed the contentment within his heart to make its way to his face in a happy grin.

The long drive to their therapist's office took them south on the 101 freeway. The stretch of highway between Santa Elena and Ventura was particularly scenic with the mountain range on one side and the sparkling waters of the Pacific Ocean on the other.

While Luis drove, Ronnie peered out the window taking in the view. She spied a group of dolphins jumping in and out of the water very close to the shore. They appeared to be playing—like children do.

"Are you scared?" she asked Luis.

"Scared about what?"

"Twins—about having two babies instead of one."

Luis turned slightly and replied, "No, I'm not scared. I am excited, nervous, thrilled, apprehensive… Maybe all those, but scared…not so much."

"Well, I am."

"Why?" he asked.

"Because I'm old and my eggs are old. We're about to move to another country. I'm leaving everything I've ever known behind. Isn't that enough?"

"Veronica Pierce, I love you and I will never let anything happen to you. It's natural to be "scared" under the circumstances, but leave everything to me. I'm going to take care of everything and make sure you will receive the best medical care possible."

"How are you going to do that?"

"First of all, I called my cousin this morning and told him about Kiara…"

"You did? What did he say?"

"He assured me he would locate Kiara and provide her with proper medication. Then I mentioned you were in need of the DR's most trusted obstetrician. He's very well connected in the medical community, both in Haiti and the Dominican Republic. And as we are speaking, he is making arrangements for you to see a doctor next week."

"You really are going to take good care of me, aren't you?"

"I said I would and I only say what I mean. There is no one more important to me in this world. Not counting Our Lord and Savior, there is no one I will ever put before you and our children."

"I think I just fell in love with you all over again." She leaned over and planted a kiss on his cheek. "I can't wait to be your wife."

"Speaking of which, what do you say we get hitched?"

"I already accepted your proposal." She laughed.

"No, I mean today. Let's get married today. Right now."

She sat up straight in her seat. "Seriously? You want us to get married, right now? We have an appointment with the therapist in less than an hour."

"Forget the therapist. We've already worked through our issues. Let's be spontaneous—like we use to be. What do you say?"

"Uh, I thought you wanted a church wedding—a ceremony your family could witness."

Luis took the next exit. He pulled off the road, facing her. "*How* we are married isn't as important as getting married. We can have a civil ceremony today and then a huge celebration in the Dominican Republic after the babies are born. I'll even fly your mother and your friend Joie down if it makes you happy." He took her hands in his. "I don't want to wait any longer. I want you to be Mrs. Veronica Duarte by the time the sun sets. I love you so much."

"Luis, you are so romantic."

"Does that mean we're on?"

"Okay. Let's do it. Let's get married today."

"Pick a place. Ventura, Carpintería, Ojai, Santa Elena… They're all within a couple hours."

She laughed, "I'm glad you didn't say Vegas."

"I would never, ever in my wildest nightmare, ever, ever, ever, consider taking you to that trash heap of a city to get married. Although this is going to be a civil ceremony, I want it to be special and memorable."

"Enough said." She gazed out at the ocean, wondering about the perfect location to be married. Out of the blue, the answer came to her. "Sweetheart, we live in a city where people travel from all over the world to get married. Let's go to the Santa Elena County Courthouse. It's really lovely. In fact, if I call them now, maybe we can get married outside in the Sunken Gardens surrounded by all those gorgeous palm trees."

"Call them up and make an appointment."

"I'll pull up the website to get the number. Hold on a sec." She quickly scrolled through several screens on mini *Ipad*. "Okay, got it. Can I use your phone to call?"

Luis listened in as she made arrangements. Everything was perfect. Absolutely perfect!

"Guess what, papi?"

"They have an opening?"

"That's right. A couple cancelled at the last minute, so if we can be at the courthouse by three, we have a spot."

"Good thing we already have our marriage license. That'll save some time." He paused for a moment then asked, "Ronnie, do you mind if I ask Tomas to come? At least we'll have one family member as a witness."

"No, I don't mind Tomas coming. In fact, I'd be thrilled if he can make it. That is, if he isn't in Virginia visiting Joie."

Chapter Twenty-Eight

*B*efore heading to the courthouse, they stopped by the house to dress for their impromptu wedding. Luis selected a pair of white linen slacks and a white *guayabera* shirt with blue accent stripes running down the front.

Ronnie wore a simple, white summer dress that barely hid her bulging belly. She put on the blue *larimar* stone earrings Luis bought for her during their outing in the DR, and then slid her mother's angel in her purse for good luck. They both wore sandals, as it was a typical late summer day with the temperature well into the 80's.

"What about the rings? We can't get married without wedding rings." Ronnie panicked. "Do I look okay? How's my hair? What about a photographer? Flowers? Oh no! I don't have a wedding bouquet!"

Luis tried his best to rein her in before she went down in a torrent of emotion. "My love, do not worry about the rings. We can pick up a pair before the ceremony and we can stop by a jeweler afterwards to select our real ones. As for everything else…we'll handle it as it comes. How does that sound?"

"Okay. And since we're being spontaneous and all, let's just buy them from a street vendor. They always have funky designs."

"Fine, we'll buy local." He checked the time and called out, "Sweetheart, let's get going. This is one appointment I don't want to miss. And don't forget to bring the marriage license."

"All right, I'm coming…."

Luis stood by the front door, nervously checking his watch every few minutes. He looked around his house, remembering the very first time he brought Ronnie home. The happiness he felt that day was a close second to how he felt today. His heart swelled with happiness.

"Come on, dear. We've got to go!" he shouted down the hallway. At that very moment, his cell phone vibrated. He looked at the incoming call and saw it was from Julio.

"What's up, Julio?" he answered, impatiently.

"Hey boss, I hope I'm not disturbing you on your day off, but I need to tell you something really important."

Luis stepped outside and closed the door so Ronnie wouldn't overhear his conversation. He didn't want anything to spoil their perfect day. "What is it?"

"You remember that crazy Carmen Sanchez woman? The one you fired a few months ago?"

"How could I not remember? Why?"

"When I got to work this morning, I found a notice taped to the front door. It was a subpoena to appear in court. Looks like that Sanchez woman is suing you."

"What the hell did you say? She's suing me? For what?" Luis felt his jaw muscles tense. He clenched and unclenched his free hand.

"It says in the subpoena that she is suing the *Duarte Graphics Agency* for breach of contract. The court date is set for two weeks."

"Luis, I'm ready." Ronnie sang out.

He heard Ronnie, but wanted to calm himself before answering. He said nothing was going to ruin his day, and he meant it.

Ronnie stuck her head out the door. "Oh, there you are. I'll set the alarm and be right out."

He acknowledged her and said to Julio, "I'll take care of it first thing Monday morning. Don't sweat it. Let her take me to court. She doesn't have a leg to stand on."

"That's good to know, boss. I'll let you go so you can enjoy your weekend."

"Thanks, man. Have a great weekend yourself and I'll see you on Monday." He hung up and shook what remained of Carmen's threat from his body. "You are not going to mess up my day, Sanchez. I will take care of you later."

Ronnie bounded out of the house, beaming as if she were lit up from the inside out. "I'm ready and here is the license." She replied in a singsong voice, while waving the paper in the air.

Luis swept her up in his arms and laid a huge kiss on his bride-to-be. "You look beautiful. Just like an angel."

"Um, you don't look too shabby yourself, papi. Let's get going. I don't want to wait any longer to become your wife."

* * *

They parked in a downtown parking garage. After purchasing a pair of rings from a local street vendor, they walked the few short blocks to the county courthouse.

"Did you ever reach Tomas?" Ronnie tucked the velvet pouch containing their rings in her purse.

"Yes, I did. And he said he's bringing a surprise with him—something for you."

"A surprise? I'm not too sure about that, Luis. Did you ask him what it was? I don't need any of his surprises, especially today."

"He assured me it wasn't anything bad. Once I told Tomas we were getting married, he seemed almost as excited as me. So don't worry. Everything is going to be just fine."

"I hope you're right."

"C'mon, let's confirm our appointment with the clerk." Luis nudged her towards a line with the words *County Clerk* branded on the wooden sign above.

"Look at all the couples waiting to get married. Everyone looks so happy," she remarked, noticing the dozen other couples surrounded by friends and families.

They lined up behind a couple decked out in *Harley Davidson* motorcycle gear and waited their turn to be called. When they reached the front of the line, the apathetic clerk reviewed their license and marriage application. She said, "Your paperwork seems to be in order. I'll need both of you to initial each page and sign at the end. Payment is due now and can be in the form of credit or debit card, check, or money order. No cash."

After they signed the legal documents in the proper places, Luis paid the fee. When it was completed, Ronnie felt slightly put off by how impersonal the process seemed.

The clerk told them, "Please proceed to the Sunken Garden area and wait for your names to be called. The judge is running a bit ahead of schedule, so you can expect to be called at any moment." The clerk offered a quick smile, then motioned to assist the next couple.

As they turned to leave, Ronnie felt a pair of warm hands slip over her eyes. She pulled the hands away, gasping in surprise. "Oh my goodness! What in the world are you doing here?"

"I'm here to witness my best friend get married. Again." Joie laughed, good-naturedly.

"How did you know we were getting married today?"

"Pure luck. Me and Tomas made plans for me to come out and visit a while ago. I had just landed when Luis called and told him about your wedding, so we came straight here from the airport. Didn't even stop to drop off my suitcase. Surprise!" She tossed her hands in the air.

Ronnie turned to Luis, playfully punching his arm. "You knew about this, didn't you?"

"Actually, I didn't find out Joie was here until I spoke to Tomas."

Tomas bent down and kissed Ronnie's cheek. "Veronica, you know I cannot pass up a good surprise. When I found out you two were getting married today, I was more than willing to bring Joie to witness your happy union."

Happy tears streamed down Ronnie's face. "This has got to be one of the happiest days of my life." She hugged Joie again and then Tomas. Finally, they all made it to the waiting area filled with other soon-to-be-married couples.

"Will the party of Luis Duarte and Veronica Pierce please step forward?" said another clerk, after checking her clipboard.

"You sure you want to go through with this?" Luis searched Ronnie's eyes for any sign of apprehension. He saw none.

"Yes, I'm sure. Are you?"

"I've never been more certain about anything in my entire life."

"Let's do it."

The quartet followed the attendant to a small clearing under a cluster of palm trees. The sun made its way through the leaves to warm the couple. The attending judge wore a white robe and stood with a Bible in his hand. He smiled at the couple as he reviewed their papers.

"Are you Luis Eduardo Duarte and Veronica Indigo Pierce?" he asked the couple to confirm their identity.

"Yes," they replied in unison.

He looked over at Joie and Tomas. "Are you two the witnesses?"

They both nodded.

"Great. Then let's get started, shall we?"

Despite the judge having already performed this ceremony several times that day, he acknowledged that getting married was a special occasion and should be treated with reverence. He performed each and every marriage ceremony as if it were the most important one of the day.

The judge opened his Bible and recited the marriage vows, asking Luis and Ronnie to repeat after him. When it was the proper time, they slipped the rings on each other's finger. After what seemed like only a few minutes, the judge stated, "I now pronounce you husband and wife. You may kiss your bride, sir."

Luis took Ronnie's face in his hands. "I love you, Mrs. Veronica Duarte," he said in barely a whisper.

"I love you, right back, Mr. Luis Duarte."

He kissed his new bride with such intense passion; Tomas felt the need to clear his throat to remind them where they were. Yet, for the newly married couple, they were the only ones who existed in that magical moment.

When Ronnie finally opened her eyes, she noticed the judge standing with his hands clasped and head bowed, obviously giving them privacy in their tender moment.

"Ladies and gentleman, I'm pleased to introduce Mr. and Mrs. Luis Duarte." The judge congratulated the couple, offered a few words of sage advice, and went on his way to perform the next ceremony.

Ronnie wiped a smudge of lipstick from Luis' lips with the handkerchief he'd given her earlier. And much to her delightful surprise, she discovered that Tomas had snagged a photographer, who busily snapped photos throughout the ceremony.

Joie approached the couple, wrapping her arms around them both. "Congratulations! I am so happy for you both."

"Thank you so much for being here."

"You are very welcome." Joie smiled.

"We planned this on the spur of the moment, so we didn't allow time for our family to make it here. That's why you two witnessing this is so special."

Tomas looked away to hide his emotions.

Joie said, "Hey, did you notice all those butterflies? There was a whole bunch of purple ones fluttering above you during the ceremony. I have never seen anything like that in my life. It was an amazing sight."

"You're right. Those butterflies had perfect timing—almost as if their appearance was planned. Hopefully, the photographer captured them," Tomas added.

Ronnie gazed up towards the sky, allowing the sun to kiss the single tear that streamed down her face. "I know exactly why those butterflies were here." She quietly whispered, "Thank you, Daddy for also being here."

Luis wrapped his arm around his wife's waist as she embraced the precious moment. Suddenly, she flinched.

"Whoa, what was that?"

"You okay?" he asked with concern.

"Feel my stomach. The babies are kicking me something fierce." She guided his hand to where feet, elbows, or fists nudged gently from her insides.

Luis' facial expression said it all. While his hand gently rested against Ronnie's swollen belly, a slight rippling motion under her skin caused him to quickly pull away, as if he'd touched something hot. He repositioned his hand, grinning like a child on Christmas morning. "I can really feel them moving around in there. Must be all the excitement."

Joie swiveled her neck in their direction. With eyes as large as saucers, she shrieked with excitement, "Hold up a minute, y'all. Did you say 'babies', as in more than one?"

Ronnie gripped Joie's forearms and started jumping up and down. "Yeah, girl. We just found out this morning. Can you believe it? We're having twins—a boy and a girl."

"Whaaaat? Twins? Girl, y'all are just full of surprises today. No wonder you've gotten so big. I thought you were just overeating."

Tomas pulled Luis aside and asked, "*Primo*, is it true? You guys are having *two* babies?"

Luis nodded.

"*¡Qué chévere!*" He patted him on his back again. "Considering you now have a wife who is pregnant with two babies, are you sure about this move to Santo Domingo? Seems like your timing is way off."

"Man, Ronnie and I have been discussing this move for months. The doctor says she's okay to travel right now, but in a month or so, forget it."

"Sounds like you don't have much time left. Have you told Veronica about the villa, yet?"

"No, the villa is supposed to be a surprise. You know how slow things move in the DR, especially since I'm not there to oversee the progress. It's already a few months behind and definitely won't be complete by the time we get there. Speaking of timing being way off, I'll tell you something else I just found out today…"

"What's up?"

"Your girl, Carmen Sanchez, is suing me and the company for breach of contract. After all that bullshit in San Diego went down, I tore up the contract with the Hernandez Group and fired her. I suppose she figures I owe her something."

"*Coño, primo!* I did not see this coming. I'll go visit her old man and see if he can talk some sense into her. He recently took her back because he missed his kids."

"I just want that entire situation to go away because I don't have the time or the energy to deal with her bullshit."

"Let me handle it. You just worry about taking care of your new wife and kids."

"Thanks." He glanced over at Joie. "What's up with you and ol' girl over there? Is this thing getting serious?"

"I'm not really sure. This whole long distance relationship thing is getting old, not to mention expensive. I really like Joie and I truly care about her, but her life is in Virginia with her children and her family."

"Take your time. If she's the right one, you will know it soon enough."

Tomas laughed, "In the meantime, Joie is cool. I've never had as much fun with a woman as I have with her."

"Have you spent any time with her children, yet?"

"Not yet. Joie wants to wait to see where this is going before she introduces me to her children."

"Big mistake if you wait too long. You can't truly know the mother without spending time with her children. They are a package deal and all that "fun time" you're having with mommy will change once the kids become involved."

"I see what you're saying, but for now, we're cool." Tomas didn't want to expose his true feelings about Joie to Luis. Truth was, he was absolutely head over heels with the woman and wanted to explore taking the relationship to another level.

Joie and Ronnie walked to where the guys stood.

"Hey Tomas, that photographer gave me his card and said he'll call when the pictures are ready. Did you hire him?" asked Ronnie.

"His wife is a coworker of mine. After I got the call from Luis, I called in to check on a listing and mentioned you guys were getting married. She told me her husband was free today and would give us a great discount if I hired him. I knew Luis wouldn't think about hiring a photographer, so I took care of it."

Luis said, "You know me too well, man. Thanks for thinking ahead."

"No problem. Well, Joie and I are going to leave you two lovebirds alone to enjoy your honeymoon." He wrapped his arm around Joie's waist.

"Will I see you before you leave, Joie?" asked Ronnie.

She nodded. "I'm here until Sunday evening. Give me a call so we can hook up."

"Thanks again for coming out on such short notice. I really appreciate everything you've done, Tomas." He dapped his cousin's fist and waved at Joie.

"Catch you two later. Have lots of fun tonight…newlyweds."

*   *   *

"Are you sure you don't want to go out to celebrate? Maybe just have dinner? It's not every day we get married, you know…"

"Baby, can I please take a rain check? I am soooo tired; my back hurts; and my feet have swollen up like crazy. Making matters worse, the babies have been extra active. They must know mommy and daddy made it official today. Would you be okay if we just pick up some Indian takeout?"

"Of course. Call in the order and we can pick it up on the way home. Nothing too spicy, now. You don't want to be up all night with heartburn again."

"Thanks, sweetie." She yawned. "I'm sorry. It's our honeymoon and all I want to do is go home and take a nap."

"Considering you're pregnant with twins, I can totally understand you being tired. We had a busy day today, Mrs. Duarte." He grinned. "I sure do love the way that sounds… Mrs. Duarte."

"Me too. Veronica Indigo Duarte does have a nice ring to it." She picked up his phone. "You have the restaurant's number saved?" She started scrolling through his contact list.

"Yeah, it's in there under *Bombay*. Whatever you order is fine with me."

"Found it." She provided her menu selections to the heavily accented woman on the other end. After repeating her order several times, she ended the call. "I hope she got it right. Anyway, I think she said our order will be ready in fifteen minutes."

Luis' mind was a thousand miles away. Ever since he uttered the words, 'I do', he had been in a reflective mood. He turned to Ronnie and said, "Thanks for taking my last name."

She squeezed his hand. "You're welcome. I'm your wife now. Why wouldn't I have your name?"

"My family's name is priceless and I don't give it away freely. I would have accepted you hyphenating your name, but I must admit I like the sound of Veronica Duarte a whole lot better than Veronica Pierce-Duarte. It just sounds so…"

"Like I'm sticking a knife into you?" She laughed.

He squirmed uncomfortably in his seat. "Yeah, some last names go better with others. Ours? Well…not so much."

"The way I see it, you're the last man I'm going to marry so why not take your name." She stifled another yawn. "I've known women who have gotten married, but kept their maiden names."

"Why would they do that? If they are committed to each other, why not take their husband's name?"

"Going against tradition, perhaps? Personally, I think those women who don't take their husband's names aren't really committed to the marriage and are simply waiting for it to fall apart. Why else would they hold on to their old names?" Another yawn made its way to her mouth. "And those who get divorced and hang on to an ex's name must be crazy or still in love."

"Didn't your friend Joie keep her husband's name after the divorce?"

"Yeah, she kept it. And that's a perfect example of what I'm talking about because the divorce wasn't her idea; it was Cedric's. She *said* she didn't change her name because she wanted to have the same last name as the twins. But I'm telling you, if Cedric changed his mind and wanted to come back, I think she would get back together with him in a heartbeat." Ronnie smirked. "To each his own…"

"Interesting… My ex couldn't wait to stop being referred to as *Mrs. Duarte* and honestly, that didn't hurt my feelings one bit. She remarried the first big baller who came along and changed her name before the ink was dry on the divorce papers."

"Well, I for one am glad that she did. I want to be the only Mrs. Luis Duarte on this side of the Rockies. Since I am now your wife, I am going to be Veronica Indigo Duarte until the day I die."

He gripped her hand and said, "That's right. The one and only. We are going to be together 'til death do we part. As far as I'm concerned, that is a very good thing."

Chapter Twenty-Nine

*J*oie showed up at Ronnie's doorstep the next afternoon pushing a side-by-side baby stroller overflowing with two of everything. Tomas stood behind her carrying two infant car seats. One blue and the other pink. She pounded loudly on the front door. "Ronnie? Luis? Open up you lovebirds."

Ronnie peeked out the window and couldn't help laughing. She saw Joie cuddling a little brown teddy bear in her arms with Tomas at her side. He appeared to be under duress. "What in the world is this?"

"This is your official baby shower. Since I won't be here to see you off before you leave, me and Tomas decided to spend this morning in *Babies r Us* picking up a few things. Here ya go, little mommy."

"This is so sweet! Come on in."

Once Luis heard the commotion coming from the entrance, he decided Tomas needed rescuing from the women. He entered the room carrying two beers. "What did you guys do? Buy out the entire store?"

"Blame it on Joie. All I did was push the cart."

"Here ya go. You probably need this more than me." Luis chuckled, pushing a beer towards Tomas' hand.

"Thanks for the cold one, *primo*." He sucked down the beer in one gulp.

"I couldn't let my best friend move to the DR without having all the latest baby equipment. You know these U.S. companies dump their recalled stuff down there, don't you?"

"That's an awful thought, but thank you for thinking of my babies' safety."

"You're welcome, girlfriend. I've got lots of experience when it comes to raising twins, you know."

"Ladies, us men are going to the den to watch the basketball game. If you need anything assembled, please wait until after the game is over," said Luis.

"Come on Joie. Help me put these beautiful gifts in the spare room."

After the gifts were put away, the guys retreated to the man cave to watch basketball, while the ladies ended up in the garden sipping on iced teas.

"It sure is nice out here." Joie eased herself into a lounge chair.

Ronnie tuned the radio to a local jazz station for background noise. "You and Luis look so happy."

"We really are…"

"Girl, when Tomas picked me up from the airport and said we were going to your wedding… Honey chile, I almost lost it because the last time I saw you guys, it was not a pretty sight."

Ronnie winced at the memory, "That *was* a pretty bad time. And to tell you the truth, I wasn't sure we were going to make it as a couple. If it weren't for us seeing that marriage counselor, I probably would be packing my bags and getting ready to move back home with my mama in Oklahoma instead of Santo Domingo."

Joie sipped her iced tea, tracing her finger through trails of condensation forming on the glass. "You guys are doing it the right way—raising your children in a loving, stable home. Together. As a normal family. The way it's supposed to be done."

"I'm sorry, Joie. I wish things would have turned out differently for you and Cedric. But you and Tomas seem to be having a good time. He's even got you flying out here to see him."

Joie rested her eyes on a flowering magnolia tree. She rose from the wicker chair and plucked a delicate white flower from a low hanging branch. Her words were measured when she spoke. "Cedric and I are thinking about getting back together."

Ronnie sat up in her chair. She turned the radio's volume down. "Run that by me again. I don't believe I heard you correctly."

"Me and Cedric are working things out. He's been coming by the house more regularly to see the kids. One day, one thing led to the other and he ended up spending the night."

"Joie, does Tomas know you're still seeing your ex?"

"I told him about Cedric dropping by to see the kids, but he doesn't know the rest."

Ronnie joined Joie at the Magnolia tree, avoiding a fat bumblebee buzzing from flower to flower. "What are you going to do? It's been several years since the divorce. Are you sure—is he sure, that you're both ready to make another go at it?"

"I never stopped loving Cedric; you know that. That's why I couldn't settle down with anyone else. That man was the love of my life. Always has been and always will be."

Ronnie smiled listening to Joie gush about Cedric.

"I don't believe there is a man on earth who can make me feel the way Cedric does. The twins love having their daddy around again... The fact of the matter is, me being with Cedric just feels like it's supposed to be this way."

"If that's true, then what are you doing flying out here to be with Tomas?"

"Gu-u-r-r-lll, you know how I am... Tomas is a lot of fun to be around and all, but..."

Ronnie eyed her friend, becoming more upset with her by the moment. After all this time, Joie hadn't really changed. She was still selfish, only considering her own feelings. "Tomas really cares about you, you know. I think you should tell him what's going on."

"I will... I just wanted to make sure that what I felt about Cedric was real. And for me, the best way to find out was to be with another man."

"Is that right? So you were just using him?"

Joie smiled slyly and closed her eyes thinking of Cedric. She brought the blossom to her nose and inhaled. "I really do like Tomas. We have a good time together and the sex is incredible. But gurrlll, I loves me some Cedric. He is an excellent lover and that man can make me come just by sucking on my toes. But it's not just the sex that makes me want to be with him."

"Listen to me, woman. You are playing with fire messing around with two men at the same time. You need to cut one of these relationships off."

Joie continued as if she hadn't heard a word Ronnie said. "A few weeks ago, when I was sick with the flu, Cedric did everything for me. He bathed me, even brushed my hair when I couldn't. Cedric takes care of *me* like no one else can. And he is such an incredible father. He's my entire world and I'm looking forward to getting back together with him permanently."

"Damn! From that description, even *I* would consider marrying him," stated Tomas from the kitchen doorway. His expression was as cold as ice.

Joie abruptly opened her eyes at the sound of Tomas' voice. She dropped the flower on the ground, too stunned to speak.

Luis cleared his throat attempting to remedy the awkwardness of the moment. "Uh, we were just getting a couple more beers and wanted to know if you ladies needed anything while we were up."

Ronnie dropped her head in embarrassment for Joie. "No, we're good. Thanks anyway, sweetie."

"Tomas..." Joie stepped towards him. "Uh, how long were you standing there?" She pasted a thin smile on her face, anxiously wringing her hands together. The bumblebee danced in front of her face causing her to sidestep its awkward flight.

"Long enough to know that this is good-bye," he said before calmly turning away. He stopped and added, "I'll drop your luggage off later. Veronica, Luis, I'll see you guys."

No one said a word until they heard the front door slam shut and Tomas' car start up. They all let out a collective sigh of relief that the situation didn't escalate.

"Ronnie... Luis... Guys, I am so sorry. I don't know why I keep fucking things up. I shouldn't have come out here this weekend, but I had to have one last fling. I am so fuckin' stupid!" She flopped down into the wicker chair, knocking the glass of iced tea to the deck. Luckily, it didn't break.

"Joie, calm down. Tomas will be okay." Ronnie looked to Luis for confirmation. He didn't give it.

She jumped from the chair and paced the length of the deck. "I've got to call him. Have to explain that it wasn't him. It's me. I'm the fucked up one. Since I knew I was planning on getting back with Cedric, I should have kept my ass in Virginia," she reasoned. "Why couldn't I just leave well enough alone? Got *two* good men who want to be with me and I fuck it up because I can't make up my fuckin' mind."

Ronnie didn't say another word during her friend's rant. She let Joie work out her situation on her own, because as far as she was concerned, Joie was totally to blame.

"Guys, do you mind if I stay the night? My flight leaves tomorrow evening." She hesitated before adding, "And I may need a ride to the airport."

"You're always welcome here, Joie," said Ronnie. *Even if you do keep fucking everything up.*

"That's right. We have plenty of room." Luis glanced at Ronnie and slowly backed into the kitchen. He was not about to get in the middle of any of this. "If you need me, you know where I'll be."

Ronnie gazed at Luis sympathetically. She mouthed, "I'm sorry."

He shook his head in disgust, went to the fridge for another beer, and quickly retreated back to the man cave.

"Hope I didn't ruin your evening, especially since this *is* technically still your honeymoon."

"Naw, girl. We were just chillin' and it's not like we can have much of a honeymoon—considering I'm already pregnant. Anyway, Luis always watches basketball on Saturday. It's the one day he can walk around the house in his underwear. But he did put on sweatpants since we have company."

Joie looked at her with red-tinged eyes. "You think Tomas will forgive me?"

"Honestly?"

"Yeah, will he?"

"No, I don't think so. Tomas really does care about you. I've never seen him act like this with any other woman."

"That's what I was afraid of. Give a man some good cootchie and he loses his mind. Oh well…"

"Oh my goodness! You are positively shameless!" Ronnie replied in disbelief at Joie's sudden shift in her attitude.

"I'm just telling the truth. I like Tomas and all, but don't blame me because he got pussy-whipped."

Just like that, all signs of anxiety were gone, only to be replaced with Joie's arrogance.

"You need to get down on your knees and pray that God don't strike you down. Here you are trying to get back together with Cedric, but at the same time, you got your ass over here in California getting busy with Tomas. Remember, you have a couple of planes to get on before your ass is back in Virginia."

Joie flicked her weave away from her eyes and sneered at her friend. "I was just trying to have a little bit of fun before me and Cedric settled back down for good. Don't hate the playa, hate the game…"

Shocked by Joie's attitude, Ronnie could only shake her head.

"For real tho', Tomas was just a bump in the road. I had no intentions of getting seriously involved with him. Matter of fact, all the men I've been involved with since me and Cedric broke up were just distractions to get my mind off him."

"Okay. If that's how you truly feel. I just hope you know karma can be a spiteful bitch."

Joie pondered Ronnie's words. "You're right. I'm being ornery. I've got to apologize to Tomas and then get my ass home to make this work with Cedric. I don't need no bad karma coming my way."

"Joie, I am truly happy to hear about you and Cedric. You guys were a good team and a great couple. And obviously, since he's willing to come back after all the mess you put him through, he must have forgiven you. That in itself is worth thanking the Lord for."

"You said a mouthful sister." She sighed, "I'm gonna try to call Tomas and apologize. I know he's probably not trying to hear anything I've got to say, but I've got try."

"Do what you gotta do, girl." Ronnie let out a loud, long yawn. "You have to excuse me, but I'm going inside to take a nap. The apartment is unlocked. Help yourself to whatever you need."

"Thanks girlfriend. I promise I'll make up for all the trouble I keep bringing to your door step. I don't want to be the one who always takes from this friendship and offers nothing but problems in return. It's time I start giving back."

"Just try thinking *before* you speak and show some consideration for other people some time. That's all I ask of you. And I'll accept you no matter what—including all your crazy-ass issues."

"Friends to the end?"

"And you know that!" Ronnie yawned again, before padding away inside.

Chapter Thirty

*T*ravis spent most of his weekend with his eyes glued to the television, tracking a massive hurricane barreling towards Haiti. In the last twenty-four hours, the storm had shifted directions and was now expected to arrive over the island later in the day. *The Weather Channel* indicated Port-au-Prince was probably going to suffer a direct hit as the storm made its way westward. With wind speeds approaching 150 mph, the Category 4 hurricane was projected to be downgraded to a Category 1 storm by the time it hit the Gulf Coast.

Ever since hearing about the hurricane, Travis tried calling the emergency contact numbers Kiara left with him. Unfortunately, he was unable to reach anyone who could provide any reliable information. Feeling helpless, he fought back the urge to panic.

Monique remained by Travis' side, doing what she could to allay his fears. Nevertheless, by the time Sunday morning rolled around, he was a total wreck.

"I'm going crazy just sitting here. I don't know where Kiara is and I can't reach anyone who speaks English."

"Have you contacted her teacher? What was his name…"

"Yeah, I spoke with Quinn last night. He's back in the states and hasn't been in touch with any of the group for about a week. He told me he would put out a few calls for status, but so far…nothing."

"Thank God, she's not alone. There are hundreds of volunteers from the U.S. to help make sure those kids stay safe. I have no idea what you're going through right now, but for all its worth, Kiara is a smart young lady. She'll be fine."

"I'm sure you're right. If only I could hear her voice, I'd feel a whole lot better."

"She'll call."

"Yeah, but in the meantime, I've got to get a hold of Ronnie. Maybe Luis knows someone down there who can help."

"I'll give you a few minutes."

"Thanks."

"You want me to brew some coffee?"

"Coffee sounds great." He took a deep breath and picked up the phone.

* * *

Ronnie woke up early the next morning. It was Sunday. She twisted the stylish band—her wedding ring, around her finger and smiled in contentment, listening to Luis' light snoring. Easing out from under the covers so as to not wake him, she grabbed her robe from the chair, picked up her cell phone from the dresser, and went out to the kitchen to call her mother.

Dianna picked up on the first ring. "Hello, my lovely daughter," she answered.

"Hey Mama, I see you're finally using callerID." Ronnie laughed.

"I sure am. It's nice to see who's calling before you answer because if it's somebody I don't want to talk to, I let the answering machine pick up for me."

"I have some news…" Ronnie sang out.

"You sound happy. What is it this time, child?"

"Me and Luis eloped."

"You did what?"

"We got married!"

"When did this happen? And why wasn't I invited?"

"We were married on Friday and it was totally on the spur of the moment, but that's not all the news I have."

"You mean there's more? Hold on a minute so I can take this bacon off the stove."

Ronnie's other line buzzed. It was Travis calling. She clicked over and said, "Hey Travis, let me call you back. I have my mother on the other line."

"Okay, but call back as soon as you can. It's important."

"I will." She clicked back over.

"I'm back," Dianna said. "What else you do you have to tell me?"

"Are you sitting down?"

"Child, will you pull back on all the drama and just tell me what's going on?"

"Okay." She took a deep breath. "Mama, remember when I told you that we're having a baby?"

"Yes. Is everything all right?" Dianna asked, alarmed.

"Everything is fine. We just found out a couple days ago that we're having twins."

"Twins?"

"Yes. A boy and a girl."

"Oh my! I'm going to have *two* grandkids to spoil?"

"That's right, Mama."

"Veronica, you are going to get sick and tired of seeing me, I'm going to be out there so often."

She doesn't know we're moving to Santo Domingo. "Mama, uh, there's one more thing and this isn't going to make you happy."

"What is it?"

"Luis and I have decided to move—to Santo Domingo."

"Is that another city in California? Because if it is, that isn't such a big thing."

"No, it's in the Dominican Republic—where Luis was born."

"Oh... I see. The Dominican Republic..." She paused before speaking again. Seemed like she needed the time to process the information. "When are you leaving?" she asked, sounding as if someone had let the wind out of her sails.

Luis trudged sleepily into the kitchen and headed straight for the coffeepot. He kissed Ronnie on her forehead and set about preparing his morning cup of coffee.

"We're considering moving sometime this month. Luis opened a new office down there and..."

"You mean you're moving *this* month? Before the babies are born? Is it safe to give birth in that foreign country? Will they be American citizens?"

"I know you probably think this is kind of sudden, but this is something Luis and I have been wanting as long as we've been together. I've already spoken to my doctor and she says we will be fine. Of course, she'll have to clear me to fly, but the hospitals there are very safe. And as long as we're American citizens, so are the babies."

"You sure don't let no grass grow under your feet, do you?"

"Mama, are you okay? I mean with us moving?"

"Well, considering I don't have a say in the matter, I suppose I'll have to learn to live with your decision."

"You can still come to visit as often as you like. The DR isn't that far from Florida, so it'll probably only take a couple more hours than flying out here to California."

"That's true. Well, I guess I'd better apply for a passport now because I am going to be there as soon as my grandchildren are born."

Ronnie laughed. "I wouldn't expect you to be anywhere else."

"Woo wee, you sure know how to make an impact first thing on a Sunday morning, don't you? I'm going to ask Pastor to say a special prayer for your new family."

"I'm sorry to drop this on you all at once."

Dianna interrupted. "Are you happy?"

"Oh Mama, I am so happy, I can hardly stand myself," she replied. "Me and Luis are doing great, we got a couple of babies on the way, and I've even started writing my novel. So, yes, I am so happy." She smiled at Luis fiddling with the can opener, trying to open the coffee can.

"Then that's all that matters, isn't it?"

"Yes, ma'am. After all these years, I am finally going to have my very own family. And since I now have you and Kiara in my life, it's complete."

"By the way, how is my granddaughter?"

"I haven't spoken to her in a while, but she keeps in touch with Travis. Apparently, they don't have the best phone service down there and the mission she's working for only lets them call home about once a month. But she did mention she received that package your church sent. She said the kids loved the toys and candy."

Luis was reminded that he needed to call his cousin, Fernando. He took his phone in the other room so as not to disturb Ronnie's phone call.

"That child has that adventurous streak in her and now that she's had a taste of freedom, it's going to be difficult keeping her still."

"Kiara is going to be fine. She has a good head on her shoulders."

"Well, it's getting late and I've got to get ready for church. You two found yourself a church home?"

"No, not yet."

"Don't let that slide for long. Anyhow, thanks for calling and despite how I may have sounded earlier, I am happy for you and Luis. There ain't nothing better than being married to someone who truly loves you."

"Thanks, Mama."

"Promise you'll call before you move, so I can know where you are. Like I said, I'm going online first thing today and apply for my passport. And tell my son-in-law that I said congratulations and welcome to the family."

"I will. Love you, Mama. I'll talk to you soon."

Ronnie hung up the phone and went to find Luis. He was perched on the edge of the sofa holding the phone firmly to one ear, focused on the television. He was watching *The Weather Channel* as he spoke in a combination of English and Spanish. He looked up at her with a worried expression before refocusing on the TV.

She turned to face the object of his concern. The weatherman pointed to several computer models projecting the path of a huge Category 4 hurricane. Coverage included newscasters standing in front of waves of water coming ashore and palm trees bent so low they almost touched the ground. The outer bands of the hurricane had pounded Haiti for hours and the eye of the storm was projected to pass over Port-au-Prince by the end of the day.

Luis abruptly ended his call and pulled Ronnie down on the couch next to him. He dropped his head and slid his hands over his face. It was his 'I'm-very-worried gesture'.

"What's going on?" she asked in a tentative voice.

"That was my cousin, Fernando. He hasn't been able to reach Port-au-Prince because of the storm. All the roads are closed and he can't get to town until the hurricane passes."

"Are you telling me he hasn't found Kiara? That was days ago."

"Not yet. Since he can't travel, he's calling his contacts at several of the charities. So far, no one has seen her."

"Travis called while I was on the phone. I wonder if he knows anything." She clutched his arm trying to not panic.

"Call him back. Let's find out."

Ronnie turned from the television and dialed Travis' number. He picked up on the first ring.

"Ronnie, thanks for calling me back. Uh, I was wondering if you've heard from Kiara."

Upon hearing his question, her heart sank when she realized Travis also didn't know where their daughter was. "No, I was hoping you had."

"Shit! That's what I was afraid of."

"What's going on, Travis? You're frightening me."

"There is a huge hurricane headed their way. No one seems to know where Kiara is."

"Yeah, I just found out about the hurricane."

He sighed, "Why hasn't she called to let us know she's okay? She must know we're worried."

"When was the last time you spoke with her?" she asked.

"About three days ago, when she said she needed to see a doctor. I hoped Luis' cousin had already treated her."

"Luis just spoke to Fernando. He wasn't able to get to Kiara because of the storm. Travis, is she going to be all right?" Ronnie clutched Luis' arm. Her eyes darted back to the television. A reporter strolled along a South Carolina beach interviewing surfers excited about riding the large waves.

"I sure hope so." He paused. "Ronnie, is Luis there?"

"Yes, he's right here."

"Do you mind if I speak to him?"

"Sure, hold on." She turned to Luis and handed him the phone. "He wants to speak to you."

Luis took the phone from Ronnie. He nervously paced the floor glancing occasionally at updates on the television. Obviously, Travis was doing all the speaking because all Luis said was, 'yes', 'uh huh', 'sure', 'all right', and 'will do'. He clicked off and gave the phone back to her.

"What did he say?"

"He asked me would I be willing to go to Haiti to find Kiara if she isn't found soon. For obvious reasons, he isn't able to go himself and he doesn't trust anyone else with locating her."

"Travis must be really worried if he asked you that. What did you tell him?"

"What else could I say? Of course, I'll go search for your daughter. If it comes to that..."

Ronnie turned down the volume. "You know, sometimes this station pisses me off with their weather coverage. Right now, Haiti is getting hit by devastating winds and torrential rain and all these assholes can focus on is surfing and where the storm will make landfall stateside."

Luis ran his hand over his scruffy chin. "Happens all the time. The good thing is, islanders are used to hurricanes and know how to properly prepare. I'm sure Kiara is fine and it will be just a matter of time before she's located. Look, I don't want you to worry. My cousin and his team are there. They'll find her. I promise."

"I sure do hope you're right."

"Me too, baby. Me too," he mumbled under his breath and held her in a reassuring embrace.

The kitchen door slammed shut, causing them both to jump. They had all but forgotten Joie was still there. The shuffling noise of her house shoes against the tile floor announced her presence way before they even saw her.

"Good morning Mr. and Mrs. Duarte. How are my favorite newlyweds this…?" Joie stopped midsentence when she realized she had walked in on something important.

"Hey Joie." Ronnie pulled away from Luis. She turned her face away trying to hide her growing fears.

Joie slowly backed out of the room. "I can come back later if I interrupted you guys."

"No, come on in. We were just discussing Kiara," explained Ronnie regaining her composure.

"Is she all right?"

Luis pointed to the television. "Haiti is taking a direct hit from the hurricane. No one's been able to locate her for several days."

"Can't you contact the Red Cross?"

"We tried. The phone lines are down." Ronnie fixated on the television again. "They're third world poor down there."

"I'm sure she's fine."

Ronnie smiled and replied, "Yeah, you're probably right." And to keep her mind from thinking dreadful thoughts, she busied herself with the chores of being a hospitable host. "Hey girl, you want some coffee? Luis just put on a fresh pot."

"Coffee sounds great. Thanks."

The ladies went to the kitchen and left Luis to monitor the situation in Haiti.

As Ronnie left his view, he flopped back on the sofa. He sipped his coffee and murmured to himself, "This is going to be one helluva long week. God help us all."

Chapter Thirty-One

*F*irst thing Monday morning, Luis showed up for work and headed straight to Julio's office. He wanted to clear the air as quickly as possible to avoid any potential explosive situations.

"Julio, my man! *Qué pasa?*"

He greeted Luis with a heartfelt handshake. "Boss, I hear congratulations are in order."

"Yeah, Ronnie and I finally decided to tie the knot."

"About time you made an honest woman out of her, Duarte. It was the right thing to do…especially with her being pregnant and all."

An uncomfortable silence ensued following Julio's comment. Recognizing his overly personal gaffe, he cleared his throat and busied himself gathering files.

"Where is this subpoena from Sanchez's attorney?"

Julio picked up the subpoena and thrust the crumpled paper at Luis. "Here it is. Like I said, it was taped to the front door a few days ago. Why would she do something like this? She wasn't even here a good month."

"There are many people in this world who want only a free ride. They don't put in the blood, sweat and tears to get what they want; preferring handouts from others. This frivolous lawsuit is going to go away quietly."

"I hope so, because she's suing you and the company for a million dollars."

Luis silently read the subpoena, loudly reciting the catch phrases that drew his attention and his ire. "What the hell? *Breach of contract? Sexual harassment? A million dollars?* She must have lost her fucking mind in San Diego along with her fucking morals."

"What are you talking about, boss?"

"Nothing, Julio. I'm going to get to the bottom of this today. There is no way in hell I'm giving this woman anything I've worked so hard for."

Luis returned to his office and phoned Tomas. Before he could answer, Luis changed his mind and ended the call. He pulled Carmen's personnel file to get her address. And before he could talk himself out of what he was doing, he found himself sitting in front of the Sanchez home contemplating his next move.

Common sense prevailed, causing him to phone his cousin. Unfortunately, the call went to voicemail. "Tomas, I'm over at the Sanchez's home to straighten this situation out with Carmen. I'm sitting out front and I might need backup. Hit me back."

Within seconds, Tomas called back. "Are you crazy? What do you mean you're sitting in front of the Sanchez's house?"

"Man, I am not about to let that crazy bitch take what I've worked so hard for. Can you believe she actually has the nerve to sue me for breach of contract *and* sexual harassment?" he asked incredulously.

"Listen to me, *primo*. Carmen Sanchez is an opportunist. I spoke to her husband and he promised me they would drop the lawsuit. She got some shitty advice from her hairdresser who recommended this ambulance chasing attorney. When that lawyer heard you owned your own business, Carmen made up a bunch of lies so they could try to get some quick cash."

"What the fuck, man? She's suing me for sexual harassment when *she* was the one doing the sexual harassing!"

"Calm down. I told her husband what went down in that hotel room—well, not all of the sordid details, obviously—and he wasn't surprised. Apparently, she's done this before."

"What's to stop her from going through with this and making my life a living hell?"

"*Señor* Hernandez, that's who."

"Hernandez? *The Señor Hernandez* from the Hernandez Group in San Diego?"

"One and the same. Coincidentally, one of my ladies is real tight with his assistant. I made a few calls, asked several questions, and discovered Carmen Sanchez is a piece of work. When she found out how rusty your Spanish truly was, she convinced Hernandez that she was your right-hand woman and the deal would fall apart without her being involved."

"I'll be…"

"When he discovered you tore up the contract, he figured the terms weren't favorable for you, that's all. He had no idea Carmen had set you up."

"I explained the situation and he agreed to submit an official statement outlining how Carmen Sanchez overstated her importance to your firm. I showed Hernandez's statement to her husband and rather than suffer the embarrassment, he decided they'd be better off dropping the lawsuits."

Luis closed his eyes, exhaling in quiet relief. "Tomas, I love you, man."

"Don't get all sentimental on me. After all, that's what family is for. I told you I'd take care of it, so you need to go home before you get your non-fighting ass in trouble. And I advise you to relearn your language, so this lost-in-translation shit doesn't happen again."

Luis mulled over Tomas' words of wisdom. He was absolutely right. Everything that happened was avoidable—due to his not paying attention. He started his car to leave. As he did so, he saw two little girls run out the door and into the front yard. Watching those innocent kids playing pulled at his heartstrings. They were beautiful little girls who resembled how he imagined his and Ronnie's children would look. *Is Carmen so desperate for cash that she was willing to do anything for it? Including exposing her children to a bunch of bullshit drama and court battles?*

"Tell me cousin, how are *you* doing?" Luis pulled away from the curb.

"Me? I'm as cool as two coconuts chillin' on the beach. Joie explained her situation to me. Had I known she was still wrapped up in her ex, I would never have gotten involved with her."

"That's tough luck, man. Listening to Ronnie tell it, I don't believe Joie even knew she was still wrapped up in him."

In the midst of his u-turn, the front door of the house opened and a small boy wandered out to the yard to play with his sisters. At that moment, Luis saw Carmen standing at the door shouting at her children. And rather than let himself get dragged into some drama, he pulled away from the family scene and headed back to the office.

"Did you take her crazy ass to the airport?"

"Of course, I did. Ronnie would have killed me had I put her friend in a taxi."

"How did she seem when you dropped her off?"

"We didn't talk much, but she seemed fine."

"Sorry for burdening you guys with my problems, but after hearing her speak about her ex-husband—soon to be husband, again... Really, what was the point in seeing her again? It was over as far as I was concerned."

"I understand. Like you said, that's what family is for."

Not one to dwell on the past, Tomas said, "In other news, do you remember when I borrowed that cash from you a few months ago?"

"You paid me back. No big deal. You need more?" Luis chuckled.

"Ha ha, that's very funny, *primo*. No, I don't need your money because I have just made a small fortune of my own."

"What do you mean? How?" Luis sped back to his office.

"That grand was just enough to add to my down payment on several parcels of commercial property up north. My accountant called this morning and gave me the news that a commercial developer wants to purchase the land for a crazy amount of cash. I am going to rake in millions!"

"Tomas, that's great news!"

"So what I was thinking is I can be your partner in your new office in Santo Domingo."

Luis laughed. "You don't know anything about the graphics design business. You're a commercial realtor."

"I don't need to know about graphics design, because you know all there is to know about it. You did a great job in this office and I see no reason the office down there won't be just as successful."

"I don't know what to say."

"Of course, I'm only coming in as an investor. I will be your silent partner with no plans to become involved in the daily routines of running the business."

"Now, those sound like terms I can accept. Let's get together later this week to iron out the details."

"*¡Chévere!* I'm on my way to meet with my lawyer as we speak. They're drawing up the papers for my transaction, so the next time you see me, I'll be a very rich man."

Luis laughed again. "What 'til I tell Ronnie about this. And I can't wait for her to tell Joie that she just passed up on a millionaire."

Chapter Thirty-Two

Several days passed with still no word from Kiara. No one—including Fernando—had seen, or heard from her since before the hurricane. It was time for the men to make a move.

Travis' driver pulled up to the Duarte's house a little after ten on a cloudy Saturday morning. They were supposed to be at the Santa Elena airport in less than two hours to catch their flight out.

Luis peered out the door and waved to Travis. He asked Ronnie, "Are you sure you're going to be okay here on your own? I can arrange for someone to look in on you."

"That won't be necessary. I'll be fine. I'm not due for another few months, so there is absolutely nothing to worry about. I just want you to go find my daughter and bring her back safely because I'm beside myself right now."

"Baby, we are going to find her. Fernando said the roads are now passable and he has all his people looking for her group."

"I don't know what I'll do if something has happened to Kiara." Her eyes filled with tears.

"I'll find her; I promise."

"I know you will." She wiped her eyes dry. "Are you picking up Tomas on the way to the airport?"

He nodded. "I just called him and told him we're on the way. Our flight leaves soon so I'd better get going."

Ronnie slipped her sandals on her bare feet.

"Just where do you think you're going?"

"I'm going to the airport with you. Travis can bring me back home after you guys takeoff." She raised her hand and said, "Don't try to stop me. Since I can't go down there with you, the least I can do is go to the airport and make sure you get off safely."

"I love you. You're going to make a great mother." Luis realized his gaffe as soon as the words left his mouth.

She grabbed her purse, her phone, and her keys. "I already *am* a great mother, remember? Now let's go."

The driver opened the back door for his passengers. Ronnie climbed in first; Luis followed.

"Ronnie, what a nice surprise."

"Hope you don't mind me riding along."

"Not at all. How are you, Luis?"

"I'm fine. How about yourself?"

"I'll be better once I know that Kiara is safe," he replied.

They rode in awkward silence for several minutes before anyone spoke, making their way to the main drag through town. Travis' tired eyes rested on Ronnie's very pregnant stomach and her cheap wedding ring. *Look at that ring, I wonder if his business is tanking... Damn, I'm tripping! I need to get a grip on myself.*

Ronnie felt Travis' eyes settle upon her belly. She interlaced her fingers and protectively rested her hands across what remained of her lap. And trying to ease the mounting tension inside the limo, she asked, "Have you heard anything from anyone?"

Travis snapped out of his trance. "No, nothing and no one seems to know anything about her group. Quinn is on his way back down, but he doesn't know any more than I do. I just wish I were able to go myself."

Luis rested his hand on Ronnie's thigh, and his eyes on Travis.

"Thanks for doing this, man." Travis offered Luis his hand. "I can't tell you how much I appreciate you and Tomas going down there."

"You're welcome. She's very important to all of us."

The driver lowered the privacy glass and asked for Tomas' address.

Luis leaned forward, answering, "He's right at the base of the hills on the western side of town."

"Is that on the outskirts of Santa Elena, sir?" asked the driver.

"Yes, near the old restaurant on the road to Ojai."

"Got it. Thank you." The driver raised the window and returned the privacy back to his passengers.

"How long is the flight?" asked Luis.

Travis handed him the itinerary and explained, "The father of one of my patients owns a private jet that he's willing to let us borrow. He can get you as far as Miami. After you get through customs, you'll catch an American Airlines flight that will get you to Haiti in less than two hours."

"Then what?" asked Ronnie.

"My cousin Fernando will pick us up from the airport. He's standing by for the flight info."

"Oh…that's good," she said.

Travis exhaled in frustration. *This damn paralysis! I can't even go find my own daughter. All I can do is sit idly by and wait for the fucking phone to ring. Why did I agree to let her go to that hell hole of a country, anyway?*

Fifteen minutes later, the driver pulled up in front of Tomas' condominium and tooted the horn once. Tomas ran down the stairs, opened the rear door and climbed in. He was stylishly dressed in a safari outfit straight from a *Land's End* catalog.

"¡*Hola*!" said Tomas.

Luis noted Tomas' get up and laughed inwardly at his cousin's sense of fashion. "Travis, I don't believe you've met my cousin, Tomas De La Cruz."

Tomas reached over. He shook the hand extended by Travis.

"Thank you for going along with Luis. I hope this isn't too much of an imposition."

"Not at all. Once Luis informed me of the situation, there was no way I could not go. I used to visit Port-au-Prince quite often, so I am very familiar with the area."

"I don't know how I can ever repay you for your kindness," Travis said in all sincerity.

"My payment will be safely returning your daughter to you and Veronica."

Travis also noticed Tomas' outfit—complete with a canteen bottle made of a sturdy material, strapped across his shoulder. He also wore an expensive pair of hiking boots. "I see you're well prepared for the trip."

"Hey man, there's no telling what kind of terrain we'll be traveling over. You can't beat having a good pair of boots to protect your feet. I also know that fresh water can be hard to come by, so I want to be prepared for anything." He turned to Luis. "I also brought an extra pair for you, *primo*."

Ronnie patted Tomas' hand in gratitude and smiled at the man she had misjudged for so many years. Now, he was not only family, but was also her friend.

The driver drove past the Santa Elena airport to the small regional airport on the outskirts of town to meet up with the private jet. A line of luxury jets were parked on the ramp with various company names and logos spanning their sides. The airport looked like a parking lot for the filthy rich's expensive playthings.

The pilot, copilot and their male flight attendant stood poised to accommodate their guests. A leathery-faced white man, dressed in well-worn jeans, a blue polo shirt, and a St. Louis Cardinals baseball cap perched atop his head, stood talking to the pilots. An unlit cigar hung from his lips. All, except Travis, assumed the man was the chief mechanic doing a final walkthrough with the pilot. He waved at the driver and pointed to where the limo should park.

Tomas whistled out loud when he saw the private company jet. "That is what I call traveling in style."

As the driver slowly inched the limo closer to the airplane, Travis leaned over and shook both men's hands. "Luis, Tomas... No matter what it takes, please bring my daughter back home..."

"We will find Kiara. And please don't beat yourself up. Kiara will understand why you couldn't make it."

Travis nodded, yet didn't say another word. Instead, he pushed back the awful thoughts that competed for space in his mind.

The driver put the limo in park and hopped out to open the passenger door. Tomas, Luis, and Ronnie stepped onto the tarmac, surveying the airplane. The man, who had spoken with the pilots, acknowledged the trio before climbing into the limo to speak with Travis.

Ronnie threw her arms first around Luis' neck and then Tomas'. "I want you both to promise me you're going to be careful. I want you all three of you to come home safely. Promise?"

"Yes. *Si*. We promise," they replied.

The copilot approached them. "Gentlemen, I hate to rush you, but we need to get going."

"Okay, we'll be right there," Luis replied.

The man, who they all wrongly assumed was the mechanic, got out of the limo and walked towards them. In a gravelly voice, the man said, "Name's Duncan. I want you to know that y'all have got my best pilot flying you to Florida. He's been with the company fifteen years without incident." He nodded in reference to the pilot.

"Nice to meet you, Duncan," all three replied in unison.

He turned to Ronnie and said, "So you're the mother, huh? You've got a great little girl in Kiara. Smart as a whip..."

Ronnie added, "Yes, she is. Thank you so much for the use of your plane."

He tipped his hat to Ronnie. "Pleased I'm able to assist, ma'am. Travis' rehabilitation center helped my boy learn to live with his spinal cord injury, so helping him locate his little girl is the least I can do to repay him. If it weren't for that man sitting in that limo..." His voice cracked and he quickly diverted his gaze. "Just make sure y'all bring that little darlin' back home safe and sound, ya hear."

"We'll do our best, Duncan." Luis shook his hand.

"Sir, we need to get wheels up in ten minutes," called out the pilot.

"Well, you'd better get going. He does not like to be late." The old man laughed.

All three men shook hands again. Duncan left the group and went to talk to the pilot.

Ronnie gripped Luis' arm. "Baby, I love you, so much. Please be safe."

"I love you, too. Now go home and try to relax. I will call you when I find her. Don't worry."

She acknowledged him; unable to speak because of the lump stuck in her throat. After a brief kiss, Luis embraced Ronnie one last time and then headed for the plane.

Tomas also gave Ronnie a hug before catching up with Luis. They bounded up the stairs leading into the plane.

Ronnie watched as they disappeared into the plane. After dropping off Joie yesterday, and now watching Luis and Tomas leave, she suddenly felt more alone than she had in a very long time. With tears streaming down her face, she returned to the limousine.

Travis had always hated to see Ronnie cry—today was no exception. "Are you going to be all right?" He reached for her hand—held it tight.

"Yeah." She watched the airplane's door close tight. "I'll be fine."

Although her heart was heavy with her own worrisome thoughts, she also knew how difficult this ordeal was for Travis. She noticed the dark circles under his eyes, and the deep lines from worry, embedded in his forehead. She wasn't alone after all. Somehow that realization lessened the stress.

"I don't think either one of us will be okay until we know Kiara is safe and sound."

Travis nodded in agreement as he watched the jet make its way towards the runway.

Chapter Thirty-Three

*T*he flight from Miami touched down in Santo Domingo shortly before midnight. After a slight delay caused by not having return airline tickets out of the country, Luis was tasked with explaining the purpose of their trip to the custom officials. Once they were cleared by the Dominican authorities, with confirmation calls made to Fernando and the Red Cross, the men boarded a smaller plane headed to Haiti. The last leg of their flight took less than an hour to reach Port-au-Prince.

The small plane taxied and parked near the main terminal building. When the flight attendant opened the door, Luis followed Tomas down the mobile staircase into the night air.

Luis wiped the sweat from his brow with the back of his hand. "I forgot how humid this island can be—even at this time of night."

"You'd better get used to it, especially since you'll soon be moving here."

"It's not me I'm worried about. Ronnie still has a couple of months to go before the babies are born. I'm not sure she will be able to get used to the heat, especially after coming from California."

They followed the line of passengers inside to the customs counter. A customs agent stamped Luis' passport and waved him through with no problems. Tomas went next. They picked up their luggage from the baggage carousel and headed outside to wait for Fernando.

As they waited for their cousin to arrive, a young boy who should have been home in bed approached them. He was carrying a box filled with chilled water bottles. He thrust the box at the two, and in perfect English said, "Water. One dollar each, please."

"Good thing we'll be up in the mountains. It's much cooler up there." Tomas reached into an inside pocket of his safari vest and retrieved a thick wad of bills. He peeled off three and handed them to the child in exchange for the water. "That extra dollar is for you, *amigo*."

"*Gracias, señor*," replied the grateful child.

"Thanks." Luis took the bottle from Tomas. He sucked the water down in one gulp. "You still do that?"

"What?"

"Carry a roll of one dollar bills when you come home."

"You know everybody wants a tip. Plus, I don't have to pull out my wallet every time I need to buy something."

Luis chuckled, "I've been in the United States way too long. I can't wait to get back home and reconnect with my roots, again."

"I hear ya, *primo*. There is nothing like being on this island. Nothing like coming home again."

People of every imaginable hue hung outside the terminal awaiting transportation. Many were European aide workers coming down to volunteer in the cleanup efforts. Puerto Ricans were there to visit relatives. A few Black Americans were indistinguishably scattered in amongst the Dominicans. Several passengers were Haitian, possibly returning home to reclaim whatever remained of their family's possessions.

A tall, thin, dark skinned, very attractive man, dressed in blue slacks and a white short-sleeved shirt approached them. The man's casual stride was reminiscent of President Obama's—it projected the quiet confidence of a self-assured man comfortable in his own skin. He smiled revealing a mouthful of perfect white teeth. On closer inspection, a small tuft of hair protruded from beneath the middle of his lower lip. The men back home referred to it as a *soul patch*.

The man, filled with unabashed excitement, reached out towards Luis, enveloping him in his long arms... "*¿Qué pasa,* Luis?"

"Fernando Doucet! What's up, man?" Luis returned his cousin's embrace with the same enthusiasm.

Fernando pulled back. "Tomas De La Cruz? I didn't know you were coming. Good to see you too." Fernando hugged him as well.

"You know I couldn't let Luis come down and search for Kiara on his own."

"He is not by himself; I am here." Fernando's smile faded.

"You know what I mean. Good to see you, Fernando." Noticing his cousin's vapid reaction to his presence, Tomas stopped short of saying anything further. He let the other two men speak.

Luis sensed tension between his cousins, but didn't have the inclination to delve in further. His primary concern was finding Kiara. Whatever was going on between his cousins would have to wait. "Have you heard anything?"

"Sorry. Nothing."

The full moon brilliantly lit the night sky. Luis gazed up at the silhouette of the mountains looming in the distance. From where he stood, the country was peaceful, serene, and beautiful. But from previous experience, he knew that a false reality existed when looking at a situation from afar.

"That's what I was afraid of... I hoped you at least knew of her general location by now."

"There are many people, including my own, which are currently searching for your daughter and the two other girls. Actually, their entire group is missing and hasn't been heard from in over a week."

"What do you mean? The entire group?"

"When the hurricane hit, the girls took it upon themselves to vacate their group of school children from the town to find better shelter. They left the other volunteers behind and headed elsewhere."

"Are you telling me that they're out there with a bunch of kids?"

"Yes. I've spoken with the missionaries they were assigned to. Neither they, nor any of the other volunteers, have any idea where the girls went. They told them to stay in the school where it was safe and to wait for the hurricane to pass. They did not listen. So now they are lost."

Luis passed his hands over his head in frustration. He knew all too well that hard-headed streak that Kiara possessed, because he had witnessed it many times in the past from Ronnie.

None wanted to discuss the danger three young American girls traveling with a bunch of kids had put themselves in. Most Haitians were decent, hard-working, honest people—but not all. Having grown up on the island, they all knew that the possibility for the girls to be sexually assaulted, or worse, existed. Since the earthquake, the molestation of young girls had become a much too frequent occurrence in the tiny nation. Sadly, it had become a way of life.

Luis sighed wearily, "What do we do now? Where do we start?"

"My jeep is parked over there. I guess we can drive to the camp first thing tomorrow morning and question the people she worked with."

"Fernando, one more thing... Ronnie said Kiara had cut her arm. She mentioned she needed medicine for the cut because of the potential for infection."

"How badly was she hurt?"

"I don't know. She didn't say..."

Fernando lowered his head. "That's not good. A simple cut can become infected quite easily in the jungle leading to all sorts of complications."

"Like what sort of complications?" asked Tomas.

He looked away. "At the moment, I'd rather not say. Come with me. I've arranged for lodging a few miles from here. I'll let you both get cleaned up and afterwards we can get something to eat. We will head out at first light."

They got into Fernando's jeep. He drove about thirty minutes through the city, stopping when he reached a small town on the outskirts. The town was so quiet that only an occasional barking dog disrupted the absolute silence. They parked outside a quaint hotel covered in pink stucco. The structure resembled an apartment complex more than a hotel and it appeared some residents were more long-term than others. The moon illuminated the path to the front desk where a tired looking man awaited their arrival.

After they had received their room keys, Fernando asked about the possibility of finding food. The hotel clerk pointed across the street. Though late, it appeared the restaurant was still open for business, because the air was filled with pungent, aromatic, garlic-laced scents.

The men wandered across the street. They discovered the restaurant was not normally open that time of night. However, as it goes in most small towns, the owner of the restaurant had gotten wind about the men's quest to locate Kiara. Thus, he decided to stay open to provide them with a good hot meal.

After dinner, Luis checked into his sparsely furnished room. He plucked his cell phone from his pocket and called his new wife to provide her with an update.

* * *

After Travis dropped Ronnie off at home, she spent the remainder of the day piddling around the house trying to find the motivation to continue working on her half written novel. She wandered to the guest house, pushed open the door to her office, and stood staring at the computer screen for a full ten minutes before finally giving up. *At the rate I'm going, I won't finish this book until the twins are in kindergarten.* Feeling defeated, she returned to the main house.

Although she knew it would be hours before she heard from Luis, she continued to check her phone every fifteen minutes. By the time nightfall had arrived, she was a nervous wreck. As a distraction, she tuned in a boring movie and stretched out on the sofa to watch. She must have dozed off because when the house phone rang after ten o'clock, she nearly jumped out of her skin.

The callerID flashed on the television screen. It was Luis. Stilling her nerves, she picked up the phone. "Did you find her?"

"I'm sorry, darling. Not yet."

Disappointment seeped into her bones. "Oh…"

"We're going out first thing tomorrow morning, though. Fernando has a good plan of where to begin."

"Oh, okay… That's good. How was your flight?" She wiped the tears from her eyes and focused on Luis.

"The flight was fine. Fernando picked us up at the airport. We just returned from dinner and now I'm sitting in a hotel—if you can call it that." He glanced around the room at the austere conditions, painfully aware how he had become accustomed to luxury.

"Be careful, baby. I don't want anything to happen to you."

"I will. Now try to get some sleep."

"I'm so worried about Kiara; Travis is too. I told him I'd call as soon as I heard from you."

"Hopefully, I will have good news tomorrow. It's late and we're getting an early start in the morning."

She looked at their wedding photo sitting on a shelf. "I love you."

"Love you, too. I'll call you tomorrow."

"Okay. Goodnight." While she listened to the dial tone on the other end, she gripped the phone tightly in her hands. Despite the late hour, she knew Travis was waiting for her call. She dialed his number and as expected, he picked up immediately.

"Ronnie? Did you talk to Luis?"

"Yeah, he just called. They still don't have any news."

"I'm not surprised. They probably just landed."

"They're going out first thing tomorrow morning."

"Good. That's real good."

"I'll call you as soon as I hear something."

"I'll do the same. Thanks for calling."

"You're welcome. Try to get some sleep." She parroted Luis' advice to him.

"You too. Goodnight." He hung up and rolled over in bed. Monique's warm body was a nice contrast against the cool sheets.

She asked, "Anything?"

He closed his eyes tightly and replied, "Not yet."

"Maybe they'll find her tomorrow."

"Yeah, maybe… Let's get some sleep. I have a feeling tomorrow is going to be a long day."

"I'm more than happy to stick around, if you need me."

"We'll see about tomorrow, but I'm glad you're here now." He pulled Monique close and kissed her goodnight.

Chapter Thirty-Four

*E*arly the next morning, Luis, Tomas, and Fernando assembled in the hotel lobby. They trekked across the street to the restaurant for a hearty breakfast of bacon, fried eggs, *mangu*, local pastries, and tropical fruit. They washed it all down with strong black coffee. Due to the time change and the early morning activity of the locals, no one managed to get a good night's sleep. Yet, in spite of their fatigue, they were all raring to go find Kiara.

Fernando pulled out a map of the area and plotted their course. "We can begin at the camp and gradually work our way outwards. Several of my colleagues have also spread the word about our search, so hopefully by this evening we will have news of her whereabouts."

Luis sipped his coffee, feeling troubled by the hesitancy in his cousin's voice last night when he spoke about Kiara's condition. "Fernando, when you said Kiara's cut can lead to complications, what did you mean? I want to know what we're up against."

His cousin took a deep breath and explained, "Left untreated, a minor cut can easily become infected and lead to what we call jungle-rot. If it *remains* untreated, the infection gets so bad the victim can lose a limb or eventually die. It's pretty common down here." In his mind, he also wanted to add, *so let us go find this girl before it's too late.*

Tomas asked, "What is common down here? The infection or dying from it?"

He looked his cousin squarely in the eye. Without missing a beat, he replied, "Both."

"*Coño!*" Tomas exclaimed, while staring off into the distance.

The three men once again piled into the jeep and headed to the camp where Kiara was last seen. Upwards they climbed on a mountainous dirt road that seemed to defy the laws of gravity. One minor mistake at the wheel could easily send the vehicle veering off the road and into the jungle floor, hundreds of feet below.

Finally, after the tortuous ride ended, Fernando stopped at a place that looked like they had landed at the edges of the earth.

Taking it all in, Luis was totally dismayed by the living conditions in the camp. Though he had seen images of many relief camps on the evening news, seeing the devastation that still existed up close and personal was a surreal experience. For miles upon miles, tents stretched as far as the eye could see. Hundreds of orphaned children milled around with nothing to do in the squalid camp. Starving dogs, with rib cages showing through their skin, nosed through piles of garbage that were virtually everywhere.

A dozen or so women stood in line with buckets, bowls, or tin cans to get water from a water faucet installed by the Red Cross. Soldiers carrying M-16's patrolled the camp, intimidating those who dared cross their path, with the threat of jail. And disease carrying raw sewage trickled into makeshift gutters, some spilling over in the streets.

Tomas was equally disturbed at the sight of crumbling buildings being propped up by fragile tree limbs and rotted boards. Trash was everywhere the eye could see. He closed his eyes and shook his head at the horrible conditions.

And yet, amidst all the squalor and misery, they saw the resilience of the Haitians shining through. Many industrious entrepreneurs had set up makeshift stores to sell whatever foodstuffs they could lay their hands on. Several people, unperturbed by their surroundings, were gathered at a food tent, laughing and telling stories. A group of school children dressed in raggedy, soiled uniforms trailed each other to school, as if it were just another normal day.

Fernando watched his cousins' astonished reactions to the conditions he encountered on a daily basis.

"What happened to the billions of dollars that were donated right after the earthquake?" Luis posed the question to Fernando. "Where did the money go?"

He simply shrugged and replied, "The way it is now, is the way it always has been, and the way it most likely will always be."

"Isn't that an awfully fatalistic attitude to take about your own country?" Tomas smirked.

Fernando turned to Tomas. "We make do with what we have. And it's not like the Dominicans are doing anything to help now, is it? They are deporting Haitians and shutting down the border faster than I can blink my eyes. Their attitude seems to be, the quicker they get rid of them, the better off the country will be. Unless of course, they need somebody to pick their crops."

"Hey, don't blame me for how the Dominicans treat your people. I live in the United States, remember?"

Fernando scowled at Tomas and kept walking. He stopped to speak with another doctor who had his hands full with a sick child.

"What is up with you and Fernando?"

"It's a family thing." He pursed his lips in disgust.

"What do you mean *a family thing?* Why don't I know about this?"

"It began years ago as a spat between his mother and mine. My mother denied her Haitian roots and anything to do with Haiti."

Luis furrowed his brow. "What are you talking about?"

"You do know our family was originally from Haiti but moved to the Dominican side when our grandfather found a good job over there, right?"

"So what? Lots of Dominicans have Haitian roots."

"My mother's sister—your aunt and Fernando's mother, moved to Haiti to be with her husband, Pierre Doucet. He was Haitian so they decided to stay and make this their home. One of their kids got sick and from what I can gather, my mother turned her back on Fernando's family."

"Why haven't I heard about this before now?"

"*Yo no se,*" Tomas responded.

"What happened between you two?"

"*Primo*, my mother was so fucking color struck. With her light skin, wavy hair and European features, she didn't want any of her friends to know our family was originally from Haiti. My mother married my light-skinned father and pretended we were straight up Dominican—as if we only had Spanish ancestry. Guess they didn't plan on me coming out caramel colored." He chuckled. "Anyway, you remember when his brother, Charles got sick with cancer?"

"Yes, I remember. He almost died."

"Fernando's mother needed money to help get treatment for Charles. Well, as the story goes, my mother ignored her calls and pretended she didn't know anything about them needing our help."

Luis narrowed his eyes. "I know exactly when that happened because our church raised money to send to their family. I didn't know that about your mother, though. That's messed up."

"Now you know why he hates me. I didn't have anything to do with how my mother treated his, but he still holds it against me." Tomas shrugged.

"I am aware of the disgraceful history that divides our two cultures; it has existed for centuries, but I didn't realize it was in our own family. I guess I put the family drama out of my mind when I moved away."

"So did I, but Fernando hasn't." He watched a young girl sashay past him carrying a young child perched on her waist. She couldn't have been more than fourteen, but winked at him as if she were a grown woman.

Luis grimaced at the deplorable conditions and hypothetically asked, "How can anyone live like this?"

Tomas exhaled loudly, stepping over a dead chicken. "I don't know, *primo*. I really don't…"

Fernando strolled back to where they stood. He addressed Luis. "One of the workers said she used to talk to Kiara all the time about her village up in the mountains. She is convinced they were headed there."

"How far is it?" asked Tomas.

"About twenty miles."

"You're telling me that these girls walked twenty miles in the jungle?" Tomas stared at the terrain stretched out before him.

Luis scratched his head. "What in the world possessed Kiara to think she could take a bunch of kids on a twenty mile hike when a hurricane was headed their way?"

"The last time a hurricane hit, hundreds of people died in flash floods and landslides. I guess she was afraid she would be one of them if she stayed," replied Fernando.

"Has anyone checked the village?" Luis asked.

"No. Up until yesterday, the road was impassable."

"What about now?"

Fernando smiled at last, "The roads are finally open. That means we can do one of two things. We can send someone up there to check or we can go there ourselves."

"Her friend seemed pretty confident they're there, huh?" asked Luis.

"Yes, very…"

"I don't want to wait. I say let's go see for ourselves."

"I agree. Let us go find your daughter."

Neither Luis, nor Tomas corrected Fernando's mistaken reference to Kiara, because at that moment, his daughter was exactly what she was.

* * *

The ride to the mountaintop village took several hours due to storm debris remaining in the dirt road. Though the road was passable; it was…just barely. Several times during the journey, Luis and Tomas got out of the jeep to clear the road. One time, they roped a chain around a fallen tree while Fernando used his jeep to haul it away. With all the unexpected stops, it was almost nightfall by the time they reached the village.

They were greeted by the village elders who confirmed the children were there. A young girl took them to where Kiara and her friends were housed. Fernando conferred with the woman who was treating Kiara. She called herself a doctor, but Luis had his suspicions. The woman in question was also the village shopkeeper, postmaster, and most surprisingly, a mother of twelve.

Luis and Tomas stood over the makeshift hospital bed in the tiny clinic. Alarmed, they peered down at Kiara, lying there unconscious, noting how frail she seemed. According to the other volunteers, she had been in that state for three days.

A freckle-faced girl, who appeared to be about eighteen years old, sat next to Kiara holding her hand. She was reading scripture from a small Bible. She looked up when she saw the men. "Hi, I'm Sarah."

"Hi Sarah, my name is Luis Duarte, I'm a family friend."

"Yeah, I remember Kiara mentioning you. You married her mom, right?"

"That's right." He smiled and glanced over at Kiara. Luis stooped down to the girl's level. "What happened? How did you girls end up here?"

Sarah dropped Kiara's hand and started wringing her own. "Mr. Duarte, we were so scared. The locals kept saying the storm was going to hit. That flood waters would come wash us away... They told us about the last hurricane... People were killed... Mudslides and tornadoes and such..." She looked up with the eyes of a frightened child.

"It's all right. Take your time," Luis said.

"Most of the children in the school were orphans because of that earthquake. So when the hurricane was forecast, those kids thought they were going to die. We didn't mean to get anybody in trouble. We just wanted to save the children so we left the camp and followed a guide up the mountain. The weather turned really bad. When we couldn't keep up with him, he left us behind."

"No one is blaming you for protecting the children. What happened to Kiara?"

"We don't know. Kiara kept saying her arm hurt. She started feeling hot and got really sick. We thought it was because of the humidity, but it was really because she had a fever. Kiara even passed out and me and a couple of kids had to carry her. Thankfully, we found the village." She wiped away the tears now streaming down her face.

"Everything is going to be all right." He looked over at Kiara's motionless body, watching for signs of any potential change. "Did that "doctor" give Kiara anything? Like medicine or drugs?"

She frowned. Lines of worry creased her forehead. "I don't think so. We've been here for almost a week. Kiara has been sick the whole time. I think she was delirious and she kept complaining about her arm hurting. Kept asking us to cut it off."

"I'm glad you all are safe." He sighed in obvious relief.

"Is she going to be all right, Mr. Duarte?"

Luis looked at the frightened teenager and replied, "I think so, but just in case, why don't you keep praying. God is always listening."

A slight smile found its way to the corners of her mouth. "A couple of days ago, the cut on her arm got really gross. It started to ooze out this yucky green pus. Maggots got into the sore, but she was unconscious by then, so she probably didn't feel anything. The doctor crushed some leaves and made a paste. She spread the stuff over the cut. It seemed to make it better."

Luis tenderly touched the girl's arm. "We're going to get you girls out of here tomorrow. Okay?"

"Mr. Duarte, I'm glad you found us."

"So am I, Sarah. So am I."

Fernando walked in with the local doctor at his side. As the "doctor" watched, he opened his medical bag and examined Kiara, asking the doctor several questions throughout the process. He removed the bandage and exposed what he thought would only be a small cut.

Luis and Tomas frowned when they saw the open wound. Her tiny arm was now swollen with the infection. Angry yellow and black splotches covered her forearm. It was not a pretty sight.

His cousin replaced the instruments inside his bag and walked Luis outside away from earshot of Kiara and her young friend. Fernando's grave expression promised a bleak outlook.

"We've got to get her out of here as soon as possible. The village doctor was able to stop the spread of the infection on her arm, but I'm afraid it may possibly have entered her bloodstream."

"Oh my God, Fernando. That doesn't sound good…" Luis said.

Tomas joined the men and stood silently listening to the prognosis. He crossed his arms and asked point blank, "What exactly are you saying?"

"I'm saying that if we don't get her to a hospital soon, she may not survive the night."

Luis gasped. "You mean…" His thoughts immediately went to Ronnie as he stared at Kiara's ashen face.

Fernando crossed his arms across his chest; let out a long, sigh of frustration.

There is no way I can deliver this awful news to Ronnie. I can't. "Then we must move quickly. What do we need to do to make this happen, Fernando?"

"I've already called back to the camp. They have dispatched a med-evac helicopter, but they don't have the proper facilities to treat her in Port-au-Prince. I can get her stabilized, but she's going to need more immediate medical treatment than I can provide. I believe it may be *sepsis.*"

"*Coño!*" exclaimed Luis.

Tomas interjected, "We'll have to get her to Santo Domingo. It's the nearest city with the proper facilities."

Fernando glared at Tomas. "I have to admit, you're right. One of the doctors from the *Doctors Without Borders* team can use his credentials to get her transported to the DR. We already have the helicopter, so the rest should be rather simple. I'll make the arrangements."

"Thank you, Fernando," said Luis.

"Do whatever you need to, man. Money is no object. We've got to get her treated right away." Tomas returned to Kiara's side.

Luis joined him. "I've got to call Ronnie. How am I going to tell her that her daughter may not make it?"

"Don't call her yet. Wait until we get her to the hospital." Tomas picked up Kiara's limp hand and squeezed.

"I promised to call when we found Kiara" He pulled out his phone. "Figures… No reception."

Tomas grabbed Luis' arm. "Listen to me. You are not thinking clearly. Veronica is at home. Alone. She is also very pregnant. You cannot give her this kind of news over the phone."

"I have to tell her something…"

"Call Travis and tell him we've found Kiara. After we get Kiara safely to the DR, then you can phone your wife and tell her that her daughter is being treated at the Santo Domingo hospital."

"You're right." He shook his head. "Tomas, man, she has to pull through this."

Tomas tilted his head towards the young woman sitting next to Kiara's bed. "You told her to pray… Now would be a really good time for us all to pray."

The med-evac helicopter arrived within thirty minutes of Fernando's call to his base camp. Fernando remained in contact with the doctor in Port-au-Prince who made the necessary arrangements to grant the helicopter clearance into the Dominican Republic's airspace.

Less than an hour after loading Kiara onboard the helicopter, the pilot landed safely on top of the Santo Domingo hospital. They were met by a team of doctors and nurses who went into immediate action to assess her condition. The emergency crew unloaded their precious cargo and rushed her to the emergency room. Fernando, Luis, and Tomas followed the gurney into the elevator. Fernando briefed the emergency room doctor as much as he could, then he stepped back to let the local experts take over.

"Is she going to be okay?" Luis asked Fernando.

"I think so, but we may have run into a kink. Technically, because you are not directly related to her, the hospital requires permission from a parent to treat Kiara, past providing emergency care. However, if that isn't possible, they will accept a medical-power-of-attorney."

Luis rubbed his hands over his five o'clock shadow. "Getting a parent here isn't possible. Travis can't travel all this way; Ronnie is in no condition to either. Power of attorney takes too long."

Fernando shrugged helplessly. "I understand. However, they can only provide her with basic emergency care. They need the next-of-kin's permission to do more. I'm sorry, but those are the rules."

"I need to call Travis." Luis found a quiet spot in the busy waiting room to make his call. He glanced over at a young woman who held an infant in her lap. The poor boy's head was wrapped in a bandage with bright traces of blood seeping through. Two small children were stretched out on the same bench sound asleep.

"Hello?" answered Travis.

"Travis, it's me, Luis."

"Please, tell me you've found my daughter." Desperation was evident in his voice.

"Yes, we found her…"

"Thank God! Can I speak to her?"

"There's more I need to tell you."

Travis had already mentally prepared himself for whatever the outcome of Luis' call would bring. "Just give it to me straight; is Kiara all right?"

"Not really. That cut she had…Well, it became very infected. They believe it may be *sepsis*."

"Oh God!" Was all he could say as he imagined the worst.

"We found her in a little village in the mountains. They told us that she had been unconscious for several days before we found her. My cousin examined Kiara and made the decision to have her airlifted to a hospital in Santo Domingo."

"How is she?"

"Thankfully, she's stable at the moment."

"What are they doing for her?"

"That's the problem, Travis. Since she's unconscious, they must have permission from the next of kin to continue treating her."

"What? How the hell am I supposed to get down there in time?" Travis felt absolutely helpless. "My child is dying in some fucking foreign country and I can't even get to her."

"I didn't say she was dying. I said she has an infection…"

"Do you have any idea how fatal that type of an infection can be once it enters the bloodstream? Well, do you?!" he screamed. "Jesus! Am I the only sane person in this world?"

Luis felt Travis' frustration blast through the phone line. His children were yet to be born, but once they were, he would move heaven and earth to protect them. "Travis, I was thinking that you can draw up a legal document giving me medical power of attorney for Kiara."

"Of course. I'll do whatever you need me to do. Just tell me where to send it."

Luis relayed the information for the hospital. "Send it to the attention of my cousin, Dr. Fernando Doucet. He'll make sure it gets to the right people."

"I'll get right on it." He took a deep breath to regain his composure. "I apologize for my outburst, Luis. I am not upset with you; in fact, I am grateful you found my daughter. It's just that I feel so fucking helpless…"

"I understand." He watched the young woman stroke her child's faces. She whispered something to him, causing the child to smile. "After you get the power of attorney done, I need to ask you a favor."

"Sure, Luis. What is it?"

"I haven't called Ronnie yet, because I don't want to give her this kind of news over the phone. Especially in her condition. Can you please drop by the house and tell her what's going on?"

"Yeah, yeah, sure. Of course…"

"She doesn't need to be alone when she receives news such as this."

"Don't worry; I'll go right over."

"Travis, don't give up on your daughter. She's a fighter."

"Thanks. Please call me as soon as you find out more. In the meantime, I'll take care of Ronnie."

Chapter Thirty-Five

*T*ravis understood his physical limitations when it came to breaking bad news to a mother about her child. He needed backup support, so he phoned his friend.

"Monique, I need to ask you a huge favor."

"Sure, Travis. Anything," she replied.

"They found Kiara…"

"That's wonderful news! How is she?"

"According to Luis, she's not well at all. That's why I'm calling."

"I'm listening."

"I need to see Ronnie to give her the news about Kiara. She's over there by herself and…"

"Say no more. Trudy is doing better so I think the kids will be okay with her for a few hours. I'm on my way."

"Thanks, I'll see you soon."

* * *

Ronnie had expected Luis' call with an update hours ago. He told her they were going out first thing that morning to begin the search. When his call didn't come, she once again tried different methods of distraction. For most of the day, she attempted to work on her novel, but mostly ended up staring at blank pages.

When six o'clock rolled around and she still hadn't heard from Luis, she called her mother. Talking to Dianna always made her feel better.

"Mama, Luis said he would call as soon as they found her, but I haven't heard a thing. I'm worried sick."

Dianna replied, "Give him some more time. That's a whole lot of country to search through trying to find one person."

"I just feel so helpless sitting here." *Thankfully, he has Tomas and his cousin with him.*

"You have got to have faith. God is watching over your daughter. He will lead Luis to her."

"What if she's hurt or…?"

"Veronica, now you listen to me. Don't you go down that road and start playing that 'what if' game. You will absolutely drive yourself insane if you do. Trust me, Kiara is going to be fine."

"I just don't know what I'd do if something bad has happened to her."

"Well, ain't nothing going to happen that the Lord can't fix. Quit your worrying or else your babies are going to come out being fretful and colicky. Get yourself a cup of chamomile with honey and put your feet up. Relax."

"Don't tell me you were full of worry when you were carrying me. Is that why I turned out this way?" Ronnie laughed, allowing the good feelings to take hold.

"How else do you think I know what I'm talking about?" Dianna joined in the laughter.

"Actually, a cup of tea sounds perfect."

"No matter what happens, you have to take care of yourself for your babies' sake."

"You're right... I'll try not to worry; it's just that I should have heard from Luis by now." Ronnie went to the kitchen to make a cup of tea. As she set the tea kettle on the stove, the doorbell rang followed by a burst of knocking. "Hold on, Mama. There's someone at the door."

She padded down the hallway to the front door and peeked through the peephole. "It's Travis and his friend, Monique. What the hell...?"

"Is everything okay, Veronica?" asked Dianna.

Ronnie tried to remain calm as fear gripped her heart. "I don't know. Travis just showed up at my front door. Let me call you back, Mama."

"Remember what I said, the Lord is watching over your child. Watching over *and* protecting her. He ain't going to put you through nothing you cannot handle."

"Thanks, Mama. I love you." She ended the call and then unlocked the door.

"Travis. Monique. What are you guys doing here? Did you hear from Kiara?" she asked, eyes wide with fright.

"Can we come in?" asked Travis.

"Of course..." Ronnie stepped aside as Monique maneuvered Travis' chair inside. The dogs circled the two, sniffing at them as they did so.

"Hi," said Monique, nervously biting down on her bottom lip. She stood still while the dogs checked her out.

When one of the boxers placed his paws on Travis' lap, Ronnie shooed the dogs away. "Sorry about that. They're just making sure you're not here to harm me."

"That's all right." Travis gazed around the beautifully decorated living space. He cleared his throat. Stalling for time. "Nice place. This is my first time inside, you know."

Ronnie hugged her body protectively, bracing herself for whatever news he was about to deliver. She studied his face. Worry lines creased his forehead and he looked like he hadn't had a decent night's sleep in weeks. "What is it Travis? Is it Kiara? Did they find her? Have you spoken to Luis?"

"Do you have someplace we can all sit comfortably?"

The tea kettle whistled loudly as if providing a warning of impending doom. She knew when Travis was trying to find a way to deliver bad news. This felt as if it was one of those times. And an impromptu visit with Monique in tow was definitely not a good sign. To keep her wits about her, she held on to the prophetic words her had mother imparted to her, moments ago.

"Yeah, sure. How about the kitchen? I was just about to have some chamomile tea. Care for some?" Ronnie headed down the hallway. On one hand, she was anxious to hear what news had brought Travis to her doorstep; on the other, she didn't want to know.

"Sure, I'll have a cup," Monique chimed in.

Travis easily steered his wheelchair over the bamboo floors that covered the majority of the house and then over the ceramic tiles in the kitchen. Monique walked behind like an obedient child put in an uncomfortable situation.

Ronnie busied her hands preparing the tea while Travis sought the right words to say. With her hands shaking uncontrollably, she set three cups on the counter, placing a tea bag in each one. As she picked up the tea kettle, Monique stepped in to assist.

"Here, let me... Why don't you sit down?"

"Thanks," Ronnie took a seat on a bar stool.

Travis interlaced his fingers. He took another deep breath and said, "Luis called me a little while ago…"

"Did they find her?" Ronnie's eyes darted wildly around the room.

"Hold on a minute and let me finish."

She exhaled trying to calm her nerves. "Okay."

"They found Kiara and the rest of the group last night in a small Haitian village. She was very sick and they had to airlift her to a hospital in Santo Domingo."

"What's wrong with her?!" Ronnie jumped to the floor.

"Apparently, she and a couple other volunteers left the camp in search of a safe place—away from the storm's path. They found shelter in a village up in the hills."

"Why is she in a hospital in the DR?"

"Remember when I told you she had a small cut?"

"Yeah. She wanted Luis' cousin's info…"

"Well, that cut got infected while she was in the jungle."

"Infected? How bad is it?"

"Don't be alarmed, but Luis' cousin thinks she may have developed sepsis."

"*Sepsis*? Oh God!" Ronnie lurched over and grabbed the counter to keep from falling. The room began to spin and a wall of darkness closed in on her.

Monique ran to Ronnie's side. She eased her down to the padded window seat. Travis wheeled his chair to Ronnie's side and took her hand.

"Before you panic, just remember they don't know for sure what type of infection it is. That's why Luis' cousin wanted her in a hospital—as an added precaution."

"How is she? Did Luis talk to her?"

Travis shook his head, "She's unconscious…has been for several days."

"What? She's unconscious?" She let Travis' words slowly sink in. "Oh my baby!" Ronnie howled. "God, please…"

Monique sat down beside Ronnie and comforted her as quiet sobs wracked her body. Travis held Ronnie's hand until the first wave of emotions had passed.

"Ronnie, there's more…"

She looked up with swollen red eyes. "More?" she asked bewildered. "What more can there possibly be?"

"They couldn't treat Kiara until they had a medical power of attorney signed by the next of kin."

"What do I need to do?" She tried to stand, but Travis held her hand and eased her back to her seat.

"I've already faxed a signed copy to the hospital in the DR giving power of attorney to Luis. I'm sorry I didn't talk this over with you first, but she needed to be treated right away."

"I've been waiting for Luis to call me all day. Why didn't he tell me all this was going on?" She sniffled.

"He didn't want you to be alone when you got the news, so he asked me to come over."

A smile found its way through her sorrow, landing on her face. "That's my Luis."

Monique went to the built-in desk they used for office space. She retrieved a box of tissues from the shelf and handed it to Ronnie. .

"Thank you," Ronnie replied gratefully, blowing her nose. She then turned to Travis and asked point blank, "Is Kiara going to be all right?"

"I wish I knew… I haven't received any updates yet…since I sent the fax." He looked Ronnie straight in the eye and said, "I hope you know that if I weren't in this fucking wheelchair, I'd be on the first plane down there."

"I know you would… Kiara also knows." Ronnie squeezed Travis' hand and stated, "Know what? Since you can't go to Santo Domingo, I will. I want her to see one of our faces when she wakes up."

"Excuse me if I'm out of line, but are you able to fly in your...condition? Is it safe at this stage of your pregnancy?" said Monique.

"I saw my doctor just this past week. She said I should be okay to fly for another few weeks. But you know what? I'm going whether the doctor says it's okay or not because my daughter needs me. Travis has been there for Kiara her entire life and I know that if it were possible for him to be there now, he would." Ronnie went to her desk and started typing on her laptop.

"Don't be reckless. Luis and Tomas are with her," advised Travis.

"You know good and well that is not the same as having her mother with her," Ronnie protested.

"Kiara is in good hands with the doctors. I don't want you to fly all the way there on your own. It may not be safe for you or your baby."

"That's *babies*, Travis. As in twins. And I don't care what anyone says. I'm going. Now you can help me get to the airport, or I can call a taxi. Your choice."

"Slow down Ronnie. If you are intent on flying to the DR, let me help you." Travis picked up his phone and wheeled down the hallway.

"Uh, is there anything I can do?" asked Monique. "Since you've obviously made up your mind to go, the least I can do is help."

"Great. You can help me pack. The suitcases are in the garage, on the shelf above the car. Take down the medium-sized black one and the small carry-on. Bring them inside. That will be a big help."

"Okay," she headed towards the garage and then stopped. "Are you sure about this? I mean, you look like you're pretty far along…"

"You got kids, right?"

"Yeah, I have three. Why?"

"If one of your kids was laid up unconscious in a hospital somewhere, wouldn't you want to be with them?"

She tilted her head to the side. "I'll be right back with the suitcases."

"Thank you."

While Monique found her way to the garage, Ronnie pulled up the flight info and discovered the next flight to Santo Domingo didn't leave until the next day.

Staring at the computer screen, she cried out, "Tomorrow's not soon enough. I can't wait that long."

Travis returned to the kitchen with a smile on his face. "Good news, Ronnie."

"What? Did Luis call?"

"No, I'm still waiting to hear from him, but in the meantime, I found a way to get you to the Dominican Republic."

"How?"

"I contacted my friend, Duncan the businessman who owns the private jet. He agreed to fly you all the way to Santo Domingo. He's going to send one of his managers with you, both to make sure you're comfortable and so the trip can be written off as a business expense."

"So he is the consummate businessman. When do I leave?"

"In a few hours."

"Really?" she asked, jumping from her seat.

"Yes, really," he replied.

Luis' two Boxers padded into the kitchen. Ronnie took one look at the dogs and said, "I can't leave them here alone. Travis, I hate to ask for another favor, but can you arrange for the dogs to be taken to the kennel?"

"We'll take care of everything. Just write down the name of the kennel you use and I'll make sure the dogs are taken care of."

Ronnie ran over to Travis and threw her arms around his neck. She planted a huge kiss on his cheek. "Thank you, thank you, thank you!"

"You're welcome. I only wish I could go with you."

"Travis, I am going to be there when our little girl wakes up. I'll tell her everything you did to bring her back safely. I know she will be okay. And just like my mother said, God is watching over and protecting Kiara."

*   *   *

Ronnie's flight touched down at the Santo Domingo airport shortly after six in the morning; just as the first blush of the sun peeked over the mountain range. If the sunrise was any indication of how things were going to progress, it was going to be a beautiful day.

Luis patiently awaited her arrival, holding a huge bouquet of native flowers in his arms. And when he got a glimpse of Ronnie come through customs, his eyes lit up. He greeted her as if it had been years, instead of days since he'd last seen her.

"There is my lovely wife." He held her at arm's length, taking in her beautiful face before embracing her. "Are you all right? Was the flight okay?"

"Hey baby, I'm fine. Tired, but fine," she whispered in his ear. "I am so glad to see you." She stepped back and chuckled. "Oops, I'm sure the flowers were beautiful before we crushed them."

"Don't worry about the flowers; there's more where they came from. C'mon, I borrowed a car from one of Fernando's friends. He's letting us use it for today. You can wait there while I get your suitcases."

"How is she?"

"The doctor says we got her here just in time."

Ronnie closed her eyes and looked towards the sky. She whispered, "Thank you Lord for watching over my child."

"Let me get you out of the sun."

She waddled from the blazing hot parking lot to the air conditioned car, fanning herself. "Whew! Is it always this humid here?"

"Actually, it isn't so bad right now. Just wait until the rain comes in the middle of the afternoon. Then you can call it humid."

"Can't be much worse than it is now... Lawd have mercy!" She continued fanning herself.

"Here's a bottle of water. You're going to want to remain hydrated, especially with the load you're carrying."

"Thanks." She grinned, "Hey, while you're getting the bags, I'm going to call Travis and let him know I made it."

"Okay, be right back."

Ronnie switched the A/C to high and let the cold air do its thing. Even at this early hour, the airport's parking lot was ablaze with activity. While she watched tourists locate their hotel vans or jump into taxis, she took a long swig of water and dialed Travis' number. The phone rang several times before the answering machine picked up. He was probably knocked out. After all, it *was* the middle of the night in California. She left a message.

"Travis, its Ronnie. I made it… I'm here… In Santo Domingo. We just landed a short time ago. I'm headed to the hospital and I'll call just as soon as I see Kiara. Talk to you later."

In no time flat, Luis returned to the car pulling two suitcases behind him. He popped the trunk and then got in the driver's side. "Little mama, are you ready to go see your daughter?"

She eased her head back until it touched the headrest. Closed her eyes to let the realization of what she was about to encounter sink in. "I can't begin to tell you how ready I am. Were there any changes during the night?"

"No, she's still the same. They pumped her full of antibiotics to fight the infection and it seems to be working."

"Thank God."

"She is a fighter. Even though she's still unconscious, she has impressed the hell out of the doctors with her quick reaction to the medicine." Luis squeezed the car between two taxis with literally inches to spare on either side.

"Thanks for being here for her; especially for tracking her down and getting her medical attention. I can't imagine how difficult that must have been."

"It was tough, but you can thank my cousin, Fernando, when you meet him. He made finding Kiara his own personal project."

Luis expertly maneuvered the car through the city, driving as if he had never left the island. He laid in on the horn when a group of teenagers on scooters blocked the street, swearing at them in Spanish.

Knowing that Kiara was doing better allowed her to relax. "Oh, I see you're retained some of your language skills," Ronnie chuckled.

"Oh that? Well, you never forget the cuss words no matter how rusty your language gets. Don't worry *chica*; my *Espanol* will be *muy bien* in no time at all. And don't be surprised at how easily you pick it up once we move here full time."

"Uh well, speaking of moving... By the time Kiara recuperates, I'm not sure if I'll be able to make that return trip back to California. Even on that luxurious private jet, flying was pretty brutal. I cannot imagine traveling on a commercial plane being this pregnant."

Luis lovingly patted his wife's hand and said, "First things first, let's go get your daughter well."

"As usual, you're right. Let's go see my child."

Entering the hospital, Ronnie was pleasantly surprised with how modern the facility appeared to be. After checking in with the reception desk, they were informed the *vigilancia intensiva* unit was on the fourth floor. The place smelled of antiseptic. *Nice*, she thought, taking it all in. *In fact, if weren't for the signs in Spanish, I would have thought I was still stateside.*

After exiting the elevator, they checked in with the nurse on duty. The woman was busy reviewing patient prescriptions, barely glancing at them as she pointed towards Kiara's semi-private room.

Tomas came up from behind. "Veronica, I see you made it." He had been sitting in the waiting room for their arrival. He gave her quick embrace.

The nurse looked up when she heard Tomas' voice. Then she took one look at Ronnie's pregnant waistline and began speaking in rapid bursts of Spanish. First she gestured at Tomas and then back to Luis before settling on Ronnie.

Luis motioned for to relax. He attempted to explain the situation.

"What is it? Is something wrong with Kiara? What did she say?" asked Ronnie with a frightful look in her eyes.

"Kiara is fine. I had to explain that you are Kiara's mother because she didn't want to let you in. The nurse says that because you are pregnant and Kiara is being treated for a serious infection, we should both wear protective gowns, masks and gloves to avoid exposure to bacteria. It's really for the protection of the babies."

"Oh, I see... Of course, I'll wear the protective clothing. By all means."

The nurse retrieved three gowns from a cabinet behind her desk and handed the items to Luis. He helped Ronnie into the gown, then dressed himself. After he secured the mask behind her ears, he told her, "My love, don't be frightened by Kiara's appearance. Remember, she's been in Haiti for several months and she has lost a lot of weight. Because she is still in intensive care, they're monitoring her very closely. She's hooked up to several machines, but it is all normal."

"I understand."

Luis held his hand up towards Tomas, "Wait here for a moment, okay?"

"Sure. Let me know if you need me."

"Thanks, man." He looked at Ronnie. "You ready?"

"Yes." Ronnie trailed Luis into the room. In spite of Luis' warnings, she was not prepared for what she saw. She gripped his arm to steady herself.

Kiara's frail body was hooked up to a multitude of instruments that measured her vital signs—heart rate, blood pressure, and oxygen levels. An IV bag hung from a stand at her bedside, dripping a cocktail of vital antibiotics and precious fluids into her veins. A plastic tube was inserted into her nostril to pump in oxygen. Her right arm was bandaged from wrist to elbow.

Her daughter's previously athletic body now appeared gaunt—as if she had lost over twenty pounds. Her once healthy glow was now tinged a sickly yellow and it looked as if her hair hadn't been combed for weeks. Dry, chapped skin, with tiny little cracks covered her previously luscious lips. Ronnie plucked an ice cube from a glass on the tray and dotted Kiara's lips.

The image of her child lying in that bed nearly brought her to tears, but she willed them away. She looked to Luis for answers, but he could only shake his head, for he had none. Ronnie leaned over and gently picked up her hand. No matter what she was feeling at that moment, Ronnie knew she needed to be strong…if only for Kiara's sake.

Ronnie collected herself. "Kiara, honey… Mommy's here. Wake up, sweetheart," she whispered over and over again, gently stroking her hand. "I love you. We're here, baby. Open your eyes, sweetheart."

She relentlessly tried to coax Kiara awake. As she did, she experienced a strange sensation of déjà vu, reminding her of that last visit with Derek when he was on his death bed—the day before he passed. Standing at his bedside, monitoring his weak heartbeat, she actually felt his life slowly slipping away. What she felt with Kiara it was totally different. There was no spirit of death in the room. Only life. And being filled with a mother's intuition, she knew Kiara would be okay. She whispered quietly, "Baby, you're going to be fine. Open your eyes."

The door of the semi-private room opened slowly. Fernando walked in with a big grin on his face. He was followed by a nurse carrying fresh linens and a clean gown. "Good news, Luis."

"Fernando, this is Veronica, Kiara's mother."

"Veronica, I am so pleased to meet you." He shook her hand.

"You too… What is the good news?"

"The antibiotics are working against the infection. Thank goodness, it wasn't sepsis. Her white blood count is returning back to normal."

"You mean she's going to be all right?" Luis felt like throwing his arms around his cousin.

"We believe we caught the infection just in time. Of course, we'll keep her in the ICU for another week or so to continue monitoring her progress and pumping her with antibiotics." Fernando made a cursory check of her vital signs. "We also had to remove the infected tissue around the wound. She'll have a slight scar—nothing to be overly concerned with."

"When do you think she'll regain consciousness?" Ronnie asked, still holding on tightly to Kiara's hand.

Fernando merely smiled. "Why don't you ask her?"

Ronnie turned her attention to Kiara who lay in bed with her eyes open, but only partially focused.

"She's waking up," Ronnie whispered loudly.

Kiara tried to speak, but was unable to due to the tube inserted down her throat. Unsure of where she was or why she couldn't speak, she squeezed her mother's hand.

"Honey, it's okay. Don't try to talk. You're going to be fine." Ronnie shed tears of joy. She bent down and kissed her child's forehead through the mask.

Kiara blinked several times, as she struggled to speak.

The nurse readjusted the IV. In a heavily accented voice, she spoke to Kiara first, reassuring her after seeing panic make its way to her eyes. "Honey, you're in the hospital. Don't worry. You're going to be just fine."

Kiara blinked again. Only this time, a tear made its way down her face. Her eyes searched Ronnie's for answers.

"Okay, folks, she's had enough excitement for this morning and needs her rest. Since she's awake, we'll take the tube out and the next time you see her, you should be able to speak with her for a few minutes. Dr. Doucet, here's her chart."

Ronnie squeezed her hand again. "I love you, baby. Your daddy sends his love, too. And I can't wait to tell Travis that you're going to be okay."

Kiara tried to smile before closing her eyes and falling back asleep.

"C'mon love, she needs her rest. And for that matter, so do you." Luis guided Ronnie from the room.

After they disrobed and scrubbed up using a special disinfectant soap, they returned to the waiting room with Tomas. He jumped up and met them.

"*Primo*, I just saw Fernando." He gripped his cousin's shoulder. "That's great news about Kiara."

"Yes, it is." Luis exhaled and passed his hands over his scruffy face. "Man, I need a shave."

"I think you look wonderful," Ronnie said before giving him a proper 'I missed you' kiss.

Tomas cleared his throat. "Are you headed back to your hotel?"

"I think that would be best for today, especially since Ronnie hasn't had a good night's sleep. We can do the other thing tomorrow."

"Well, I'm going to stop by Mom's house and crash there for a while. Call me if you need anything."

"Will do. And thanks again. I couldn't have done this without yours and Fernando's help."

Tomas made gestures as if he'd done nothing special. Ronnie gripped his arm and added, "Yeah, thank you so much for coming down with Luis. You guys were amazing."

He kissed her cheek and said, "It was my pleasure. After all, you are part of the family now. Kiara too."

Ronnie's cell phone rang. A picture of Travis popped up. She turned to Luis and said, "It's Travis. I'm going to give him an update. Reception is pretty bad here."

"Try standing next to the window. The reception is much better over there." Tomas pointed towards a sunny area of the waiting room.

Luis watched his wife waddle away. It seemed as if she were having more difficulty walking every passing day. He silently wondered if bringing her down here to live was the right decision.

Tomas watched Luis' gaze follow his wife.

"When *are* you going to introduce Veronica to your mother? Once Mom knows we're both in the DR, yours will expect you to stop by for a visit."

"I will get over there soon, but first Ronnie has to get her rest. Did you see how tired she looks?"

"Stress is taking its toll. It has to be difficult carrying twins… And now she must worry about her daughter, too."

"I'm going to do everything possible to eliminate those stressors from her life. Therefore, I will bring my bride to my mother's house all in good time and not a second before."

"Good luck with that. You know how these Dominican mothers are when it comes to their sons." Tomas smirked and headed for the elevator, waving at Veronica on his way out.

"Travis, I'm here at the hospital with Kiara. I just left her room." Ronnie pressed the phone against her ear, placing a finger in the other. She watched on in sorrow as a doctor delivered what was obviously bad news to a family, because they all broke out in loud tearful sobs.

"How is she?"

"She's much better. I just spoke with Fernando, Luis' cousin and her doctor. It wasn't sepsis. He says the prognosis is good. They think they caught the infection in time."

"That's wonderful news," Travis exhaled.

She heard his audible sigh of relief come through the line. "She woke up while I was in her room. I have never in my life been so happy to see those beautiful brown eyes of hers."

"Did she tell you what happened?"

"She wasn't able to speak just yet because she had a tube inserted in her throat. The nurse told me they're going to remove it since she's awake. I should be able to talk to her later today. Tomorrow at the latest."

"What a relief…"

"Travis, she is so thin. It looks like she hasn't had a decent meal since she left home."

"She mentioned a few times that she had lost weight. Is it that noticeable?"

"She was never big to begin with... I'll take care of fattening her up just as soon as they release her."

"Did the doctor say how long it will be before she is discharged?"

"They're going to keep her in ICU for another week and after that, we'll just have to wait and see. By the look of things, I wouldn't plan on her being able to return to California any time soon."

"I was afraid of that. She must be pretty weak, huh?"

"Considering what she's been through, she's doing better than expected."

"How long do you plan on staying in Santo Domingo? I don't want her to be alone, if we can help it."

Ronnie spoke haltingly. "Um, Travis, I didn't mention this to you before, but Luis and I have made plans to move to Santo Domingo in a few months."

"You don't say... You're moving to Santo Domingo permanently?"

"Uh huh, and because of the situation with Kiara, our timetable may have to be moved up, because very soon I won't be able to fly."

"Hmm, well, I suppose its best that you are there. At least Kiara won't be alone."

"Travis, I'll make sure she receives the best treatment possible. I know you want to be here. Just know that I am not going to leave her side." Ronnie caressed her stomach trying to ease the babies' activity. It seemed as if feet, hands, and elbows were coming from everywhere. Plus, she had to pee again.

"Do me a favor, please."

"Sure. Anything. Name it." She scanned the hallway for signs of a restroom.

"Can you please check around the city to see if there are any wheelchair friendly hotels in the area? I can't just sit here and wait any longer. I need to see my daughter."

"I understand. I'll ask Luis to check around. We'll locate appropriate accommodations for you."

"Thanks, Ronnie. And in spite of everything, I really am happy you're there."

"Me too, Travis. Me too. I'll call you again after Kiara is able to speak."

"Thanks. Be sure to send her my love. And give her a hug and a kiss for me, please."

"Sure Travis. I'll be happy to. Talk to you soon." Ronnie felt as if a huge weight had been lifted from her shoulders. "Now to get rid of this pressure in my bladder." She hurried off towards the sign touting a woman's silhouette, making it to the *baño público* just in the nick of time.

* * *

Luis was concerned noticing how worn out Ronnie appeared. With the combination of stress, the intense heat, and lack of sleep, she was pushing herself way too much. "You need to rest. I have checked us into a local hotel for a few days. It's nearby, so we can see Kiara whenever visiting hours are in effect."

She yawned loudly. "Sleep does sound like a good idea. Since I know Kiara is going to be okay, I feel as if I can sleep for days."

Leaving the hospital, the heat and humidity of the afternoon had once again built to its fullest intensity, making Ronnie feel as wilted as the lettuce on a sandwich Luis offered her.

"Where did you find this piece-of-shit car? Ugh! What happened to the other one?" Ronnie pushed the roof's drooping fabric up and away from her face. It quickly dropped back down. She fiddled with the air conditioner, but it refused to turn on. "What the hell, Luis? No air?"

"Here, let me try." He was also unsuccessful.

"Never mind, I'll roll down the window." She gripped the handle only to have it come loose in her hand. "You have got to be kidding me!"

"This is Fernando's spare. I didn't have time to rent a proper car, but I promise I'll get another one later today." He chuckled at his oh-so-American wife's reaction.

"Damn, it's hot down here! Baby, I don't think I can take this heat." She used an old magazine to fan the hot air around. As she was in the middle of complaining, her cell phone rang.

"Who is that?" asked Luis, concerned it may be the hospital.

"It's my mother. Hold on, I need to let her know Kiara's okay."

"Hey Mama." Beads of perspiration trickled down the length of her back.

"Veronica, I've been trying to call you since last night, but my calls kept going to voicemail."

"I'm sorry, I didn't call you. I'm in Santo Domingo with Luis."

"What in the world? You shouldn't be flying nowhere by yourself in your condition." Dianna scolded.

"I know but I had to get here."

"I understand. Please tell me they found Kiara."

"Yes Mama, they did. Luis and Tomas found her two nights ago and the doctor had her airlifted to the Dominican Republic…" Ronnie explained everything that had occurred over the past forty-eight hours. By the time she was finished explaining, Luis was pulling up to the hotel's parking lot.

"Thank you, Jesus!" Dianna exclaimed.

"I agree."

"How long are you going to be there?"

"Since I'm already here, I'm staying. I'm not going back to California."

"What? Does this mean you really are going to have the babies there?"

"Yes, ma'am. We are looking for a good obstetrician."

"What are you going to do with your house? Your furniture? Your things?"

"Luis is going to arrange for it all to be moved."

"And when are you supposed to give birth?"

"My due date is January 10th. I have about another ten weeks to go."

"All right," Dianna's voice broke. "I've already sent out my application for my passport. It should be back before then."

"Mama, we'll still see each other soon and you'll have lots of opportunities to spoil your grandbabies."

"I'll let you go, just please keep me updated with any changes. And tell my handsome son-in-law I said 'hello'."

"I will. Bye, Mama."

Ronnie turned to Luis and exhaled. "My mother says hello." She peeled her sweaty legs from the seat and latched on to Luis' hand to help her from the small car.

"You really are miserable, aren't you, mama. Let me get you upstairs to cool off."

Chapter Thirty-Six

*T*he following afternoon, Luis dropped Ronnie off at the hospital's entrance to visit with Kiara while he went to take care of business. "I'll be back in an hour. Then we'll go visit my mother."

"I'm really looking forward to meeting your mother and the rest of your family."

"I told them all about you and they can't wait to meet you, too." He thought to himself, *I hope this meeting goes better than the first time I brought a wife home. That was a total disaster; much like the marriage itself.*

"I'll see you in an hour."

"Give Kiara my love."

"I will." Ronnie waddled into the hospital, making her way past an emergency room that seemed filled to the max.

After she donned her protective clothing and before entering Kiara's room, she mentally prepared herself for whatever story her daughter was willing to share. She approached Kiara's bed. "Hey sweetie, how are you feeling today?"

"I'm still like really tired, but I'm feeling much better than last night. Guess I fell asleep on you, huh?" she said in a weak, raspy voice.

"That's all right. We just needed to know that you're going to be okay. Luis couldn't make it today, but he sends his love." Ronnie ran her hands through Kiara's unkempt, tangled hair. She reached in her purse and pulled out a brush. Using her fingers, she made a crooked part down the middle.

"Did he like really come all the way to Haiti to find me?" She coughed several times.

Ronnie picked up the sippy cup and offered her a drink of water. "Yes, he did. Your father arranged the entire trip to get Luis and Tomas here. Their cousin Fernando, your doctor, helped them locate you girls."

"Awesome! That is so cool. I have to like thank him and Tomas for all they did to find me."

"You'll have a chance to thank them both very soon."

"How is Daddy? Have you spoken to him, yet?"

"Now that you mention it, Travis should be here later today. He's flying down to see you."

"Daddy is coming here?" Her eyes lit up in excitement.

"Yep. He said he had to come check on his baby." She braided her hair into two braids, patting them down. "There, that's better."

"I can't wait to see him." Kiara looked at Ronnie. "I am so glad you're here, too, Mom."

"So am I. Everyone tried to discourage me from coming—with my being pregnant and all, but there was no way I was going to leave you down here on your own."

"You're *really* showing now."

"A little over two months to go..."

Kiara reached for Ronnie's hand. She closed her eyes tight. When she opened them again, the tears started to flow freely.

"What is it, sweetie?" Ronnie wiped the tears away with her free hand.

"Mom, I was so stupid. I thought I was protecting those kids, but actually I just made a huge mess out of everything. We all could have died up there." She shook her head from side to side.

"You only did what you thought was right. No one will fault you for that."

"They were so scared when they heard that a hurricane was headed our way. Many of those children lost their parents in the earthquake; and then more in the floods that came afterwards. When Kasheba told me about her village up in the mountains, I thought it would be better there. But it wasn't, because we got lost and...and... Mom, I've never been so frightened in all my life." She cried so hard, she got the hiccups.

"Shhh, it's all right. Everyone's fine, now. Fernando saw to it that your friends were safely returned to the school."

"I couldn't let the kids know how scared I was. After the guide left us, me and Sarah got turned around and ended up lost in the jungle. We heard wild animals in the bushes. Snakes slithered over our feet—some were even in the trees."

"Oh boy! I know how you are with snakes. You must have been terrified!"

"Uh huh, but snakes weren't even the worst of it. A group of men carrying guns and machetes passed us by. We told the kids to lay face down in the dirt and covered them with vegetation because... Well, we didn't know what they would do to us... We stayed like that for hours to make sure those men were gone. "

Ronnie did not let on how truly afraid for Kiara she had been. The news was filled with stories about young girls who lived in those camps being raped at the hands of unscrupulous Haitian men. If she had heard the stories in California, she was sure Kiara had also been warned.

"The weather started to turn really ugly. We were like wet, cold, and hungry. And so very tired. Rain was coming down in sheets and the ground was difficult to walk on because it was slippery. My arm started to hurt so much. I knew that cut was like infected because of the awful itch. Then I got really weak and feverish."

Ronnie could only imagine what she had gone through.

"Somehow we located the village and those really nice people took us in." She looked at the bandage on her arm. "I held on because I didn't want to leave Sarah alone with all those kids. After the people in the village let us stay, that's the last I remember...until waking up and seeing you here."

Ronnie didn't tell Kiara that she had almost died the night Luis found her. After she was well, maybe they would go into more detail. But then again, maybe they wouldn't. "All that matters now is you're going to be fine. A few more days in intensive care, then they'll put you in a regular room. After that, I'm going to take you home to our villa and fatten you up."

"Villa? What villa?" Her eyes grew heavy.

"Kiara, sweetheart... There is so much I want to tell you—need to tell you. For now, let's just focus on getting you well. Okay?"

"Okay, Mom. I...love...you," she replied before falling fast asleep.

"I love you, too."

*   *   *

Luis picked Ronnie up from the hospital and headed to his family home. The one hour trip took them past buildings that towered high above the crowded city streets of downtown Santo Domingo. Dominicans in various shades of black and brown filled the streets going about their business.

A group of school children, dressed in uniforms, trailed one another as their teacher led the way to a statue of Christopher Columbus pointing towards the sea. As Luis drove, Ronnie marveled at the historic buildings that sat side-by-side with modern architectural feats.

"Luis, you didn't tell me Santo Domingo was so beautiful. It's like a paradise." Her eyes trailed a line of palm trees extending down the main drag filled with exclusive boutiques, fine restaurants, and ritzy hotels.

"Paradise? I wouldn't exactly label Santo Domingo as paradise, but it is a very nice place to live."

"Everything you need is so close—within walking distance."

"That's true to a point. Or you can take a taxi or bus, however, my mother lives closer to the country."

Ronnie sat back and grinned, "I think I'm going to like living here. This is the place that is going to make me finally settle down and raise a family."

"That is right, mama. You…me…and our two little babies." He lovingly rubbed her stomach.

"Whoa! You made one kick."

"That was probably our future soccer star." Luis grinned.

"Or it may have been her little brother." Ronnie joined in the laughter.

"A daughter who ends up being a soccer star. Now wouldn't that be something?"

*   *   *

"We're here." Luis glanced over at Ronnie as he punched the four-digit entry code into the keypad. For as long as he could remember, the code had always been his father's birthday.

They pulled up to a contemporary two-story house surrounded by a decorative wrought iron fence. A massive wooden door, accented on all sides by beautiful stained glass, graced the entrance of the home that was finished in mango colored stucco with white accents.

"Your mother's home is absolutely lovely," Ronnie whispered, taking in her surroundings. "Did you grow up here?"

"No, and to tell you the truth, I have never lived here. After my father passed away, my mother used the insurance money—plus a little extra from me, to purchase this house. I told her this place was too extravagant for a woman living on her own, but she explained that all her life she had lived in modest homes. For once in her life, she wanted to have something nice. So, I ended up putting in more than I initially expected, but if it makes her happy…" He shrugged as he opened the front door.

His mother, a petite, light brown skinned woman of average build, came running down the hallway. She had a dishtowel wrapped around her hands, but quickly tossed it aside when she saw her son.

"Luis! *¡Bienvenido a casa!*" his mother exclaimed before embracing her son.

Trailing behind his mother was his sister and all four of her children. They encircled Luis and began speaking Spanish. Loudly, quickly, and all at once. Ronnie stood back and waited patiently for them to acknowledge her.

After a few moments of hugging and kissing, Luis was able to divert their attention to Ronnie. He pulled his wife close and introduced them. "Mama, Sophia, *mi esposa*, Veronica.

"Ah, Veronica… *Encantada de concocerte.*" They politely shook hands. And when his mother noticed Ronnie was pregnant, she asked with a shocked expression on her face, "*¿Está embarazada?*"

"*Sí*, I'm going to have twins." Ronnie held up two fingers.

Once that fact was known, she was instantaneously accepted into the family. The women whisked her away into the kitchen, set her down, and proceeded to place all sorts of food in front of her to encourage her to eat.

"Baby, why didn't you tell me your mother had such a good sense of humor? Even though I barely understood what she said, she was so funny."

Luis opened the car door for Ronnie while balancing a bag filled with leftovers.

"I didn't know she did," remarked Luis. "It must be you; she really likes you."

"What's not to like?"

Luis was not about to get caught up in a conversation of comparing his first wife, whom his mother absolutely could not stand, to Ronnie. Instead, he did the right thing and answered, "Nothing, my love. Nothing at all."

"Know what? I had a great time with your family. It's going to be so much better once I learn to speak Spanish. Do they always talk so fast?" She took the bag from Luis, placing the still warm food on her lap.

He walked behind the car and got in the driver's side. "Yes, everyone speaks fast. Spend enough time around my family and you'll be speaking Spanish as if you were a native." He waved to his mother standing in the doorway. "Ready to go?"

"Yes, it's been a busy day and I'm beat." Ronnie also waved good-bye.

Luis tooted his car horn and pulled away. Strains of his mother saying good-bye continued to be heard halfway down the block.

"So, I take it they were excited when you told them you were moving here?" asked Ronnie as she rested her eyes.

"Oh yeah, but not as excited as us having twins."

"That's good, baby. Real good." Ronnie closed her eyes and drifted off to sleep.

Chapter Thirty-Seven

*R*onnie warmly embraced Tomas as they stood outside the small airport terminal. "I wish you could stick around a little longer."

"I've already been away for a week. I need to get back to California to close out a few deals. Time is money, you know." He took a step backwards, taking a long look at her growing belly. "I think the babies have grown since you've been here."

"Unfortunately, all this..." She laughed out loud while caressing her round stomach, "...is not all baby. Luis' mother loves cooking for us. We've eaten over there every day for the past week."

"You'd better watch out for those rice and beans, especially if you're not used to eating them. Dominican food can pack on the pounds very quickly," he teased.

"Listen, I know you have to get back, but we loved having you around. We're going to miss you, won't we, honey?"

Luis swaggered over to where Tomas stood. "Tomas needs to get back home. He has lots of important things to take care of."

"That's right. Luis has given me a laundry list of items that needs to be completed." He tapped a folded piece of paper in his front pocket.

"Oh, I get it... You fellas must have something up your sleeves."

"Business, my love. Strictly business," Luis replied.

"Uh huh...right..." she replied.

Over the speaker came the announcement. "Flight 4690 to Miami will be boarding in fifteen minutes at Gate four. I repeat..."

"That's me. I'd better get going." Tomas retrieved his carry-on from the chair next to Luis. He hugged Ronnie one more time and fist-bumped Luis. "Keep in touch and let me know when those beautiful babies are born."

Ronnie waved. "Bye Tomas. We'll miss you."

After seeing that Tomas' plane was safely airborne, they headed directly to the hospital to visit Kiara.

The attending nurse recognized the couple, offering them both a warm greeting. "*Hola, Señor y Señora Duarte. ¿Cómo está ustedes?*"

"We're fine. How are you?" Ronnie answered.

The nurse shrugged and replied in English, "I could complain, but why bother. Oh, I almost forgot... She has a visitor, already. Only one of you can go in."

"Who's in there with her?" asked Luis, confused.

"Her papa," replied the nurse.

"It must be Travis. Remember, I told you he was flying down? That's why I asked you to look up those hotels. I guess he finally made it."

"*Si, Senor* Bradford is here. Sorry, we allow only two at a time in the ICU. Hospital rules."

Luis touched Ronnie's elbow. "You go on in. I'll wait here."

"Are you sure? We can come back later..."

He waved her off. "No, we're already here. Go on in."

"Okay. I shouldn't be very long. Just want to see how she's doing today."

"Take your time. I'll be fine." Luis pulled out his smart phone and began checking his messages.

Ronnie changed into the required protective gown, mask, and gloves and quietly opened the door. Travis and Kiara were engrossed in a private conversation. Not wanting to eavesdrop, she announced her presence.

"Ronnie, hey, good to see you," said Travis.

"Hi Travis. I see you made it." She gave him quick hug. "Hey Kiara, how are you today?"

"Hi Mom. I'm much better since Daddy's here." Kiara glanced behind Ronnie. "Where's Luis?"

"He's in the waiting room. Only two at a time in ICU…"

Travis listened to the exchange. "C'mon in. We were just discussing moving Kiara back to California for her follow up treatment."

Ronnie crossed her arms and tried to speak in a pleasant voice, however, her words came out sounding like she was pissed. "Um, Travis, that's not what her doctor suggested. He said it would be best if she remained here for a while."

"I know that is what he *suggested*," Travis stated. "I just think it would be better if Kiara were back in the states where she can receive *proper* care. Even though the facilities seem to be clean enough and the staff appears competent, I still prefer our daughter be under the care of an American doctor."

"She's getting the best care available according to Fernando. Have you even spoken with him yet?"

"No, I only got here last night. I was hoping to speak to him today, though. So, do you really think they are providing her with the proper medical treatment? You feel comfortable with all…this?" He swept his arm across the room, focusing on the signs written in Spanish.

"Yes, I do. I've met the doctors and the nurses. I've toured the facility and watched how well they treat Kiara. She *is* receiving proper medical care. And because the type of infection she had is commonplace in this part of the world, *this* is probably the best place she can be to receive the best treatment."

Kiara waved her good arm trying to get her parents' attention. "Hey guys, I'm still here… Don't I get a say so in this?"

"I'm sorry. I guess I got carried away. Tell me, dear. What do you think about remaining in Santo Domingo?" Travis said.

"I like it here. The doctors are wonderful and the nurses are really nice. Dr. Doucet says I will be moved to a regular room probably like tomorrow. Then after a few days of observation, I can go home with Mom… I'm not ready to take that long plane ride home to Santa Elena."

Ronnie tightened her arms over her belly. "We're moving into our villa in a few days and Luis says it will be well equipped to take care of Kiara until she heals. He'll even bring in a private nurse, if necessary."

"Is that right?" Travis frowned. "You guys already have this figured out, huh?"

"We had to come up with a plan. She can't stay here in the hospital forever and a hotel is out of the question. Since she won't be able to travel for several weeks, we had to do something. Travis, we weren't trying to push you out of the equation…"

"I know you were just looking out for her."

A nurse stuck her head in the door and announced, "Visiting hours are over in five minutes."

"Daddy, can I talk to Ronnie for a few minutes? Alone?" asked Kiara.

"Sure sweetheart. I'll be back to see you tomorrow. I love you," he said through the surgical mask.

"Love you, too, Daddy."

The nurse held the door as Travis wheeled himself out. "Ronnie, I'll be in the waiting room when you're done."

"Okay, Travis." She turned her attention to her daughter. "Young lady, what's so important that you couldn't discuss in front of your father?"

Kiara looked towards the window as if the answer to her problems resided outdoors. "Can I stay with you and Luis for a couple of months to get well? You know… After I get out of here?"

"I'll talk it over with Luis, but I don't think it will be a problem. Why? What's going on?"

"Don't tell Daddy I told you this, but he asked that Monique woman to marry him."

"He did what?" Ronnie's eyebrows shot upwards in surprise.

"Yeah, that was my reaction, too. He's only known her for a few months." Kiara pouted like a spoiled child.

Ronnie tried to hold her laughter in, because obviously this was a very sensitive issue. "Sweetheart, your father getting married will in no way affect the way he feels about you. And for your information, Luis and I didn't know each other very long either before we moved in together."

"But that was different." She sighed. Misery was written all over her face.

"Really? How so?"

"Because I've known Luis practically all my life, so I knew he was a good person. And you… Well…even though it was my first time meeting you… I didn't mind you being with Luis. You know what I mean?"

"You mean it was no big deal when Luis and I got together, because in some ways we both were already part of your family. However, since you don't know anything about Monique, you feel she may be a threat to you?"

"That's right *and* she has three kids. I was the only child all my life and now I'm getting lots of brothers and sisters all at the same time. She'll probably move all my things out of my room to make room for one of her little brats."

"Listen Kiara, your father must obviously love Monique, otherwise he would not have asked her to marry him. Neither she, nor her kids, will ever take your place. Don't you know that by now?"

"I suppose…"

"You are growing up and your father deserves to be happy. If marrying Monique will make him happy, then you should offer him your support."

"I know…" Kiara faced her mother with tear-filled eyes. "I still don't want to go home and live in that house while I'm recuperating. Not if she's living there. Can I please stay here with you and Luis? In a couple of months, the babies will be born and I can help you out."

"What about school?"

"I am going back eventually, but I've already missed so much of this year that I'm going to have to start over next year. In many ways, it was worth missing school, because what I've learned this year in Haiti was priceless."

The nurse entered the room and said, "I'm sorry ma'am, but visiting hours for ICU are over. You can return tomorrow morning when she will be moved to another floor. The regular rooms have less restrictions so you can visit with your daughter much longer."

"Well, sweetheart, I guess that means goodnight, but we'll talk more about this tomorrow."

Kiara reached for Ronnie's hand. "I love you, Mom. See you tomorrow."

* * *

Travis was on his way to the waiting room. Preoccupied and slightly perturbed by his conversation with Kiara, he almost ran into one of the doctors. If he had run over the doctor's foot, it wouldn't have been entirely his fault. The doctor had his head down immersed in reading a patient's file.

The doctor stopped walking when he came upon the American in a wheel chair. From Luis' and Kiara's description, he assumed the man's identity. "Pardon me sir, but might you be *Senor* Bradford, Kiara's father?"

"Yes, I'm Travis Bradford."

He extended his hand. "Hello, I am Dr. Fernando Doucet. Your daughter, Kiara, is my patient."

Travis accepted his handshake. "I am so pleased to finally meet you, Dr. Doucet. You're Luis' cousin, right?"

"Yes, that's correct. Luis and I are cousins."

"I want to thank you for everything you've done to help find and take care of my little girl. I can't begin to tell you how much I appreciate what you've done."

"It's been my pleasure. She is a delightful young lady."

Travis exhaled, "So, please tell me, Dr. Doucet…"

"Please, call me Fernando…"

"All right, Fernando… How is she really doing? And when can I take her home?"

"She is doing very well under the aggressive antibiotic treatment we have her under. Her last tests indicated the infection was completely gone, but we'd like to take another blood test today to make sure. Because of her quick recovery, she will be moved out of the ICU and into a regular room tomorrow. I would like to keep her under observation for another four days to treat the flesh wound to ensure it doesn't become re-infected. After that, I'd like to see her once a week for about a month, just to make sure she does not have a relapse."

"Is she going to make a full recovery? I'd really like to take her home as soon as possible."

"I believe so. She was in relatively good health, albeit rather thin, prior to becoming sick, so her chances of making a full recovery are in her favor. As for traveling long distances… I would advise against that for at least a month. Strange things have been known to happen in the bloodstream during a flight."

"Is that your opinion or a medical diagnosis, doctor?" Travis asked, skeptically.

"Sometimes, an opinion is worth more than a diagnosis. Call it superstitious or an old wives tale, but I highly advise against your daughter flying for at least thirty days unless it is a true emergency."

After Ronnie left Kiara's room, she ran into Fernando and Travis talking in the hall. Fernando greeted her with a quick embrace. "Veronica, *hola*."

"*Hola*, Fernando. I see you've met Travis."

"Yes, I was just giving him the good news about Kiara. She will be placed in a regular room tomorrow."

"That's good to hear," replied Ronnie. "Will we see you later?"

"Of course. Luis has my number. Now, if you will excuse me…"

"Nice meeting you, Fernando. And thanks again. For everything," Travis added.

"You are very welcome. I'll be in touch," he said and went on his way.

"Nice guy…" remarked Travis.

"He sure is. The Santo Domingo hospital gave him special privileges just so he could oversee Kiara's treatment."

"You mean he's not on staff here?"

"No, he lives in Haiti. And did you know he was named as the most influential doctor in Port-au-Prince's best hospital? That is until it was damaged in the earthquake. He also attended one of the best medical schools in the country at Washington University in St. Louis *and* graduated at the head of his class. In exchange for his temporary privileges in Santo Domingo, he agreed to teach a few seminars on the treatment of tropical diseases."

"Impressive credentials... So, he decided to stay here to treat Kiara? Why?"

"I guess that's what families do. I am just glad Fernando was willing *and* able to be here for Kiara."

"I'll be..." Travis replied, shaking his head in bewilderment. "Top of his class? Well, I'll be..." he repeated.

Ronnie poked Travis' shoulder. "Hey, I hear you have some big news? Wanna share? Hmm?"

Travis saw the look on Ronnie's face and immediately knew what she was referring to. "I suppose Kiara told you I'm getting married, huh?"

"Well? Is it true?"

"Yep, it's true. I asked Monique before I flew down here and she accepted."

"Travis, that's wonderful news! Congratulations!"

He sat there grinning like a kid on Christmas morning. "I don't believe it myself. I never expected to meet anyone who was so perfect for me. It was like she fell out of nowhere and landed into my lap. Before I realized it, we were in love."

"People say, 'Happiness happens when you least expect it'."

Travis stared at her with a twinkle in his eye. "I tried to talk myself out of it, especially since she already has three young children, but the more time I spent with them, the better we got along. I discovered her kids are great."

"I'm really happy for you, guys. Truly, I am."

Travis glanced sideways at her. "What did Kiara have to say anyway? I know she hates the idea, but I can't go on living my life trying to please my grown daughter."

Ronnie chose her words carefully. "Well... She was understandably upset and feels she is being replaced by another woman. Honestly, I think she was more upset because Monique has children who may invade her private space. I wouldn't be too concerned…she'll get over it."

"I hope so, because Kiara proved to me how grown she actually is by coming to Haiti against my wishes."

"I hope *that* didn't have anything to do with you asking Monique to marry you." Ronnie raised her eyebrows questioning his decision. "What? I'm just saying."

"I know it may look like that and quite possibly Kiara's defiance might have played into my decision. The truth is, I love this woman. She is the only woman, besides you, who ever truly *got* me. Monique understands me… We have a wonderful time together. My being in a wheelchair doesn't seem to matter at all."

"For what it's worth, she seems like a nice person." Ronnie thought about something her mother used to always say. *'There's a lid for every pot.'* "As long as you're happy; I'm happy for you. And don't worry about Kiara… She'll come around."

"Thanks… I appreciate you saying that."

She turned when she heard Luis calling to them. "Oh, here comes Luis."

"There you two are. Travis, how you doing, man? When did you get in?"

"I got in last night and have been here in the hospital most of the day. I'm doing much better since I spoke to your cousin."

"Cool." Luis placed his hand on the small of Ronnie's back and gave her a gentle massage upon noticing her obvious discomfort. "You need a ride somewhere?"

"Since you asked, I could use a lift. I've arranged for a private driver to transport me around the city, but he's not able to start until tomorrow morning."

"It's not a problem. Where are you staying?"

"I'm staying at the Hilton. It's just a few miles from here."

Luis laughed. "That's where we are."

"That makes it easy, then. Lead the way." Travis steered his chair alongside the couple as they headed towards the elevator.

"Maybe we can get a bite to eat on the way back. I'm starving," said Ronnie.

"What about you, Travis? You hungry?"

Travis replied, "Hey man, I'm in your backyard, so whatever you want to do is fine with me."

"How long are you staying?" asked Ronnie.

"Just until day after tomorrow. I had to see with my own eyes that Kiara was in good hands. And now that I've seen it, I'm okay to head back."

Chapter Thirty-Eight

*L*uis and Ronnie headed up the scenic mountain to tour their villa. Despite being in the DR for almost two weeks, it was her first trip to view their new home. Most of her time was spent in the hospital. However, since Kiara had been moved to a regular room and was doing much better, the greatest danger seemed to have passed.

"You think Travis is going to be okay leaving Kiara here for an entire month?" asked Luis.

"I think so. He seemed to have taken it all in stride after seeing the facilities and discussing her status with Fernando. And I think he'll appreciate this time alone to really get to know his wife-to-be. I just hope he's making the right decision about getting married," she said.

Secretly, Luis was thrilled that Travis had finally found someone of his own. Now, he could finally stop fawning over Ronnie. "That Monica woman will have him tied up with making wedding arrangements, so he shouldn't have time to think about Kiara not being around."

"Don't be so sure about that. Monique is not going to replace Travis' little girl. No way, no how…"

"He must really love her. Three kids? That is a lot of responsibility to take on."

"I'm sure they both understand what they're getting into. They seem to complement each other very well."

"Yeah, I'm sure you're right. It's just that it's a big deal marrying a woman who has small children."

From out of the blue, thoughts of Derek's kids came into mind. She recalled how her initial enthusiasm of being their stepmother gradually waned once she realized his children didn't hold the same enthusiasm as she. Derek's behavior didn't help matters because he let his kids do whatever they wanted—making her the disciplinarian when they came to visit. She quickly pushed the sad memories aside. "I suppose… Speaking of kids, are you sure you don't mind Kiara staying with us after she is discharged from the hospital?"

Before he could answer, their conversation was interrupted by the ringing of Luis' phone. "Hold on a minute, mama." He saw it was from Tomas. "I've been waiting for this call."

Ronnie raised her eyebrows wondering what was so important.

"What's up, man? I expected to hear from you days ago."

"Sorry I didn't call sooner, but I've been working on completing your list."

"How *is* that coming along?" Luis smiled at Ronnie.

Luis was acting suspiciously. She glared back at him and started pulling up sites for local obstetricians Fernando had suggested.

"I made all the arrangements to get your furniture packed up and shipped down. You would not believe how expensive it is to ship furniture to the DR, but I was able to get a good price and it should be there in a week or so."

"That's good. I'm driving Ronnie to the villa now to show her the place. Having furniture will be a nice touch."

"I found you a great property manager. She's a good friend of mine and is great at what she does."

"I suppose I will need a property manager, huh?"

"She will be contacting you shortly about leasing out your house. She told me that you should able to rent it quickly and at a profit, even after her fee is taken out. The apartment should go pretty fast also. I made the arrangements to have both dogs transported. They'll have to spend a month in quarantine if you decide to have them shipped to Santo Domingo; otherwise, the woman who owns the kennel says she'd be more than happy to adopt both of them."

"That's great man. Thank you. That's less stuff I have to worry about. Anything else?"

"Yes. I've also coordinated with Julio to transfer several of your Central American accounts to you at the new location."

"Anything *else?*"

"*Si!* I closed the deal on my commercial property sale. I'm rich, bitch!"

Luis chuckled at Tomas. "Cousin, that's great news. I'm happy for you." He mouthed to Ronnie what Tomas had said.

She laughed imagining Tomas' expression.

"Uh, what about that other urgent matter? What's going on with that?"

Ronnie's ears perked up at the suddenly suspicious tone Luis' conversation had taken. He rarely ever spoke in code.

"That's something we need to discuss further and if Ronnie is in the car, I assume you won't be able to speak freely."

"No, please tell me." He glanced over at Ronnie, noticing the way she cut her eyes at him.

"I spoke with Carmen Sanchez and she agreed to drop the lawsuit after realizing Mr. Hernandez wasn't going to play ball. One thing though, she keeps insisting that you promised her a ten thousand dollar bonus for helping you land the contract. She is not willing to let that drop."

"Technically, that is correct. Those were the original terms of the transaction. What does the client want?"

"Oooh, Ronnie must *really* be listening…"

"Yes, that is correct. You are right on the money with that."

Tomas laughed, "Why don't you just tell her what's going on? You know what happens when you try to keep stuff like this in the dark."

"You may be on to something with that observation. Draw up the plans and call me tomorrow with the details."

"Just tell her what's going on. She will understand."

"Thanks for taking care of that for me. I'll talk to you later, Tomas." Luis hung up and glanced over at Ronnie.

She glared at him with fire blazing from her eyes. Her lips were pursed and he could hear her sucking her teeth.

"What?" Luis feigned innocence, keeping his attention squarely focused on the road. As a matter of fact, with the intensity of his concentration, you would have thought he was driving on the edge of a treacherous, mountain pass, instead of a modern four lane highway with light traffic.

"Don't you *what* me. I know when you're up to something. What's going on?"

"You and your female intuition. *Coño!* Can I please just drive? We're almost there."

"Fine, but this conversation is on pause. It ain't over yet, *papi*!"

"I'll tell you what's going on later. I just don't want anything to spoil the surprise of seeing our new home. Okay?"

"Okay. This time I'll let it go, but we promised to be honest about everything. Remember? That's the only way *this* is going to work."

"Ronnie, I said we'll discuss it later. Please, just sit back and relax."

She sat back, but she did not relax.

Luis exited from the highway and turned on to a country road that wound up the side of a hill. They drove past a horse ranch that had a tour bus parked near the entrance. A group of tourists trailed a man wearing a straw hat.

"Hey, I remember this place." She watched as the man wearing the straw hat lined up the tourists. "We went horseback riding there. Don't your relatives own the stable?"

"That's right. You have a great memory." He kept driving, but now with a smile.

"Where are we going, anyway?"

"Almost there. You'll see. Just a little further…"

"Oh, I'm so excited. And I've got to pee so bad."

Luis followed the dirt road to the top of the hill and turned into a gravel driveway bordered by tropical foliage. When he broke through the vegetation and entered the clearing, he parked the van and turned to gauge Ronnie's reaction.

"Is this it?" she whispered. She stared ahead—sitting motionless. "Is this our new home?"

It was not the reaction Luis had anticipated. "Yes. What's wrong? Don't you like it?"

All of a sudden, she burst out in tears. "Luis…"

Confused by her reaction, he hopped out from the driver's side and ran around to hers. He opened the door and she fell into his arms.

"Ronnie, I am sorry. I thought you would be pleased. I didn't mean to upset you."

She gazed into his eyes, overcome with emotion. "This is the place you showed me years ago when we first met. You told me you wanted to buy this villa and raise your children here."

"You *do* remember…"

"Of course, I do. I thought about this place whenever you spoke about settling down in Santa Elena. I always knew that *this*—here, is where you wanted to live, not out there—in California. That was supposed to be… *temporary.*"

"You're right. I almost lost sight of my dreams."

"But you didn't. You followed through and I am so proud of you." She fell into his arms again.

"Why are you crying?"

"I'm overwhelmed that you did this for us. You told me you were going to buy this villa and you did." She took in the magnificent 360 degree view and exclaimed. "It's absolutely beautiful up here. So peaceful… I can't think of a better place to raise our children." Her eyes overflowed with happy tears. "Luis Duarte, I love you so much."

"Whew, you had me going there for a minute. I thought I had messed up horribly."

"No baby, you did fine. This place is absolutely amazing. And you've had everything renovated? Including the guest house and the swimming pool?"

"It's not totally finished, yet. I thought we would have a few more months to work with, but with all that's happened we had to move the timetable up. The main house is livable, though." He took her by the hand. "C'mon, let me show you around."

Luis took Ronnie on a tour of the villa. The two-story, four bedroom house had been completely gutted and renovated from the ground up. It now included all the modern amenities and appliances. The home included two master bedroom suites, one on the lower level and another on the upper.

They climbed the stairs. Two bedrooms were on the opposite side of the hallway from the upstairs master. Ronnie walked into the second master and glanced around the beautiful room. "There's a balcony up here, too?"

"Yes, it overlooks the swimming pool."

"When did you do all this?" she asked, looking around at the ongoing construction.

"During that time we were apart, I knew I had to get us out of California if *we* were going to work, so I contacted my late father's business partner and asked him about purchasing the villa."

"Luis Duarte, you are truly an amazing man."

"Look, I made a promise to you that we were going to live our lives in the offbeat and that's a promise I intend to keep."

"It's gorgeous." She grimaced. "Was it terribly expensive?"

"Not so much. After I sold half the business to Tomas…"

"You what?!" She stopped dead in her tracks. "You sold half your business to Tomas?"

He nodded.

"Why didn't you discuss this with me?"

"Sweetheart, I've been successfully handling my business for years now. Tomas made a few commercial deals and is now a wealthy man. He wanted to branch out and knew I was looking for a business partner. Julio is still going to run the business, but Tomas will be like a silent partner. So what I was saying is, after I sold half the business, I had a good chunk of money to buy the villa outright."

"We should have discussed this… That's a lot of money."

"Okay, if it will make you feel better, we will discuss all personal financial transactions that involve a thousand dollars or more."

"Uh, let's make that five hundred since I'm no longer working."

"Agreed. Anything over five hundred dollars will be discussed."

"Tomas is your business partner, huh? Well, color me impressed. He was actually telling the truth about hitting it big."

"Let's go back outside. I want to show you something I'm working on…just for you."

He led her across a pathway paved in stone. It was obvious the landscapers had been very busy because the last time she saw the villa over three years ago, it was practically overrun with weeds.

They stopped in front of a small unfinished building with a view of the kidney-shaped, inground swimming pool on one side, and a panoramic view of the valley below, on the other.

"*This* is for you." Luis made a sweeping motion towards the structure. "What do you think about turning this into your writing studio? It's not much, but I think it will provide the seclusion and privacy you need to write."

Ronnie clasped her hands together. "Oh my! If I don't find inspiration to write, I have no business calling myself a writer. This is perfect."

"I hoped you would like it. The other structure is slightly larger, so I thought we should keep that as the guest house."

She imagined placing clay pots filled with rosemary bushes outside the windows. And an outdoor rocking chair would be a perfect touch to lending itself to providing moments of inspiration. Or rocking the babies to sleep. "I love it. When will the rest of the construction be completed?"

"Everything moves slowly here in the DR, so I wanted the primary focus to be on finishing the main house. Since that is almost complete, you get your choice on what gets renovated next—your writing studio or the guest house?"

"I think the guesthouse should be next." She hopped from one foot to the other, squeezing her legs together. "My bladder is about to burst." She asked, "We *do* have running water?"

He laughed. "The water comes from a well, so we will never run out. Also we're on a septic tank system. In the winter, we will use oil for heating, but I can tell you more about that later. Go on before you wet yourself."

Ronnie hurried inside to the downstairs powder room. After emptying her bladder, she toured the house again. The workmanship and the attention to detail were remarkable, beginning with the portico at the villa's entrance.

Suddenly an idea came to her from out of nowhere. *The villa is the perfect place to renew our vows. We can have the ceremony in the garden.*

Meanwhile, Luis cut a stalk of sugarcane from a plant growing in the yard and began to chew on it. He took a seat on a concrete bench facing the garden awaiting Ronnie's return. Taking note of her joyful reaction to the villa, he contemplated how he would break the news about paying off Carmen Sanchez. *Uh oh, here she comes. Whew! This is not going to be fun...*

Ronnie rushed towards him with a huge grin on her face.

"Better?"

"Yes, much better." She sat down beside him. "This is really nice. I'm going to love living here."

"Ronnie, I need to discuss something with you."

"Before you say anything, I want to ask you a question." She bit her lip, nervously.

"Okay, I'm listening."

"What do you think about renewing our wedding vows here—at the villa? We'll invite our families down and we can do it before the babies are born."

"You want to marry me, again?" He gripped her hands. "I think that's a great idea and I'm all for it. However, before we nail down the specifics, I need to clue you in on what's going on..."

"Is this about your conversation with Tomas?"

He nodded.

"Should I brace myself?" She cut her eyes at him.

"What I have to say is going to upset you, but I promised total honesty."

"All right, I'm listening."

He explained the gist of Tomas' call. "I owe Carmen Sanchez some money in exchange for her dropping a lawsuit against my company."

"Say that again, but this time, speak slowly."

"About a month ago, Carmen filed a lawsuit against me and my company—for sexual harassment and breach of contract."

Ronnie listened carefully, feeling her anger rise. Although it was hot outside, her internal heat had nothing to do with the external temperature. The urge to lay into Luis was powerful. However, she held her breath *and* her tongue.

"Tomas spoke to Carmen's husband. He convinced his wife to drop the lawsuit, but now she wants money."

"Is she blackmailing you? Call the police on that bitch!"

"No, she isn't blackmailing me. Not exactly. She dropped the lawsuit because Mr. Hernandez, the president of the company I saw in San Diego was going to provide a statement in my defense indicating how Carmen tricked him into adding a clause that secured her position with my company. When she found that out she dropped the lawsuit."

"Then what's the problem?"

"I promised her a ten thousand dollar bonus if she worked with me to seal the Hernandez deal. I didn't tell her how to do it, and I for damn sure didn't expect her to do what she did, but technically she fulfilled her part of the agreement. Regardless, I'm leaning towards fighting this lawsuit... What do you think?"

Ronnie rose from her seat, picking up a piece of the sugarcane Luis had left on the bench. She chewed on the sweet stalk as she wandered from one side of the villa to the other, trying to clear her mind. Perhaps, it was adrenaline, or maybe it was the sudden rush of sugar flooding into her bloodstream. Whatever it was, both babies began kicking her something fierce, bringing her back to a harsh reality.

Gazing over the gorgeous villa, she recalled her visit with Carmen. She thought about Carmen and her children residing in a dwelling one step above living in the projects. Even though Tomas mentioned she had moved back in with her husband, for the very briefest of moments, Ronnie developed empathy towards the woman—for someone who had such low self-esteem, that she would prostitute her body. She returned to Luis' side and plopped down on the bench.

Luis dropped his head, preparing himself for whatever followed.

Several moments passed before she finally spoke. "Is she still working at that grocery store?"

"I have no idea. Tomas said she got back together with her husband. Why? What difference does it make?"

Ronnie sighed wearily. "Just pay her the ten grand and be done with it."

"You want me to pay her? That's it?"

"I want to put all that bullshit behind us. After you take care of this "little matter", I never want to hear that woman's name ever again. Agreed?"

"I'll have Julio get our attorney to draft a statement of understanding tomorrow along with issuing the check," he replied in relief. "Thanks for being so understanding. I love you, baby." *Wow! This woman never ceases to amaze me. I am one lucky SOB.*

"Good, now let's go inside and talk about our renewal ceremony. December might be nice—right before the Christmas holiday."

"Sweetheart, just give me a date and I'll push the construction guys to meet it."

"The more I think about it, the middle of December will be perfect, because I'll still have another month before the babies are due." She led the way inside the house. "Oh, one more thing… We were going to discuss Kiara staying here…"

"My love, Kiara can live with us as long as she wants. Anyway, once the babies are here, it will good for you to have her around to help you out."

"Thanks, papi. I love you so much. And I love our new home."

Chapter Thirty-Nine

When Ronnie wasn't at the hospital visiting Kiara, she was at her mother-in-law's home, assisting Luis in his new office space, or overseeing the renovation at the villa. No matter what she was doing, she came to the conclusion that living in Santo Domingo was just like coming home again.

After weeks of interviewing dozens of obstetricians, Ronnie finally settled upon one. After her first official appointment, she took a taxi to Luis' office to provide him with an update. She breezed into Luis' office, noticing dozens of paint samples spread out on the table. She planted a huge kiss on his face and told him, "I really like Dr. Anderson-Santana."

He joked, "I thought you were going to interview each and every obstetrician within fifty miles of Santo Domingo. I'm happy you finally found a doctor you like."

"Hey, choosing our baby's doctor is very important. And taking my time paid off. Dr. Anderson-Santana was born in the states, but she moved here to be with her husband about a decade ago. Apparently, many of her patients are ex-pats, so everyone in her practice speaks English and is experienced with the ins and outs of stateside insurance."

"Well, after listening to her talk for over an hour, she definitely sounds like she knows what she's doing. How'd you find her, anyway?"

"Actually, she was one of three doctors who Fernando recommended. I even had a chance to tour the hospital's obstetrics ward." Ronnie perused the paint colors Luis had preselected for the office. "I like this color. What do you think?"

"No. Too feminine. How about this one?" he asked, while watching the sign painter stencil the name of his company, *Duarte Diseñador Gráfico* on the glass door.

She shook her head. "The sign looks very nice. How much longer before you can open for business?"

"Technically, I am already open. I've been working on a few accounts I managed to pick up here and there. There is just the final inspection left before I can officially open the door. It's scheduled for Friday. After that's done, we're in business, my love."

Strains of Tone Loc's 1980's hit, *Funky Cold Medina* came from Ronnie's purse.

"What in the world is that?" said Luis.

"That's my new ring tone. You like?"

"It's definitely unique..." He laughed.

"Oh my goodness, it's Joie. I haven't spoken to her since she left Santa Elena."

"Go ahead and answer. I'll be out back checking on the phone and internet installation."

"*Hola?*" answered Ronnie.

"Ronnie? Is that you?"

"*Si, esta, Veronica.*"

"What's up with the Spanish? Luis finally got you brainwashed, huh?" Joie laughed.

"When in Rome..."

"What in the world are you talking about, woman?"

"Girl, we moved to Santo Domingo. I've been here almost three weeks."

"For real?! Are you shittin' me?"

"No, but it's a long story..." Ronnie filled her in on all the events.

"Dang! Kiara and those kids must have been terrified in that jungle. I'm glad Luis and his cousins found them when they did."

"Me too, girlfriend."

"So she's going to be okay?"

"Yeah, we're picking her up tomorrow and taking her home to the villa. She'll be with us for a couple of months. More if she wants to stay longer."

"Life seems like it's going pretty well for you. You two finally got to that place you're always talking about. What did you used to call it? Living in the offbeat?"

"That's right, only now I'm calling it *loving in the offbeat.* So tell me... What's going on in Joie Parker's world?"

"Remember when I told you me and Cedric were working things out?"

"Yeah, how is that going?" Ronnie placed a mauve color paint chip against the wall. *Naw, that's still too girlie for Luis.*

"Girl, he asked me and the kids to move back into our old house. We're getting remarried in a small ceremony this weekend."

Ronnie stopped what she was doing, giving Joie her full attention. "Did you just say you're getting remarried?"

"Cedric proposed to me a few days ago. He said he's been lost without me and the kids ever since we split. He said he forgave me for what I did and wants us to be a family again."

"Joie, are you sure…"

"We went to our pastor a few months back and told him everything. Since then, we've been in counseling sessions twice a week working on our issues. Lord knows, I have got me some issues…"

"That's great that you two are working things out…" Ronnie replayed the past several months in her mind.

"Thanks."

"Hold up a minute, girlfriend. Were you in counseling all the time you were seeing Tomas?" she asked incredulously.

"Yeah, we were trying to decide if we wanted to get back together."

"You are a straight up trip, you know that?"

"I told Cedric about my dating Tomas. He was disappointed, but he said he understood because we were just dating."

"Joie, you'd better hold onto that man and do everything in your power to treat him well, because he is priceless."

"You are so right. He is a great catch. I also know how much I love him. We plan on continuing the counseling because its helping me understand some of the crazy shit I've done."

"I always thought you guys were the perfect couple. Tell him I said 'hi' when you see him."

"I will. So when are you going to pop?"

"My due date is in January."

"It will be here before you know it."

"My delivery date can't get here soon enough. I don't remember pregnancy being this difficult before." Ronnie caressed her huge belly.

"Well, you were twenty years younger, don't forget… And you're carrying twins this time."

"Right…" she laughed. "Hey, while I have you on the phone, I want to ask you a huge favor."

"Sure. What's up?"

"Luis and I are planning a marriage renewal ceremony. I'm looking at the middle of December. Do you think you and Cedric can attend?"

"Hell yeah, I'll be there. I'll have to check with Cedric because he just started a new job, but I know he'd love to see you again."

"I know its short notice, but we want to do this before the babies are born. Luis is designing the invitations so we can mail them out in a few days. It's not going to be a large ceremony—mostly family and a few friends. And don't worry about having a place to stay. We've renovated the villa so there'll be plenty of room."

"A villa? Ooh la la! Haven't we come up in the world?" she teased.

Ronnie bristled at Joie's comment regarding her living a lavish lifestyle. Joie knew her at a point in her life when she was willing to give up all her material possessions in exchange for peace. She had no intention of ever going back to being materialistic. "It's probably not what you think. All right... I ain't gonna lie. The villa is nice!"

"I ain't mad at you. If your man can work it like that, more power to you."

"Thanks, Joie. Well, I'd better go. I'm helping Luis select paint for his office and so far I'm striking out zero for three."

"Okay. I'm looking forward to seeing you again. I'll catch you later."

* * *

By the beginning of third week in the hospital, Kiara was finally well enough to go home. Fernando met Ronnie and Luis at the nurse's station.

"Dr. Doucet, Miss Bradford is all ready to go. All I need is your signature on her discharge papers," explained the nurse.

Fernando signed the papers attached to the clipboard, returning the documents to the nurse. "All right, Kiara is all yours. I gave her a ten day prescription for antibiotics. Make sure she takes the full course of treatment. And I want to see her every week for the next four weeks."

"Fernando, you shouldn't have to travel all the way back to Santo Domingo just to see Kiara," Luis said.

"I agree. Can't one of the local doctors take care of the follow up treatment?" asked Ronnie.

Fernando shook his head. "My patient. My follow up. My decision."

Luis threw his hands up in defeat. "Fine, you win. Just let me know where and when and I'll have her there."

"I will, cousin." Fernando asked Ronnie, "Did you contact Dr. Anderson-Santana, the obstetrician?"

"Yes, I did."

"What did you think? Does she meet your expectations?" he asked.

"Yes, I was quite pleased with her and I'm really happy she is going to deliver the babies. Here—in this hospital."

"You are in very good hands with her."

"I think so. Thanks again for everything, Fernando. And I hope to see you at our renewal ceremony in December."

"I wouldn't miss it for the world."

Ronnie and Luis watched as Fernando advised another doctor on the care of a very ill patient. He was so comfortable in his role that they both wondered if he had ever done anything else other than be a doctor. He was a natural.

"C'mon, let's go get Kiara."

Ronnie slowly made her way down the hallway, stopping every few feet to catch her breath.

"Hi Mom. Hey Luis. Are you guys coming to rescue me from this place?" Kiara greeted them both with a warm smile.

"Hmmm, I don't know. Luis, what do you think? Should we take her home with us?"

"Absolutely!" replied Luis.

"Everyone has been like really nice to me, but I am so ready to get out of here." Kiara sat on the edge of the bed, fiddling with her cell phone.

"Well, let's get out of here then." Ronnie lovingly stroked her daughter's hair.

A male attendant knocked on the door, pushing a wheelchair. Luis gathered up her suitcases and the rest of the luggage Fernando had requested be retrieved from the Haitian camp. The attendant helped Kiara into the chair and steered her towards the entrance with Ronnie and Luis following closely behind.

"Kiara! What are you carrying inside your luggage? Bricks?" Luis tried to straighten his back as he struggled with a duffel bag.

"Those are the books I brought with me to donate to the Haitian children."

"Why are you taking them back with you?" Luis asked, still struggling.

"I guess the volunteers got confused and sent them to me. I certainly don't need them. Maybe we can donate them to the children's hospital."

As they crossed the threshold of the hospital exit, the overstuffed duffel bag slipped to the floor with a loud thump. Luis exhaled in exasperation as he tried in vain to pick it up.

Ronnie spied a bench outside the door and headed for it. "Honey, why don't you see if they'll accept those books for the children's wing? There's no use in us keeping them." She motioned for the attendant to park Kiara in the shade next to the bench.

Luis took one look at the duffel bag blocking the entrance, causing the automatic doors to open and close, over and over again. He set the remaining suitcases on the ground near Ronnie and dragged the book-filled bag over to the reception area.

Ronnie said to Kiara, "How are you doing over there?"

Kiara sat in the wheelchair with her face turned up towards the sun to soak in its warmth. "I'm happy to be alive. One of the nurses explained that I nearly died when I was in that village in Haiti and if it weren't for Dr. Doucet… Like I said, I'm happy to be alive." A lone tear fell from her eye.

Ronnie reached over and embraced Kiara's good hand in her own. "We were all so worried about you. You gave me, Travis, Luis—everyone a good scare."

"Yeah, I know. Guess I ended up making a huge mess out of everything. I should have like stayed in Santa Elena and just went back to school. Then none of this would have happened."

"Kiara, don't go beating yourself up over this. There was absolutely nothing wrong with your decision to go to Haiti. I'm sure you made a huge difference in those children's lives."

"Yeah, like getting them lost in the jungle…"

"Think about it, sweetie. You may have gotten them lost, but you also taught them some very important survival skills. I'll bet most of those kids will remember you for the rest of their lives. So don't be so sure you messed up. God puts us in tough situations to see how we'll react and you did great. I am so proud of you."

"Thanks, Mom. I just feel so different since I've gone through this." She absentmindedly picked at her bandage, trying to calm the itch.

"Oh yeah? How so?" Ronnie squinted at the bright sunshine. She fished two pairs of sunglasses from her purse and handed one to Kiara.

"I feel older now—more mature. Living in Port-au-Prince—in that camp, under those conditions, seeing how those kids had basically nothing, changed me. Some kids lost their entire families, yet they were still happy. And then when we were lost in the jungle, Sarah and I were responsible for their safety. I think about how I grew up and I feel...well...sort of... embarrassed."

"You have no reason to feel embarrassed about what you have. Being an American offers distinct advantages that people from other countries don't have. In American, people can start with nothing and end up being extremely successful—much like your father."

"Daddy is pretty amazing, isn't he?" She smiled.

"Now that you've experienced what it feels like to have nothing, you will appreciate everything you have that much more. What you can take from your time in Haiti is that you can make the world better by contributing to it, rather than taking from it. And by giving of yourself to those children, you have contributed more than you will ever know."

"I think I understand... Leave the world better by adding something worthwhile?" She pondered the notion.

Ronnie nodded, "That's right, sweetheart. The world will always be full of takers—people who want everything handed to them, but aren't willing to work for what they have. But you—my sweet, smart and beautiful daughter—you are a giver."

Kiara accepted her mother's wisdom, finally able to understand how she had been changed.

"Look, here comes Luis." Ronnie pointed to the door.

Luis was all smiles as he returned—with hands empty. "Guess what? They were happy to take the books. The receptionist says her son's school is always looking for books written in English. So she was thrilled with the large donation. Kiara, they told me to tell you, *gracias*, because it isn't very often they run across a young person with such a generous heart."

Kiara glanced at Ronnie, offering a weak smile because Luis' news warmed her inside. Turns out it really did feel better to give than to receive.

The women looked at one another and shared a private moment.

"You girls sit tight. I'll be back with the van in a few minutes." He handed each a bottle of cold fruit juice. "A gift from the receptionist..."

Chapter Forty

Six weeks later…

"**M**om, I'm home!" Kiara yelled out, as she dropped her bags by the front door.

"Welcome back, sweetie!" Ronnie threw her arms around Kiara. "How'd you get here?"

"I took a taxi."

"Luis could have picked you up on his way home from the office. Why didn't you call him?"

"I did. He said he would come get me, but since he was busy working, I told him I'd be fine. Anyway, I felt empowered being able to take a taxi on my own," she joked.

"Well, I'm glad you're back. I missed you." Ronnie gave her another warm embrace.

"That was a good idea having me move to his mother's house for the past couple of weeks. You are in no condition to be driving me back and forth to my doctor appointments. I'm supposed to be helping you out, remember?"

"I was fine the first month you were here. But lately, it's becoming more and more difficult for me to get around—walking or otherwise."

"Luis was right about it being easy to get to the hospital from his mother's house. It only took me fifteen minutes on the bus."

"Speaking of the hospital, what did Fernando say? Did he give you a clean bill of health?"

"Yes, he did. I had appointments with him a few times over the past couple of weeks. He says I'm fine now and can return to the states whenever I want to. The infection is completely gone."

"Thank goodness you're going to be okay."

Kiara surveyed the room. "I can't get over how great the villa looks," Kiara remarked. "They did a really great job on the landscaping. Those plants by the entrance are beautiful!"

"While you were away recuperating for those two weeks, they came in and finished everything," Ronnie explained. "C'mon, let me show you around."

Ronnie strolled through the house pointing out the changes that were made in Kiara's absence.

"You guys had the house painted; the floors refinished, and even completed the pool—all this was done in a couple of weeks? Amazing…"

"Just so you know, it wasn't me pushing the completion. After you went to stay with Luis' mother, he wanted everything to be finished before our ceremony took place."

Kiara reiterated, "I am thoroughly impressed. You guys did like a really great job."

"So… How was it staying with Luis' mother?"

"At first it was kinda awkward because I had trouble understanding her. I used to think Spanish was Spanish, but I have since learned that they have different dialects between nationalities. The Spanish I learned in California is a whole lot different than Dominican Spanish. But as far as his mother is concerned, she is like so sweet."

"Yes, she is. I felt welcomed the moment I met his entire family."

"I love that I also have a Dominican family," Kiara beamed. "It makes me feel so—exotic."

"Luis has lots of relatives in Santo Domingo, and many more throughout the country."

"I'm looking forward to meeting them all." Kiara's face temporarily clouded over.

Ronnie noted her daughter's sudden change of mood. "What's wrong, sweetie?"

"Mom, even with all that's happened, I've had such a wonderful exciting time on this island—both in Haiti and now the DR. I love spending time with you, Luis…his family… I'm not ready to return to Santa Elena—not yet, anyway."

"Ah, honey. You know you have to go back eventually to complete your last year of school."

"I know…" she sighed. "It's just that half of my family is here, and the other is in California with Daddy."

"After you graduate, you can make your decision on where you want to live. The world is at your feet right now, so there is no telling where you will end up. Just know that wherever I am or Travis is, that's where your home will be."

"Thanks, Mom. And you're right. I have my entire future ahead of me… Although I have some time before school starts again, I'd better register for next year, huh?"

"Yes, you should." Ronnie carefully studied her child. She seemed different—more mature now. "I know you've changed your degree several times, but what did you finally decide upon?"

"For years, I had my heart set on becoming a graphics designer. But since volunteering in Haiti...I don't know...I think my calling may be elsewhere. I have to think about it..."

Ronnie allowed a smile spread across her face. "Whatever you decide upon, I already know I'm going to be proud of you."

Kiara picked up her suitcases and headed towards her room. "You have no idea how happy that makes me."

"I know you have a lot of decisions to make, but for now, you can enjoy the rest of your time here." Ronnie rubbed her back, groaning in discomfort. "Go ahead and put your bags in the guestroom. I need to sit down for a moment."

"Are you okay, Mom?"

"I'm fine. Just ready to deliver these babies is all..." She eased into a chair.

"Let me know if you need anything..."

The ringing of the doorbell interrupted their conversation.

"Who can that be?" Ronnie made an unsuccessful attempt to get up.

"I'll get it. You just sit," ordered Kiara. She padded down the hall to the living room and opened the door. At first, she didn't recognize the woman behind the dark sunglasses, but once she opened her mouth...

"Kiara? Is that you? Girl, you look great!"

"Uh, hey..." Kiara replied. "Miss Parker, I didn't know you were coming." She looked over the woman's shoulder. A man she didn't recognize paid the taxi cab driver, and then headed towards them.

"Child, there is no way in the world I was gonna miss seeing your momma get married again. Now, where is my girlfriend hiding?"

"She's inside. Come on in." Kiara stepped aside and welcomed in her mother's obnoxious friend and the man who trailed behind her.

"Oh, this is my husband, Cedric Parker," Joie said. "Cedric, this is Kiara Bradford, Ronnie's daughter."

"Pleased to meet you," Kiara replied.

"You too," said Cedric.

Hearing the commotion coming from the living room, Ronnie managed to hoist her body from the chair. When she saw her best friend, she screamed, "Oh my God! Joie! You made it!"

Joie ran over to Ronnie and threw her arms around her. "Told you I would. Look who I brought with me." She motioned towards Cedric.

Cedric took one look at Ronnie, allowing a huge smile to spread across his face. "Veronica, you look…g-g-great." He hugged her tentatively.

Ronnie laughed, "Cedric, it's good to see you again, especially after all these years."

Cedric raised his eyebrows, surprised at how large Veronica had become. "Uh, Joie told me you were expecting, but…"

"You just didn't know I was this big, right?" She laughed. "It's okay to be shocked. I'm kinda surprised I could get this huge myself. But I suppose that's what happens when you're carrying twins. Right, Joie?" Ronnie placed her hands on her back trying to get rid of a kink.

"I think you are absolutely stunning," he said. "And thanks for inviting us."

"I am so glad you both made it. It means the world to have you both here. And congratulations on the remarriage."

"Thanks." Cedric grinned.

She plopped down in a recliner near the door. "Oow wee! But you can see, I'm not exactly in my best shape right now."

"Pregnancy really does suit you. I remember when Joie was about to deliver. I felt so sorry for her. The poor woman could barely walk, sleep, or get around on her own."

Ronnie told Cedric, "Yeah, I remember how miserable Joie was. She would call me at work and ask me to run all kinds of errands when you weren't able to. One time, she even asked me to put nail polish on her toe nails. I was so glad when she finally had the babies, so I could get me some rest." Ronnie laughed at the memory.

"I was quite the pregnant diva, wasn't I?" Joie cringed. "I must have put on at least sixty pounds when I was pregnant with Maya and Trey. But don't worry about losing the weight. Just make sure you breast feed so the pounds will melt right off."

Ronnie told her, "Yes, you were. But anyway, I'm so glad you're here, this way you can help with the preparations for the ceremony day after tomorrow."

"We actually landed yesterday. We spent a day of sight-seeing in the city. This is our first trip to the Dominican Republic, you know. I had no idea this country was filled with black and brown people," said Cedric.

Ronnie laughed, "Yeah, that's what most Americans discover upon visiting for the first time."

Joie slipped her arm through her husband's. "Soooo... Cedric just started working for the city of Newport News, but they agreed to give him a week's vacation. He's a teen counselor."

Kiara's interest perked up. "You counsel youth?"

"Yes, I do," answered Cedric.

"I spent a few months in Port-au-Prince, Haiti. I was kinda sorta like a teacher."

"You don't say... Well, I'd love to hear about your experiences down there."

"It was an experience all right..." Kiara chuckled. "Those kids were amazing. So resilient."

Ronnie addressed Kiara. "Sweetie, why don't you show Joie and Cedric to the guesthouse so they can freshen up?"

"Sure, Mom. No problem." She picked up a small carry-on and told them, "Grab your bags and follow me."

Cedric smiled. "Fine. Lead the way."

* * *

The day of the ceremony finally arrived on the heels of a glorious sunrise. Even though it was early in the day, the villa was busy with exuberant activity. Luis' male relatives tended an outside pit where a whole pig had been roasting since the night before, while the women fussed over decorations inside the house.

Luis' mother and sister busied themselves making *pasteles* for the dozens of guests who would arrive later in the day.

"How you feeling today, little mama?" asked Joie, as she sipped on a cup of coffee.

"My back is killing me, my feet are swollen, and I can't stand more than five minutes at a time. Other than that, I'm doing just fine."

"Girl, you'll have so much fun today, you'll soon forget about how tired you are now."

"I hope so." Ronnie glanced around her home. "Little did I realize when I sent out those invitations a couple of months ago, that I'd be feeling so crappy today. All I want to do is get this day over so I can go back to sleep." She leaned against the kitchen counter, trying to catch her breath. She picked up a knife and cutting board with every intention of helping.

"Good morning, Mom." Kiara took one look at her mother who looked like she would pass out at any moment. "Mom, why don't you sit down? There are plenty of people to help cook."

Once Luis' mother saw Ronnie in the kitchen trying to help, she also ran over to Ronnie, speaking in rapid bursts of Spanish. She took the cutting board from her hands and shooed her away.

Although Ronnie didn't understand what her mother-in-law was saying, she certainly got the gist of it.

"Well, since y'all won't let me help…guess I'll make myself comfortable over here." Ronnie eased into a comfortable chair in the sitting area of the kitchen. "Anybody seen Luis this morning?"

Kiara answered, "I think he said something about going to the airport to pick up Grandmama Pierce. He should be back anytime, now."

"Great. Have you guys eaten yet?"

"Don't you worry about us. What would you like to eat?" asked Joie.

"Something light. I don't think I can stomach anything heavy this morning. Maybe some toast and fruit…"

The front door opened. It was Tomas accompanied by his parents. "Veronica?" he shouted out from the living room. "Veronica! Where are you?"

"We're in the kitchen," Ronnie shouted back.

Tomas walked in, looking as handsome and debonair as ever.

"Tomas! What a nice surprise. I'm so happy you made it."

"You know I wouldn't miss seeing you marry *mi primo*. Again."

"Excuse me if I don't get up, but my back is killing me."

"No need to get up on account of me. I'll come to you." He bent down and greeted her with a kiss on both cheeks. "Veronica, I'd like to introduce my parents. Everyone this is *Señor* y *Señora De La Cruz*, but you can call them *Tía* Sophia and *Tío* Tomas."

"*Hola*," Ronnie replied.

"Spanish is fine, but just in case you're still learning, we both speak English," offered his father.

Ronnie chuckled, "Thanks, I've still got a lot to learn."

Joie took one look at Tomas and went into panic mode. *Oh shit! Ronnie didn't tell me Tomas was coming, too.* She looked around in search of Cedric.

Tomas noticed Joie leaned over the kitchen sink. In spite of how they last parted, he hoped that she would be happy to see him. He headed her way.

In all the confusion of renovating the house and preparing for the ceremony, Ronnie had all but forgotten that Tomas and Joie were ever involved. Unfortunately, that little slip up hit her like a ton of bricks. *Luis, where are you when I need you?*

"Hey Joie, I'm surprised to see you here." Tomas stood back and allowed his eyes to glide over Joie's body from head to toe. He casually glanced down to her left hand. She wasn't wearing a ring. *Hmmm, maybe she didn't remarry her ex after all. She sure is beautiful, though.*

"Uh, hey Tomas. W-w-what are you doing here?" she asked, nervously looking around for Cedric.

"What am I *doing* here? Did you forget Luis is also my cousin? He invited me."

"Oh yeah, that's right. You guys are cousins. Well, it's nice to see you. Uh, I see you brought your parents with you."

Noticing the potential for trouble now existed, Ronnie grabbed Kiara's arm as she was headed to the backdoor. She whispered, "Where is Cedric, Joie's husband?"

"Um, I think he's outside helping set up chairs. Why, do you want me to go get him?" Kiara asked.

"No, no, that's all right." She continued to watch Tomas as he inched closer to Joie. He leaned over, then kissed her neck.

"Oh, I almost forgot to tell you, Daddy and Monique are on their way. He said they should be here by the time the ceremony begins at three."

"Great! I can't wait to see them."

"Are you still going to put them in the downstairs bedroom?" Kiara asked.

"Yeah, yeah, that's fine. Let me know when they arrive. Thanks, sweetie." Ronnie kept her eyes on Joie and Tomas.

Kiara followed her mother's gaze. *Oh gawd, how disgusting!* "Mom, I'll be back in a few. It's starting to feel a little crowded in this house."

Joie's heart rate picked up when she felt Tomas' soft lips on her neck or maybe it was the thought of Cedric seeing them together. "Tomas, I'm sorry about how it all went down with us, but I've got something important to tell you." Joie took a step backwards.

At that very moment, Luis flung open the front door and shouted out, "Ronnie, I'm back! Come and see who I brought with me."

Tomas shushed Joie. "Hold that thought. I'm going to go say hi to Luis. Be right back."

Joie let out an audible sigh as Luis' mother and sister looked on, whispering in Spanish. Although she didn't understand what they were saying, she knew it was about her. She smiled at them sweetly. And feeling like she was suffocating, she went outside for some much needed air.

Ronnie slowly shuffled to the living room, dragging her feet, holding her belly. "Hey Mama, I am so happy to see you."

"Hello, my dear." Dianna took one look at Ronnie's girth. "Oh my! You look like you could pop at any moment. You sure that doctor got your due date right?"

Ronnie embraced her mother. "I'm carrying twins, remember? But I sure do wish this was already over. I feel awful," Ronnie complained.

"Aw, baby, I know you're miserable…" Dianna caressed Ronnie's arm. "But them babies will come out when they are good and ready and not a minute before."

"I know. Problem is, I think they've gotten way too comfortable up in here." Ronnie laughed.

Dianna noted the décor, much as everyone else had. "This sure is a lovely home you two have. It's even nicer than the one in California."

"Thank you, Mama."

"Where is my room? I want to get freshened up." Dianna used a handkerchief to dab away the perspiration gathered above her lip.

"You're upstairs in the last room on the left." She pointed to the staircase. "Baby, can you take Mama's suitcases up?"

"Sure can." Luis bent down and kissed Ronnie's forehead. "How are we doing today?"

"If I had known then that I would be feeling like this today, I swear I never would have planned this ceremony." She whispered to her husband, "Baby, I think we may have a slight problem on our hands."

"What's going on?" Luis leaned in close.

"I don't think Tomas knows that Joie and Cedric are back together. And from the look of things, Cedric probably didn't know that Tomas was going to be here."

"Don't worry. I'll speak to Tomas before he does anything stupid."

"Thank you. I just don't want no drama today."

"Neither do I." He kissed her again and asked, "Can I get you anything?"

"Joie was fixing me a light breakfast... I think it's still on the kitchen table."

"Be right back." Luis brought Ronnie her plate and then took Dianna's bags upstairs to her designated guest bedroom.

Meanwhile, Joie returned to the living room. She perched on the edge of the ottoman where Ronnie rested her swollen feet. She whispered, "Girl, why didn't you tell me Tomas was going to be here?"

"I'm sorry, Joie. With everything that's going on, I forgot about you two being involved. Why don't you just tell him you're married to Cedric?"

"That's the least of my worries. It's not Tomas I'm concerned about. It's Cedric. I told him about Tomas, but he probably never expected to actually be in the same room with him. What am I going to do?" She wrung her hands anxiously.

"Luis is going to speak to Tomas. And Cedric didn't come all the way down here to get in no mess. Just tell him the truth so he won't be caught by surprise."

"I suppose you're right. At least, I hope you are."

Joie noticed the dark circles under Ronnie's eyes. "How are you doing? You don't look so good."

"It's my back. I had trouble sleeping last night because I couldn't get comfortable." She used her fist to massage a kink that wouldn't go away.

"Why don't you lay down for a bit? Try to relax..."

Ronnie glanced at the anniversary clock above the stone fireplace. "That's a good idea. I have another couple of hours before the ceremony. I think I will go upstairs for a nap."

"Call out if you need anything." Joie helped pull her to her feet.

Ronnie climbed the stairs and headed to her bedroom to escape the noisy activity in and around the house. The women in Luis' family were in the kitchen busily adding the finishing touches on the meal. And the men finished tending the roasted pig. As she looked around, she noticed that everybody seemed to be having a great time—well, everyone except her.

* * *

After about an hour of sleep, she was awakened by a cramping sensation in her lower back. She tried to massage the pain away with her own hands, but was unable to reach it. Thankfully, Luis was in the closet selecting his clothes.

"Baby, can you come here?" She groaned.

"Yeah, be right there," he replied. "You okay, love?"

"I have a really bad cramp in my side. Can you just rub it for a minute? I can't get to it."

Luis sat on the bed and gently kneaded her lower back. "How's that? Better?"

"Yeah, much better. Thanks. At least I can sit up now."

"It's almost time. You should probably start getting dressed." He laid out his suit on the bed.

"Is the minister here, yet?" She yawned.

"Yes, he arrived about half an hour ago. Pulled up about the same time as Travis and Monique."

"Oh good, they made it. I was beginning to get worried." Ronnie rubbed her eyes. The short nap hadn't made much of a difference in how she felt. She still felt like shit warmed over.

Luis noted his wife's weary appearance, feeling sorry for her. "You need some help, baby?"

"Probably. Can you please ask Joie and my mother to come up in about ten minutes?"

"Sure can. I'm going to jump in the shower. You want me to draw your bath?"

"Yeah, that'll be nice. Maybe it'll help relieve this cramping in my side."

"Oh, I almost forgot to tell you. While you were sleeping, Tomas decided to take his parents to the horse ranch. They spent most of the afternoon horseback riding. And, they brought back a present for us."

"Really? What is it?"

"Unlimited access to the horses—well, as soon as you are able to ride again. Isn't that cool?"

"Yeah, that is very cool!" *Tomas was gone most of the day? Well, at least I know he and Cedric didn't get into it. That's a relief.* "I can't wait to go horseback riding again."

Luis leaned over and kissed her. "I'll go downstairs so you can finish getting dressed. Call me if you need me."

After Luis left the bedroom, Ronnie hoisted up from the bed, barely making it to the closet. She pulled out a white dress that she and Kiara had selected from a maternity catalog a few months back. Ronnie had deliberately ordered the dress in a larger size to accommodate any potential weight gain. The dress was made from spandex and lace and it did nothing to hide her pregnancy. In fact, the dress was designed to accentuate it.

As she undressed, she was caught off guard by another strong cramp. She struggled to get into the bathtub. *My goodness, that hurts. What the hell is going on?* Unfortunately, she was unable to maneuver her hefty weight over the side of the tub. Instead, she opted for the shower.

* * *

"Veronica, you must have really packed on the pounds because there is no way you're going to squeeze all *this* in that little dress," Dianna said. She stood back and watched Joie attempt to close the zipper.

Joie shook her head from side to side. "She's right, Ronnie. This dress ain't gonna work. You got something else to wear?"

"No, I don't. I'm too fat to fit in anything except those oversized muumuus. I can't get remarried in one of those ugly things!" Ronnie started to cry.

Dianna took a seat on the bed. "Sugar, it don't really matter what you get married in. That man ain't looking at your clothes. Trust me. He is looking at the beautiful woman inside." She pointed at Joie and instructed. "Girl, get in that closet and see if you can find something for my child to wear."

Joie widened her eyes in surprise. She was this close to responding in her usual who-the-hell-do-you-think-you-talkin'-to manner. She wasn't used to being spoken to that way, but since it was Ronnie's mother, she got off her butt and said, "Uh, uh, yes, ma'am."

Kiara was in the upstairs bathroom fixing her hair. She overheard the women's conversation and ran downstairs to explain the situation to Luis. Upon hearing of Ronnie's predicament, one of Luis' aunts, who also just happened to be a seamstress, ran up the steps. She burst into the master bedroom, quickly approached Ronnie, and began speaking in rapid bursts of *Spanglish*.

Not knowing much Spanish, Ronnie had no idea what the woman was saying, but she understood the motion to take off her clothes. With the assistance of both Dianna and Joie tugging and pulling, they were able to get her out of the dress. Luis' aunt retrieved the dress, ran from the room, down the stairs, and out the front door in under five minutes flat.

A few minutes later, Luis stuck his head in the bedroom and explained, "My aunt says to wait here. Not to worry… She's going to take care of everything."

After watching the drama unfold, Dianna stated matter-of-factly, "These are some very industrious people down here in the Dominican Republic. You don't get service like this back home."

"I know that's right," Joie agreed. "It would take a whole lot of cash to get somebody to move that fast."

"All I can say is, I'm part of the family." Ronnie grinned.

A knock at the door drew the women's attention.

Ronnie told Kiara, "Sweetie, can you please see who that is?"

Kiara went to the door. "Mom, it's Monique."

"Well, let her in, child," Ronnie said.

Monique walked in, holding a small package in her hands. "Hi Ronnie. Since Travis and I didn't have the chance to see you earlier, I wanted to come up here to offer you our congratulations."

"Thank you, Monique. I am so happy you guys were able to make it." She motioned to her. "Come on over here and join us."

Monique sat down beside Ronnie while the other women looked on. Monique handed her a small gift box. "It's from grandmother. She sends her best wishes—on the marriage and your becoming a mother."

"Trudy sent me a gift? How sweet." Ronnie opened the small jewelry box. Inside was an antique brooch. "Wow! It's beautiful!"

"Grandmother says it belonged to her mother. It's a family heirloom that has been passed down for several generations."

"I can't keep this," Ronnie exclaimed, trying to hand the brooch back. "This should remain in your family."

"Grandmother insisted. She said she always considered you as a daughter." Monique smiled. "And you know how stubborn grandmother can be. If I came back with that, she'd personally fly down here to deliver it herself."

"In that case, I will wear it today with honor." Ronnie gave the brooch to her mother to help pin it to her dress later.

While Luis' aunt was away working miracles, Dianna and Joie tackled Ronnie's hair. In about fifteen minutes, they transformed what she called her bird's nest, into a cascade of flowing locs, piling it atop her head.

Thirty minutes later, Luis' aunt returned with the dress. She had magically transformed the back of the dress by removing the zipper and attaching lace extensions across the back to add more room.

Ronnie pulled the dress over her head and modeled the results to the women who watched and waited.

"Now *that* is a beautiful dress!" exclaimed Dianna.

"Wow!" exclaimed Monique.

"Oh yeah... You are wearing that dress, girlfriend," added Joie.

"Mom, you look wonderful," Kiara gushed as she placed a veil attached to a tiara atop her mother's head.

"*¡Qué vista tan hermosa!*" Luis' aunt clapped her hands in delight.

Ronnie looked at her reflection in the mirror, liking what she saw. She ran over to Luis' aunt and gave her a grateful hug.

"*Muchas gracias, tia.* It's absolutely perfect." She used her mother's handkerchief to wipe away the tears. "I want to thank all of you for your help—for making this day special. Each of you has made me so happy in your own unique way..."

"Don't go getting mushy on us just yet, girlfriend. You've got a ceremony to get through." Joie slipped a string of pearls around Ronnie's neck.

Ronnie stepped into a pair of low heeled pumps.

Dianna pinned Trudy's brooch on the dress, and then handed her a small bouquet of flowers picked fresh from the garden. Ronnie took one last look in the mirror. "All right, ladies. I guess I'm ready."

Chapter Forty-One

*I*t ended up being a beautiful winter afternoon in the hills high above Santo Domingo by the time the ceremony finally rolled around. The warming rays of the sun shone brightly in the deep blue sky; the temperature hovered in the mid-70's; and a gentle breeze stirred the warm air, heavy with the fragrance of tropical flowers. In other words, it was a perfect day for a remarriage ceremony.

As Ronnie waited for her cue to begin the wedding procession, she surveyed the small crowd. Kiara was seated next to Travis and Monique. Joie and Cedric had their heads huddled together, probably planning some sort of risqué rendezvous. Dianna sat next to Fernando and his family, because she was so impressed by how well he had taken care of her granddaughter. Luis' mother, sister, and about thirty or so other relatives filled in the remaining seats. The only one missing was her father, Vernon Pierce. *Daddy, I wish you were here to see me get married. You would absolutely love Luis.*

Soft jazz music was piped in through the outside speakers. Tomas, who volunteered to step in for Ronnie's father, ushered her down the aisle to where Luis awaited under a flower covered gazebo. As she walked past her family and friends, she looked to her left and noticed two beautiful purple butterflies flitting about in the garden. She smiled at her father's private message and refocused her gaze upon Luis' smiling face. Suddenly, a cramp in her lower back came out of nowhere, causing her to pause.

"Hey, you okay?" Tomas whispered, feeling her hesitation.

"Yeah, I just caught a cramp. I'm okay." She quickly recovered and continued her march forward.

Tomas delivered Ronnie to Luis' side and took his seat next to his parents. But before he did, he winked at Joie. *I wonder who the brother is sitting next to her. Doesn't matter, this is a wedding and weddings are made for couples to reunite. I'll catch up with Miss Joie later.*

Cedric caught the wink and glanced at Joie sideways. When she didn't react he nudged her with his elbow and asked, "Who is that brother? And what's with the winking?"

"Huh, what are you talking about?" She pretended to not notice Tomas' flirtation. On the contrary, her focus was solely on Ronnie and Luis; she wanted his to be the same.

Cedric was not about to start playing games with Joie. Not after all they had been through. "I'm talking about *Rico Suave* over there who just winked at you, that's what."

"Shhh, it's about to start." *Shit! Ronnie said Luis was gonna tell Tomas about me and Cedric. I hope this thing don't blow up in my face...*

Ronnie stood next to Luis and placed her hand in his. Luis gazed upon his wife's beautiful face and fell in love with her all over again. He looked out over his friends and family who had taken time from their busy lives to witness this special ceremony. In that moment, he felt as if he were the luckiest man alive.

The minister began to speak. "Luis Duarte, Veronica Duarte, family and friends... We have gathered here this afternoon to witness Luis and Veronica's remarriage ceremony. Whereas these types of ceremonies typically take place years after a husband and wife have been together, Luis and Veronica have only recently taken their sacred oath to love, honor, and cherish one another. Unfortunately, at that time, only a couple of friends were able to attend. Today, they want to renew their vows in front of everyone and proclaim to the world their commitment to one another. In lieu of me performing the sacred marriage ritual, they will each say a few words and I shall then offer God's eternal blessing upon this union." He looked at the couple and quietly whispered, "You may begin whenever you are ready."

Luis spoke first. "Veronica, Ronnie... I want to begin by saying I love you so very much. You are my best friend, my lover, my wife... God delivered you to me over three years ago and for that I shall forever be grateful. My darling, a day without you is like a day without air and the moment you pulled me from the ocean is the day my life truly began. You recently reminded me of the dreams I used to dream. But you not only reminded me, you also encouraged and supported me each and every step of the way to pursue them. And because of you, here we stand today. I also want to praise God for blessing us with our two unborn children. I pray they look just like you. You have given me so much already...Your love, your joy, a beautiful stepdaughter who I am so very proud of... All I have left to say is I love you and I am proud to be your husband."

Ronnie wiped the tears away and cleared the emotion from her voice. "Luis, my love, my friend, my husband... I also want to praise God for delivering you to me at a time when I needed someone. You were there. Like an angel who fell from Heaven just to be with me. You spoke of the day I rescued you from the ocean… Well, my dear, you rescued me from drowning in my own life."

She paused and took a deep breath before continuing. "Because of your love, patience, and understanding during that long, long, cross country drive, I discovered what true love is. And the past three years have been the best years of my entire life. I got my daughter back, I found my soul mate, and I am being blessed with two little babies who can't wait to make their way into this world. My love, you are the alpha to my omega, the yin to my yang, the apple of my eye… I love you and I am in love with you, Luis Eduardo Duarte. I am so proud to be your wife."

The minister smiled and said, "Luis, Veronica, today you have chosen to renew your wedding vows and have asked to be blessed by God." He placed his hands on both their heads and said, "As it is written in the book of Ephesians, *Be kind and compassionate to one another, forgiving each other, just as in Christ God forgave you.* And from the book of Peter, *Above all, love each other deeply, because love covers a multitude of sins.*" He removed his hands from their heads and made the sign of the cross over them both. "May the Lord keep you and bless you both with love and joy every day of your life. May peace be with you."

"And also with you," they replied in unison.

"You may kiss your wife."

Luis gripped Ronnie face with both hands and murmured, "I love you, mama." Afterwards, he planted a huge kiss on her luscious red lips.

"Ladies and gentlemen, please join me in receiving Luis and Veronica Duarte."

The group erupted in applause and shouts of joy. Most everyone stood and headed towards the happy couple to offer congratulations.

All of a sudden, from out of nowhere, Ronnie felt a sharp pain shoot from her back across to her waist. She lurched towards Luis. Her hands went to her stomach.

"Baby, are you all right? What's wrong?" A panicked look spread over his face as he steadied her.

She grimaced in pain. "Probably nothing. I guess I was standing too long. Help…me…make…it to a chair."

* * *

From the moment the ceremony was over, Tomas continually stared in Joie's direction, willing the man to leave her side. He saw his chance when the man sitting next to her went inside the house.

To Joie's credit, she had managed to avoid Tomas by remaining surrounded by his family members. Each attempt made to be alone with her was thwarted by an aunt or another cousin. However this time, she was alone. Cedric had gone inside to use the restroom.

Tomas swaggered over, taking two glasses of champagne from a tray. He handed a glass of the bubbly to her. "Joie, why have you been avoiding me? I'm the same Tomas De La Cruz you loved spending time with in Santa Elena. What gives?"

"Uh…hey, Tomas. I…uh…well, I've got something to tell you," she stammered.

"Tell me later. How about a big hug for your old friend? I'm not upset about our last get together." He enveloped her in his arms.

"Tomas…wait."

"C'mon, baby. Let's start over and let bygones be bygones." Tomas bent over and tried to kiss her.

Joie turned her head to the side, avoiding his kiss, allowing it to land on her cheek, instead. "Tomas, I'm not alone. I'm here with my husband."

He took a step back. "*¿Qué dices?* You're married? Since when?"

Joie held her hand out and showed him her ring. "Since about a month ago. To Cedric. He used to be my ex."

Tomas held his hands up. "Joie, I'm sorry… I had no idea." He slowly backed away as if she might bite him at any moment. "I didn't see a ring on your finger earlier."

"I took my rings off when I was preparing the food. I thought Luis spoke to you…"

"No, Luis didn't mention anything about your being married. Why didn't you?"

Joie stared at the beautiful ring Cedric had placed on her finger. "I should have told you earlier—as soon as I realized you had come down for the wedding."

"Well, you must admit it was fun while it lasted." Tomas felt a light tap on his back. He glanced over his shoulder and immediately felt a fist connect with his jaw. He stumbled backwards, breaking his fall by latching on to a chair. Tomas glared at the man who had the nerve to punch him. Staring back with fire in his eyes was the man Joie had sat next to during the ceremony. Her husband.

From where Ronnie sat nursing her discomfort and receiving hugs and kisses from her new family, she saw Cedric punch Tomas. She gasped, "Oh no, Luis! They're fighting!"

"Who?"

Ronnie pointed towards the trio tussling near the side of the pool. They bumped into a table sending hors d'oeuvres flying everywhere. "Oh shoot! Cedric just punched Tomas and it looks like Joie is trying to break them up."

"*¡Maldita sea!* Not today…" Luis left Ronnie's side and quickly strode over to his cousin's side.

"Muthafucka! I advise you to keep your goddamn lips off my wife unless you want some more of this." Cedric pushed up on Tomas.

Though his jaw ached, Tomas felt like laughing at the absurdity of the situation. He looked from Joie, and then back to her husband. *I know this little pendejo didn't just sucker punch me! He obviously doesn't know I held the national boxing championship title for Santo Domingo, three years running.* "Look man, I don't want any trouble. I didn't know she was married. I made a huge mistake."

"Damn right you did." Cedric glared at Joie. "Who the hell is this muthafucka you let kiss on you?"

"Cedric, t-t-this is Luis' c-c-cousin, T-Tomas," Joie stammered.

"Tomas? Is this the same muthafucka you were messing around with in California?"

Tomas had enough of the name calling. "Listen man, I apologized to you once, but if you keep calling me out of my name, I promise you will regret it."

Joie inserted her body between the men. Facing Cedric, she explained, "Tomas is a friend of mine. I met him before you and I officially got back together…"

Luis strode over to break it up. "Hey fellas, what's going on here?"

Tomas rubbed his jaw. "Your, ahem…guest…sucker punched me because I kissed his wife. Problem was, I had no idea she was his wife," explained Tomas.

Luis remembered he promised Ronnie he'd talk to Tomas and let him know what was going on. "Cousin, it's my fault. Ronnie asked me to tell you that Joie had gotten married."

Joie piped up and said, "It's nobody's fault but mine. I should have told Tomas about Cedric. And I should have told Cedric who Tomas was. I was just trying to keep the drama at a minimum for Ronnie's sake."

Cedric backed down after hearing the explanation. "Hey man, I'm sorry for punching you."

"We're cool." Tomas grabbed Luis' arm. He looked towards Veronica. "*Primo*, uh, I think you'd better get back to your wife."

Luis glanced over at Ronnie. Fernando was at her side, helping her to stand. Luis rushed back to his wife, forgetting all about Tomas, Cedric and Joie. "What's going on, Fernando?"

"Her water broke," he explained.

"Huh? What does that mean?" asked Luis, gawking at the puddle under Ronnie's feet.

"It means you need to get my daughter to the hospital. These babies are ready to be born." Dianna wrapped a towel around Ronnie's waist.

"But it's too soon. She still has another month to go," Luis rationalized.

"I've been in labor most of the afternoon. Those back cramps I had earlier were actually labor pains." Ronnie draped her arm across Luis' shoulders. She noted Luis' wild-eyed look. "Honey, are you going to be okay to drive me to the hospital?"

Luis gulped, trying his best to remain calm. "Yeah, I'm fine. Help me get her to the van."

Fernando said, "Luis, I'll drive. You can ride with Veronica in the back seat to help keep her calm." He looked at his wife and said, "You and the kids can catch a ride home with my parents."

"Thanks, cousin," he exhaled, "I really appreciate this."

"No problem. I'll give Dr. Anderson-Santana a call and have her meet us at the hospital."

Dianna clutched onto Luis' arm. "Hold on, I'm going, too. I was there when Kiara was born and I'm going to be there when these babies are born, too." Dianna called Kiara over. "Honey, go get your momma's hospital bag. Most likely it's in the master bedroom closet."

Kiara rushed into the house, headed up the stairs to the master bedroom, and went in search for a packed bag. She was surprised to find it at the foot of the bed. She ran out of the house yelling, "Got it!"

After the ceremony was over, Monique and Travis had retreated to their room to change, missing the excitement. Once Monique heard all the commotion coming from outside, she went into the living room to check on things. She saw Kiara running down the stairs with a suitcase in hand. "Hey, what's going on?"

"Mom's water broke. She's about to go to the hospital! The twins are about to be born!" Kiara jumped up and down in excitement.

Monique smiled. "There's never a dull moment around here, huh? Well, go, don't let me stop you. Get that bag to your mother."

"Tell Daddy, I'm going to the hospital. See you guys tomorrow." Kiara dashed out the door and headed to the van.

Travis approached Monique after her overhearing the conversation. He asked, "Is this what happens when a child is about to be born? Everyone loses their minds?"

Monique frowned, "Weren't you there when Kiara was born?"

"No, I guess that's one story I haven't told you yet. You got a few hours?"

"Sure. We have all night."

Kiara handed the bag to Luis and stared at him with a sad, puppy dog expression. He tossed the bag in the backseat, took one look at her and said, "All right. Get in."

Everyone from the ceremony was gathered outside to see them off. They shouted out good luck wishes in both English and Spanish as Fernando carefully maneuvered the van down the dirt path and headed towards the highway for the thirty minute drive to the hospital.

Chapter Forty-Two

*R*onnie bore down as if she were having the most awful bowel movement of her life. She grunted and strained and continued pushing until she could barely breathe. "I can't do this anymore. I'm so tired... Luis, make the pain stop. Please..." she cried out.

"One more good push and the first baby will be out," Dr. Anderson-Santana explained. "Okay Veronica. On the count of three I want you to bear down as hard as you can. Ready! One. Two. Three. Push!"

"Baby, you're almost there. Don't give up, yet," encouraged Luis.

"I can't... I'm so tired..." Ronnie's hair was plastered to her face with sweat. Tiny blood vessels burst in her eyes, making her eyes appear bloodshot. She was exhausted.

"I need another good push. Push hard! Now!" instructed the doctor.

Ronnie felt like passing out. She didn't remember Kiara's delivery being so difficult. However, just when she thought she couldn't take anymore, she dug deep and found the strength to give one more push. She pushed and pushed. And just when she thought she couldn't push anymore, she heard a strong cry.

"Good job, Veronica. It's a boy!" She handed the first baby to the nurse and concentrated on Ronnie. "Now, let's focus on getting his little sister delivered. Take a few minutes to catch your breath..."

"Luis, how does he look? Is he all right?"

"He's beautiful, absolutely beautiful..." Luis marveled at the birth process, never imagining it to be so difficult. He kissed his amazing wife.

"Oh my goodness! What a perfect little angel!" Dianna gushed. She stayed at Ronnie's side. There was no way she wanted to see what was going on *down there*.

"Mama, is everything okay?" asked Ronnie. She wanted to do nothing more than sleep. Unfortunately, she was only halfway done with the delivery.

"Yes, baby. He is perfect."

Dr. Anderson-Santana returned to the delivery stool. "Okay Veronica. Break is over. Let's get your daughter delivered. I'm going to count down again, then I want you to push with all your might. You ready?"

Ronnie looked at Luis with an uncontrollable, wild look in her eyes. She shook her head from side to side. "Baby, I don't think I can do this. I'm too tired. I want to go home." She cried.

Luis grasped her hands. He whispered, "You can do this, Ronnie. Think about your little baby girl who wants to come out to meet you. I want you to concentrate on me. Find your focal point and listen to the doctor."

"Veronica, we need to get going, honey. You ready?" said the doctor.

Ronnie used a tiny freckle on Luis' nose as her focal point. She hadn't noticed it previously, but was glad she spotted it now. She murmured softly, "Okay, I'm ready."

"Good girl. On my count… One. Two. Three. Push!" shouted the doctor. "Don't stop! She's almost out!"

Ronnie squeezed Luis' hand and continued pushing with all her might. She didn't stop pushing until she heard a baby's shrill cry and the doctor's order to stop.

"You can stop now," stated the doctor in a calm voice. "Veronica, meet your baby girl. She's a real beauty." The doctor held up the baby so Ronnie could see her and then handed the baby off to the nurse.

"She's positively beautiful!" Luis exclaimed with tears running down his face. "She looks just like her mommy."

Ronnie gently stroked his arm and said, "Congratulations, papi. You're a daddy."

Dianna approached the bed and kissed Ronnie on her cheek. "You did real good. Those are two beautiful little babies you two got there. My grandbabies. Lord have mercy!"

"Thanks, Mama." Ronnie squeezed her hand tight. "Can you let Kiara know it all went well? I'm sure she's worried."

"Sure will. I'll be back later. Try to get some rest."

"I am so proud of you." Luis beamed.

"Thanks, I couldn't have done it without you and your freckle." She laughed. "I am so I glad that's over."

"Was it very bad?" Luis grimaced. He wiped her hair from her forehead.

"You don't know the half of it," she whispered before closing her eyes to take a ten minute nap.

The nurse brought the babies in and laid both on Ronnie's chest. One baby tried to clutch her finger with its tiny pink hand.

"Their fingers are so tiny," Ronnie remarked in amazement.

"They were a few weeks early and twins are usually smaller than single births, but they're both fine," explained the doctor. "Perfectly healthy."

"Look Luis, she opened her eyes."

"Yeah, and her brother is sound asleep."

The doctor continued working on Ronnie, delivering the afterbirth and putting in needed stitches. After a few minutes she stated to the nurse, "All done."

"The nurse will transfer you to the recovery room and then you'll be taken to your room where you can see the babies. Great job in there!"

"Thanks," said Ronnie.

"Six hours of active labor is tough, but especially difficult on the older moms." Dr. Anderson-Santana pulled off her gown and tossed it into a bin.

"Thank you, doctor." Luis said.

"My pleasure. I'll see you later today."

* * *

Kiara quietly entered the room. She leaned over her mother's bed to give her a hug, while Dianna watched over her family from a chair strategically placed near the window. Both babies were sound asleep in their bassinets. Luis sat hunched over in his chair quietly snoring.

Ronnie turned to face Kiara. "Ready to meet your baby brother and baby sister?" she whispered.

"I sure am." She peeked at the twins. "Awww… They're so cute and so tiny. Can I please hold one?"

"Sure, take a seat." Ronnie looked to her mother. "Mama, can you please help her?"

"Come on over here next to me, chile." Dianna got up and reached into the bassinet. She picked up her grandson and handed him to Kiara. She told her, "Make sure you support his neck."

"Hey little man, I'm your big sister, Kiara." She tenderly stroked her brother's soft cheek.

He opened his little eyes as if he recognized her voice.

"Have you guys decided upon names?" she asked Ronnie.

"Your little brother is named after his father and your sister is named Isabella Indigo."

"Isabella Indigo Duarte and Luis Eduardo Duarte, Jr.? Awesome! Very good choices. I approve," Kiara remarked, lightheartedly. "So, when can we take them home?"

Epilogue

*O*ver the next few days, a steady stream of relatives stopped by with well wishes for the couple and gifts for the babies.

Travis and Monique stopped by the hospital on their way to the airport to offer their sincere congratulations to the happy parents. They also invited Luis and Ronnie to their wedding. Cedric and Joie checked into an exclusive resort to finish out their honeymoon holiday, making up for all their lost time.

Tomas returned to Santa Elena, alone, but very rich. He and Fernando never did clear the air about their ongoing family feud, but then again, the De La Cruz and Doucet feud had been going on for over thirty years and wasn't about to end. Especially, since most couldn't remember why it began in the first place.

Kiara decided to remain in the DR for another month to help Ronnie with the twins, before heading back to Santa Elena to finish school. And with Luis and Ronnie's persistent requests for her not to leave, Dianna ended up staying for three more months before she finally went home. After all, when it comes to grandbabies, there ain't nobody better to have around than grandma.